LOVING
THE
HIGHLANDER

JANET
CHAPMAN

POCKET BOOKS
New York   London   Toronto   Sydney

An *Original* Publication of POCKET BOOKS

POCKET BOOKS, a division of Simon & Schuster, Inc.
1230 Avenue of the Americas, New York, NY 10020

ISBN-13: 978-1-4165-2342-0
ISBN-10:   1-4165-2342-1

This Pocket Books paperback edition December 2005

10 9 8 7 6 5 4 3 2 1

POCKET and colophon are registered trademarks of
Simon & Schuster, Inc.

Front cover illustration by Min Choi
Photo credit: Gail Shumway/Getty Images
Back cover illustration by Jon Paul Ferrara

Manufactured in the United States of America

For information regarding special discounts for bulk purchases,
please contact Simon & Schuster Special Sales at 1-800-456-6798
or business@simonandschuster.com.

For my two sons,
Ben and Nick,

who are as comfortable in the civilized world
as they are in the woods. What remarkable men
you've become. Thank you for the laughter, for
keeping me grounded, and for constantly reminding
me to trust you. It has definitely been an adventure.

Oh, and thank you for stacking the firewood.

Acknowledgments

As I travel along the pathway of my life, I realize that I've been blessed with the greatest of family and friends, as well as with the many dynamic people I find myself working with now.

And so, I would like to thank Grace Morgan, my agent, for guiding me (with energy and patience and just enough compassion) through the wonderfully exciting—and to me, mysterious—world of publishing.

And thank you to everyone at Pocket Books—especially Maggie Crawford, Selena James, and Micki Nuding. Your confidence in me, your enthusiasm, and your encouragement, has made my journey most rewarding.

And thanks also to the Publicity and Art Departments at Pocket, and to the enthusiastic Sales Team who did such a great job of making sure my books reached all corners of the country.

Blessings to you wonderful people.

LOVING
THE
HIGHLANDER

Chapter One

Present day, deep in the Maine woods

The old wizard sat in reflective silence on the tall granite cliff, oblivious to the awakening forest around him, the roaring waterfall that shot from the precipice, and the churning pool of frothing water a good hundred feet beneath where he sat. Daar scratched his beard with the butt of his cane and sighed, his troubling thoughts completely focused on the lone fisherman below. He had done a terrible disservice to that young man six years ago. Aye, he was solely responsible for turning Morgan MacKeage's life into the mess it was now.

Daar had cast a spell that had brought Morgan's laird and brother, Greylen MacKeage, forward to the twenty-first century. It had been the wizard's greatest blunder to date. Oh, Greylen had made the journey safely enough, but so had six of his enemies, two of his men, and his younger brother, Morgan. Even their disgruntled war horses had managed to get sucked into the spell, catapulting them all on an unimaginable journey forward through time.

Daar blamed the mishap on his advanced age. He was old and tired, a bit forgetful on occasion, and that was the reason his magic sometimes went awry.

Morgan MacKeage should have been eight hundred years dead, having had the joy of a couple of wives and a dozen or so kids. Instead, the Highland warrior fishing below was now thirty-two, still unwed, and lonely. It seemed nearly a sin to Daar that his wizard's ineptness had caused such a fine, strong, intelligent warrior to be cast adrift without direction or purpose.

Daar hunched his shoulders under the weight of his guilt. Aye, that young man's malaise was all his fault, and it was past time he fixed things.

A woman might help.

Then again, a woman might only add to the young warrior's troubles.

Daar had discovered that twenty-first-century females were a decidedly peculiar breed. They were brash, outspoken, opinionated, and stubborn. But mostly they were simply too damned independent. They dared to live alone, they worked to support themselves, and they quite often owned property and held positions of power in business and government.

How was a man born in a time when women were chattel supposed to deal with such independent women? How was a virile twelfth-century warrior supposed to embrace his new life in such an outrageous time?

The MacKeages had lived in this modern world for six years. Six years of adapting, evolving, and finally accepting, and still Morgan MacKeage stood alone. Morgan's brother, Greylen, was happily settled with a wife, a daughter, and twins on the way. Callum was courting a woman in town, and Ian was secretly seeing a widow two nights a week. Even their sole surviving enemy, Michael MacBain, had fathered a son and was getting on with his life.

Only Morgan remained detached, not only from the company of females but also from the passions of life itself. He hunted, fished, and walked the woods incessantly, as if searching for something to settle the ache in his gut.

"Give a care, old man, lest you fall and become feed for the fish."

Daar nearly did fall at the sound of Morgan's familiar voice behind him. He stood and faced the young warrior and gave him a fierce scowl.

"You're a pagan, Morgan MacKeage, for scaring ten years off an old priest's life."

Morgan lifted a brow. "When I next see a priest, I'll be sure to confess my sin."

Daar attempted to straighten his shoulders and puff his chest at the insult but gave up as soon as he realized it made little difference. "You're seeing a priest now."

Morgan lifted his other brow. "What church ordains a *drùidh* into its ranks?"

"I was a priest long before I became a wizard," Daar shot back, pointing at the warrior. "And one is not contradictory to the other. Both roads lead in the same direction."

Morgan merely chuckled as he turned and started

up the path that led to Daar's cabin. "Come on, old man, if you want breakfast," he said without looking back.

Eyeing the string of trout swinging from Morgan's belt, Daar decided he'd school the warrior on his manners later. After all, this argument had been repeated often over the last two years, since Daar had been forced to reveal his wizard's identity in order to save Greylen MacKeage's wife from kidnappers.

And what thanks had he got? None. Not even an "I'm sorry" that his precious old staff had been cut in half and thrown into a high mountain pond. It was that same pond, by the way, that was the source of the waterfall shooting out the side of the cliff from an underground stream, creating the crystal-clear pool that had produced the tasty trout he was about to have for breakfast.

"Does that puny new cane have any real power yet, *drùidh*?" Morgan asked as he settled into a comfortable, unhurried pace toward Daar's cabin.

Daar snorted. "As if I'd tell you," he muttered, eyeing the leather-sheathed sword tied to Morgan's backpack. The sword was more than three feet long, extending from Morgan's waist to a foot above his head, the hilt cocked to the side for easy access. That sword was as large as Greylen's sword and just as capable of destroying Daar's new cane.

Morgan stopped and turned to help Daar over a fallen log in the path. "Can it even toast bread yet?" he asked.

"It's powerful enough to gather stars in your head if I smack you with it."

Apparently not worried by the threat, Morgan turned his attention to something he pulled from his pocket. "What do you know of these?" he asked, holding up a three-foot-long orange ribbon of plastic.

Daar squinted at the ribbon. "What is it?"

"I don't know." Morgan leaned his fishing pole against his chest and used both hands to stretch the ribbon to its full length to show off the writing on it. "I found this one and several like it tied to trees all over the valley. And each one has numbers written on it."

Daar dismissed the ribbon with a negligent wave, eyeing the trout instead. His stomach rumbled, loudly announcing his hunger. "It's probably surveyors marking ownership lines," he said. He started toward home again. He was hungry, dammit, and had no patience for puzzles right now. "That's what they do in these modern times to mark their lands," Daar continued. "A man's word that he owns up to a river or to the crest of a mountain is no longer enough."

Daar stopped when he realized Morgan was not following. "Hell, boy. Your own land has lines drawn on a map and marked in the woods. They're even written in the deed you got when your brother purchased TarStone Mountain. It's what makes things legal today."

"They're not borders," Morgan said, stuffing the ribbon back in his pocket as he moved to follow Daar. "They don't run in any line I can discern."

"Then maybe they're logging markers," Daar offered next, mentally planning what he would fix with the trout. He started scanning the forest floor as they walked, looking for edible mushrooms. "Maybe they're doing a cutting in the valley," he absently continued. "Those numbers could be directions for the cutters."

"No. I found some of the ribbons on MacKeage land," Morgan countered, moving ahead to block his path, forcing them to a halt yet again. "And we are not cutting trees in this valley. The loggers we've hired are working east of here."

Daar looked up into Morgan's intense green eyes. "What is it you're wanting that's so important you're letting a fine brace of trout grow old?"

"I want you to use your magic and tell me what's happening in my woods."

Daar lifted his cane and used it to scratch his beard. "Ah. So it's okay to cast spells when it's convenient for you but not me? Is that how it works now?"

Morgan's eyes darkened. "There are rumors of a park being built in this valley, and I want to know if they're getting ahead of themselves and presuming to start work."

"And if they are, what does it matter?"

"I don't want the park to be here. A quarter of this valley is MacKeage land, and I'm against selling any of it."

"Why?"

"It's ours."

Daar lost hope that he was going to get breakfast anytime soon, unless they simply built a fire here and roasted the trout on spits. He sat down on a stump, cupped his hands over the top burl of his cane, and stared up at the young warrior.

"What's a few thousand acres to you, when your clan already owns four hundred thousand?"

"They can build their park someplace else, as long as it's not near this gorge."

Daar finally got his mind off his belly and focused on the man standing in front of him. Was that a faint spark he saw in those usually indifferent spruce-green eyes? Had something in this forest finally captured the attention of Morgan MacKeage?

"What's so special about this particular gorge?"

Morgan unhooked the trout from his belt. "These," he said, holding them up. He waved his fishing pole to encompass the forest. "This entire ridge. The stream that mysteriously appears from nowhere out the side of the mountain, cutting this gorge down to the valley. These trees. Have you even noticed their size, old man? Or their health? And these fish," he said again, shaking them slightly. "They're brook trout the size of salmon."

Daar frowned as he slowly looked around the forest. Aye, the trees did seem rather overlarge when compared with the others of the area. "They are big," he admitted. "I never noticed that before."

"That's because they were just like the rest only two years ago."

That number pricked at the wizard's memory.

"It's when your staff was thrown into the pond," Morgan continued at Daar's look of confusion. "It's the mist," he added, waving his fishing pole again. "See? It boils up from the falls and covers this gorge."

Daar nearly fell off the stump he was sitting on. The mist from the stream that ran from the mountain pond where his old staff lay?

Well, hell. Daar knew the water was special in that

pond, since it held his magical staff, but he had never stopped to consider consequences such as this. Huge fish? Towering trees? A veritable rain forest where none should exist.

"It's magic," Morgan said in a whispered, almost reverent voice. "This entire gorge is the result of what happened two years ago. And I don't want it to become part of a park. Hundreds of people will come hiking through here and discover the magic."

Daar stood up. "And neither do I," he quickly agreed. "We must do something about this."

"You've got to talk to Grey," Morgan said. "And make him understand that our land must not become part of this park."

"Me?"

"He'll listen to you."

"He will not. He's mad at me right now. His wife just had some test for her pregnancy, and the blasted doctor told Grey that Grace was carrying twin daughters, not sons."

Morgan looked startled. "They can tell if an unborn child is a boy or a girl?"

Daar shrugged. "It seems they can now." He started walking back the way they had come, totally resigned now to missing his breakfast. He chose a path that would lead them above the falls to a ridge that overlooked the valley below. "Come on. Let's go see just how strong my staff has grown."

Morgan quickly fell into step beside him. "Will it tell me what the plastic ribbons are for?" he asked.

"Nay. It's not a crystal ball. It's only a conductor of energy."

As they walked along the path, Daar fingered the smooth, delicate cane he had been training since his had been lost. It sported only a couple of burls so far, which indicated that its power was not yet strong. His old staff, the one Grey had severed with his sword and thrown into the pond, had been riddled with burls, carrying the strength of fourteen hundred years of concentrated energy.

"Then what's the point?" Morgan asked. "If it can't do anything yet, why are we climbing the ridge?"

"Hush. I'm trying to remember the words," Daar instructed as they walked along. It was not that easy, reciting spells by rote. The last time he had tested the new cane for something more intricate than lighting a fire, it had rained dung beetles for more than an hour. He could only thank God that it had been dark outside at the time.

Surprisingly, Morgan obeyed his request, and they quickly reached the top of Fireline Ridge. Two miles behind them was the pond where his old staff lay on the bottom, and in front of them was the deep gorge that fingered its way to the vast valley below.

Daar was stunned. From this vantage point the stream's path was blatantly obvious. Large, lush hemlock and spruce and pine trees, draped in a mantle of mist, towered up from the forest floor in a carpet of vivid evergreen splendor.

The cane in his hand suddenly began to hum with delicate power. A warm, familiar energy coursed up his arm, and Daar closed his eyes to savor the distinct feel of his long-lost staff.

"What is it, old man? What's happening?" Morgan

asked, taking a step back, eyeing the humming cane as it twisted and grew in length and thickness.

"Here. Touch this," Daar said, holding out his staff. "Feel it, Morgan. 'Tis the energy of life."

"I'm not touching that accursed thing."

"It won't bite," Daar snapped, poking the warrior in the belly.

Morgan instinctively grabbed the cane to protect himself, his eyes widening as the warm cherrywood sent its vibrations up his arm and into his body.

"There. That's what it's about, warrior. That's the life force. Have you forgotten what passion feels like?"

Morgan let go and stepped back, rubbing his hand on his shirt as he did. "I've forgotten nothing, old man. Now, point that thing at the valley and say your words. Tell me what's happening down there."

Daar pointed his staff toward the valley below and began to chant his ancient language. The burls on his cane warmed. The breeze kicked into a wind, sending the mist into swirling puffs of chaos around them. Birds and squirrels scurried for cover, and the distant roar of the falls turned to a whisper.

Daar opened one eye to peek at Morgan. The man had his hands balled into fists, his eyes scrunched closed, and his head pulled into his shoulders, his jaw clenched with enough force to break his teeth. And the poor warrior appeared to be holding his breath.

"It would go much better if you helped," Daar said. "Grab hold of the staff with me, Morgan, and concentrate. Feel the energy first, then see it in your mind's eye."

Morgan MacKeage slowly laid his hand over the second burl on the cane, his grip tight enough almost to splinter the wood. Together they waved the staff, which had nearly doubled in length, over the valley.

"Now. Tell me what you see, warrior. Tell me, and I will interpret it for you."

"Light. I see blinding light, yet it does not hurt my eyes."

"What color is the light?"

"Can you not see it yourself, *drùidh*? It's white. I can feel the heat, but I don't feel burned. And yellow. I see yellow sparks."

"And what is the yellow light doing?"

"It's dancing through the white light in dizzying circles, as if searching for something."

"What else do you see?"

"There is green also, chasing the yellow light."

Daar swept the staff into an arc farther afield, then stopped, bracing himself for the jolt of energy he knew was coming. The light intensified, swirling the colors into a blinding rainbow. The staff jerked, tugging at their hands as the new energy hit with the force of a tornado.

The warrior was not prepared. He staggered back against the assault but did not let go of his powerful grip.

"Holy hell. What's happening, *drùidh*? There's a great blackness swirling through the light now, driving against the yellow sparks. The yellow light is disappearing."

"And the green, warrior? What is the green doing?"

"Chasing the blackness. But when it reaches it, nothing is there."

Daar released his grip on the staff and stepped back. The wind stilled, and the mist immediately returned, as did the roar of the falls.

Morgan turned to face him, still clutching the once again normal-sized cane in his hand. Pale and shaken, Morgan threw the now silent piece of wood to the ground.

"Few mortal men have experienced what you just did, warrior. What think you of my gift?"

"It told me nothing, old man. I saw only colors."

"It told you everything, Morgan. You just had a glimpse of the energies roaming this valley. The emotions."

"Emotions?"

"Aye. Did the green light not feel familiar to you? Was it not the same shade of green in the MacKeage plaid you wear?"

"If the green light represents me, then who is the yellow?"

Daar grinned. "Someone you have yet to meet."

"The ribbon planter? Is that the yellow light?"

Daar widened his grin. "Possibly."

Morgan frowned at his answer. "And the black?"

"Ah, the black. That is another life force. Something visiting your valley."

"Something? Or someone?"

Daar shrugged and bent to pick up his cane. "Evil usually takes a human form when it wishes to plague humans."

"So the black represents evil, then? And it's coming?"

"Nay, warrior. It's already here. And so is something good. Don't forget the yellow light, Morgan. That covered your valley as well."

"But I couldn't catch it, either."

"Because you became more busy chasing the black."

Morgan's sigh blew over Daar with enough force to make him take a step back. Morgan MacKeage looked ready to explode in a fit of frustration. Good. There was certainly no lack of passion now.

Daar held up his hand to stop Morgan's outburst. "Talk to your brother," he quickly suggested. "Ask Greylen's permission to claim this valley as your own. Then build your home here. He'll not deny your request."

That suggestion took the bluster from the warrior's expression. "A home? You think I should build a house here?"

"This is a good place to raise a family," Daar said, then added speculatively, "I'm guessing you've got two months at least, judging by the strength of the lights we saw, before you must truly become involved in this mystery. You should be able to have a house up in that time. And then your claim will be unmistakable. It will put an end to the threat of a park in this gorge."

Morgan's face reddened. "I'm not having a family," he muttered. "So I don't need a house."

Well now, Daar thought. He wasn't having children, huh? That was news. Very disturbing news, considering the strength of the passion Daar had seen in the lights just now.

Not that he intended to tell Morgan that. No, some things were better left discovered on their own.

Such as the gender of unborn children, to name one.

"But why?" Daar asked. "Every warrior wants sons."

Morgan rubbed the back of his neck with one large hand. "I'm not a warrior anymore, *drùidh*, thanks to you. I'm just a man who shouldn't even exist now. I'm nothing."

"That's not true. You are alive, Morgan MacKeage, whether you wish to be or not. You are a landowner and a member of this community now. You run a ski resort with your clan."

Morgan actually laughed at that. "I sit people's asses onto a ski lift by day and spend every winter driving a machine up and down the mountain, grooming perfectly good snow. You call that noble work?"

"And fishing and hunting is?"

Morgan actually growled. "I feed you, old man."

His growl was suddenly answered by another, coming from the mist just below them. Morgan pivoted and drew his sword in one smooth motion.

"You'll not harm Faol," Daar said, moving to place his hand over the hilt of the sword. "He's my pet."

"A wolf?" Morgan asked, recognizing the Gaelic name for the beast. He tried to peer through the rising mist, then looked briefly at Daar. "You have a wolf for a pet?"

"Aye, it seems I do now. He arrived on my doorstep just last week."

"There are no wolves in this land."

Daar shrugged. "Maybe they're just wise enough not to be seen."

Faol finally showed himself, stepping silently out of the mist, his head low and his hackles raised. Morgan grabbed Daar by the shoulder and quickly pushed the wizard behind him. Morgan raised his sword again.

The wolf growled.

Daar snorted. "Two warriors, each protecting me from the other. Now, cease," he said, stepping back between them. He faced Morgan. "Faol can help you."

"Help me what?"

"Your valley, remember? The lights? The blackness? Faol can help you discover what's happening."

Morgan looked incredulous. "He's a wolf."

"Aye, warrior, he is that. But, like you, he's without direction. He's wanting a good fight to stir his blood."

Morgan looked over Daar's head at Faol, then back at the wizard, his eyes narrowed in speculation. "Is he one of your spells, *drùidh*? Have you conjured the wolf to plague me?"

Daar raised his hand to his heart but cocked his head to keep one guarded eye on the heavens. "May God strike me dead if I'm lying. Faol is as real as the hair on my face. He just showed up at my cabin eight days ago."

Morgan still looked skeptical. He slowly lowered his sword until the tip touched the ground. With his free hand he ripped one of the trout from his belt and tossed it to the wolf.

Faol stepped forward until he was standing over the fish and growled again.

Morgan snorted. "Some pet."

Alarmed that Morgan was giving away their breakfast, Daar moved to gather wood for a fire. By God, they would eat now before he fainted. He quickly set several branches into a pile, touched his cane to it, and muttered under his breath.

The wood immediately caught fire.

"I'll be more civilized if you toss one of those trout to me," he said then. "Ignore the beast, and whittle some spits to roast our breakfast on. A man could starve to death in your company."

It took Morgan another good minute to move. Finally, satisfied that Faol was more intent on guarding his trout than on eating the two of them, Morgan sheathed his sword and drew out his dagger. He stripped a maple sapling of its leaves and fashioned two intricate circular spits, skewered the three remaining fish, and walked over to the now crackling fire. Not once throughout his chore did Morgan take his attention off the wolf.

"Will you lend me your dagger, please?" Daar asked, once the trout were roasting.

Morgan studied the hand held out to him. "What for?" he asked, darting another brief look at Faol.

"I've a chore that needs doing while breakfast cooks."

Obviously reluctant to give up his weapon, considering he was within lunging distance of a wolf, the Highlander hesitated.

"He's more intent on eating the trout than us," Daar assured him, still holding out his hand. He grinned at the warrior. "Or is it me you're afraid of arming?"

He was answered by a green-eyed glare strong enough to turn a man into stone. Daar had a moment's concern that true passion in this warrior might very well turn out to be a dangerous thing for anyone on the receiving end of it.

Morgan finally handed his dagger to Daar, then quickly drew his sword and laid it across his knees. Faol lifted his head at the motion.

"Have you noticed his eyes?" Daar asked, using the dagger to point at Faol. "And the way he cants his head slightly to the right? Does he not seem familiar to you?"

Morgan's and Faol's gazes locked, each seemingly determined to outstare the other.

"No," Morgan said, not breaking eye contact. "He's just a wolf."

Daar sighed and set the sharp blade of the dagger to the small burl in the middle of his cane. Morgan had been only a lad of nine when Duncan MacKeage had died. And nine-year-olds had no time for noticing things like the color of their fathers' eyes.

"What are you doing?" Morgan asked, his attention suddenly drawn from the wolf when he realized that Daar was using the dagger on his cane.

"I'm thinking you should have some help as you set out on this path you seem determined to travel," Daar said, prying at the stubborn knot. The cane hissed in protest and started to vibrate.

"I want nothing to do with your magic," Morgan said, quickly moving back to tend the trout. "Keep your precious cane intact. You need its powers more than I do."

Daar ignored Morgan. His snarling cane was trying to scorch his hand as it twisted and sputtered to avoid the blade of the dagger.

Faol whined and stood up, leaving his trout and backing away toward the woods. Morgan also stood, his sword at the ready in his hand. He, too, began moving toward the safety of the forest.

With the deep roar of a wounded animal, the burl suddenly popped free of the cane and rolled across the forest floor, igniting a path of snapping red flames. Faol yelped and disappeared into the woods. Morgan grabbed Daar around the waist, lifted him off his tree stump, and pulled him into the forest. They stood together behind a giant spruce and watched as the angry knot of wood rolled around in frantic circles, spitting and hissing a rainbow of sparks.

"Are you insane, old man?" Morgan whispered. "You shouldn't piss off the magic."

Daar wiggled himself free of Morgan's grip and walked back to the stump. He picked up his now maimed staff and stroked it gently. "Give me that cord from around your neck," he told Morgan as he soothed his trembling cane.

"Why?"

Daar looked up. "Because it's time you let go of that pagan charm. It's been a worthless crutch and does nothing for you."

Morgan grasped the stone at his neck. "It's been with me for years."

"Old Dorna was not a true witch, Morgan. See her here today, alive and practicing her black magic? The old hag is eight hundred years dead. She preyed on simple-minded men and desperate women for her living. The stone is useless."

"I am not simple-minded."

"Nay. But neither are you quite ready to let go of your old beliefs. Have you learned nothing in six years? This thing called science has disproved what Dorna practiced and what you call magic."

"Then how does science explain you?"

"It can't. Nor will it ever. Some things must simply be accepted on faith."

The Highlander did not care for that explanation, if Daar read his expression correctly. Morgan gripped his amulet protectively, then finally tore the cord from around his neck. "Here," he said, handing it to Daar.

The wizard let the smooth stone slide free and fall to the ground. "Hand me that burl, would you?" he asked, using his cane to point at the now silent knot of cherrywood.

Morgan paled. "You pick it up," he whispered.

The burl was sitting against a rock, softly humming. With a sigh of impatience, Daar pushed himself off the stump and picked up the burl. He closed one eye and squinted the other to thread the rawhide cord through the burl.

"There's no hole," Morgan said, coming up behind him. "You can't push a soft rope through solid wood."

The rawhide smoothly slipped through the swirling cherrywood. Daar quickly knotted the cord and turned to Morgan.

The warrior stepped back, holding up his hand. "Keep that thing away from me."

"It won't bite," Daar snapped. "Now, lean over so I can put this around your neck."

"I said I don't want your magic."

"And I'm thinking the time will come when you will need it," Daar countered. "If not for yourself, think of the valley. And the yellow light. Remember? The blackness was consuming it."

Daar pointed at Morgan. "And although you may have survived your journey six years ago, there's no saying you'll survive this one. You are a fierce warrior, Morgan MacKeage. But hear me well. You are not invincible. The blackness is a powerful life force void of goodness, compassion, or conscience. It will devour anything that gets in its way—you, the yellow light, and eventually this whole valley if it manages to get past you. This small piece of my cane will be your greatest weapon against it."

It took the warrior some time to digest Daar's words. Finally, Morgan leaned forward and bowed his head, allowing the wizard to place the cord around his neck. Daar then centered the burl over Morgan's chest as he straightened.

"If you want this to work, you're going to have to give it your faith," Daar told him, stepping back to admire his gift. "And your intelligence. This burl is not strong by itself. You must discover the best way to add to its strength."

Standing as still as the mountains themselves and holding his breath again, Morgan scowled at him. "How—" He swallowed hard. "How do I do that?"

Daar waved his question away. "You'll figure it out when the time is right."

He handed Morgan back his dagger. As if afraid any quick movements would fry him on the spot, the warrior carefully held out his hand and took his weapon, then slowly placed it back in his belt.

"Oh, one more thing, Morgan. You're not to whisper even a hint of what's happened here today. Especially not to your brother. Not one word about the unusual state of this gorge, your vision, or my special gift to you," Daar said, pointing at the burl. "I don't want Greylen knowing that any part of my old staff still exists, and I surely don't want him knowing that my new one is gaining strength."

The first hint that Morgan was beginning to relax appeared when one corner of his mouth turned up in a smile. "You have no worry I'll tell anyone about this, old man."

Daar's nose suddenly twitched. What was burning? He looked around. The small fires the sparking burl had started were gone. The campfire, however, was burning brightly.

"Dammit! The fish!"

The burl around his neck suddenly forgotten, Morgan rushed to the fire and pulled the trout free of the flame. He held them up and turned to Daar, grinning.

"No worry. They're only charred on the outside a bit."

Morgan kicked at the fire with his foot, dousing the flame to leave only the smoldering coals, then placed the trout above the coals to finish cooking more slowly. Daar joined him, and together they sat once again facing the fire.

Morgan looked off into the forest, in the direction Faol had run. "Do you think he'll return?" he asked.

"Aye. I doubt he went far. He's probably watching us now."

Morgan hesitantly lifted his hand to the rawhide cord at his neck and slowly closed his fist over the burl. His eyes widened.

"It's warm."

Daar nodded. "Aye. It was angry for being ripped from the collective energy of the staff," he explained. "But now it is content. If feels your strength, warrior. It will work hard to protect you."

Faol silently returned to the edge of the clearing, lying down beside his trout. Morgan did not unsheathe his sword this time or pull his dagger from his belt. Instead, both warrior and wolf turned their attention to the burl hanging around Morgan's neck. Faol watched as Morgan fingered it briefly before he tucked it out of sight beneath his shirt.

Daar smiled. It was good, all that had happened today. Morgan had found his passion for life again in a mystery that promised a battle worth fighting.

Faol had found a new purpose as well.

And Daar's guilt was somewhat assuaged.

After ten long minutes of waiting, the trout was finally ready to eat. Daar watched as the Scot expertly pulled their breakfast from the spits, and the wizard was reminded of a similar moment nearly eight hundred years ago. There had been another campfire then, with old Laird MacKeage teaching his two young sons how to cook their catch.

What would Duncan MacKeage think of his sons today, of their predicament and their incredible journey? Would he be proud of how they had comported themselves through it all and how they were coping with their new lives now?

Or did Duncan already know?

Daar looked over at Faol. The animal rested much as Morgan did, relaxed but ready to spring into action if need be. For the tenth time in the last eight days, Daar wondered what power had lured a wolf in from the wild to walk among humans. And for the tenth time, he decided he didn't really care enough to inquire.

Daar finally took his first bite of the delicious trout the warrior handed him, and not a moment too soon. His stomach rumbled with thanks. He leaned back against one of the magically tall pine trees and watched Morgan MacKeage eat his breakfast.

Should he mention the fact that there was a woman involved in this valley mystery? And that she had shiny yellow hair that sparkled with the sensuous promise of passion?

Nay, probably not.

Better to leave some things a surprise.

Chapter Two

Seven weeks later

Sadie Quill squinted through the brightness of the noonday sun, her attention focused on the opposite shore of the narrow cove of the cold-water lake. Holding her breath, careful not to make any noise, she watched the young moose calf slowly step into the water where its mother stood. The calf was only three months old and already had learned a few lessons about survival, judging by his reluctance to move into the open.

Mama moose lifted her head to watch his progress, water pouring from her mouth as she chewed on the succulent growth she had pulled from the lake bottom. Startled by the cold water dripping onto his face, the calf staggered backward and fell on his rump on the slippery bank. His angry bleat of protest was lost on his mother, however, as her head was underwater again.

Sadie stifled a chuckle and raised her camera,

pointing the long lens through the honeysuckle bush where she hid. This scene was priceless, exactly why she loved her job so much.

She was still in awe of her luck. She was being paid to help put together a proposal for a wilderness park. She was scouting locations for trails and campsites while cataloging both geographical areas of interest and animal activity. These last ten weeks had been a pleasant dream she never wanted to wake up from.

Well, most of it had been a dream job, except that some of her work was being sabotaged. But having her trail markers stolen was more of a nuisance than a setback. The orange ribbons were nothing more than a visible tool for her project. She had the coordinates written on the large wall map back at her cabin, and she still could locate them by satellite, using her hand-held global positioning system device.

It was only an inconvenience that some short-sighted fool thought he could slow down the progress of a wilderness park by stealing the ribbons. Still, Sadie had turned her attention away from scouting trails for the time being, hoping the jerk would think he had won.

This week she had been exploring the flora and fauna of the valley, noting in her journal areas that future hikers would want to see.

At the urging of his mother, the calf again stepped into the shallow water of the protected cove. Sadie depressed the shutter on her camera, captured the shot, and advanced the film. No noise betrayed her position, thanks to her father's ingenious skill with equipment, which made the mechanics of the camera silent.

Sadie and her dad had walked these woods for years, taking pictures as she was doing now, and Sadie's heart ached with sadness that he was not here with her today.

Frank Quill had taught Sadie the fine art of moving silently among the animals and had instilled in her not only an appreciation of nature but a respect for it as well.

And now she was thanking him by the only means she could find, by helping to build a park in his memory.

The mother moose suddenly lifted her head and looked toward the open water of the lake. Sadie used the telephoto lens of her camera to scan across the calm lake surface. And there, near the opposite shore, she saw the movement.

Something was swimming toward them.

Sadie leaned forward to get a better view. The mother moose heard her, whipped her head around, and stared directly at Sadie. For a moment, their eyes locked.

There wasn't much in these woods that worried a full-grown moose, but a mother had to be more cautious of the vulnerability of her calf. Sadie's presence and whatever was swimming toward them were apparently more than the mother moose was willing to deal with. She gave a low grunt of warning and stepped out of the cove, pushing her baby ahead of her.

With a sigh of regret for scaring the moose, Sadie

turned her attention back to the lake. She couldn't imagine what was swimming directly across the widest expanse of water, when walking around would be much easier. Most animals were lazy by nature or, rather, more efficient with the energy they were willing to spend.

Whatever was swimming toward her was too small to be another moose and too large to be a muskrat or an otter. Sadie sharpened the focus on her lens and watched, until finally she saw the rise and fall of arms cutting a path through the water.

Arms? There was a person swimming across the lake?

Sadie could count on her fingers and toes the people she had run into this summer: kayakers taking advantage of the last of the spring runoff nine weeks ago, a biologist, a game warden, a small fishing party, and a middle-aged couple from Pine Creek searching for mushrooms to eat.

Sadie settled herself deeper into the bushes, making sure she was well hidden as he moved ever closer. Yes, she could see now that the swimmer was male. And that he had broad shoulders, long and powerful arms, and a stroke that cut through the water with amazing ease.

The cove she was hiding in, and that he was heading toward, was strewn with boulders. The swimmer moved with lazy, rhythmic grace, right up to one of the larger rocks. He placed two large hands on the rock and pulled himself out of the water in one strong, seamless motion.

Sadie blinked, then tore her eye away from the

viewfinder. She no longer needed the vivid clarity of the telephoto lens to see that the man was naked.

She looked through her camera again and adjusted the focus. He was as naked as the day he was born. He sat on the boulder, brushing the hair from his face and wringing it out in a ponytail at his back.

Well, heck. The guy's shoulder-length, dark blond hair was almost as long as hers. Sadie pushed the zoom on her lens closer, aiming it at the top half of the man. She almost dropped the camera when he came into focus. He was huge, and it wasn't an illusion of the lens, either. His shoulders filled the viewfinder, and when he lifted both hands to push the water away from his forehead again, his chest expanded to Herculean proportions.

Sadie noticed then that the guy wasn't even winded from his swim. His broad and powerfully muscled chest, covered with a luxurious mat of wet, dark hair, rose and fell with the steady rhythm of someone who had merely walked up a short flight of stairs.

Who was this demigod of the woods?

Sadie zoomed the lens of her camera even closer, on his face. She didn't recognize him from town. She'd been back in the Pine Creek area for only a few months now and had gone into town only six or seven times for supplies since returning, but she would have remembered such a ruggedly handsome face on a man his size. She definitely would have remembered such startling green eyes framed by such a drop-dead gorgeous face. His jaw, darkened with a couple of days' growth of a reddish-blond beard, was square, stern, and stubborn-looking. His neck was thick, with a leather cord around it that dangled an odd-shaped ball of some sort over his chest.

Sadie zoomed the lens out again until his entire body filled her viewfinder. His stomach was flat and contoured with muscle. He had long, powerful-looking thighs, bulging calves, and even his feet dangling in and out of the water looked strong.

The man could have been made from solid granite.

And he was turned away just enough to keep his modesty intact. Too bad. It wasn't every day she was treated to such an exhibit of pure, unadulterated maleness. And despite her own sense of shame for being a blatant voyeur, Sadie wished he would turn just a bit more toward her. She was curious, dammit, and made no apology for it.

She liked men. Especially big ones, like this guy. Sadie was six-foot-one in her stocking feet, and she usually spent most of her time talking to the receding hairlines of the men she knew. Since she had hit puberty and shot up like a weed, Sadie had wished she were short. Like the heroines in the romance novels she loved to read, she wanted to be spunky, beautiful, and petite. And she was tired of having only one of those traits.

About all Sadie could say for herself was that she did possess a healthy dose of spunk. She may have come close to beauty once, but a deadly house fire eight years ago had ended that promise. And no matter how much she had willed it, she hadn't stopped growing until her twenty-third birthday. She was taller than most men she met, and every bit of her height was in the overlong inseam of her jeans.

She'd bet her boots that the guy on the rock had at

least a thirty-six inseam and that he wore a triple-extra-large shirt he had to buy from the tall rack.

The vision in her viewfinder suddenly began to fade, and Sadie had a moment's regret that it had all been a dream.

Until she realized that the viewfinder had fogged up.

Well, she did feel unusually warm. And she was breathing a bit harder than normal.

Wow. Either she was having a guilt attack for being a peeping tom, or she was experiencing a fine little case of lust.

Sadie didn't care which it was, she wasn't stopping. She used the back of her gloved right hand to wipe the viewfinder dry before she looked through it again.

The man was now laid out on the boulder, his arms folded under his head and his eyes closed to the sun as he basked in its warmth like an overfed bear.

Sadie suddenly remembered that she was looking through the lens of a camera. If this guy was willing to parade around the forest naked, why should she feel guilty about a couple of pictures? She just wondered where in her journal of fauna she should place his photo.

Probably at the top of the food chain.

Feeling pretty sure that the man had fallen asleep, Sadie snapped the shutter on her camera and quickly advanced the film. She zoomed in the lens and snapped again.

But just as she advanced the film for another picture, the man leaped to his feet in a blur of motion. And suddenly he was looking directly at the bushes where she hid.

Dammit. He couldn't have heard that. Animals couldn't hear the damn thing, and their lives depended on their ears.

Sadie sucked in her breath and held it; she wasn't sure if she was doing so from fright or because she now had a full frontal view of the man.

She snapped the shutter down one last time and scurried backward to free herself from the bush. She foolishly stood up, then immediately realized her mistake when she found herself face-to-face with the giant, with only a hundred yards of water between them.

She couldn't move. He was magnificent, standing there like a demigod, his penetrating green stare rooting her feet into place.

"Come on, Quill," she whispered, her gaze still locked with his. "Move while you still have the advantage."

He must have heard that, too, because he went into action before she did. He dove into the water and began swimming toward her.

Sadie snatched up her backpack and headed into the forest. She broke into a run as soon as she hit the overgrown trail and set a fast, steady pace toward home.

She grinned as the forest blurred past.

The swimmer didn't stand a chance of catching her. He had to get to shore first and then find the trail as well as the direction she had taken. Sadie's long legs ate up the ground with effortless ease, and she actually laughed out loud at the rush of adrenaline pumping through her veins.

This was her strength; there were very few people she couldn't outrun. Especially a barefooted streaker who looked as if he outweighed her by a good sixty pounds. It took a lot of energy to move that much weight through the winding trail, ducking and darting around branches and over fallen logs.

Yes, her long legs would give her the edge this time, rescuing her from the folly of trespassing on a stranger's right to privacy.

Sadie slowed down after a while, but she didn't quite have the courage to stop yet. Only a maniac would have followed her, but then only a crazy person would be swimming naked in a cold-water lake.

So Sadie kept running, easing her pace to a jog.

Until she heard the branch snap behind her.

She looked over her shoulder and would have screamed if she could have. The man from the lake was fifty feet behind her. Sadie turned back to watch where she was going, the adrenaline spiking back into her bloodstream.

There was nothing like seeing a fully naked, wild-haired, wild-eyed madman on her heels to make a girl wish she had stayed in bed that morning. Sadie ran as if the devil himself were chasing her. She could actually hear the pounding of his feet behind her now, could practically feel his breath on the back of her neck.

She grabbed a small cedar tree to pivot around a corner, and that was when he caught her, hitting her broadside in a full body tackle. Sadie wanted to scream then, too, but he knocked what little air she had left out of her body. They rolled several times, and

Sadie swung her camera at his head. He grunted in surprise at the blow and grabbed her flailing arms as they continued to roll.

When they finally stopped, he was on top of her . . . and her wrists were being held over her head . . . and her back was being crushed into the ground . . . and she had never been so scared in her life.

Sadie thought about really screaming now, but her throat closed tight. She pushed at the ground and tried to buck the man off her, at the same time as she lashed out with her feet.

That was when he shifted from sitting on her to lying on her, trapping her legs with his own.

Sadie instantly stilled. This was going from bad to worse; she now had a naked madman on top of her—and she was wearing shorts.

Oh, God. Now that she had such a close look at him, he was no longer a demigod. He was a full-blown god, Adonis, maybe. His broad shoulders and amazingly wide chest blocked out the sunlight. His warm breath feathered over her face. Sadie could feel every inch of his muscled legs running the length of hers. And she could feel something . . . something else touching her bare thigh. Something firm.

He was excited, either from the thrill of the chase, their suggestive position, or the anticipation of what he was planning to do. Sadie didn't want to scream anymore. She wanted to faint.

She did close her eyes, so she wouldn't have to look at his triumphant, very male face. Why didn't he move?

Then she opened her eyes to find him staring at her hands, which he still held firmly over her head. She immediately opened her bare left hand and let the camera fall onto the ground.

Still, he kept staring over her head.

He reached up and tugged at the glove on her right hand. Sadie closed it into a fist, to keep her glove on. Momentarily deterred from his task, he turned his attention to her face.

She turned her head away.

He pulled her chin back to face him, then gently ran his thumb along her bottom lip, watching as if fascinated.

Good Lord. Was he going to kiss her?

His finger trailed down her face, over her chin, to her neck, and Sadie felt him touch the opening of her blouse. She twisted frantically and tried to bite the arm holding her hands over her head.

He lowered the full force of his weight onto her then, and Sadie fought to breathe. Well, heck. She hadn't realized he'd been holding himself off her before. She stilled, and he lifted himself slightly, allowing her to gasp for air.

Their gazes locked.

His long blond hair dripped lake water on her chin and throat. The heavy object dangling from his neck nestled against her breasts, causing a disturbing sensation to course all the way down to the pit of her stomach. Sadie could feel her clothes slowly sopping up his sweat, his hairy legs abrasive against hers, his chest pushing into her with every breath he took. The heat from his body scorched her to the point that she couldn't work up enough moisture in her mouth to speak.

Not that she could think of anything to say to the brute.

As if sensing her discomfort, he slowly turned up the right corner of his mouth, and his gaze broke from hers and returned to her right hand. This time Sadie was unable to keep him from pulling the glove off. She balled her now bare hand into a fist as she felt her face flush with embarrassment.

And that made her mad. Why should she care that this man found her disgusting? Her disfigurement could well be half of her salvation.

He sat up suddenly, still straddling her, and released her wrists. Sadie instinctively rushed to push down her twisted clothes and cover her stomach, but her hand bumped into his groin. With a gasp of dismay, Sadie jerked, hiding her scarred right hand in her shirt.

The other side of the brute's mouth turned up, setting his face into a cocky grin, his forest-green eyes sparkling with the pleasure of scaring her spitless.

Dammit. Why didn't he speak?

He leaned forward, and Sadie froze in anticipation of his kiss. But he only picked up her camera. He carefully lifted the rewind and popped it open. He was not so gentle, however, when he ripped the film from it. He tossed the exposed film and the camera onto the ground beside them.

He opened her pack next, spilling the contents onto the ground. He poked around in the mess he'd made and found her handheld GPS. He turned it over, pushed several buttons, and tossed it back onto the ground. He picked up her cell phone, flipped it open, then discarded it like trash.

Next, he picked up her roll of orange surveyor tape.

He stared at that tape for several seconds, turning it around in his hand as he looked from it to her. He pulled a three-foot section free and tugged it between his hands until it snapped in half. He threw both pieces down onto the ground next to the GPS and the cell phone.

And then he picked up the small roll of duct tape she used for emergency repairs.

Now, Sadie had heard that victims often were killed with their own guns. She suddenly understood that concept when the man freed a length of her own tape and grabbed her wrists. He stopped, though, when he saw the eight-year-old scars on the palm and wrist of her right hand.

He handed her back her glove. Sadie struggled to put it on, the chore made difficult by her uncontrollable trembling. He was still sitting heavily on top of her, he was still disturbingly naked, and he still hadn't uttered one single word.

He took both her hands as soon as she finished putting on her glove and taped them together. He slid down her body and started to take hold of her legs.

Sadie kicked him hard enough in the stomach that he grunted, then she rolled and scrambled up to run. She didn't make it past her camera before he grabbed her by the ankles and pushed her back to the ground, on her face this time. Sadie looked over her shoulder as he wrapped duct tape around her legs.

The damn crazy man was grinning again.

She kicked out at him again with her bound feet.

He smacked her on her fanny.

Sadie closed her eyes and gritted her teeth, burying her face in her arms. God save her, Adonis was a sadistic brute.

Sadie flinched when a sharp, carrying whistle suddenly rent the air. She snapped her head around to see what he was doing.

Was he calling a friend?

Sadie looked at the scattered contents of her pack. Where was her knife? She needed something, a weapon, to defend herself. She checked to see that he was still looking off into the forest, watching for someone, while she rolled toward a group of young pine trees. She found a lower limb devoid of bark and wiggled to sit up beside it. She looked up at the man again, only to find him looking over his shoulder at her, still grinning, not at all worried that she would get far being trussed up like a turkey ready for cooking.

Ha. This turkey was not going into the pot without a fight.

He turned back and whistled again, and Sadie broke off the small branch at the same time, his signal covering the sound of the snap. She quickly tucked the sharp little stick under her arm.

The ground started to rumble beneath her. A sound, faint at first, slowly gathered in volume until it was like thunder moving closer. A huge, solid black horse appeared suddenly, galloping through the forest and sliding to a stop a mere two feet in front of the man. Sadie had to shield her face from flying debris.

A horse?

Holy Mother of God. The brute had a horse?

Sadie also remembered hearing that a victim should

never let her assailant take her to a second location. She almost snorted at the absurdity of that useless warning. Where could he take her that was any more remote?

The horse was the largest animal of its kind she had ever seen. It had a funny-looking saddle on its back, and tied to that saddle was a bundle of clothes, a back-pack, and a long, leather-wrapped stick that must be a fishing pole.

With an almost negligent look back to see that she was still there, the man patted his fidgeting horse and pulled the clothes free of the saddle. Turning to face her, he started dressing.

The jerk had no shame.

Once dressed, he pulled some socks and boots out of the pack and walked over to sit down beside her.

Sadie decided the man didn't look any less scary fully clothed. If anything, he appeared even larger. Still as silent as a mime—which was really starting to get on her nerves—he wiped off his feet and dressed them.

Sadie dismissed the fact that she hadn't exactly been a fountain of words herself. She was the victim here. She had a right to be scared speechless.

His chore finished, he stood up, put his hands around her waist, and picked her up to stand in front of him. Sadie pulled her stick free and drove it at the center of his chest.

She hit that odd-looking object he wore around his neck. It deflected her blow and allowed him to wrest the stick from her hands. Staring at her with forest-green eyes now laced with laughter, he snapped the stick in half and tossed it to the ground. He ducked and lifted her over his shoulder.

Sadie kicked and twisted as if her life depended on it.

And then she finally screamed at the top of her lungs.

Her assailant was so startled he dropped her onto the ground like a sack of wormy meal and covered his ears. His horse backed up a good five paces, shaking its head as if his own equine ears had been damaged. Sadie dug at the tape binding her legs.

"You bastard!" she yelled, pleased with herself for finally finding her voice. "You get the hell out of here, before I claw you to shreds!"

His hands still covering his ears, the man just stood there staring at her. He shook his head slightly, then turned and calmly walked over to his horse. He untied the fishing pole from the saddle and pulled it free of the leather case.

Sadie snapped her mouth shut. It wasn't a fishing pole, it was a damn big, scary-looking sword.

She kicked her feet and scurried back as fast as she could, until she bumped into a tree. The man advanced on her, his eyes narrowed, and stopped when his booted feet touched hers.

That was when Sadie realized their little game of cat and mouse had come to an end. She closed her eyes and waited.

But instead of the prick on her skin that she was expecting, Sadie felt his warm, tender mouth covering hers.

She opened her eyes and found herself staring into deep, evergreen eyes. The giant raised his hand and cupped the side of her face and pressed closer, his sweet-tasting lips compelling her to respond.

Sadie shoved him away.

He laughed as he fell backward, the sound a deep, boisterous rumble that echoed through the forest. He stood up, brushed himself off, and turned and walked back to his horse. Goose bumps shivered over Sadie's skin as she watched him walk away, that long sword held so casually in his hand, his stride almost swaggering. He vaulted into his saddle with effortless grace, then moved his horse closer. He brought his sword up to her hands and cut the tape.

"Take a care, *gràineag,* until we meet again," he whispered with a nod, swinging his horse around and thundering away in the direction of the lake.

Sadie sat in stunned silence as she watched horse and rider disappear into the woods. Holy Mary Mother of God and all the saints and angels in heaven. Who was that lunatic?

And that word he'd used—had he just cursed her?

And what did he mean when he said "until we meet again"?

Hell, not in this lifetime.

Not unless she was carrying a gun.

It took Sadie a good ten minutes before she could will herself to move. She was still trembling so much she had to use a tree to help herself stand. As she gripped the branch and fought to keep from falling, she brushed at her clothes, more or less patting herself down to make sure she really was okay.

She started walking back to her cabin.

For the first time in a lifetime of growing up in these mountains, Sadie realized how arrogant she had been to think she could protect herself from any danger the woods might offer. By the time she reached her cabin, she had worked herself up into a full-blown frenzy aimed more at herself than at anyone else.

She could have been raped or even killed. But instead she'd been chased down by a naked giant who was way too handsome to be real. He hadn't been angry, or even all that rough; he had just been determined to teach her a lesson.

And he'd succeeded, more than Sadie cared to admit.

For all of her own anger at having put herself in such a vulnerable position, she couldn't help but remember the feel of his rock-solid body pressing against hers, couldn't help but think about the sensuous touch and taste of his lips.

And she couldn't decide if her shivering was the lingering remnants of her initial fear or the awareness that she had found the encounter exciting.

She ran up the steps and shoved open the door of her small cabin, quickly moving to close the wood shutters on each window, locking them securely, throwing the interior into darkness. She threw paper and kindling into the huge stove that sat in the center of the room and lit a fire. She left the stove door open, sat on the floor in front of the fire, and held her hands out to the heat.

Ping, Sadie's gray tiger cat, came slinking out from

under the bed, yawning and stretching as she walked, and climbed onto Sadie's lap. Purring loudly enough to wake the dead, the cat stretched up and gave her a gritty lick on the chin. Sadie hugged the cat against her chest and buried her face in the animal's fur.

"Oh, Ping," she whispered against her rumbling little body. "You won't believe what happened to me today."

She couldn't stop shaking. Her naively safe little world had been shattered by the stone-hard body of a man who had held her very life in his hands.

Sadie already had a rather low opinion of men—all except for her father. She was twenty-seven, and she had never had a relationship that lasted more than two months. And that had been before the fire had scarred her in more ways than one.

But up until now, Sadie had never actually feared any man. Never again would she be able even to go out on a simple date without realizing that she might be tall and strong, but she was not invincible.

Even her ugliness couldn't protect her.

Or had it? Had the man felt so sorry for her that he had decided to let her go?

Now, that irked.

Perversely, Sadie got angry that the sinfully handsome man might have let her go out of pity.

She stopped rubbing Ping and lifted her hand to her lips. He *had* kissed her. And after he had seen the ugly scars on her hand. Had it been a sympathy kiss?

Oh, those were the worse kind, quick little pecks that said she was likable, just not in a passionate way. She'd had quite a few of those over the last eight years.

Ping protested the loss of affection by nudging

against Sadie's arm. Sadie absently began scratching the cat again as she tried to judge the kiss she'd received today against those sympathy pecks.

Naw, the guy hadn't felt sorry for her. He'd been too amused.

Had it been a mocking kiss?

That was just as bad. Sympathy or mockery, when the kiss was from an Adonis, both were equally humiliating.

Chapter Three

It was late afternoon when Morgan guided his horse, Gràdhag, through the magical mist of the gorge. He chuckled as he remembered the expression on the woman's face when she had realized he was right behind her, when she had tried to stab him with a stick, and when she had shoved him away when he'd kissed her.

Morgan simply couldn't quit smiling. If he had known the ribbon planter roaming his valley these last ten weeks had been a stunningly beautiful woman, he would have spent less time building his house and more time plaguing her instead.

Well, he certainly had plagued her today, and it would be a long time before he found any more ribbons.

His smile quickly faded, however, when he rode into the clearing and saw Daar sitting on the steps of Morgan's newly completed home. He ignored the *drùidh* and walked his horse to the small barn and dismounted. Daar came over, took the beast by the reins, and fed him a carrot.

Morgan shook his head. Gràdhag was as fierce a war horse as any warrior could hope for. But in the presence of the *drùidh*, the animal became as docile as a newborn kitten.

"Now what have you done?" Daar asked without looking up from his chore.

"What makes you think I've done anything? I always swim in the morning."

"You were grinning like the village idiot when you rode up, which tells me something pleases you greatly." The priest cocked his head, squinting at him. "And that usually means you've been up to mischief. How did you get that cut on your head?"

Morgan briefly touched the small cut on his forehead, then began unsaddling Gràdhag. "I am smiling, old man, because I have just put a good dent in the plans to build a park."

"How?" Daar asked, turning a suspicious eye on him as he fed another carrot to the horse.

"By scaring our ribbon planter away." Morgan chuckled again. "She probably hasn't stopped running yet, nor will she likely stop until she reaches Pine Creek. She'll not be back in this valley anytime soon."

"She?"

Morgan tossed the saddle over the rail of the paddock and picked up a brush to begin grooming his horse. "It's a woman who's been marking the valley with ribbons. I found the roll of orange tape in her bag."

"And how would you know what she was carrying in her bag?"

Morgan stopped brushing. "I looked."

"Did this woman see you look?" Daar asked, looking pointedly at the cut on Morgan's forehead.

Morgan grinned again. "Aye. I was sitting on top of her at the time."

"Sitting on her?" Daar's eyes widened. "What have ya done?"

Morgan tossed the brush into the bucket and took Gràdhag's reins away from the *drùidh*. He led the horse into the paddock and opened a bale of hay.

"Tell me. What did you do to her?"

"I scared her, okay?" Morgan said, turning to face the old priest. "I ran her down and scared her so badly she couldn't even speak."

"You accosted an innocent woman you found in the woods? Are you mad, Morgan? That's unforgivable, not to mention illegal."

"She's no innocent. She's the one laying out the park in the valley."

"So you caught her tying ribbons to trees, then?"

"Ah . . . no," Morgan said, walking toward the house.

His home was a sturdily built structure, two stories tall, made of timber he'd cut from the surrounding forest and had milled in town. The house wasn't that large and, with Callum's help, had taken only two months to build. There was a porch spanning the front and several large windows facing Prospect Valley, which offered a spectacular view whenever the mist was not too heavy.

Morgan walked onto the porch and through the door, into the large single room that served as both living room and kitchen.

Daar followed close at his heels. "Then what made you go after her?" the priest asked, moving to the cooler on the counter and helping himself to a can of soda.

Morgan watched the old man fight to open the flip top on the can. With a sigh of resignation, he walked over, took the can from him, opened it, then handed it back.

"She took my picture," Morgan told him. "She was hiding in the bushes with her camera, and she took my picture while I was sitting on a rock in the middle of the lake."

Daar lowered the can from his mouth. "You were swimming naked as usual, I presume?"

"Aye." Morgan found his grin again. "She'll certainly have something to dream about tonight."

"So you chased her because of the pictures?"

"That I did."

"While you were still naked."

"Well, I didn't stop to find my clothes, old man. She's a fairly fast runner. I swear the woman has legs all the way up to her ears."

Daar sat down and placed his soda on the finely crafted maple table in front of him. He turned the can with his fingers and absently watched the label spin around. Unable to decide if the old priest was angry or bemused by his tale, Morgan went to the cooler and took out a can of beer. He leaned against the counter and opened it, taking a long drink of the weak ale as he watched the *drùidh's* back.

"What did this woman look like?" Daar asked without turning around. "Her eyes. And her hair and skin. What color were they?"

Morgan frowned at the question. "Her eyes were blue," he said, as if that detail were unimportant. He wasn't about to reveal to the priest just how captured he'd been by the woman's eyes when he finally saw them up close. "What does it matter what color they were? She had tanned skin, blond hair, blue eyes, and she stood as tall as a man."

Daar twisted in his seat to face him. "Blond hair? A red-blond or a yellow-blond?" he asked. "Do you remember seeing that color before today?"

Morgan wondered what the old man was getting at. She was a blond, dammit. Lots of people had light-colored hair and blue eyes. His sister-in-law had blue eyes. Hell, the old priest had blue eyes.

But his ribbon planter did have a distinct honey-yellow shine to her hair and flawless golden skin that looked to be kissed by the sun.

Well, flawless skin but for the scars on one hand and those he saw peeking around the side of her waist from her back.

Morgan suddenly straightened away from the counter.

"It's not the same," he said, glaring down at the priest. "This woman is not the yellow light we saw in the vision. Her work will destroy the gorge."

"Then you saw the blackness around her?"

"Of course not. I don't practice your magic. But she did try to kill me. She tried to drive a stake through my heart."

Daar glared at him. "You didn't hurt her, did you?"

Morgan glared back. "Not unless a person can actually die of fright."

The priest's stare darkened. Morgan blew out a frustrated breath, rubbing his neck. "I left her whole and hearty, old man. Just shaken, I hope, enough to leave the valley and not come back."

"Ah, warrior," Daar said with a tired sigh, shaking his head and turning back to the table. He began toying with his soda again. "You may have just scared away the only goodness this valley has seen in more than eighty years."

"Explain yourself," Morgan demanded, moving to sit at the table. "How can anything that has to do with that park be good?"

"You've claimed this land now. If the park doesn't include your gorge, what can it hurt?"

"They don't run a fence around it," Morgan countered. "People will wander, and once the waterfall—and the magic—is discovered, nothing will keep them away."

The old man sighed again. "That is true. But there must be some way for both you and this park to exist in harmony."

"I've thought about that." Morgan leaned his arms on the table. "I had our lawyer check the registry of deeds at the courthouse. The lands of the valley are still held by many owners. They haven't been combined yet to form the park. What if I buy this south end of the valley? That will keep the people miles away."

"Buy it with what?"

Morgan warmed with the excitement of saying his plan aloud for the first time since thinking of it two weeks ago. He leaned closer. "You can put me in touch with the auction house where you sold Ian and Callum's swords and several pieces of our equipment."

"You'll not sell your sword! Your brother would kill you."

"Nay. I would die before I part with it. But my dagger is a gift from my father. It's nearly nine hundred years old now and is jeweled. It might bring enough money to buy the land."

Daar leaned back in his chair and scratched his beard. He didn't speak for a full minute.

Morgan grew impatient. "What are you thinking, old man?" he finally asked.

"I'm thinking it might work, if your brother agrees."

Morgan was surprised. "What has Grey to do with this?"

"He's still your laird."

Morgan waved that away. "That means nothing today, especially in this country. It's only a hollow title now."

It was Daar's turn to be surprised. "My, my. How you do like to cling to the old ways, Morgan MacKeage, and embrace the new ones only when it's convenient for you. You should not let your brother know your opinions if you value your skin. Grey is still determined to bring this clan back to the power it once was."

Morgan grinned. "With daughters?"

Daar nodded. "Aye. But also with the sons you will give him, warrior."

"I'm not having children," Morgan snapped.

"Sometimes children appear without warning," the old priest replied, a smirk lifting the edge of his mouth. "Sometimes they're wanting to be born so badly they sneak in when you're not looking. Or do you intend to live like a monk the rest of your life?"

"Babies can be prevented."

"Aye," Daar agreed. "And sometimes they can't, no matter how careful you are. Mother Nature is a formidable force to go up against when she's wanting something to happen."

Morgan stood up and got himself another beer. He wasn't liking what the old *drùidh* was saying. He didn't want children.

Then again, he didn't much care for the celibate life he was living now.

A vision of a leggy, blue-eyed blonde suddenly rose unbidden in his mind. He'd gotten hard lying on top of her, knowing he just had to use his knees to spread her legs apart. Oh, yes, he wouldn't mind feeling those long, lovely legs wrapped around his waist.

Hell, he wanted the woman.

Morgan turned to look out the window and adjusted the fit of his pants. Dammit, he wanted her gone from this valley.

But he also wanted to see her again.

"There's something that doesn't make sense in all this," Daar said from the table.

Morgan continued to look out the window, willing his male urges to go away. "What?" he asked harshly.

"I'm wondering why they would start work on a park if they don't even own the land yet."

That changed the direction of his thoughts. Morgan turned around. "I wondered the same thing," he admitted, "when I discovered the valley was owned by several different people. Two paper mills own most of it, but five individuals own the rest."

Daar turned in his seat to face him. "Can your lawyer find out *who* is building this park? Is it the government or a group of people?"

"I'll have him look into it," Morgan said, nodding. "Now, will you give me the name of that auction house?"

"You can't really mean to sell the dagger? It was a gift from your father."

"And the land I buy with it will become his legacy. It's metal and stone, old man. Selling the dagger to gain property will not diminish my father's gift. It will only strengthen my memory of him."

"Speaking of Duncan, have you seen Faol lately?" Daar asked.

Morgan had to shift gears mentally. How had they gone from Duncan to the wolf?

"Aye. The beast has been sneaking around here for the last seven weeks. Did you not notice the scratch marks on my door?" Morgan asked, irritation lacing his voice.

That damn animal had nearly ruined his woodwork.

Daar made no more mention of the wolf. He stood up and walked out onto the porch, his cane tapping the rhythm of his steps. "I'm wanting a ride home. And not on that damn rough-gaited beast ya call Pet," he complained, though Morgan knew he shared his affection for the beast. "I want to go on the ATV."

Morgan followed him out. The old *drùidh* was fascinated with mechanical rides—trucks, snowcats, ATVs, even the chair lift that climbed TarStone Mountain. Daar insisted on riding the lift at least three times a week from May to October. But when the snows came, he stopped. He thought only idiots would ride in the winter, in the freezing weather, with sticks strapped to their feet.

Morgan settled Daar on the back of the four-wheeler and climbed on in front of him. But before he could start the engine, the old man tapped him on the back with his cane.

"You've done a fine job with the house," Daar said, when Morgan looked back to see what he wanted. "Any woman would be proud to call it home."

Morgan swung back around and started the bike, the engine drowning out his muttered disagreement. Hell would freeze over before he ever brought a woman here.

Chapter Four

*B*oth *mentally and physically exhausted* from her afternoon outrunning a gorgeous, nude maniac, Sadie spent a fitful night locked in her cabin. She tossed and turned as nightmares paraded through her mind. She was trapped inside a mountain of solid green that glowed with crushing malevolence. She was running without direction through a maelstrom of swirling black mist that sucked the very energy from her muscles. And she was trapped in a burning house, her only escape blocked by an apparition carrying a sword, mounted on horseback, laughing at her as she cowered in the corner of her smoke-filled bedroom.

Sadie woke with a scream lodged in her throat. Thunder shook the cabin with resounding force just as lightning flashed through the cracks of the shutters, splintering the wood and shattering the glass in one of the windows on the opposite side of the room. Rain flooded into the cabin, immediately soaking everything it touched.

Sadie struggled to free herself from the sheet twisted around her body. Ping shot from the foot of the bed, her snarl of displeasure lost in another crack of thunder and blinding white lightning. The cat disappeared under the table, and Sadie ran to the window to capture the banging shutter and lock it back into place.

Her heart pounding louder than the rain on the roof, Sadie slowly backed up until her knees buckled against the seat of a chair. She sat down, flinching as another shaft of pure light brought another deafening boom of thunder. She rested her elbows on her knees and dropped her head, forcing herself to take deep, calming breaths. Still bent over, she placed a hand on her chest, willing her heart to slow down before it cracked one of her ribs.

Holy hell, the storm was intense. The lightning seemed bright enough to penetrate the walls and continued to strike in rapid succession. Sadie could hear the sizzle of boiling sap when a nearby tree was hit. She sat in darkness broken only by intense flashes of light, hugging her soaked, shivering body as she waited for the storm to pass.

It seemed forever before the rain slowed to a drizzle and the thunder faded. Ping brought Sadie out of her trance by jumping onto her lap, forcing Sadie to open her arms and catch her.

"Ah, Ping Pong," she whispered, scratching the cat behind her ears. "Did the thunder scare you?"

Ping purred in answer, then moved from Sadie's lap

to the table. She sat down and promptly began cleaning herself. Sadie sighed. After the fire had burned down in the stove last night, she had simply crawled over to her bed, still fully dressed, wrapped herself in the sheets, and fallen into a fitful sleep—only to be awakened this morning by the storm.

The intermittent rumble of the retreating storm had a surprisingly calming effect on Sadie. Her energies slowly rebalanced, and the events of yesterday were finally washed from her immediate conscience.

She doubted she'd ever forget feeling that vulnerable, but this morning's storm had served to remind Sadie that nothing in this world was without risk. Such as how a candle left burning unattended in the study could spark a deadly house fire or how trespassing on a stranger's privacy could provoke him to violence.

But the green-eyed man hadn't turned violent, had he? He hadn't actually hurt her. He had only accomplished his goal of scaring the holy hell out of her, smartly teaching her a lesson she wasn't likely to forget.

Yes, the stranger had never meant her physical harm—she could see that now. Heck. What would she have done if she had discovered someone snapping pictures of her?

She might not have been quite so gracious.

Sadie started to stand up but winced at the pain in her feet. She immediately lifted one foot to her knee, saw the blood, and glanced at the shards of glass littering the floor in front of the broken window. She'd cut herself closing the shutter. She looked at her other foot.

Well, damn. Both feet were bleeding.

Sadie hobbled to the kitchen area, pulled down the first aid kit, then hobbled back to the table. She cleaned each small cut and examined her feet for any hidden shards of glass. Satisfied that there weren't any and pleased that none of the cuts was deep enough to need stitches, she bandaged both feet and covered the bandages with heavy wool socks.

She stood up and tested her work.

The salve helped, as did the cushion of the bandages and socks. And once she put on her hiking boots for support, the small wounds wouldn't even slow her down.

Sadie walked to the bathroom at the back of the cabin, stripping off her clothes and throwing them on the disheveled bed as she passed by. She checked the level of water in the overhead tank and decided there was just enough left for a lukewarm sponge bath.

Sadie turned to find a towel and caught sight of herself in the mirror. She almost screamed at the woman looking back at her. Her hair was a tangle of knots and actually had twigs and pine needles sticking out of it. There was dirt on her forehead and dried blood smeared on her cheek, and one of her little gold stud earrings was missing.

And then there were the scars. Always the scars, peeking over the top of her right shoulder, continuing down her back, and wrapping around the left side of her waist in a crazy quilt of raised patchwork.

Sadie lifted her right hand and turned it over to look at the ugly scars on her palm. The burning beam had nearly crushed her, and she had pushed at it frantically with her right hand, trying to free herself.

Frank Quill had died three years ago with both of his hands scarred—a testament to his strength and determination to leave the burning house with at least one of his daughters.

Sadie dropped her hand and turned away from the image that had been so much a part of her life for the last eight years.

She'd gone to bed that night eight years ago and left the lilac-scented candle burning in the study; her only thoughts had been of a long-dead trapper named Jedediah Plum, a camp cook named Jean Lavoie, and the obsessive dream of helping her father find Plum's gold.

Sadie soaked her washcloth in the basin of tepid water and scrubbed at her face, forcefully washing back her threatening tears. Eight years, and still the memories rose unbidden. Beautiful Caroline, teasing Sadie for locking herself in their dad's study instead of going out on dates. Frank Quill, focused on the new piece of evidence that reinforced his belief that Plum's gold really did exist. And Sadie herself, home for the summer between her second and third years of college, equally enthralled by the hunt for treasure.

Scrubbing would never wash the memories away. Regret would not bring her sister and her father back. And no amount of guilt would ever grant Sadie's wish that Caroline Quill had been the daughter her father had reached first.

Sadie fought daily to keep the demons firmly tamped down in the back recesses of her mind. And now she put her energies instead into building a park in Frank and Caroline's memory. A small measure, certainly, compared with the days, months, and years of missing half her family. But she hoped that establishing the park would bring her some semblance of peace.

Sadie quickly washed up and dried off, then walked back into the main room of the cabin and rummaged around in the bureau. She put on a pair of well-worn jeans, slipped a finely woven silk camisole over her head, and tucked it into her pants. She smoothed the wrinkles from the soft body sock until it fit like a second skin to protect her scars, before she put her bra on over it, fastening the clasp between her breasts. Over the bra she put on a simple, long-sleeved, and colorful cotton T-shirt.

She picked out a supple leather glove for her right hand from the pile she'd amassed over the years. She had another pile just like it packed in a box in the attic at home, but all of those gloves were left-handed. Sadie intended to donate the pile of unused left-handed gloves to a charity for people who also had scars they wanted to hide from the world.

Sadie walked back to the bathroom and took a brush to her hair. She worked out the twigs and pine needles and finished the job with a baseball cap, pulling her ponytail through the opening at the back.

She inspected her work in the mirror.

Not bad for having ten years scared off her life yesterday—a bit of distress showing under plain blue eyes that were too big for her face, a small scratch on her chin, probably from the tussle, and a golden tan that had grown darker over the summer. Sadie lifted her bare left hand and wiped at her face, as if she could rub away the crinkle lines at the corners of her eyes.

She needed to pluck her eyebrows.

And she also needed a haircut.

She'd neglected these rituals while living like a nun in the woods. Why bother? Ping didn't seem to mind that her roommate was beginning to look like a bag lady.

She'd get her hair trimmed when she went to visit her mom, and she'd have her eyebrows waxed while she was at it. Sadie sighed at her reflection. Heck, she'd even buy some makeup at the drugstore.

Sadie knew her mother would be telling her about the blind date she had already arranged the moment she stepped into the house.

Charlotte Quill did that a lot. Sadie visited her every week, and nearly every week there was another new man just dying to meet her. Sadie wondered where her mom kept finding them. Pine Creek had a population of sixteen hundred and twelve. Had Charlotte been placing ads in the county paper or something?

Upon returning to Pine Creek this spring, Sadie had resigned herself to humoring Charlotte's motherly need to see her daughter happily married. So she went on the blind dates without complaint. Sometimes they bombed, and sometimes they turned out rather nicely—until it came time to dance.

Five dates in nine weeks, and Sadie had danced a grand total of once. And then it had been a fast dance, not a waltz, and she really hated those. She had always imagined she looked like a cow moose on roller skates, all legs and arms and not a clue what to do with any of them.

Not one of the guys had called her again, even though she had given several of them her cell phone number.

Sadie wasn't surprised. She was taller than four of them, and the fifth guy, though taller than she was by a good inch, had been so shy it had been all he could do to shake her hand when he had left her at her front door.

Maybe this week would be different. Maybe when she went into town in two days, her mom would tell her that they'd spend a quiet evening at home instead. Just the two of them. She was even willing to spend the evening scrapbooking, if that's what her mom wanted to do.

Charlotte Quill was a scrapbook junkie. Every picture ever taken of her family, every fingerpainting or tattered ribbon won, every newspaper list of honor-roll students that had Sadie's or Caroline's name on it, every birth certificate, death certificate, marriage license, and fishing license was forever immortalized in one of Charlotte's scrapbooks.

Sadie turned when Ping gave a loud meow from the door. The cat was standing in the open doorway, her mouth full of feathers, grinning like a Cheshire.

"No," Sadie said, rushing over and picking her up. "You let that bird go. Give it to me," she insisted, using her fingers to pry open Ping's mouth. She squeezed the cat's ribs. "Spit it out."

With a low growl in her throat, Ping dropped the small bird into Sadie's hand. Sadie set the cat on the floor and carried the bird outside, rubbing its unmoving body. She set it up high on the old bird feeder and quietly stepped away to watch it. After a few minutes the tiny bird stirred, awkwardly sat up, and looked around in a daze. Ping rubbed against Sadie's legs. She picked up the cat and carried her back to the cabin.

"Here. You eat the food in your dish," she told Ping, setting her down on the porch. "I have to go for a little walk, but I'll be back by lunchtime. I'll give you some canned food then, if you promise me no more hunting today."

Ping blinked up at her, then lifted one of her paws and began cleaning herself. Sadie turned and faced the forest.

She had to go back in there this morning. Her father's camera was still in those woods, now soaking wet from the morning's storm, and nothing, not even yesterday's fright, would stop her from getting it back.

Chapter Five

For the entire three-mile walk to where her pack and camera were—which took longer than normal because of her tender feet—Sadie knew she was being followed. And now, as she stood and scanned the empty ground where her pack and camera should be, she still felt silent eyes watching her from the dense undergrowth.

She wasn't afraid. She knew it wasn't the stranger from yesterday, not unless the man had crawled on his hands and knees for the last three miles.

No. The presence out there just beyond her sight was four-legged, probably a bobcat or a fox, a black bear, or even a coyote. Although bears and coyotes usually shied away from humans, young ones were directed more often by curiosity than by their own good sense.

While growing up, Sadie and her dad had been followed like this on several occasions. Sometimes they caught a glimpse of their stalker but usually not. The animals hadn't been looking for a meal, they'd just wanted to see what was intruding on their turf.

Which was why Sadie ignored the eyes watching her now. She was too busy trying to decide what had happened to her stuff.

She couldn't find any signs anywhere—no pack, no GPS, no cell phone, no camera. Nothing. Not even the duct tape that had bound her hands and legs.

Sadie wanted to weep. She'd lost her father's camera, the one she had carried since his death three years ago. How could she have been so careless as to walk away from it yesterday?

But, more important, where was it now?

The stranger must have returned and taken it. He may have been merciful by letting her go, but that was probably the extent of his good will. She would never see her camera again.

A tree branch snapped in the woods behind her, and Sadie turned at the sound. Had she unnerved the animal by stopping here? Was it growing impatient for her to move on?

Sadie looked around the small clearing one last time, but when her things did not magically appear, she gave a sigh of regret and headed for home.

She walked for a good half hour before the bandages on her feet wrinkled enough that walking became impossible. She sat down on a fallen log and was just leaning over to untie her boots when she saw it.

The animal stepped silently out of the forest less than thirty feet from where she sat.

He was absolutely the largest, most magnificent, most regal-looking coyote she had ever seen. His eyes were two calm liquid pools of iridescent green. The fur around his face was full and fluffed out at the jowls, swept back against two large, alert ears. His shoulder blades would come to her waist if she were standing, and his long legs were placed solidly over huge, broad-toed feet. His dense, unruffled fur was the color of cedar sawdust sprinkled with hues of variegated grays.

He was truly the most beautiful animal she had ever seen.

Sadie didn't dare move a muscle. In fact, she nearly stopped breathing. What was he doing, showing himself to her? No coyote with even an ounce of instinct would dare approach a human this close. They were hunted animals, killed for the simple reason that they competed for the deer that humans prized so highly.

But coyotes simply weren't this large. Or this bold. A thought came to her then, that she was staring into the eyes of a wolf.

Sadie immediately dismissed that notion. It simply wasn't possible. Wolves hadn't been seen in Maine in more than a century. They'd been hunted to extinction and smart enough to never return. Until now?

Sadie didn't know if she should keep such direct eye contact with the animal, for fear that he might consider it an aggressive action on her part. Then again, she wasn't quite brave enough to look away, either.

The animal yawned, nicely showing off every one of his lethal teeth, and leaned back on his haunches, flexing his shoulders into a stretch. But instead of straightening up, he lay down right there in the middle of the path and began licking his paws.

Just as Ping did when she was bored with human company.

Sadie could only stare. He was acting as if he had stopped in for a friendly visit.

She didn't know what to do.

Could she just get up and quietly walk away?

Nope. He might consider that rude.

Unless he wasn't a coyote or a wolf at all but a domestic hybrid. There were often classified ads in the paper that offered half-wolf pups for sale. God, she hoped that was the case. If he were half domestic, he might not mind that she didn't return his desire to spend some quality time together.

Her sore feet forgotten, Sadie slowly stood up, careful not to make any sudden movements. The animal lifted his head from his chore and looked at her.

"Nice fella," she said in a calm and soothing voice. "I'm just going to continue my walk home now. You can keep cleaning your feet if you want. I can find my own way from here."

As she spoke, Sadie took small, guarded steps away from the animal, keeping her back to the trail and her eyes on him.

"That's a nice boy," she whispered, slowly turning around and widening her stride. She took at least ten steps before looking over her shoulder to see if she was being followed.

He was gone.

Sadie picked up her pace, not knowing if his disappearance was a good thing or not. A branch broke in the woods off to her left, and Sadie let out a shaky breath. It seemed they were back to the same routine as before, her walking the path and the wolf following in the shadows.

The final mile was the longest she had ever traveled before her cabin finally came into sight. Sadie decided that her career as a woodswoman was being sorely tried. The forest was suddenly crowded with all manner of beasts she wanted nothing to do with.

As if to prove her point that the valley had turned into Grand Central Station, Sadie spotted a strange-looking man, a hundred years old at least, sitting on her porch and scratching an ecstatic Ping under the chin.

"Aye, there you are, girl," he said, standing up and walking toward her.

He had a thin, delicate cane he used for support—probably to catch himself when his feet got tangled in his long black robe—and a wild mane of white hair and a perfectly trimmed beard. A crisp white collar peeked out above the top button of his robe.

A priest?

Wasn't this a bit remote for a parish call?

Sadie took the hand he offered and shook it, surprised by the strength of his grip, which was nothing compared with the direct stare of his crystal-clear, bright blue eyes.

"Are you lost?" she asked, taking a quick scan of the cabin grounds, looking for either a vehicle or a traveling companion.

"Nay. I'm right where I want to be, girl. And I apologize for showing up on your doorstep without notice," he said, not releasing her hand. "I'm Father Daar. And you would be?"

"Ah . . . Sadie. Mercedes Quill."

He cocked his head at her, his wrinkled face forming a smile. "I'd be knowing that name, Quill. Is your mother Charlotte, by any chance?"

He still hadn't released her hand. Sadie didn't really mind, though. She liked old people. She liked their old-fashioned manners, their straightforward talk, and their spit-in-the-eye attitude toward life.

"Yes. Charlotte's my mom. How do you know her?"

Tucking her hand into the crook of his arm, he began to lead her toward her own cabin. "We have a mutual friend. Callum MacKeage has been spending a wee bit of time with your Charlotte, I believe."

Yes, she knew that. As a matter of fact, Callum was all her mother had been able to talk about since Sadie had returned to Pine Creek. Charlotte had met Callum at a grange supper last winter, and the two had been dating ever since.

They climbed the stairs together, her hand still in the priest's possession, and stopped at the door. Ping rubbed up against Sadie's leg. Sadie pulled free and scooped up the cat, looking back over her shoulder at the forest.

"We should probably move inside, Father," she said, pushing open the door. "A large dog followed me back to the cabin, and I don't want him to catch sight of Ping."

"Ping, is it?" the priest asked, not stepping inside. He scratched Ping under the chin again, then looked out at the woods and grinned. "No worry, lass. Dun . . . er, I mean Faol has always had a soft spot for cats. The wolf will not hurt your friend."

"Wolf? You've seen him, then?" Sadie asked. Realizing he'd called the animal by name, she added, "Is he yours?"

The priest lifted his bushy eyebrows into his shaggy white hairline. "Wolves know no owners, girl. They're independent beasts."

The beast in question stepped out of the woods just then and sat down at the edge of the clearing, facing the cabin. The hackles on Ping's back rose in alarm, and four sets of claws dug deeply into Sadie's arms. Sadie all but ran into the cabin and pushed her frightened pet under the bed. She ran back, took Father Daar by the arm, and pulled him inside the cabin and closed the door.

"Ah . . . I just thought we'd be more comfortable sitting inside, out of the sun," she said lamely, peeking out through the broken shutter. "Have a seat, Father," she instructed.

He didn't sit down but walked over to the corner and stood studying the large four-by-eight-foot model of the valley.

"What would this be?" he asked, running his finger along the tops of the mountains.

"That's a model of this valley," Sadie explained, moving to stand beside him. "This is where we are," she said, pointing to a black dot near the center. "And this is Fraser Mountain, Pitts Mountain, Yawning Ridge, and Sunrise Peak," she added, moving her finger along the tops of the eastern range. "This side of the valley is nicknamed Thoreau's Range, made up of these six mountains," she said, pointing to the other side of the model. "And in the middle is Prospect River, running the length of the valley."

"Where's TarStone Mountain?" he asked, leaning closer and scanning the names taped onto the mountains.

"TarStone would be here," she told him, placing her hands just off the southeastern edge of the board. "It's not on the model because it won't be part of the park."

Still bent over the makeshift table, he turned his head to her and waved his hand over the valley. "This is all supposed to be a park?"

"Yes. That's why I'm here. I'm mapping landmarks and cataloging the various ecosystems, so that I can help put together a proposal for a nature preserve."

He straightened and turned fully toward her. "A proposal? So it's not really a park yet?"

Sadie shook her head, absently running her finger along the edge of the model. "No, not yet. I was hired by a group of people who are working up a feasibility plan to present to our state legislature. It's still in the early stages. Surveys have been done only on paper, not in the field yet. It's my job to propose a basic layout for the park, with suggestions on where to put the trails and campsites and roads, locate the best place for a visitor center, and highlight prominent landmarks."

"All by yourself?" the priest asked, looking back at the model. "It's a mighty large task for one person alone."

"I'm only the beginning of what will take years to develop," Sadie explained, walking toward the window.

She looked outside, and, sure enough, the wolf was still there, lying down now, grooming himself again.

"I'd be liking a cup of tea, Mercedes, if you have some," Father Daar said, heading back over to the door and opening it. "You got anything sweet to go with it?"

Sadie smiled as she moved to put the kettle to boil on the gas range in the kitchen area. "I have some brownies that my mother made," she told him, getting two cups down from the shelf and quickly rinsing the dust off them.

"Would you be having something Faol could eat?" he asked.

Sadie looked past Father Daar at the napping wolf. "I don't think we should feed him, Father. He might hang around if we give him free handouts."

He turned and smiled at her. "You would not care for a wolf as a pet?" he asked, lifting one brow. "You don't think a great beast like Faol would be handy to have around on occasion?"

"If he really is a wolf, then he's wild. And it's dangerous to endow him with human emotions."

Father Daar left the door open, returned to the table, and sat down. "You haven't much magic in your soul, have you, girl?" he said, taking a sip of his tea and setting the mug back on the table. His eyes suddenly lit with speculation. "How about this? What if I tend to those cuts on your feet and promise they'll be completely healed by tomorrow? Would that not seem magical to you?"

Sadie was dumbfounded. "But how did you know?" she asked, looking down at her boots.

"You're limping. And I see the glass on the floor," he said, using his cane to point at the broken window littering the floor. "And I see tracks of blood," he added, now pointing at the obvious path leading from the table to the counter and back.

Sadie sat down so she could untie her boots, thankful for the opportunity to straighten her bandages at last. They did hurt, but she had thought it would be rude to undress her feet in front of a guest.

"Thank you for the offer, Father, but I can tend myself. You sit back and enjoy your tea."

She used the table to conceal the mess of her feet and slid out of her boots. The socks did not come off quite so easily. They were stuck to the bottoms of her feet.

"Here, child. Let me do that," Father Daar said, slowly getting down on his knees in front of her.

Sadie was horrified. She hid her feet under the chair.

He looked up at her and grinned. "You're a mite shy when it comes to your perceived flaws, aren't you, Mercedes? I promise not to laugh if you have six toes."

"You're not tending my feet, Father. You're a guest in my house."

"The Son of God was not above washing a man's feet," he said, grabbing her by the ankle and pulling her foot out to inspect. "Besides, how can I make you believe in the magic if you don't let me do my work?"

Her face flooded with heat. Lord help her, she would either have to kick the man or let him clean and bandage her feet.

"Where's the salve?" he asked once he had the bandages off. "Ah, here it is," he said, seeing the first aid kit on the table. "And now for the magic," he whispered, opening the salve and ceremoniously dipping the head of his cane into the jar.

Sadie was fascinated as well as entertained. He was a funny old priest, making a production of magically healing her feet.

Well, if he'd wanted to put her at ease for his doctoring, it was working. She didn't mind so much anymore that he was doing this humble chore for her.

"Mercedes is a beautiful name," he said as he fingered the salve from his cane and worked it into the cuts. "Is it a family name? From a grandmother or great-aunt, maybe?"

"Yeah, something like that," Sadie said, tucking her crossed fingers under her thighs. She wasn't about to tell this man she was named after a car. Especially not the car she had been conceived in.

Frank Quill had had a warped sense of humor.

"There. How does that feel?" he asked, patting the last bandage into place and straightening up, giving her an expectant look.

"Hot. My feet feel warm as toast."

And they did. Warm and tingly and wonderfully soothed. Sadie wanted to hug him, they felt so good. She smiled instead.

"Thank you, Father. You really did work magic."

He narrowed one eye at her suspiciously. "You think I'm jesting about the magic, don't you?" He lifted his cane and showed her the salve-covered burl of wood at the top. "I wish I could be here to see your face in the morning, when you wake up and find your feet completely healed."

Sadie patted his shoulder. "Magic is the stuff of fairy tales, Father. I'll put my faith in modern medicine. And your kindness, too, because I know it helps."

Still kneeling in front of her, his eyes not quite level with hers, he gave her a fierce glare. "The magic isn't here," he said, touching her forehead with his finger. "It's here," he continued, touching her just below her collar bone. "It's deep inside, in your heart. It's the belief that anything is possible, against any odds, as long as you're open to the gift."

"You're very sweet."

"Nay. Never call an old man sweet, child, unless you're wanting to prick his temper. Even priests have pride," he finished, leaning on his cane to stand up. He walked around the table, sat back down, and took up his tea again.

Sadie ignored his scolding and sipped her own tea as she stared at the strange man sitting across the table. Where had he come from? And why was he here?

"Why do you call him Foul?" she asked, waving toward the wolf. "He doesn't stink."

"It's spelled *F-A-O-L*, and it means 'wolf.' "

"In what language?"

"Gaelic. I'm a Celt, girl, in case you haven't noticed."

The man did have a mean accent. Gaelic, huh? Maybe he would recognize the word the giant had used yesterday when he'd told her to take a care until they met again.

"Father? Do you know what 'gray-agch' means?"

He scrunched up his face. "What language would that be? You sound like you have a frog in your throat."

"I don't know what language it is."

"Where did you hear it? That might help me decide."

Well, now. What to tell him. She wasn't saying spit about yesterday's encounter. "It's just something I heard someone say," she prevaricated. She shrugged. "It's not important. I was just curious."

He finally put his brownie into his mouth, chewing and grinning and then taking a sip of his tea. He stood up suddenly.

"I've enjoyed our visit, Mercedes. And now I was thinking ya could give me a ride home in that comfortable-looking truck you've got parked out back."

Sadie stared up at him. What had been the point of his visit? And now he wanted a ride?

"Did you walk all the way out here from town?"

He started for the door, waving his cane in the air. "Nay. I live on the west side of TarStone Mountain."

"Good Lord. That's nearly ten miles away, cross-country. And a good fifteen miles by road. You walked?"

He turned to her and thumped his chest with his cane. "Walking is good for the heart, not to mention the soul. But then you already know that, don't you, Mercedes? You've covered every inch of this valley in the ten weeks you've been here, most of it on foot, I would guess."

Now, how had he known that?

Dammit. Who was this strange man?

He suddenly turned and was out the door and already down the steps before she could respond. The wolf—Faol—stood up and watched as Father Daar quickly walked around the cabin and disappeared from sight. Sadie heard the door of her truck open and then slam shut.

She could only stand there, immobilized with confusion, finding herself with many more questions than answers for a visit that had lasted less than an hour.

Chapter Six

Sadie wasn't waiting two days to visit her mother, she was going home tonight. She was taking a long weekend, hoping that was enough time for the green-eyed stranger to move on, the wolf to move on, and the priest to forget where she lived.

Talk about weird. The old man had eaten her food and drunk her tea, doctored her feet, urged her to make a pet of a wolf, and scolded her for hiding her scars. It hadn't been Sunday, but Sadie felt as if she had sat through a four-hour sermon.

So, with all her dirty laundry loaded in the truck and her empty cooler packed, all she had left to do was convince Ping that there was nothing ignoble about riding in a cat carrier.

Just as Sadie finally caught Ping and put her in the carrier in the front seat of the truck, another truck pulled up to the cabin. Sadie quickly closed the cage before the spitting-mad cat could escape and cursed her terrible timing. Heck. It was *worse* than Grand Central Station out here.

At least she knew this visitor. Eric Hellman, her boss, jumped out of the truck before it had fully shut off, his hand full of papers and his expression saying he was a man on a mission.

"You're still alive, I see," he said by way of greeting as he strode toward her.

Sadie looked down at herself in mock surprise. "I guess I am," she agreed, giving him a broad smile she hoped would disarm his obviously bad mood.

He stopped in front of her and glared at her answer. "I've been calling your cell phone since yesterday morning. Why haven't you answered it?"

"Because it's broken?" she offered, still forcing a smile but bracing herself for the outrage she knew was coming.

His face turned bright red. "That's the third phone in two months! What are you doing, chopping wood with the damn things?"

Sadie wanted to tell him that this last one wasn't her fault, but she remained mute. It was nobody's business what had happened in the woods yesterday—not the priest's and not Eric's.

"This is the last one," Eric told her angrily. "They said they would cancel the insurance the next time I brought them a smashed phone." He held out his hand. "Give it to me so I can get it replaced. But the next one you break is coming out of your paycheck."

Sadie looked at his hand, shifting her feet uncomfortably. Damn, she knew he needed the ruined phone to get the credit from the insurance.

"I don't have it. It's at the bottom of Prospect River, probably halfway to the Penobscot by now." She steeled herself for the next explosion. "And so is the GPS. I lost my backpack overboard when I dumped at Portage Falls."

Instead of the explosion, there was silence. Eric's gaze shot to the kayak strapped to the roof of her truck. His face incredulous, he looked back at her.

"You're a class four kayaker, Quill. You don't dump your boat on class two rapids."

She shrugged. "Hey, anyone can have a bad day."

"Why wasn't your pack in the dry hatch?" he asked, looking back at the nineteen-foot-long yellow kayak.

The boat was really an ocean or calm-water kayak, since Sadie usually traveled lakes and dead-water streams, but she did need to get down swift water on occasion, and she wasn't lugging around two different boats to do the job. This poor kayak carried the scars of rough use, but it was still an excellent vessel, a gift from her dad on her sixteenth birthday.

"The hatch popped," she said, straight-faced.

The bluster seemed suddenly to go out of Eric. He shook his head. "What were you doing at Portage Falls? Do you think Jedediah's gold is that far north?"

"I was mapping the river, looking for possible campsites."

"That kind of stuff can come later," he said, dismissing her work with a wave of his hand. "You need to find that gold, Quill. It's going to be the focal point of the park."

"I'm looking, Eric. Honest to God, every day I'm out there, I'm looking for it." She sighed and rubbed her forehead. "It was Dad's obsession to find Plum's gold, before the fire. You know that. I spent every school vacation and summer and every weekend looking for Jedediah's claim."

"And that's why I suggested the consortium hire you, Quill. You have the best chance of finding it. You know this valley, and you know your father's research. So why can't you find it?"

"It might not exist, you know. Even Dad was aware of that possibility. Maine is not a state known for gold."

"It exists," Eric said through gritted teeth. "Frank spent the better part of his life looking for that gold."

"As a hobby, Eric. He found some writings on Jedediah Plum, even unearthed an old journal. But it all could have been the romantic delusions of an eccentric old hermit. Jedediah claimed he'd found the source of Prospect River's placer gold, but the man died a pauper nearly eighty years ago."

Eric's face suddenly brightened, and he handed her the papers he was holding. "I've been doing some research of my own," he said as Sadie took the papers and unfolded them.

She gasped when she saw what they were. "Where did you find this?" she asked, leafing through the photocopies of an old handwritten journal. "This is the diary Dad found just before . . . well, just before the fire."

"It is?" Eric asked, moving to look over her shoulder. "Frank had this diary? I found this in an obscure little logging museum about sixty miles north of here and got permission to photocopy it. It's the journal of a logging camp cook who lived in Jedediah's time. It seems that just before the old hermit died, he came back out here one last time. The cook, Jean Lavoie, thought he was after some of the gold. But Jedediah disappeared a few days later. They found his body after the spring thaw."

"Yes. They also found that he had been shot," Sadie added. "That part of Plum's life—or, rather, his death—is well documented. I can't believe you found this." She looked at Eric, smiling sadly. "I tried cajoling Dad into gathering back his research, but after the fire he lost his passion for the hunt."

Eric moved back to face her, smiling sympathetically. "I'm sorry, Quill. But maybe now you can study this diary and finally come up with a location. I've read it at least a hundred times, but I don't know this valley as well as you do. Maybe you can find where these logging camps were, and that will tell you the vicinity of Plum's claim."

"I wish I had the rest of Dad's research. We'd been so close eight years ago."

"Everything burned?" he asked, tempering his voice with kindness.

"Yes. The fire started in the study where he kept his research," Sadie confirmed, turning away and walking to the driver's side of her truck. She opened the door and put the papers inside.

"You're going home? It's only Thursday," Eric said, seeing that the truck was packed with her belongings.

"I need a few days off. And I want to contact the geological people in Augusta."

"Why?"

"I've been studying my model and began wondering about approaching the mystery of Plum's gold from a different angle."

"A geological angle?" he asked, suddenly not looking so disgruntled about her self-approved vacation.

"Yeah. Instead of only trying to follow Jedediah's path, which is all but nonexistent, why not see where Mother Nature would most likely have set her gold?"

He looked skeptical. "Frank never tried that approach?"

"Sure he did. But all his maps and aerial photos burned with his research."

Eric got a far-away look in his eyes as he rubbed the back of his neck and stared over the hood of her truck. "I never thought of that. And I wasn't aware Frank had, either."

Sadie climbed into her truck and looked at Eric, still standing in the open doorway.

"Come by my store Sunday," Eric said. "I'll have a new cell phone for you. And you can pick out a new GPS while you're at it." He gave her a stern look. "You pick out a waterproof one, and you wear the damn thing tied around your neck. The budget we've allocated for this phase of the project is nearly spent. And until we can raise more funds, or you can find that gold, anything else you lose is coming out of your paycheck."

She gave him a salute. "Gotcha. I'll cherish my new equipment as I would my own child," she promised, reaching to close her truck door. Eric stopped her by grabbing the handle.

"Oh, one more thing," he said. "The Dolan brothers are in town. It seems they're actively looking for the mine again. You keep an eye out for them, Quill," he told her. "You also be sure you stay one step in front of them, not behind them. If they find that gold before we do, our plans for the park will be set back by several years. We're counting on that gold for funding."

That reminder given, he closed the door, walked back to his own truck, and headed back toward town as quickly as he had arrived.

Sadie was about to start her own truck when the wolf stepped out of the woods right beside her. Only he wasn't looking at her but in the direction Eric had gone. His hackles were raised on his back.

Goose bumps lifted on Sadie's arms. What had Father Daar said? Something about Faol protecting her from strangers?

Oh, she needed to get out of here. Now.

But even before Sadie realized what she was doing, she rolled down the window and actually spoke to the wolf. "Thank you, big boy," she said in a whisper.

Faol turned his head and looked up, his regal green eyes calm and direct, and whined.

Sadie gaped at the animal, then shook her head to clear it. She was acting more foolish than the priest, endowing the wolf with human emotions.

It was definitely time to go home.

But home had its own host of surprises, not the least of which was a very tall, very naked man standing in her mother's darkened kitchen. He was peering into the fridge, singing rather loudly and off key as he sorted through its contents.

Sadie yelped and nearly dropped the cat carrier on

the floor. The man's song turned to a shout, and he spun around as if ready to fight. His eyes wide and his mouth frozen open in shock, he suddenly grabbed one of the kitchen chairs and held it up in front of his waist. The man turned as red as his hair, from his forehead to his feet, as they stared at each other in silence so thick Sadie actually could hear her heart beating.

"Why did you yell, Callum? Did you drop the milk?" Charlotte Quill asked as she walked into the kitchen.

Sadie's jaw dropped. Her mother was dressed in the sexiest, most beautiful nightgown she had ever seen.

"Mother?" Sadie croaked. She looked back at the man. This was Callum? In her mother's kitchen? Naked?

She looked back at her mother, who had stopped dead in her tracks and was blushing to the roots of her blond tousled hair.

"Oh, dear," Charlotte whispered.

It was Callum who broke the triangle of stares. Still holding the chair like a shield to protect what modesty he had left, he sidled over to Charlotte, then backed through the doorway before disappearing into the darkness of the hall. Her mother walked over and closed the refrigerator door, then walked over to Sadie and took the cat carrier out of her hands and set it on the floor. Charlotte leaned up and kissed her still shocked daughter on the cheek.

"Hi, sweetie. I wasn't expecting you home tonight."

"I see that."

"He's a fine figure of a man, don't you think?"

Sadie stared at her mother, then suddenly broke into laughter. She gave her mother a huge hug. "Oh, Mom. Only you would ask your daughter what she thought of your lover's bod."

"Well, you did get a good look, I take it," Charlotte said into her shoulder, hugging her back.

"I guess I did."

Charlotte pulled away and took Sadie by both hands, absently running her thumb over Sadie's glove-covered scars. "He's so embarrassed, sweetie. He's probably dressing right now and practicing what to say to you when he comes back out here."

"Maybe I have something to say to him. Like asking what his intentions are toward you."

"I intend to marry your mother, lass," Callum said from the entrance to the hall.

He was fully clothed now and no less impressive for being dressed. He had obviously tried to smooth down his hair with his hand but had fallen quite a bit short of taming it. Charlotte let go of Sadie's hands and crossed the kitchen to stand at Callum's side.

"Hush, Callum. Now is not the time."

"Not the time, woman?" he asked in a growl, looking down at her with a gleam in his eyes. "Your daughter has just caught us in a compromising position. Her question is fair."

He wrapped one arm around Charlotte in an embrace that said he wanted no more interference from her. He looked at Sadie.

"I've asked your mother to marry me, lass, at least once a week for the last two months. But she's being stubborn about giving me an answer."

Sadie lifted her shoulders into a shrug. "Don't look at me. It took two years of coaxing just to get her to visit me in Boston."

"Two years!" he said, looking a bit sick in the face as he glared down at Charlotte. "I'm getting old, woman. I can't wait two more years."

Charlotte patted his shirt, then ducked out from under his arm to move away. "Well, Callum MacKeage, you're going to have to wait a while longer," she said, going to the kennel.

Charlotte's cat, Kashmir, had silently come into the kitchen and was standing with her nose pressed up against the kennel. As soon as Charlotte freed Ping from her carrier, both cats took off at a run to the nether regions of the house.

"Well," Sadie said into the awkward silence. She held out her gloved right hand. "It's nice to finally meet you, Callum. I'm surprised we haven't met before now."

Callum took her hand in a warm, gentle embrace. "I've wanted you and your mom to have some time alone together," he told her. "I know you've been living away since college." He looked at Charlotte and smiled. "She's glad to have you back."

"And I'm very glad to be back. I think I'm going to stay this time."

Callum looked back at Sadie, the rugged planes of his face softened by the warmth of his smile. "Good. Now, I must be going. You two have a good visit together."

"You don't have to leave," Sadie quickly assured him. "I can go down to Nadeau's and have a beer."

"Alone?" he asked, looking somewhat scandalized.

Sadie refrained from laughing out loud, but she couldn't stop a smile from escaping. "But I won't be alone once I get there, will I?" she said, holding her mirth in check. She didn't want to tease her mother's friend. At least, not until she knew if he had a sense of humor.

Charlotte groaned and came to Callum's rescue by physically pushing him toward the door. "I'll talk to you soon, Cal. Thanks for the . . . um . . . lovely visit," she said, standing on tiptoe and pulling his mouth down to meet hers, giving him a quick kiss on the lips and then pushing him again.

Only he wouldn't be hurried. He kissed her a bit more thoroughly and then straightened and smiled at Sadie. "It was nice to finally meet you, lass. I'll see you again this Saturday evening."

That said, he allowed Charlotte to send him out the door. Sadie moved to stand beside her mother, and they both watched Callum walk to the truck parked a short way down the street.

"What's happening Saturday night?" Sadie asked.

Charlotte turned to her, excitement lighting her already beautiful face. "We're going to double date."

"You, Callum, me, and who?"

"His cousin, Morgan." Charlotte clapped her hands together. "Oh, I don't know why I didn't think of the two of you together before now. Morgan is perfect, Sadie. He's taller than you. Well, actually, he's a lot taller than you. And he's handsome and well mannered, and he seems very interesting to talk to, the few times I've met him."

"If he's so perfect, why isn't he already taken?"

A worried frown creased Charlotte's brow. "He's—ah—Morgan is a bit of a loner, sweetie, from what Callum has told me. He's building a house someplace in the middle of the woods, and that's taken up most of his time."

"Great. A hermit. You've matched me up with a tall hermit this time." Sadie kissed her now fretting mother on the cheek and then walked to the table and sat down. "Don't worry, Mom. I'll go on a date with you and Callum and Morgan-the-hermit," she assured her once Charlotte had joined her at the table. "Why won't you marry him?"

Charlotte looked startled, if not a little confused, by the change of subject. "You wouldn't mind if I got married again?" she finally asked.

Sadie leaned back in her chair and stared at her mom for a full minute. "You've been holding the man off because of me?"

"Of course I have." Charlotte reached out and took hold of Sadie's hands. "You didn't just love your father, sweetie, you adored him. I always assumed you would never want anyone to take his place."

"Oh, Mom. No man ever will. But that doesn't mean I expect you to spend the rest of your life alone, as some sort of shrine to Frank Quill. You're only forty-three years old. You're not even halfway through your life yet."

Charlotte pulled back, fingering the folds of her gown nervously. "It's been only three years, Sadie. How can I live with a man for twenty-four years, then suddenly expect to move on with a new life so soon, as if he never existed?"

"Because Daddy is dead, and you're not. Because nothing says you stop feeling, or wanting, or needing human contact. Because even though you have me, I know that's not enough. If you love this guy, I say go for it."

"I still can't marry him," Charlotte said in a barely audible voice, still toying with her gown.

"Why not?"

"Because I'm pregnant," she whispered, looking up finally, her eyes two stricken circles of worry-washed blue.

For the third time in thirty minutes, Sadie was rendered speechless.

"I married Frank when I was sixteen because I was pregnant with you, Sadie. And even though I loved you and Caroline and your father with all my heart and have never regretted a day of my life, I just can't start another marriage that way."

Sadie still couldn't think of a thing to say.

"Oh, Sadie," Charlotte cried, burying her face in her hands. "I'm so foolish. How could I let this happen again!"

Sadie dove from her seat to her knees, wrapping her arms around her mother, hugging her fiercely. "You're not foolish," she assured her, lifting her mom's face and wiping her cheeks. She gave her a warm, affectionate smile. "You just have the damndest luck with men. What is Callum, the second guy you've dated in all your life?"

Wiping her tears with her gown, Charlotte nodded. "Can you believe it? Two boyfriends, and both of them knocked me up."

"But how?"

Charlotte blinked at her. "The usual way," she said, her face turning bright red. She wiped at her tears again, and Sadie let out a frustrated breath.

"I know how. What I mean is, weren't you using something? You're old enough this time to know about birth control. What did you and Daddy do all these years?"

"Frank had a vasectomy just after Caroline was born," Charlotte told her through a short round of hiccups. "In my entire life, I never used birth control. And I didn't even stop to think this time. It just . . . it just happened," she ended with another round of weeping, burying her face in her hands again.

Sadie let her mother cry instead of asking if Callum hadn't at least been bright enough to use something himself.

Sadie stood up and decided her mother needed a cup of tea. Personally, she needed something a little stronger. It was as she was getting the brandy down from the top shelf of the cupboard that Sadie suddenly realized what all this meant.

She was going to be a sister again.

The bottle of brandy forgotten on the counter, Sadie ran back to her mother, pulled her up out of the chair, and hugged her fiercely.

"We're going to have a baby, Mom. I'm going to be a sister again."

Charlotte looked up, blinking in surprise. Slowly, and with the immense power of love behind it, she smiled the smile of a woman coming to terms with her condition.

"You are, aren't you? You're going to be a sister again because I'm going to have a baby."

"This is wonderful, Mom," Sadie whispered, as if she could keep their precious secret just between them, not even wanting the house to hear it. "You can marry Callum if you truly love him, but you can also raise this baby yourself. You know I'll help you. No pressure. No history repeating itself. You're not a scared girl of sixteen this time. You have me."

"Oh, sweetie. You have no idea how hard it was back then and the struggles we faced, what with your father trying to finish school and working at his family's mill to support us."

Charlotte hugged her quickly and then moved to put the kettle on to boil before she placed the brandy back in the cupboard, taking down two teacups instead. She talked while she worked.

"I do love Callum. I've known that for months now." She turned and pointed a china cup at Sadie. "I wouldn't have gone to bed with him if I didn't," she said firmly. "I'm not that kind of girl."

Sadie took a seat at the table, recognizing her mother's need to be busy. She quickly nodded agreement as a dutiful daughter should.

"It's just that I don't want to *have* to marry him," Charlotte continued. "Your father loved me, Sadie. But I always felt that he could have gone on to greater things if he hadn't had us to slow him down."

"Dad loved running the lumber mill," Sadie quickly interjected. "And it never stopped him from pursuing his hobby of Maine history."

"He could have been a professor," Charlotte countered, turning to take down the teapot.

"He could have been," Sadie agreed. "But that would have meant leaving these woods, and you and I both know that never would have happened."

Her mother turned to her again, her tear-swollen eyes hopeful. "Do you really think that's true, Sadie? That I didn't hold Frank back?"

Unable to sit any longer, Sadie got up and went to her mother, taking the forgotten teapot from her hands and setting it on the counter with the cups. She took her mom by the shoulders and looked her square in the face.

"Dad loved you, me, Caroline, and his life here. How can you doubt that?"

Charlotte pushed the hair from her face with a trembling hand and let out a tired sigh. "I don't. It's just that I'm so confused right now. And scared. How am I going to tell Callum he's fathered a child? The man's forty-eight years old. He'll practically be on Social Security before our kid even gets her driver's license."

Sadie dismissed that worry with a chuckle. "I'll teach her to drive if Callum can't handle the stress. It's okay, Mom. People are having children later in life now. You won't be the only gray-haired lady at the PTA meetings."

"I'm going to have to tell him soon, aren't I?"

"Yes, you've got to tell him. But that does not mean you have to marry him."

It was Charlotte's turn to laugh. "Of course I do, sweetie," she said, patting Sadie's cheek and then moving back to pour the boiling water into the teapot. "Callum MacKeage is one of those old-fashioned men. Once he knows I'm having a baby, he'll probably drag me to the minister before I've even finished telling him."

Charlotte shot a grin over her shoulder that said she found that idea amusing. "If he doesn't have a heart attack first. The poor man is so *hung up* on proprieties. That's why he always parks his truck down the road instead of in my driveway, so people won't know he's visiting me so late," she said, waving at the window facing the street. "And he tried hard not to show it, but he was mortified that you found us together tonight." She winked at her daughter. "And naked, at that."

Sadie laughed. "Then he really would have keeled over if I'd arrived earlier and actually found you in bed together. And I would have, if Eric hadn't shown up at camp."

"Eric actually ventured into the deep woods?" Charlotte asked, tongue in cheek.

Everyone in Pine Creek knew that Eric Hellman hated the woods. And everyone thought it ironic that the man owned an outfitters store.

"He only took a few steps on actual dirt," Sadie assured her. "And he drove like the devil to get in and out as fast as he could."

"But why make the trip? He knows you come into town on the weekends."

"He found an old diary that belonged to a camp cook who knew Jedediah. And he couldn't wait for me to see it."

"I tried calling you today," Charlotte said, bringing the tray of tea to the table. She lifted one brow. "Did you forget to charge your cell phone again, or did you break another one?"

"I—ah—I sort of lost this one," Sadie admitted.

Charlotte sighed into her tea on the pretense of cooling it off. She looked over the rim of her cup, and Sadie could see that her mother was trying very hard not to laugh.

"Hey. It's physical work that I do," Sadie defended herself. "But the cell phone's nothing. You should have seen Eric's face when I told him I lost the GPS at the same time." She suddenly sobered. "I lost Dad's camera, too, Mom."

"Oh, honey, I'm sorry," Charlotte quickly consoled, understanding what the loss meant to Sadie. She reached over and patted her hand. "You still have the one Frank gave you for your tenth birthday."

"But it's not the same. And now I don't dare use it. I don't want to risk losing that one, too."

"Then I'll buy you a new one," Charlotte said, sitting up and smiling at her plan. "And you can have it fixed so it doesn't make a noise when you use it."

"Then I'll be worried about losing *your* gift." Sadie blew into her own tea. "I'm better off just buying my own. That way, I won't feel bad if something happens to it. I'm too damn sentimental."

"No, sweetie. You're too damned absentminded," her mother said, not unkindly. "You're always so busy being curious about everything that you keep overlooking the details of life. And that's why you need a husband."

Sadie didn't respond to that half-truth; she might need to work on getting her act together, but she sure as heck didn't need a husband to do it for her. So, instead of arguing the point, Sadie drank the soothing chamomile tea and basked in the warmth of her mother's kitchen.

Yes, this was why she had come home today. Charlotte's mothering was a balm to her soul. Her mom was grounded in reality, always able to put things in the proper prospective for Sadie, always able to give Sadie the confidence she needed to continue moving forward despite the guilt she wore around her neck like a granite tombstone.

It was her fault that Caroline and her father were dead. She had caused the fire that had killed Caroline and disabled her dad to the point that he had only lived five years, until he died from a weakened heart at the young age of forty-one.

Frank Quill had returned to the burning house, and it had been Sadie, not the innocent Caroline, he had pulled from the flames.

A preventable, senseless tragedy. And not once, ever, in the eight years since had her mother or father condemned Sadie for the loss of their younger daughter. In fact, they had both gone out of their way to convince her that they cherished the one child God had left them while they mourned the one they had lost.

Sadie loved them both so much for that.

And she loved her mom's friendship now. Charlotte Quill always met whatever life gave her head-on, since finding herself pregnant at the age of sixteen, through the tragedy eight years ago, through her husband's death three years ago, and now as she found herself pregnant yet again.

Sadie only hoped that someday she could be half the woman Charlotte Quill was. Because she needed very much to be the sort of big sister this unborn child could look up to.

Chapter Seven

Sadie was out of bed and halfway down the hall before she realized she should have been feeling bare feet touching the hardwood floor. She stopped in the doorway of the bathroom and stared down at the bandages covering her feet. She wiggled her toes, then shifted her weight from one foot to the other, testing for pain.

There was none. Not a twinge or even the memory of pain.

Sadie sat on the edge of the tub and lifted one leg to her knee, quickly unwrapping the bandage and twisting the bottom of her foot toward her.

Well, hell. There weren't even any scars.

She quickly unwrapped the other foot and examined it closely, stretching the skin and running a finger from her toes to her heel, looking for the tiny little cuts that should have been there.

There wasn't even any redness.

Sadie dropped her foot to the floor and stared out at the empty hall. Cuts didn't heal, much less disappear, in twenty-four hours. It wasn't possible.

And it sure as heck wasn't magic.

Sadie looked down and wiggled her toes again. If she hadn't pulled the small pieces of glass from her feet herself, she would say that it had all been a dream—or a really good advertisement for the salve she had used.

But it was not magic.

She had to see that priest again. She had to sit him down and make him explain how rubbing some over-the-counter medicine onto his cane could heal her feet. And she also would insist that he explain why he wanted her to believe it was magic in the first place.

"Sadie? What are you doing sitting on the tub and staring at nothing?" her mother asked, walking into the bathroom. She pointed at the floor. "And what are those?"

Sadie grabbed the bandages and tossed them into the trash by the sink. "They're just some padding to help prevent blisters on my feet," she quickly lied. "I've got to get some new boots this weekend. Do you remember that Dad used to own a small handgun? Do you still have it?"

Charlotte frowned at her. "A handgun? What's that got to do with blisters?"

"Nothing. It's just that I remembered Dad always carried a gun whenever we hiked. And I was wondering if you'd kept it."

Her mother's face wrinkled with worry. "Why?" she asked, sitting down on the closed toilet, facing Sadie.

"Are you having trouble at the cabin? Has someone been bothering you out there?"

Sadie shook her head. "No, Mom. Nothing like that. I just thought I should probably have some sort of protection with me."

"You can't mean to carry a gun, Sadie. Frank only kept that for emergencies."

"And that's all I want it for. What? You think I'm going to walk around with it strapped to my hip like a gunfighter? Mom, I'm miles from nowhere out there. I just want to know that I can take care of myself if a problem arises."

"But a gun, Sadie? Do you even know how they work?"

"Now, that's a sexist remark."

"You know what I mean. Gender has nothing to do with ignorance. You're going to shoot yourself in the foot."

"Dad taught me to use a gun when I was twelve." She grinned at her mother. "And he also made me promise never to tell you."

And she still shouldn't have told her, judging by the scowl her mother gave her just then.

"I don't have it anymore," Charlotte told her. "After Frank died, I gave it to Sheriff Watts to get rid of."

"Why?"

"Because I don't like guns."

Sadie rolled her eyes. "Mom, you're living smack in the middle of hunting country. Every damn pickup in town has a gun in the back window."

"That's different. Those are rifles, meant to put meat on every damn table in town," she shot back, standing up and glaring at Sadie. "And if you don't feel safe in the woods anymore, then maybe you should move home and forget about that stupid park."

Sadie also stood up, mostly from surprise at her mother's outburst. "I thought you supported the wilderness park."

"Not if it means my daughter has to live in the woods like a hermit and carry a gun in order to feel safe."

Sadie blew out a frustrated breath and scrubbed her face with her hands. She pushed her hair behind her ears and forced herself to smile. "Well, jeez. If it bothers you so much, forget I even mentioned the gun. I am perfectly safe doing my job."

"But that's just it, Sadie. It's not just a job to you. That park has become an obsession. From the time Eric Hellman called you in Boston, you've become a driven woman. You left a perfectly good career and all but ran up here in less than a week. And just look at you," she said, grabbing Sadie by the shoulders and pivoting her around to face the mirror. "You've lost weight."

"I've toned up," Sadie countered, glaring at her mother in the mirror.

"And you're not taking care of yourself," Charlotte continued, as if she hadn't spoken. "Your hair hasn't seen a pair of scissors in six months. You're not using any sunscreen, and you have two hairy caterpillars for eyebrows."

"I'm going to the salon today."

Charlotte lifted Sadie's left hand and turned the palm toward the mirror. "Look at that," she said.

"Calluses the size of quarters. Scratches. Bug bites. Broken nails." Her mother examined the fingers on the hand she was holding. "Or are you chewing your nails again?"

Sadie pulled free and stared into the mirror, unable to utter a word.

Charlotte spun her around to face her. "You're so obsessed with this park that you're ignoring the details of life again. You're not even thirty yet, and you're already becoming one of those addlebrained old spinster cat ladies."

Sadie could only gape at her mother. "I date," she snapped, pulling away.

"You go through the motions," Charlotte said fiercely, not backing down. She waved an angry hand in the air. "And you spend those dates systematically driving the poor guys away before they can even get to know you."

"Those poor guys are dorks. I gave three of them my cell phone number, and they never called."

"You gave them the number of a cell phone that is always broken." Charlotte waved her hand again. "It's those damn details, Sadie. You've got to start living in the present, not the past. And not in some future shrine to your father and sister. I want you to live in the *now.*"

Deciding it was definitely time to end this conversation, Sadie moved forward and took her mother into a fierce embrace. "I will, Mom. I promise. Starting today." She leaned back and smiled. "I'll go to the salon, spiff myself up real pretty, and I'll even buy a new outfit for our date tomorrow night."

Charlotte's expression was skeptical.

"And I promise," Sadie said, placing a hand over her heart. "I'll be the epitome of charm and grace for Morgan MacKeage."

Morgan MacKeage tightened the knot at his neck with a severe jerk, then tugged at the front of his silk tie with an impatient hand. He lifted his chin to free his throat and scowled at his reflection in the mirror.

"Ya can't mean to wear those braids in your hair tonight," Callum said, walking up and looking pointedly at the small braids running down both sides of Morgan's head.

Morgan turned slightly and examined one of the braids. "And why not?" he asked, glaring back at Callum in the mirror.

"Because men don't wear braids in this time." Callum snorted and tapped the back of Morgan's head. "Nor do they wear their hair so long. You look like a heathen."

Morgan walked to the dresser and picked up a short leather strap. "I am a heathen," he acknowledged. He pointed at Callum. "And I've agreed to go on this accursed date only because you nagged me into it. But it will be a cold day in hell before I cut my hair for a woman."

Callum raised both his hands in surrender. "I appreciate the favor you're doing for me. And I'm not asking that you cut your hair. I'm just wishing you could be a bit more . . . well, more civilized. Just for tonight? Is that asking too much, Morgan, for you to dig out some of that charm you were once famous for?"

Morgan pulled his hair to the back of his neck and tied it with the leather strap. He grinned at his cousin. Poor Callum had definitely been bitten by the domesticating bug—and she was named Charlotte Quill.

"And what, pray tell, is wrong with Mercedes Quill, that she needs her mother to find her dates?" Morgan asked. "Does she have pointed ears? Or is she missing some teeth?" His grin turned into a scowl. "Dammit, she'd better not be five feet tall. I get a crick in my back dealing with short women."

Callum suddenly paled. Morgan watched, surprised, as his cousin nervously smoothed down the front of his shirt and looked every place but at him.

"Ah, no. Sadie—she prefers Sadie to Mercedes—is a comely lass," Callum said in a pensive voice. "And she's tall, Morgan," he added a bit desperately, taking a step forward and finally looking at him. "But there is something I want to warn you about."

Morgan slapped his hand down on the bureau. "Dammit, I knew you were setting me up. What woman reaches the age of twenty-seven and still needs her mother to find her a date?"

"A perfectly fine woman," Callum said, getting defensive. "But nobody is flawless."

"And this Quill woman? What is her flaw?" Morgan asked, feeling a bit defensive himself. He'd agreed to this date only because he owed Callum for helping him build his house. Hell, one evening out with a woman, even if she stood five feet tall and was missing some teeth, was well worth two months of free manual labor. Or was it?

Morgan was getting an ache in his belly.

"Sadie Quill is perfectly normal," Callum said, not looking at him again. His cousin began fidgeting with his own tie, tugging at the knot at his throat. "It's just that . . . well, she was in a fire eight years ago," Callum said to the floor. He looked up, his hazel eyes worried. "She has some scars."

"She's disfigured? From the fire?" Morgan asked, his defensiveness suddenly gone. It was replaced by suspicion. And a sudden thought. "Where are these scars?"

Callum waved a negligent hand in front of his body. "Her back, mostly, Charlotte told me," he said. "Her left side and the inside of one arm."

"And?" Morgan asked, his suspicion more focused.

Callum frowned at him. "And her hand," he added. "She wears a soft leather glove on her right hand to hide her scars." He pointed at Morgan. "You cannot back out on me now," he said, his expression threatening. "I promised Charlotte. And I swear I'll tear your house down board by board with my bare hands if you renege on our deal."

Morgan rubbed his own hands together and started for the door. "Don't worry. I've no intention of missing this evening." He looked back over his shoulder to find that Callum wasn't following. "What? We're going to be late."

"One more thing," Callum said, his eyes narrowed in suspicion. "When I introduce you to Sadie, don't offer to shake her hand unless she offers first. She may be self-conscious with you because you're her date, and I don't want her to be embarrassed."

Embarrassed? Hell. Morgan doubted embarrassment would be the first emotion the woman would feel. Shock was more likely. And a healthy dose of discomfort.

"Don't worry, cousin," Morgan quickly assured him, slapping himself in the chest. "There. I just put on my mantle of charm," he said with a smile. "For my date with your woman's daughter." He held his hand up in salute. "Long hair, braid, and all, tonight I will be a perfect gentleman."

"Are you sure Callum warned this guy about my scars?" Sadie asked for the tenth time in as many minutes.

Charlotte walked over and rearranged Sadie's newly trimmed, gently permed hair over her shoulders. She smiled with motherly satisfaction.

"Callum promised me he'd discreetly broach the subject," Charlotte warmly assured her. She straightened Sadie's new silk blouse next, undoing the button at her throat. "Here. You don't need to look as if you're being strangled. You have an elegant, long neck and a beautiful throat. Show them off."

Sadie automatically reached up and pulled the edges of the collar closer together, but she didn't redo the button.

Charlotte smoothed down her sleeves next, ending up by taking hold of Sadie's hands and smiling at her again. "The color of that blouse sets off your eyes. And that new camisole is much prettier than those old body socks you're always wearing. It was worth the drive to Bangor to go shopping for your outfit and find a professional salon. You're beautiful, Sadie."

Sadie felt her cheeks heat. She pulled her hands

free and finished her mother's job, smoothing down the front of her black linen pants. She tested the fit of her new shoes. It was the first time in her life she'd worn anything other than flats. Her mom had insisted that her blind date was a good bit taller than her, and so Charlotte had talked Sadie into two-inch heels.

She only hoped that she wouldn't break her long, elegant neck trying to walk in them.

And that Morgan MacKeage wouldn't turn out to be a dork.

Sadie couldn't explain it, but she was actually nervous about tonight. She would never in a million years admit it to her mother, but she was also worried that she was slowly becoming one of those addle-brained old spinster cat ladies. How many more frogs was she going to have to kiss before she found her prince?

The really sad part was, Sadie was starting to consider herself lucky if even the frogs wanted to kiss her.

"You're sure Callum prepared the hermit for what he's getting tonight?" Sadie asked again, suddenly filled with anxious energy. "I mean, not just my scars but that I'm a bit of a klutz sometimes?"

Charlotte walked to the kitchen door and snapped on the porch light. "You're not a klutz," she said fiercely, turning back to face Sadie. "You can be graceful when you want to be. You just refuse to bother most of the time."

"The point being?" Sadie asked, disgruntled that her mother had all but agreed with her.

"The point being that your abilities change in direct proportion to your interest in something. When you're kayaking rapids, you're not a klutz," Charlotte said more softly, coming to stand in front of her again. "When you're photographing wildlife, you never make a mistake." She fluffed the padded shoulders of Sadie's blouse. "And with the right partner, you could dance like Ginger Rogers."

Somewhat mollified, Sadie turned to present her back to her mom and used both hands to point at her body. "Does the camisole drape properly to hide my scars?" she asked, looking over her shoulder at her mother. "Does it give my back a smooth line?"

Charlotte gave her a critical inspection, her brows furrowed. "As smooth as a baby's bottom. All six-foot-one-inch of beautiful woman."

Sadie grinned and turned back to face her mother. "Did I just get all gussied up for another dork?" she asked.

Charlotte shook her head. "No, sweetie. You got gussied up for yourself. Because even if you and Morgan don't hit it off tonight, you can safely assume it's his shortcoming, not yours."

Sadie walked over and kissed her mother on the cheek. "And that's why I need you," she whispered. "You keep things in perspective for me."

Charlotte's smile was warm. She started to say something but stopped suddenly at the sound of a truck pulling into the driveway.

"They're here," Charlotte said, her face immediately lighting with pleasure. She turned and rushed to the door, opening it wide before smoothing down her own outfit.

Sadie followed at a more sedate pace, shaking her

head and smiling at her mother's excitement. Charlotte Quill really was in love again. And she positively glowed, not only from that love but from the promise of the secret little life nestled securely in her belly.

Sadie only wished she could be a fly on the wall when that secret was finally revealed to Callum MacKeage.

Truck doors slammed, and Sadie peeked over her mother's shoulder to see two men walking toward the porch. She sighed with relief. Morgan-the-hermit really was tall. That was one awkward obstacle out of the way.

He certainly wasn't a dork, if that manly swagger was any indication. Even from this distance, Sadie could see that the man carried himself with confidence, apparently not at all put off by finding himself on a blind date.

Sadie backed up to let her mother greet their guests, at the same time quickly smoothing her cuff over the hem of her glove, hoping to calm the butterflies now rioting in her belly.

Callum stepped through the door first, stopping in mid-stride to stare at Charlotte. "I swear, woman," he said, his voice gravely serious. "You get prettier every time I see you."

With that declaration, he swept Sadie's suddenly flustered mother into a bear of an embrace and kissed her soundly on the lips. Charlotte, her face flushed red, pulled away and quickly turned her attention to smoothing down her clothes again. She tried fussing with her hair then, but Callum pulled her under his arm and turned them both to face Sadie, Callum grinning like a cat who had just polished off a large dish of cream.

"Sadie," he said, "I'd like to introduce you to my cousin, Morgan." He turned slightly, moving a still flustered Charlotte with him. "Morgan, this is Sadie Quill."

Sadie barely heard what Callum was saying. Her feet were lead weights stuck to the floor. Her vision had narrowed and dimmed, her heart was trying to pound a hole in her chest, and the loud buzz of pumping blood rang in her ears. She couldn't work up a drop of moisture in her mouth, and a lump the size of a basketball was lodged in her throat.

She could only stare, open-mouthed, at her date.

The man stood just inside the kitchen door, his broad shoulders nearly touching the woodwork on both sides, his hands negligently thrust into his pants pockets, and his unforgettably familiar, forest-green eyes making Sadie think the butterflies in her stomach just might escape.

Her date wasn't a dork. He was the madman from the lake.

And she was supposed to spend the evening with him?

He took a step toward her.

Acting on instinct alone, Sadie took an equal step back.

His eyes suddenly lighting with unholy mischief, Morgan MacKeage took yet another step forward. He pulled a hand out of his pocket and held it out to her.

The jerk. The silently laughing, defiantly challenging jerk was just daring her to put her gloved right hand in his.

Callum gave a deep cough into his fist. Sadie looked over to find him glaring at Morgan MacKeage with enough force to knock the man over. She looked back at her date from hell. He wasn't paying any attention to his cousin. He was still staring at her, still holding out his hand.

Sadie looked at her mother then. Charlotte appeared horrified. But was her mother horrified *for* her or *at* her for not politely greeting her date?

Anger suddenly came to Sadie's rescue. Morgan MacKeage had been born a jerk and would likely die a jerk. But that didn't mean she had to let him be a jerk to her tonight.

He had no right to toy with her this way. Even if she had caught him swimming naked, he didn't have the right to continue punishing her for what was really no more than a minor indiscretion four days ago. It had been an innocent mistake that any person would have made given the circumstances. If their roles had been reversed, she'd like to have seen Morgan MacKeage simply turn his back on a naked woman swimming in a lake.

Which meant she had two choices here. She could shake the hand that he was still insistently holding out to her, or she could spit on that hand—if she could somehow get the glands in her mouth to work again—and run screaming up to her room.

Both choices made her stomach knot.

Lifting her chin and steeling herself for the feel of his grip, Sadie reached out with her right hand and firmly placed it in his. He gently closed his fingers over her glove and bent slightly at the waist.

"It is certainly my pleasure, Mercedes," he said in a soft brogue, his polite tone a stark contradiction to his laughing eyes. "I can't tell you how much I've been looking forward to meeting you. Again," he added in a soft whisper that only she could hear.

The right corner of his mouth turned up in a grin, and he looked at Callum. "You could have warned me, cousin, that she was beautiful enough to take a man's breath away."

Callum arched one bushy eyebrow. "I believe I did mention that fact," he said, smiling tightly.

Sadie gently tugged on her hand, hoping to get it back sometime tonight. Morgan MacKeage shot her a mischievous wink that silently said he clearly knew her discomfort. Instead of releasing her hand, he moved one long finger past the hem of her glove and rested it on the inside of her wrist, directly over her racing pulse.

Sadie flinched at the intimate contact and shivered at the fire that shot up her arm and into the center of her chest. She tugged more frantically to free herself.

His smile now decidedly wicked, Morgan MacKeage refused to release her. He moved instead to stand beside her, tucking her arm through his, anchoring her to his side.

"Shall we go, then?" he said to the room at large. "I believe our reservations are for eight o'clock."

"I need my sweater," Sadie said. She made another attempt to free herself.

He started walking to the door as if she hadn't spoken, her entire arm as well as her hand still entrapped. "You won't need it," he said as he all but dragged her along. "It's a perfect late-summer night."

He led her through the door and onto the porch, where he stopped briefly. "If you get chilled, lass, I'll gladly warm you up," he said in a lowered voice, for her ears only.

Sadie was already chilled, all the way down to her bones. She couldn't possibly spend an entire evening with this man, considering what she'd done to him four days ago. Especially considering that she knew exactly what Morgan MacKeage looked like without his clothes on.

A bead of sweat trickled between Sadie's breasts. How was she supposed to spend an entire evening with this Adonis and not make more of a fool of herself than she already had? How did a woman smile and talk and share food with a man when she knew that his tie and jacket were merely a civilized veneer covering the body of a god?

Then again, how could she bow out on her mother now?

She was smartly trapped—in more ways than one.

Her arm still in his possession, he led her off the porch toward the monstrous four-door truck he and Callum had arrived in. He finally did release her, but only after he had opened the back door of the truck. He let go of her arm, grabbed her around the waist, and lifted her into the seat. He then gently closed the door before she finished gasping in shock.

Sadie found herself sitting beside her mother. Charlotte quietly handed Sadie her purse, a bemused smile warming her face.

"Morgan seems to be one of those take-charge kinds of men," Charlotte said, approval obvious in her voice. She patted Sadie's knee. "Just what you need."

Sadie smiled at her mom. "You mean the kind of man who puts his date in the backseat?" she asked. She waved at the still empty front seats. "What is this, 1955?"

Charlotte smiled back, shaking her head. "I told you Cal was old-fashioned," she said. "And it's kind of sweet, when you think about it. Cal is always worried about getting into an accident when we go out and having the airbag hurt me if it deploys." Charlotte leaned over and said in a whisper, "He saw something on the news about them being dangerous to small people." She actually giggled. "Cal says I'm a tiny thing, and it worries him. Can you believe that, thinking me tiny?"

Sadie refrained from rolling her eyes. "You are small, Mom, compared with Callum."

Sadie shot a look through the windshield to see their two dates now standing at the front of the truck, exchanging words. She couldn't hear what they were saying, but both men wore darkened expressions. It appeared that Callum was scolding Morgan. Good. The arrogant jerk needed a set-down. And since Callum was more of a size to do it, Sadie basked in the hope that her mother's boyfriend was up to the task.

Chapter Eight

On the pretense of smoothing down his tie, Morgan petted the cherrywood burl softly humming against his chest. The *drùidh's* charm had started to warm and gently vibrate the moment Mercedes Quill had placed her hand in his.

And now the damn thing was still not wanting to settle down.

Morgan sat at the tiny table of the restaurant nestled on the shore of Pine Lake. The dining room was dotted with only a few late diners, as most of the people had already moved to the adjoining dance floor and bar. Morgan absently listened to the lounge music and idle chatter between his cousin and his cousin's woman, but his attention was definitely focused on his date.

The woman had cleaned up rather nicely from the woods sprite he'd encountered four days ago. He had almost forgotten how tall she was. But not how beautiful. Mercedes had shiny blond hair that fell in waves to the small of her back, golden skin that had been kissed gently by the sun, and an utterly feminine body that made his own skin tighten in response. She was arresting, and Morgan had noticed more than one man glancing at her during dinner.

Not that his date noticed. She seemed completely oblivious to her effect on men.

And that pleased him.

Morgan was also pleased that Mercedes was a woman of very few words. He'd gotten maybe a dozen sentences out of her all evening, and most of those had not been directed at him.

But what he really liked, what most drew him to Mercedes Quill, was the thing that most disturbed him: her eyes. They were the color of an autumn sky freshly washed by a fast-moving rain. Sparkling. Energized. Alive.

And he wanted to possess them.

To possess her. He wanted to wrap his arms around Mercedes, pull her lovely, supple body against him, and focus all five of his senses on her beauty.

Morgan stood up and held out his hand to Mercedes—his left hand this time. "I'd enjoy your company on the dance floor," he said, making sure his voice didn't betray his thoughts.

She appeared downright appalled by his invitation, her gaze darting from him to the dance floor, then swiftly back to him. She looked as if he had just asked her to take off all her clothes.

Now, that irked. Except for demanding that she give him her scarred hand back at the house, he'd been a perfect gentleman all evening. Hell, he'd set her in the backseat of the truck where she'd be safest, he'd ordered a delicious dinner of salmon for her, and he'd just ordered her a nice glass of sweet red wine, of which she'd only taken one sip.

He saw Mercedes suddenly jump as if she'd been kicked, and she snapped her gaze to her mother and scowled. Tired of standing there with his hand out and not getting the response he wanted, Morgan simply moved to the back of her chair and pulled it out. Mercedes shot to her feet as if he had pinched her and leveled her scowl on him.

"I'd rather not dance," she said.

He took her arm and guided her to the dance floor. "I promise not to step on your toes," he assured her, turning her into his embrace.

This was the nicest thing Morgan had discovered about modern society, the slow dancing. It was like courting in public. Perfectly acceptable. Encouraged, even.

Aye. He definitely liked dancing.

Except that dancing with Mercedes Quill was like wrestling with the ridge pole on the roof of his house. She was as stiff as a board and uncooperative. And Morgan soon discovered it was *his* feet that were in danger of being stepped on.

Holy hell. The woman didn't know how to dance. He would subtly guide her in one direction, and her feet would head off in another instead, trying to lead him. Morgan couldn't keep his smile from tugging free. And that little quirk seemed to deepen her scowl even more.

"Ah, lass. Just this once, just for five minutes, give me your trust," he entreated, firming his grip on her waist and moving them into a rhythm that matched the music.

"I don't like dancing."

"In general, or just with me?"

"Both."

He chuckled and pulled her closer, tucking her head under his chin. It was definitely nice to dance with someone he didn't have to bend over to hold.

"Maybe you'd enjoy yourself a bit more if you had drunk your wine," he suggested.

She snapped her head up. "I don't like wine."

Morgan blew a sigh over her head, praying for patience. It was difficult being a gentleman to a gràineag.

"Then why didn't ya say so?" he asked, trying his damndest not to sound disgruntled, shoving her head back down so she wouldn't see his own scowl.

"Because you didn't give me a chance," she muttered into his jacket. She popped her head up again. "Just like you didn't give me a chance to order my own dinner."

"You ate the salmon."

"Because I happen to like salmon."

"Then what's the problem?"

She blinked at him, started to say something, then suddenly sighed and returned her head to his shoulder. Morgan grinned. She was still having trouble finding her words. That was fine with him. Her body language was all that mattered.

The woman in his arms slowly began to relax, and together they moved to the soft music, slowly learning to sway in harmony.

He wanted her. That simply, that urgently; he wanted Mercedes Quill with the passion of a man long lost and needing the anchor of a special woman. But what Morgan really wanted was for Sadie's own simmering passion to ignite in his arms. Together they could probably light up the entire valley.

"Hey, Moose Woman!" someone hollered from across the dance floor.

His date's feet stopped moving, and Mercedes stiffened into a pole again. Her fingers dug into his back, and Morgan wasn't sure, but it felt as if she were trying to crawl inside his jacket.

"Moose!" the voice repeated, closer this time. "When did you get back?" the man asked as he and three other men and two women approached.

Mercedes stopped trying to hide and finally pulled free of his arms and turned around. The quick glimpse Morgan got of her expression told him that this was not a welcome reunion with old friends. Her entire face was scorched red.

"It is you," the man said. "I thought you had a job in Boston. What was it? Oh, yeah. Meteorology. You make it as a weather girl yet?"

"Ah, no. I've moved back home," Mercedes said, darting an embarrassed look around the room.

"Hey, that's good. That you've come back, I mean. We're just headed over to Nadeau's for a beer. Want to join us?" The guy looked briefly at Morgan, then back at her. "You can bring your friend if you want."

"No, Peter. We're here with my mom and her date," she told him.

"Aw, come on, Moose. We can catch up on old times," he said, aiming a cajoling punch at her arm.

Morgan stepped forward and caught the man's hand before it could connect with his date.

"Peter, is it?" he asked.

Peter nodded, trying discreetly and unsuccessfully to get his hand back.

"Well, Peter. My date's name is Sadie, not Moose. And if you try to punch her again, I'm going to break your hand," he finished softly, squeezing Peter's hand just enough to get his point across before he released him.

Now, as warnings went, Morgan thought this one had been nicely delivered according to modern rules. His date, however, appeared to take exception. She whirled on him, her eyes wide with disbelief.

Peter the idiot was even less believing. He actually took a step closer. So did the three men behind him.

Morgan gently pushed Mercedes behind his back. She stayed there all of three seconds before she came bounding back around to stand between him and the four now defensively postured men.

"I'm going to help them beat you up if you cause a scene," she whispered in a much more threatening voice.

"You want to go with them?" he asked, trying to keep his smile from escaping. His date was flaming mad—and obviously unaware of the scene she was creating all by herself.

"No, I don't want to go with them. And I don't want

a fight breaking out, either. It's an old nickname from high school," she said, leaning up to whisper her confession. "Peter didn't mean anything by it. And he didn't try to punch me to hurt me. Now, stop being a caveman, MacKeage."

He had two choices. He could shove the spitting-mad woman into the arms of his now approaching cousin and give in to his urge to punch Peter the idiot in the nose. Or he could finish dancing with his date.

What to do?

Both actions stirred his blood.

Both would be equally satisfying.

With a grin sent to Callum, Morgan reached out and pulled Mercedes back into his arms, turning them both so that his back was to the intruders, smartly dismissing them as a threat to his evening. He ignored her squeak of surprise and nodded his head to Callum, who had now stopped his advance through the dancers. But his cousin didn't return to his seat until the four men and two women, obviously confused by the sudden loss of a fight, simply walked away.

"Never issue threats you can't back up, lass," Morgan whispered into her hair. "It's a bad habit that might prove dangerous someday."

She popped her head off his shoulder and stared at him in silence. Her blush had calmed down slightly, but still her entire face glowed with lingering anger.

Morgan lifted his hand, entwining his fingers in her hair so she couldn't look away, while he gently continued to coax her body to sway with his to the music.

"If I apologize for terrorizing you the other day, will

you call a truce to our silent war?" he asked. "And maybe start enjoying yourself tonight?"

"No."

Why didn't her answer surprise him? "Will you kick me in the shin if I tell you how beautiful you look this evening?"

Her gracefully arched brows puckered together, and her eyes narrowed, as if she suspected he was toying with her. Morgan gave up trying to make pleasant conversation. Instead, he urged her head back down to his shoulder before he gave in to his own urge to kiss her—right here on the dance floor, in front of God and all these people.

It was damn prickly business, trying to possess a *gràineag*.

It was also damn fun.

Sadie didn't know what to make of her date. One minute he was pricking her temper, then defending her from an embarrassing nickname, and the next minute he was telling her she was pretty.

And he was a bossy date. The guy hadn't stopped manhandling her all evening. He was constantly leading her here and there, ordering dinner and drinks for her, then guiding her over the dance floor like a drill sergeant.

And now they were walking the two miles back to her home because Morgan had decided it was a beautiful evening for a moonlit stroll.

Sadie still couldn't understand why she liked him.

Can a man actually smell sexy? Sadie had been around plenty of men, but when she'd found herself in Morgan's arms on the dance floor, all she could think about was how sexy he smelled. Warm in a masculine sort of way, with just a hint of the woods.

And he felt the way he smelled—just as sexy and very inviting. Sadie couldn't believe she'd been able to relax enough actually to snuggle against him. Heck, what girl wouldn't be enchanted to find herself in the arms of a tall, powerful, very handsome god? She'd have to be insane not to take advantage of the moment, to rest her head on his broad shoulder and sway to the music as if she were a goddess.

Which was why Sadie had said her goodbyes to her mom and Callum and had gone along with Morgan's plan to walk her home.

She was in no hurry for this dream date to end.

Sadie sighed into the stillness of the peaceful night. She was going to have to admit her actions four days ago had been wrong. Morgan had proven himself a gentleman tonight, and she could at least act like a lady. She would have to apologize.

"I'm sorry I took your picture the other day," she said, keeping her eyes straight ahead on the road. "I had no right to invade your privacy that way."

Sadie stopped when she realized she was speaking to empty air. She turned and looked. The man was standing several steps back, staring at her. And he was not smiling.

"Dammit, MacKeage. I wasn't thinking, okay? It's just that you . . . well, you surprised me, and I didn't stop to think about what I was doing."

Without responding to her not-so-gracious apology, he slowly slipped out of his jacket and walked up to her. He swung the jacket past her head and settled it over her shoulders, gathering the lapels together and tightly entrapping her.

Sadie caught her breath as she stared up at him, just as trapped in the depths of his moonlit evergreen eyes.

"Did you like what you saw through the viewfinder, lass?" he asked, his gaze never wavering from hers.

She couldn't have answered that question if she dared.

He suddenly smiled and released his hold on his jacket. He touched the end of her nose with one finger and shot her a wink. "It doesn't matter if you did or not," he said, moving to continue their walk toward home. "It's the only body I've got, and you'll just have to get used to it."

Sadie blinked at his back, watching him walk away. She ran to catch up, tripped on her heels, and started skipping as she pulled first one shoe and then the other one off. She ran into him then, when he unexpectedly stopped and faced her.

"Ya can't be baring your feet," he said, reaching to take her shoes from her. "There might be glass or metal on the road."

Sadie quickly tucked her shoes into the pockets of his jacket she was wearing and moved past him, walking on the pavement now, once more leading the way home. "I went barefoot the first ten years of my life," she said over her shoulder. "Besides," she said as his stride quickly brought him beside her, "I know a priest with a magic cane who can heal me just like that." She snapped her fingers in the air.

She was suddenly brought to such an abrupt halt

and spun around that one of her shoes fell onto the road.

"What do you know of a priest with a magic cane?" he asked.

Sadie blinked again. Morgan had gone deathly pale and frighteningly still, but for the fire of inquest in his now emerald-black eyes.

"I . . . I met the old priest who lives up on TarStone Mountain," she said, not knowing what to make of his reaction.

"When?"

"The other day. Thursday. He came to visit me."

Morgan's hands on her shoulders tightened. "You stay away from Daar," he told her. He shook her slightly. "Understand, Mercedes? You stay away from that old priest."

She could only gape at him.

He shook her again. "You're not to believe anything he tells you."

And with that command issued, Morgan turned on his heel and started toward her house again. And again, Sadie found herself gaping at his back. His moods changed more often than the weather.

She ran to catch up. "Wait," she said, grabbing his arm. "There's something I want to ask you."

He stopped and turned to her.

"I want to know if you're the one stealing my trail markers."

"Trail markers?"

"My orange ribbons. You said so yourself, earlier tonight, that you didn't want a park built in Prospect Valley. Are you taking my ribbons, hoping to stop it?"

"And will taking the ribbons stop it?"

"No."

"Weren't some of those ribbons on MacKeage land?" he asked, crossing his arms over his chest as he looked at her.

Sadie dropped her gaze to the knot in his tie. "They might have been," she quietly admitted. "But stealing ribbons won't stop the park."

He took hold of her hand and started walking again, this time across the grass, in the direction of the town pier that jutted into Pine Lake. Sadie allowed him to lead her to a bench, aware that he hadn't answered her question and resigned to the fact that he probably would never admit to stealing her trail markers.

"Why a park in Prospect Valley?" he asked as he settled her on the bench and then stood across from her, leaning against the pier rail.

"Why not? It's a beautiful valley with plenty of recreational features. We have the opportunity to offer four-season use—camping, hiking, kayaking, snowmobiling, fishing. You name the sport, and the public can come here to do it."

"We? Who is this 'we' you speak of?"

"Right now it's a group of businessmen from around the state who have formed a consortium. Eric Hellman hired me to help work up a proposal to present to our legislature."

"These businessmen, what is their gain? Why have they come together with the hope of building a park here?"

Sadie frowned at his question. "Maybe because they

want to see this vast wilderness preserved for future generations."

"Or maybe they hope to profit?" he asked very quietly. "Will they donate all the land to this park, or are they intending to sell lots for vacation homes?"

"But that's the point," Sadie said, leaning forward to make her own point. "Not only will the park open a beautiful piece of land to the public, it will also help grow the economy of this area. Just as your ski resort has done. Look at all the shops and inns that have cropped up since you opened. The population of Pine Creek is nearly double in winter. With a new park, that economic boom could be year-round."

"And then what do you have, Mercedes? Another small city with hordes of people overrunning the wilderness, crowding the animals onto smaller and smaller tracts of land?"

Sadie stood up, pulling the lapels of Morgan's coat tightly around her. Morgan stepped away from the rail and took hold of her shoulders.

"I know why the businessmen have come up with this plan, Mercedes. But I don't understand your connection. What is it you hope to gain?"

"Nothing," she said, torn between pulling away and wanting to lean into his broad chest.

The man was making her angry.

But he still smelled sexy.

"Since I learned to walk, I've been hiking that valley," she continued, looking up into his serious, deep green eyes. "And I want to be part of preserving it."

"Has the valley not been happily existing all these years without your intervention? Can a person not hike and fish and hunt there now? And will turning it into a park not ultimately destroy the valley, if more and more people come here?"

Dammit. She hated that his argument made a certain kind of sense. Hadn't she had that very worry herself? Wasn't it still a concern?

"Why are you so against the park?" she asked. "Your family will likely profit the most. Your hotel will be full winter and summer. Your restaurant on the summit could be open year-round."

"It's already open year-round. And how much profit does one family need? Especially at the expense of the land."

Morgan suddenly released her shoulders, took hold of her right hand again, and started walking them toward her house.

"My camera. I want it back," she said, deciding it was time to change the subject and probably better to keep a line drawn between them.

He was too handsome and tall and masculine and . . . and too damned sexy to be attracted to her. She would bet that when Morgan MacKeage made love to a woman, they both got naked, sweaty, and completely consumed by each other. All the lights would be on. The covers would be stripped from the bed, with no place to hide. Everything would be exposed.

Well, if she lived to be a hundred, she was never getting undressed in front of a man.

Especially a man who could give Adonis a run for his money.

"What camera?"

"What?" Sadie asked, completely lost in her train of thought. "Oh. The camera I had with me the other day, that you took the film out of. I want my pack, my GPS, and my camera back."

"I don't have your camera. I left it on the ground."

"You must have come back later and gotten it, along with everything else." She squeezed his hand which was holding hers. "I want my stuff back."

"On my honor, lass. I didn't return and take your belongings," he said softly. "Did you go back and look for them?"

"Yes." Sadie sighed into the night. "I'm never going to see my stuff again, am I? Someone else must have come along and found it."

"I'll buy you a new camera, Mercedes. It's my fault yours got lost."

"It doesn't matter. The camera can't be replaced, anyway. It was my dad's."

He used his grip on her hand to stop them again. "I'm sorry," he said simply, staring down at her with serious eyes.

Sadie straightened her shoulders. "It was my fault. I walked away without even thinking about my stuff."

He raised a finger to her cheek and brushed a strand of hair off her face, tucking it behind her ear.

"We didn't get off to a very good start, did we, lass?"

Sadie balled her left hand into a fist and shoved it into her pocket, determined not to run her own finger over his cheek.

Lord, she was attracted to this man, and it had nothing to do with having seen every naked inch of him four days ago.

Well, maybe that had a little bit to do with it. But it was more than this unfamiliar stirring of lust she was feeling right now as she stared up into his warm, mesmerizing forest-green eyes. It was the warmth of his touch, the way he held her gloved hand as if it were a perfectly normal act, the way he looked at her, smiled at her, and made her feel . . . well . . . special.

"The start of what?" she asked.

"Excuse me?"

"You said we didn't get off to a very good start. The start of what?"

He tugged her forward, pulling her off balance toward him, and released her to wrap both of his arms around her. He hugged her to him tightly, and his chest heaved with another deep sigh.

"The start of a cautious but important friendship," he whispered over her head, his arms tightening around her.

Sadie wanted to bury her face in his shirt and weep.

Friendship.

Dammit. She was lusting after his body, standing in his arms in the middle of the moonlit road, foolishly hoping that he had been talking about starting a flaming affair.

And he was offering her friendship.

Sadie pulled away with a jerk. She shot him a good glare to let him know what she thought of his offer, then turned and started walking toward home again.

Morgan quietly fell into step beside his obviously angry date, not knowing whether to be amused or angry himself.

He did know he was damned frustrated. He wanted the woman with a fierceness that was almost painful. There was nothing casual about his feelings for Mercedes. He didn't just want to bed her, he wanted to possess her, to capture and hold on to that powerful energy he felt whenever she was close.

He rubbed the softly humming burl on his chest again as he walked along the dark road, keeping pace with the silent woman beside him. If he were a gentleman, he would not be starting anything with her tonight but ending things by taking her to her door, politely saying good night, and walking away and never seeing her again.

Aye, that is what he should do.

If he were a gentleman.

By the time they reached Sadie's front porch, she was dreading the sympathy kiss on the cheek Morgan likely would give her and his wan smile and false declaration that he'd had a nice time tonight, that maybe they'd see each other around sometime soon.

Well, not this time. And not with this man.

Sadie had actually had a wonderful evening. Morgan MacKeage had been a nearly perfect date—attentive, considerate, amusing, and entertaining. He had danced like Fred Astaire and made her feel like Ginger Rogers. Heck, even the near brawl on the dance floor had been invigorating.

She didn't want a peck. Not from a guy who could probably lay a kiss on a girl that would blow her socks off.

And she was not going to let this man ruin the first

truly wonderful date she'd ever had, because she was not going to let him kiss her at all.

But before Sadie could complete her thought, one of Morgan's large hands came around the back of her neck and slowly drew her closer. With his other hand, Morgan lifted her face toward his. "I've been wondering if you taste as good as you look," he whispered just before he touched his lips to hers.

Sadie stopped breathing as he completely engulfed her in his embrace, tightening his hand on her hair, wrapping his arm around her back with fierce intent. He canted her head and deepened the kiss, urging her mouth open, sweeping his tongue inside.

Sadie was so overwhelmed she completely lost all train of thought save one: she didn't want him to stop.

Because her arms were being held at her sides, she could only move her hands to grip the back of his waist. And, glory of glories, she actually had to stand on tiptoe to kiss him back.

The guy rumbled an earthy, approving growl at her tentative action and tightened his hold on her, taking her breath away again. Their tongues introduced themselves, forgoing the pleasantries and getting immediately down to business. Sadie kneaded her fingers into his back, wondering if she might simply crawl into his skin beside him.

He broke the contact suddenly and tilted her head to expose her neck. Sadie whimpered the moment his mouth touched her throat.

Light flashed in the back of her eyes, and she wiggled her arms free to reach up and grab his shoulders.

He lifted her then, bringing her feet completely off the ground, and stepped forward until her back was pressed against the side of the house. He moved even closer, nestling himself between her thighs.

With only the fleeting worry that she might burst into flames, Sadie wrapped her legs around his waist and welcomed the storm brewing deep inside the pit of her stomach.

His mouth trailed a path of fire down her throat, to the opening of her blouse. His teeth rasped against her skin briefly, and then a button popped. Sadie felt his hot mouth touching the sensitive skin at the base of her throat.

"Morgan," she whispered, closing her eyes, letting her head fall back against the house. She pulled at his hair, tugging it free of its ponytail, running her fingers through the length of it. She finally gave in to the urge she'd had all evening and fingered one of the small, thin braids that now ran loose down the sides of his face.

He lifted his head and stared at her, then took possession of her mouth again, just as deeply and far more intimately than before. The vision of evergreen eyes swam through Sadie's dizzily reeling mind.

Her hands trembled with building passion as she held Morgan to herself, savoring his taste. Their tongues sparred. Their lips molded together. And their pounding hearts beat against each other.

He tore his mouth free, taking a shuddering breath that rocked her like a small earthquake, and blew it out harshly as he rested his forehead on hers.

"Two choices, Mercedes. We make love right now,

right here on this porch, or you run like hell into your house and lock the door."

He thrust his hips forward, forcefully, backing up his ultimatum with hard, blatant evidence that clearly said which choice he preferred.

Heat scorched her cheeks, and Sadie couldn't decide if it was radiating from him or from inside herself, as she realized just how close she was to committing emotional suicide.

And just how much she wanted to.

She immediately reversed her grip on his shoulders and pushed at him frantically as she unwrapped her legs from around his waist and dropped her feet to the porch. She pushed him again when he continued to hold her tightly, staring down at her with a look that said he wanted to take the choice out of her hands.

He suddenly let go, dropped his arms to his sides, and took a step back.

Sadie shivered. With his hair loose and tangled in waves, his face harsh from lust denied, and his dark eyes unreadable, her date had lost his mask of civility.

He was that same madman again who had chased her through the woods four days ago.

And she suddenly felt just as vulnerable as she had then.

Sadie spun around and groped for the knob, twisting it violently and throwing her weight against the door until it opened and she could run inside and slam it shut behind her. And, as he had so kindly suggested, she threw home the bolt with a desperate twist and backed away into the safety of the kitchen shadows.

She stood there in the dark, breathing heavily, listening for his footsteps on the porch stairs. They were five minutes in coming, and in that time every touch, every sensation, every emotion his kiss had evoked ran through her head like sparks of energy gathering strength. Sadie touched her trembling fingers to her lips and shivered again.

Holy heck. That had been one hell of a sympathy kiss.

But it wasn't until she was lying in bed later that night, stark naked because every inch of her skin was super-sensitive, her heart still pounding in her chest and her mind still reeling with confused emotions, that Sadie realized Morgan MacKeage hadn't simply kissed her socks off—he'd blown them clean past the summit of Fraser Mountain.

Chapter Nine

𝒥t had taken Sadie most of the morning to wiggle gently out of her mother's clutches. Charlotte had wanted to know how Sadie could have lost one of her shoes, why Morgan's jacket had been found crumpled in a ball on the kitchen floor, and what she thought of her date last night.

Sadie still couldn't believe the lame excuses and raving praises she'd come up with to appease her mother.

She was glad she'd made Eric open his store early this morning, so she could pick up her new GPS and cell phone, backpack and supplies, as well as a new, overpriced camera.

Now she was finally back at her cabin. She was going to miss Ping, though. She had left the cat at her mother's house, afraid the wolf might return and decide Ping would make a tasty lunch. No matter what the priest had said, she wasn't trusting Faol with her pet.

Sadie opened her cabin door and set her new backpack and supplies on the table. She walked over to the model of the park and studied the eastern mountain range.

Morgan MacKeage had built his house halfway up Fraser Mountain, he'd told her last night. He owned a good chunk of land there that ran all the way down to Prospect River.

Which meant he owned the southeastern corner of the proposed wilderness park.

Sadie pulled out the map she'd been given the day she took this job. She spread it on top of the model and studied it again. The boundary of the park, traced in bright green marker, definitely included the western slope of Fraser Mountain. It was nearly five thousand acres—a small part of the park but a very important part. The south access road would be going across the MacKeage land, bringing people in through Pine Creek.

Sadie suddenly straightened from looking at the map, pushed her hair behind her ears, and listened. She heard it again, a gentle, barely audible *woof*.

She closed her eyes and dropped her head. Damn. She'd been hoping that damn wolf would be gone by now. Had he been hanging around for three whole days, waiting for her to return?

And now he wanted her to come out and say hello?

Sadie moved to the window and peeked out. And there he was, sitting just on the edge of the forest, staring at the cabin. With a gasp, Sadie ran to the door and threw it open.

He was holding her old backpack his mouth.

The one she'd lost.

And it looked to be full.

Faol stood up and took several steps forward, his tail wagging. Sadie slowly walked down the steps and stopped a good ten paces from the wolf when he let out another muffled *woof*.

"What have you got there, big boy?" she asked. "Where did you find that?"

He took a step closer to her, giving a soft whine.

Sadie took a step back.

Faol immediately sat down and gently laid the pack on the ground at his feet. He lifted his head, and this time his bark was stronger, almost demanding.

Not for all of Plum's gold would Sadie move an inch closer to the huge, powerful-looking animal. She was not bending down to take her pack, putting her face mere inches from Faol's teeth.

He wagged his tail as he sat there staring at her, sending a cloud of dust wafting into the air. He whined again, stood up, and took several steps back.

Keeping ten paces between them, Sadie moved forward, matching his retreat. But he stopped suddenly, only a few feet from the pack.

She darted a look at her pack and almost cried with relief when she saw the camera lens peeking past the zipper. Sadie looked back at the wolf. His tongue was lolling out the side of his mouth, his eyes—a crisp, iridescent green—round and sharply focused as he softly whined again, darting his own look from her to the pack, then back at her.

Sadie took another cautious step forward, then

waited, watching him. He lifted a paw and started to lick it clean.

She took another step forward.

He yawned, then walked his front legs forward until he was lying down, for all the world looking as if he couldn't care less that she was there.

Two more cautious steps, then Sadie used her toe to hook the strap on her pack and slowly pull it toward her.

Faol laid his head on his paws.

The pack now on the ground at her own feet, Sadie bent her knees and blindly felt for the strap, grabbing it and then slowly straightening. With her back to the cabin and her eyes trained on the still reclined wolf, Sadie retreated until she felt the porch touch her thighs. Then, keeping one guarded eye on her visitor, she sat down, opened the zipper, and looked inside.

The wolf completely forgotten, Sadie stared at the contents of the pack. She lifted her father's camera out, then dumped the rest onto the porch.

It was all there: GPS, cell phone, surveyor's ribbon, knife, water bottle, even the shredded duct tape she'd been bound with.

Everything. All there.

And all dry.

Sadie looked over at Faol. He was sitting up now, staring at her, his tongue lolling out again, his eyes unblinking, and his head cocked as if he were expecting her to speak to him.

And say what? *Thank you for returning my things, wolf?*

Sadie hugged her father's camera to her chest and

laughed out loud. She was going nuts, and she didn't care.

"Thank you, big boy," she said, waving the camera at him. "I don't know where you found this stuff or how you knew to bring it here, but thank you from the bottom of my heart."

She wiped at the unexpected tears that suddenly welled up in her eyes. Her daddy's camera. She had it back.

Sadie went into the cabin and rummaged around in her supplies on the table. She found the bag of beef jerky she'd bought from Eric this morning, tore it open, and grabbed a handful of the dried meat. She headed back outdoors and down the steps toward the wolf.

"This might go against everything I believe about feeding wild animals, you big, beautiful wolf, but I've never met anyone who deserves a reward as much as you do. Here," she said, tossing the beef onto the ground in front of him. "I promise there'll be more where that came from. Next trip into town, I'm buying you the biggest bag on the shelf."

Faol sniffed the food at his feet but didn't actually touch it. He lifted his head and looked at her.

"Hey. That's not the cheap stuff," Sadie told him. "That's prime beef."

He suddenly raised his nose into the air and gave a long, plaintive howl before he turned and trotted away, disappearing into the forest.

Shivers ran down Sadie's spine as the last echo of the haunting cry faded into the air around her. She stared at the spot where Faol had disappeared. He couldn't have known the pack belonged to her. He was just an animal who had found something in the woods and brought it here, the same way Ping brought hunting trophies to Sadie to show off.

That must be it. Faol didn't like the food because it carried a human scent. And he had just found the pack, and because it had *her* scent on it, he had brought it here.

Yeah. That was a perfectly logical explanation.

Morgan forced more power to his tired muscles and pushed his overheated body through the calm waters of the cold lake. He was on his second trip across the lake, and still he couldn't seem to outswim the emotions driving his thoughts.

Mercedes Quill. She was responsible for his mood this evening. He'd spent the entire day thinking about her. It didn't seem to matter that she was independent, prickly sometimes to the point of rudeness, and determined to open this valley to hordes of people who needed wilderness parks in order to play at primitive living.

Mercedes was beautiful.

Intelligent in a most challenging way.

He'd walked off her porch last night frustrated to the point of pain and decided on the point that he would have her—on whatever terms it took, by whatever means he could find.

Mercedes Quill was his. Morgan had declared that she belonged to him in the late hours of last night as he'd stood in the mist-shrouded moonlight overlooking the waterfall. He'd told God, the forest, and anyone who could hear him that the blue-eyed woman who walked this valley was his.

Morgan pulled himself onto the boulder in the middle of the cove and let the setting sun wash over his body. He wrapped his fist around the cherrywood burl hanging from his neck and watched the sky dance in a brilliant display of colors that arced from soft blue to a warm, vibrant red.

And somewhere in the middle he saw Mercedes.

Aye. After last night on the porch, aroused by his kisses, her eyes had been the same deep blue of tonight's sky. And Morgan made another vow then, that he would see that same color again, fired by the passion of their lovemaking.

But first he must find a way to explain to Mercedes that when she had walked into his valley and planted her first ribbon, she'd entered the world of an ancient and possessive man.

A world she would never be leaving again.

A gentle bark carried over the water toward him. Morgan turned in the direction of the sound and saw Faol standing on the shore of the lake, staring at him.

"Go away, you accursed beast," Morgan said, turning his back on the wolf. "I'm not in the mood for your company."

Faol barked again, louder this time, more urgently.

Morgan dove into the water, swimming back across the lake, away from the wolf. His stroke less rushed, his breathing barely labored, he thought again of the *drùidh's* vision and the blackness that had swarmed through the valley, chasing the yellow light.

He couldn't tell Mercedes that she was in danger,

because he couldn't explain to her how he knew such a thing. Nor could he let her discover his gorge. The woman was too intelligent, too curious, and too knowledgeable about this forest not to realize that something more than just the fickleness of nature was at work here. And she was too modern to comprehend that the magic of an aging *drùidh* was responsible.

His kicking feet suddenly touched bottom, and Morgan stood up, brushing the water from his face and wringing it out of his hair. He walked onto the gravel beach but stopped at the sight of Faol standing at the edge of the forest, staring at him.

"Dammit. Go away," he said, turning to walk down the beach towards Gràdhag. His horse took several steps back as he approached and began to prance nervously in place. Morgan stopped and looked behind him.

Faol was matching his steps, ten paces back.

Morgan pulled his sword from its sheath tied to the saddle and turned to face the wolf. He raised the weapon threateningly. "I want nothing to do with you tonight."

Faol lowered his head and dropped something out of his mouth. Morgan lowered the tip his sword and squinted at the ground. "What is that?" he asked, taking a step closer.

Faol whined, nosing it forward in the dirt.

Morgan bent down in front of the wolf, set his sword across his knees, and picked up the metallic object. A hot, wet tongue suddenly ran up the side of his face.

Morgan fell back in surprise.

"Damned beast," he said, wiping his face with the back of his hand. "You'd better not be seeing if I'll make a good meal."

Morgan reached out and touched the wolf on the side of his face, just below his right ear. Faol nosed the palm of Morgan's hand, then rumbled a contented growl deep in his chest. He took a step forward and nudged the forgotten object in Morgan's hand.

Morgan turned his attention to what looked like the ammunition clip of a hunting rifle. A powerful rifle, judging by the size of the bullets.

"Where did you get this?" he asked, turning it over in his hand. He looked at the wolf. "Where did you find this?"

Faol turned and started into the forest but stopped and looked back. Morgan stood up, placed his sword back in its sheath, and pulled clothes down from his saddle. He dressed quickly, tucking Faol's gift into his pocket, then mounted Gràdhag and turned them into the forest to follow the now running wolf down the narrow, darkening path.

Faol turned onto a tote road and headed north, deeper into the valley. Morgan followed Faol for several miles along Prospect River, then pulled Gràdhag to a halt when the wolf suddenly left the road and leaped onto the crest of a knoll. Morgan followed on foot, making no sound as he moved through the woods.

The voices of men carried softly across the stillness of the evening. The wolf abruptly stopped and lay down; Morgan did the same and watched the two men in the camp below.

"Jesus Christ, Dwayne. A bigger idiot was never born. How in hell can you lose an entire clip full of bullets?"

"I swear, Harry, I left the clip right here," the man named Dwayne said in a whine, pointing at the tarp spread out on the ground. "I was cleaning our guns and went to the truck for a polishing rag. But when I tried to put my gun back together, I couldn't find the clip," he continued, holding up the gas lantern as he scanned the ground. "It's got to be here somewhere."

The man named Harry also scanned the forest floor, using a flashlight. Morgan looked around the camp the men had erected. It appeared they planned to be in the valley for quite a while. They had boxes of supplies stacked against the outside wall of a large tent, several gas cans, backpacks, and a canoe strapped to the rack of their truck.

They'd set up camp near the river, just far enough back that anyone coming down the Prospect by boat would not see them.

Morgan didn't like this, that these men were here in Mercedes' valley, looking for all the world like a pair of poachers. Hunting season was not for several more weeks in this area, but there were two high-powered hunting rifles leaning against a tree near the tarp.

And poachers, in Morgan's experience—both from eight hundred years ago and from these last six years—were unconscionable men who thought only of themselves and were a danger to anyone who crossed their reckless paths.

Which Mercedes was bound to do, eventually, if she kept planting her ribbons.

With a silent sigh, Morgan retreated down the knoll and headed toward Gràdhag, leaving Faol to watch the men. And as he rode through the night, Morgan tried to decide how he could protect Mercedes while trying to protect this valley from her—and not let his wanting to possess her distract him from either duty.

Chapter Ten

When it came to the weather, September and March were transition months in Maine, and Sadie had decided long ago that they were also the most interesting. It had to do with the equinoxes, when the sun sat directly over the equator, equalizing the hours of daylight and darkness. It was the turning point of the seasons, the final push of the air masses that moved with the tilt of the earth, producing great battles between the warm airs of the south and the cold airs of the north.

And September, in Sadie's estimation, was the greatest time of year to be living in Maine, caught in the middle of those timeless meteorological wars.

So this morning she packed accordingly and filled her kayaking dry bag with shorts, T-shirts, jeans, and heavy sweaters. She also packed a pair of long johns, a full rain suit, a tent, and enough food for several days.

She checked her equipment next—GPS, cell phone, new camera, five rolls of film, matches, lighter, knife, water bottles, duct tape, two flashlights, and several lengths of rope. In another dry bag she placed her carefully folded maps and the copy of the diary of Jean Lavoie that Eric had brought her, as well as her own journal of the last ten weeks.

Finally, satisfied that she had everything, Sadie headed to the cabin door. She was driving to the headwaters of the Prospect, a good eight miles upriver past Fraser Mountain. Then she'd make the eighteen-mile run down the river, in three days if she didn't dawdle too much.

And if she were really lucky, she'd talk her mother into driving to the end of the valley to pick her up. If not, well, she'd have a mighty long hike back to her truck.

Sadie opened the cabin door with her foot and had just stepped onto the porch when she suddenly halted and dropped everything she was carrying. She stared at the note skewered to the nail on the porch post: DON'T GO INTO THE WOODS TODAY.

Sadie ripped the paper down and glared at the boldly scrawled letters of an obviously masculine hand: DON'T GO INTO THE WOODS TODAY. That was all it said. No name of the writer. No explanation. Only a dictate that she was expected to obey.

Morgan MacKeage was manhandling her again, from a distance this time. And, as in every minute of their date two nights ago, he was expecting her cooperation.

Sadie frowned into the forest in front of her cabin.

What was this about? The guy just leaves a note and expects her to obey meekly?

Sadie crumpled the paper in her hand, crushing it with angry force and then throwing it at the woods. Dammit. She was being paid to do a job here. Morgan couldn't expect her to change her plans simply because he was in the mood to test their *friendship*. She didn't care if she still hadn't found the socks he'd kissed off her feet; she was not playing his game.

He had plenty of nerve to leave such a note, instead of having the decency to knock on her door and explain his reasoning.

What to do? What to do?

If she stayed in camp today, what message would she be sending him? That she was a good, obedient little lass whom he could bend to his will on a whim?

Yet Morgan didn't strike Sadie as a man who issued idle orders. Nor was she a woman to ignore a sincerely given suggestion if there was sound reasoning behind it.

"Dammit, MacKeage!" she hollered, shaking her fist at the woods. "You're an arrogant jerk!"

Her echoing outburst unanswered, Sadie let out a frustrated breath and returned to her fallen gear. She picked up the dry bag that had her papers inside and took out Jean Lavoie's diary and her own journal. Then, still angry at herself for letting six simple words rule her day, Sadie stomped down the steps and strode to a pair of towering maple trees with a hammock strung between them.

She pretty nearly hung herself getting into the hammock. As it was, she ended up on the ground, creating a cloud of dust that made her cough.

She had to get a grip here before she did herself bodily harm. Oh, she would stay out of the woods today, but Morgan MacKeage would be getting a rather scorching lecture on *friendship*—if and when she ever saw him again.

It amazed Sadie the amount of work she could get done when driven by a healthy dose of anger. She had spent more than three hours lying in the hammock, completely engrossed in Jean Lavoie's diary, furiously scribbling notes in her own diary that would help her map out Jean's movements through the valley.

Now she was giving her old kayak a good waxing and replaying Jean Lavoie's diary through her mind. This entire valley had been heavily cut in the early 1900s. The logging camp where Jean cooked had slowly migrated upriver with the cutters. There seemed to be three camps at least, maybe four, she'd been able to discern from the diary, erected over a six-year period.

But all of this had taken place more than eighty years ago. The remains of the camps would be mostly rotted back into the forest by now.

And Jean Lavoie, for all his attention to detail, was not a very gifted writer, especially considering that the diary was laced with enough French-Canadian words to make the reading downright impossible in places.

Still, it seemed that Jedediah Plum had visited camp number three during the fourth year of Jean's stint as camp cook. And camp number three appeared to have been set someplace on the west side of Fraser Mountain, away from the banks of the Prospect River.

Sadie turned her kayak over on the picnic table and began rubbing wax on the top surface. She needed to find camp number three. That was the last known place Jedediah had been seen alive. And the west side of Fraser Mountain was also the area near which Frank Quill had suspected the gold was located.

Her daddy's years of research had only been able to pin the location down to about a two-thousand-acre area, however. And finding a small pool full of placer gold in two thousand acres was like trying to find one particular grain of sand in a desert. There were hundreds, maybe thousands, of tiny streams running down off these mountains, and any one of them could be the source of Jedediah's gold.

Sadie tossed the wax-covered rag onto the table, picked up a clean rag, and began wiping the kayak with strong, circular strokes. She would travel to the base of Fraser Mountain tomorrow and set up her camp there. She'd search not for Jedediah's stream, though, but for the site of the third logging camp. If she could find it, then maybe, just maybe, she could also find a clue that would lead her to the gold.

The sound of a fast-moving truck broke into Sadie's thoughts, and she looked up to see Eric Hellman arrive in a cloud of dust-laden gravel and pine needles, making a mess of her newly raked yard.

"It's Monday," he said as he jumped out of the truck and strode toward her. "Which means you're on the clock, Quill. Why aren't you out looking for Plum's gold?"

Sadie set her fists on her hips and glared at her boss. "Because I'm just now deciding where to look. And the question is, Eric, if you thought I was out hunting for gold, what are you doing here now?"

Her words, and quite possibly her posture, stopped him in mid-stride. "I . . . er, I brought the aerial photos you asked for," he said, lifting his empty hands and staring at them. He turned around and returned to his truck.

"I drove to Augusta this morning," he said over his shoulder. He opened the truck door, took out a cardboard tube, and walked back to her. "I didn't want to wait until they mailed them out. After you came by my store yesterday and told me which sections you needed, I decided it was easier simply to drive down this morning."

He held the tube out to her. "And here they are. I was going to leave them in your cabin."

Feeling a bit foolish for snapping at him, Sadie took the tube and pulled the photos out, unrolling them on top of her kayak.

"You take good care of these," Eric said, looking over her shoulder at the photos. "They cost a small fortune."

Sadie turned in surprise. "Didn't you tell them in Augusta that they were for the park? They shouldn't have charged you a penny."

Eric shook his head. "Not a chance, Quill. The consortium is footing the bill until the park is accepted. Then the state will take over the costs. Which is why you need to find Jedediah's gold, so we'll have all the funding we need."

"The gold might not exist," she shot back through gritted teeth, not liking what he was implying. "Dammit, Hellman. I was never told the consortium was counting on that gold for funding."

"How in hell do you think we intend to buy the land? Do you have any idea what productive timberland goes for?"

Sadie set her hands back on her hips and narrowed a level gaze on Eric. "Are you saying a group of intelligent businessmen is actually putting up the money for this proposal based on a legend?"

"Jedediah Plum is not a legend," Eric countered, getting angry himself. "The man roamed this valley for nearly sixty years. He knew every inch of it. And he did find gold. My great-grandfather saw it himself when the old prospector came into town. Hell, Jedediah bought beers for everyone that entire summer."

Eric suddenly sighed and sat down on the picnic table, looking up at her. "And the plans for the park are real, Sadie. It will help this area in countless ways. And we'll eventually pull together the funding we need to buy the land. But finding Jedediah's gold will make it happen that much sooner."

"But if we find an actual lode? We can't just walk in and take it if we don't own the land."

Eric grinned. "Even your daddy knew there's no mine, Sadie. Jedediah was a panner, not a digger. And if you pan for placer gold, you get to keep it. As long as it's not in the ground but in state waters, it's finders keepers. And that means we can legally keep the gold to build our park."

Eric stood, rolled the photos up, and stuffed them

back into the tube, then used the tube to point at her. "So if I were you, lady, I'd use every daylight hour available for hunting. If the Dolan brothers find the gold before us, it'll be years before we can raise the money we need."

"What's in it for you, Eric?" Sadie asked, remembering Morgan's accusations two nights ago. "Are you part of this as an environmentalist or a businessman?"

Eric rolled his eyes. "Get real, Quill. The consortium is made up of businessmen. It's a win-win situation. We profit from having a beautiful park in our backyard, and the land gets protected."

"If I find the gold."

"That's the plan," he agreed, tapping the tube of photos on her kayak. "So see that you keep ahead of Harry and Dwayne in this little race."

"The Dolans have been hunting nearly as long as I have," she told him. "They're no closer now than they were three years ago."

"Don't count on it," Eric said. "How do you think I got the diary?"

"How?" she asked softly.

"Harry and Dwayne actually discovered it and were foolish enough to brag about it. I snuck into their house one evening while they were out, made a copy, and returned their original."

He nodded in the direction of her hammock, where he could see her stolen copy, then used the tube of photos to point at it. "Just figure out the connection between Jedediah and the cook before they do."

But before Sadie could let him know what she thought of his business ethics, a low and ominous growl suddenly came from the woods just off to their right. Eric, a man not at home in the forest, turned in surprise, his eyes widening when he spotted the wolf standing at the edge of the clearing. Eric took a quick step back and to the side, placing first the table and then Sadie between himself and the large set of teeth the wolf was so nicely displaying.

But Faol wasn't the reason for the shiver that suddenly ran down Sadie's spine. No, it was the man standing beside the wolf that made her mouth go dry.

The note writer had returned to the scene of his edict.

Why wasn't she surprised that these two green-eyed, wild-looking males knew each other?

"Who the hell is that?" Eric asked out of the corner of his mouth. "The guy looks meaner than his dog."

"That's Morgan MacKeage," Sadie told him in a voice that wouldn't carry across the clearing. "And if you want this park to work, it's his land on Fraser Mountain that has to be purchased first. Without that acreage, there's no south access to the valley. And that's not a dog, Eric," Sadie added, just to rile him. "That's a wolf."

Eric stiffened and moved another step closer to her. Faol, apparently not liking the direction Eric had taken, stepped forward and growled again, hackles raised in warning.

"Jesus Christ," Eric said on an indrawn breath. "Get me to my truck, Quill. Now."

More from wanting him gone than from pity, Sadie moved around the picnic table and toward Eric's truck. Keeping herself between him and her uninvited guests, she tried not to laugh as Eric latched onto her side like a shadow. Together they walked the short distance, and Sadie opened the truck door. Eric quickly climbed in, slammed the door shut, and locked it, then started the engine and rolled up the windows.

Only then did he turn and glare at her. Sadie smiled back, waggled her fingers in a mock wave, and stepped away just as Eric sent the truck spinning backward, sending another cloud of dust into the air and leaving a groove in the gravel an inch deep.

Brushing herself off, Sadie turned and headed back to her cabin, completely ignoring her guests. She picked up her dry bag, her pack, and her tent and carried everything to her truck. She opened the back hatch and threw the gear inside, only to turn around and nearly run into Morgan MacKeage.

"I don't like your boss," he said, not moving out of her way.

"Neither do I, at the moment," she shot back, stepping around him. She went to the picnic table, grabbed her kayak, and hefted it onto her shoulder. She swung around, and Morgan barely had time to catch the nose of the boat before it hit him in the chest.

"Dammit, Mercedes," he said, lifting the kayak off her shoulder and setting it on his. "I'm trying to talk to you."

"The only talk I want to hear is your reason for leaving that note on my porch this morning."

He repositioned the kayak and grinned at her. "I can't believe you stayed put."

Sadie scowled at him. "Was it a test, or was there something in the woods that was dangerous?"

He sobered. "Poachers," he told her succinctly. "Or so I thought. But, according to your boss, the two men are your competition. And that makes them even more dangerous."

Sadie waved that away and headed for her truck again. "It's the Dolan brothers," she said. "Neither one of them is competent enough to tie his own shoes. They're more a danger to themselves than to anyone else."

She stopped at the truck and grabbed the end of her kayak, lifting it onto the roof rack. She left Morgan to slide it into place while she moved to stand on the running board to tether it down.

"And what do you know of this competition?" she asked as she tossed one of the straps to his waiting hands. "How long were you standing there, listening to Eric and me?"

"Long enough to know that this park you're so determined to build might not happen."

Sadie glared across the roof at him. "It will happen. Because I'm finding that gold and giving it to the consortium. The Frank Quill Wilderness Park will be built if I have to turn over every rock in this valley."

He stopped working and rested his arms on the roof, staring at her. "But why? Why a park, of all things, and why here?"

Sadie tightened the last buckle on her side of the boat into place. She also rested her arms on the roof and looked at him. "Because this is the valley my father loved. This is where I spent every summer, every weekend, and every vacation with him. Frank Quill's soul still roams these woods, searching for Jedediah's gold."

With a frown at her answer, Morgan finished fastening his side of the kayak down, then walked around and stood in front of her. Sadie got a good look at his face, and her toes instantly curled in reaction to what she realized was coming.

"I'm mighty impressed you stayed put this morning," he said just as his arms came around her and his lips made contact with hers.

Sadie stiffened, kept her mouth firmly shut, and tried not to notice how nice he smelled or how his powerful body pressed so intimately against hers made her heart race. He couldn't kiss her whenever he wanted.

But, more important, she couldn't want him to. Responding to Morgan MacKeage's kisses, she had learned on their date Saturday night, could very quickly lead to intimacy. And intimacy would mean getting naked.

And that could never happen.

Sadie felt herself spinning through space, and it wasn't until her back touched the hood of her truck that she realized Morgan had just picked her up and was all but lying on top of her.

Damn. He was pure alpha male when it came to kissing.

Sadie felt the hem of her T-shirt being pulled from her pants. She tore her mouth away with a gasp, at the same time grabbing his hand to stop its advance. She gave his shoulder a mighty shove to push him away.

It was like trying to push a mountain. Sadie found herself staring into solid green eyes, as dark and as swirling as the forest during a storm.

"That's far . . . I don't . . . you can't . . ." Sadie snapped her mouth shut and glared at him.

Morgan simply watched her for the longest time, then threw back his head and laughed out loud. He straightened and pulled her upright to stand against him, hugging her tightly.

"Someday, lass, your mouth will catch up with your brain," he told her, still laughing, still hugging her. He pulled on her hair to tilt her head back and kissed her soundly but briefly on the lips. "But you have my permission to postpone that day for several more years yet."

She tried to pull away, but he wouldn't release her.

"Now, lass. Where is it we're going in such a hurry this afternoon? Will I be needing my own boat?" He darted a look at her kayak, then back at her. "Because I'm telling you now, that's a mighty odd craft you use, and I don't have one like it."

"I'm going to the Prospect and setting up camp. You're going home and staying the hell out of my business."

He shook his head and grinned at her. "Ah, Mercedes. Haven't you figured it out yet? When you stayed put today, you gave me your trust."

"I *stayed put* because I had things to do."

Sadie wiggled free, went to the hammock, and picked up the stolen diary and her own journal. She turned to find Morgan sitting on her porch, watching her. Faol was sitting beside him. The wolf's head was cocked at an inquisitive angle, his eyes following her every movement.

And if Sadie didn't know better, she would think the two arrogant fools were grinning at her.

She strode to her truck, ignoring the male parade that silently fell into step behind her. She climbed in, but before she could shut the door, Morgan had one hand on the roof and one arm resting on the inside handle, effectively stopping her from leaving.

Sadie glared at him.

He grinned at her. "Until later, *gràineag*," he said as he softly closed her truck door.

Sadie rolled down the window. "What does that mean?" she hollered to his retreating back.

He stopped, only turning his head, and shot her a wink. "It's a term of endearment, lass. And one that fits you much better than that glove you wear on your right hand."

He walked into the woods with that nonanswer, and Sadie watched as Faol ran to catch up. The wolf stopped, though, just before he entered the forest and looked back at her. He gave a single bark, then turned and also melted into the landscape.

Sadie heard the sound of pounding hooves traveling through the woods then, and she listened until only their fading echo remained. Morgan MacKeage and his odd band of animals were gone, disappearing as suddenly as they had arrived.

Sadie turned and stared out the windshield at the road ahead of her. "An endearment, huh?" she whispered to herself. "I'm thinking of a few of my own for you, MacKeage. And I doubt you'll like them any better than I like mine."

That said, she twisted the key in the ignition and put her truck into gear. She was heading into the great woods herself, with the hope that this valley was big enough for her to avoid the Dolan brothers, her boss, the wolf, and Morgan MacKeage while she searched for Jedediah's gold.

Chapter Eleven

 $\mathcal{T}$ he problem with lust, as Sadie saw it, was that raging hormones knew no sense of discretion. They were just as happy to target the first handsome male—suitable or not—who had the unfortunate luck to step into their path. And it was exactly that sort of reck-lessness that was causing Sadie such worry now.

Because her hormones definitely liked Morgan MacKeage.

Sadie absently tossed another stick onto the dying fire and took a sip of chamomile tea as she watched the wood catch and flare into flame. The air was heavy with summer-tropical moisture, pregnant with the promise of thunderstorms. That was why she had positioned her campsite away from the threat of suddenly rising river water, towering trees that might attract lightning, and the path of falling rocks that might suddenly slip down from Fraser Mountain without warning.

The same way her heart might suddenly slip, also

without warning, over the spell of Morgan's unforgettably deep, mesmerizing, forest-green eyes.

And that was the problem. How could she casually let Morgan know that friendship was not what she wanted but that a lusty affair was more to her liking? And how could she orchestrate it all without taking her clothes off?

Her hormones didn't seem to understand that she simply couldn't undress and hop into bed—not if she didn't want Morgan hopping right out and running away in horror.

Sadie set her mug of tea on a rock near the fire and slowly worked the glove off her right hand. She flexed her fingers and turned her palm up, staring at the maze of scars that patterned the smooth skin like white lines of spider silk.

Whenever she tried to look at her scars with detachment, Sadie could almost make herself believe they weren't that ugly, nothing more than damaged skin that had done a very efficient job of healing.

She still had use of her hand. The skin, although tight and somewhat more leathery than its original version, was still nicely functioning to protect the bone and muscle and cartilage beneath it.

Sadie splayed her fingers wide. It was the romantic view of herself that made her put her glove on every morning, made her wear a body sock and long sleeves, and made her sometimes wish that her father had never reached her in time.

"Do you wear your glove so much you forget what your own hand looks like?"

Sadie fell off the log she'd been sitting on, landing

on the ground with a yelp of surprise. Her foot hit the mug of tea, sending it into the fire. The liquid hissed as it evaporated on the embers, and the plastic cup burst into colorful flames.

The laughter of a highly amused male wafted into the campsite, followed by the forms of two shadowed bodies—one impressively tall, the other short and fur-covered.

"Dammit, MacKeage. You travel these woods like a ghost."

He laughed again and hunched down in front of her. Sadie caught her breath. He appeared more formidable than the old-growth pines that towered over these woods, more solid than the mountains, and far more wild than the river that ran in rapids just a hundred yards away.

His wavy blond hair was loose, with two thin braids holding it off his face. His shoulders were broad enough to make her heart race, his hands on his knees large enough to make her mouth dry. He wore a pack on his back, the straps pulling his shirt taut against his chest, nicely showing off every muscle a man would need to make a girl's head spin.

"Come on, lass. Let me help you up."

Sadie stared at the hand he held out to her. What was it with this man, that he always insisted on taking her right hand? Ignoring his offer, a bit peeved that she was having lustful thoughts and he seemed totally oblivious, Sadie rolled over and got to her feet without his help. She immediately put some distance between them, at the same time tucking her bare right hand into her pocket.

Morgan pivoted on his haunches and sat on the log she had been occupying. He reached down, picked up her glove from the ground, and held it up to examine it in the light of the setting sun.

"It's made of fine soft leather," he said as he rubbed the glove between his fingers. He looked up at her. "Do you need it to protect your skin, Mercedes?"

She balled her hand in her pocket and gritted her teeth to keep from growling in frustration. "No," she told him succinctly, lifting her chin and holding out her left hand for the glove.

He tossed it to Faol. The wolf immediately snatched it up and looked at her, the glove dangling out of his mouth like a dead rat.

"Then why do you wear it?" Morgan asked, drawing her attention again.

Sadie glared at the man. "What is it with you people? Is it a Scottish thing, this need you have for being rude? First that nosy old priest, and now you. Why I wear a glove is my business."

He shook his head, and the corner of his mouth lifted in a crooked grin. "Ever the *gràineag*," he said, shrugging out of his pack and letting it fall to the ground behind him.

"What does that mean?"

"I'll tell you if you come sit with me," he said, patting the log beside him.

Sadie immediately became suspicious. She held her position, crossing her arms under her chest and burying her right hand in the folds of her fleece.

"What are you doing here, MacKeage?"

He picked up his pack. "I'm thinking a hunt for

gold might be a nice adventure," he said, undoing the buckles and opening the top flap. He shot her a grin. "And I'm also thinking it might be the most fun with you."

Sadie could only gape, speechless, as he then turned his attention back to the contents of his pack. He wanted to hunt for Plum's gold? With her? As in their traveling together, sharing a boat and meals?

And a campsite?

He pulled a bottle of wine from his pack, set it on the ground, then picked up the pot of tea she had set by the fire to keep warm. He sniffed the pot, made a face, and dumped the tea onto the ground.

Still unable to find her voice—not sure if it was from the shock of his stated intentions or from curiosity about what he was doing now—Sadie could only hug herself and watch. He set the now empty pot on the grate over the fire, then rummaged around in his pack again, pulling out a corkscrew. He quickly opened the bottle of wine and poured nearly all of it into the pot.

Something bumped against her thigh, and Sadie flinched in surprise. She looked down to discover Faol standing beside her, her glove still in his mouth, his iridescent green eyes unblinking as he stared up at her. Sadie quickly moved away, putting several feet between them.

"He'll not harm you, Mercedes," Morgan said, drawing her attention again. He shot her another grin. "I'm thinking the beast has taken a liking to you."

"And I'm thinking you think too much. You're not hunting for Plum's gold." She waved to encompass her campsite. "You can't just waltz in here and say you're joining me. I'm not on an adventure. I'm building a park."

"A park that will only happen if you find the gold, according to your boss. I can help." His grin broadened, and his already impressive chest puffed out a good six inches more. "I'm a very good hunter."

Sadie wanted to screech in frustration and maybe walk over and smack him on the side of the head. She rubbed her hands up and down her thighs instead. She was not sharing a campsite with him, not even for one night. She'd probably do something foolish, like throw herself on top of the man the moment he fell asleep.

"Hunting for gold is not like hunting for supper," she explained patiently. "It's tedious, frustrating work that depends on luck more often than skill."

He wasn't paying attention to her. His nose was buried in his pack again. This time, he pulled out a small silver tin, which he opened. He took a pinch of something out of it, which he tossed into the pot of now steaming wine.

"Morgan, you have to leave," Sadie said, somewhat desperately. "You can't come with me. And you sure as hell are not sharing my camp."

It was Faol who answered, since Morgan was busy ignoring her, rummaging around in his pack again. The wolf, her glove still in his mouth, walked over to the back side of the fire, lay down as if settling in for the night, put his head on his paws, and closed his eyes.

Morgan pulled two tin cups from his pack.

Sadie spun on her heel and walked into the forest.

She stopped just beyond the light of the fire and let her eyes adjust to the darkness of the woods. Once she could see, she headed for the river.

They were both denser than dirt, bullying their way into her life, fraying her emotions, neither of them heeding her petition to leave her alone. Faol, apparently, had decided he liked the company of humans and was trying to worm his way into her affections. And Morgan was much too handsome and far too self-serving for her peace of mind.

That was probably why he had accepted the blind date with her in the first place. Knowing her mother, Charlotte likely had mentioned Plum's gold to Callum, and Callum likely had mentioned it to Morgan. So the man had dated her, kissed her senseless in hopes of worming *his* way into her affections, and now he thought he could search beside her and claim his share of the gold so that she wouldn't have enough left to fund the park he was so much against.

Sadie suddenly tripped and landed facedown in the moist dirt of the river bank. She turned into a sitting position and stared back at the dark green canoe lying keel-up on the gravel.

The boat hadn't been there an hour ago.

Sadie crawled on her knees to the canoe for a closer look. It was an old boat, strongly built of cedar and canvas, at least twenty feet long. It was also heavy. It took all of her strength to turn the boat upright, exposing the canvas pack that had been stashed beneath it.

She immediately reached for the long, leather-sheathed sword lying beside the bag. She settled down on the gravel and rested her back against the canoe, then pulled the heavy sword across her lap. She undid the leather stays at the top and awkwardly slid the great weapon out of its sheath.

Moonlight glinted off the blade.

"Have a care, lass, not to slice open your hands."

Sadie looked up to find Morgan standing not ten feet away, holding two steaming mugs. He came over and sat down beside her, placing one of the mugs in her hand.

"You're thinking a sword is a strange thing to be carrying around," he said just before he took a sip from his own mug.

Sadie lifted her steaming cup to her nose, sniffed it, and involuntarily shuddered. "Whew. What is this?"

"Mulled wine. Or the closest I can get to mulled wine. Drink, lass. It tastes better than it smells."

Not wanting to hurt his feelings by refusing his gift—although she couldn't imagine why she should care about his feelings—Sadie took a small, tentative sip. And, again, every muscle in her body uncontrollably shuddered.

Morgan chuckled and took another, heartier drink of his wine. Sadie absently fingered the blade of his sword. "It is a rather odd thing to be lugging around the woods. It's very heavy. Why do you carry it?"

He stilled her fingers by covering her naked right hand with his own. "Because it is a very efficient weapon," he said, lifting her hand to his lips and kissing the palm of it softly.

Sadie sucked in her breath and held it.

He had just kissed her scars.

She didn't know what to do. What to say. How to act.

So, without thinking, she took another drink of her wine.

Tears immediately came to her eyes, and her throat closed up in defense of the powerful taste. It was all she could do not to break into a fit of coughing.

The man beside her chuckled again and set down his mug so that he could take her right hand in both of his. Ignoring her tug to get free, he turned her hand palm-up and traced a finger lightly over her scars.

"Will you tell me about the fire?" he asked, his voice soft and low-timbered, sending a shiver down Sadie's spine.

"No."

"About your sister, then. And your da."

"No."

He laughed softly and let go of her hand. He lifted his sword off her lap, set it on the ground beside him, and reached over to take her mug of terrible wine and set it beside his sword. And then he grabbed her by the waist and picked her up. In the blink of an eye, Sadie found herself straddling his thighs, her eyes level with his.

She stopped breathing again.

"Then, if you're not in the mood for conversation, what should we do with the rest of our evening, lass?"

With all the hormones in her body suddenly zinging around like sparks from a wildfire, Sadie pondered her options. She was all alone in the woods with a very handsome man, miles from nowhere with nothing to disturb them, and it might be nice to feel that tingling sensation deep in her chest again.

"I'm not asking you to solve the world's problems," he said through a grin, giving her a squeeze. "I'm only looking for suggestions on how to occupy our time."

We could kiss until the cows come home, she thought.

She truly did love the taste of Morgan MacKeage. She liked the way he smelled, the way he felt, and the way he made all five of her senses come alive.

But she just couldn't work up the nerve to start something that would end with her taking off her clothes.

Morgan answered his own question, not with words but with action. He cupped the sides of her face and pulled Sadie into his kiss, canting her head to access her mouth fully.

Her resistance faltered under the siege of his sensual, enticing lips. His hands sent shivers down her spine as they wrapped around her back and pulled her against his solid body.

Sadie quit fighting—both Morgan and herself. She trailed her mouth over his jaw, tracing the edge of his beard with her lips. She felt his groan rumble through every inch of her own trembling body, felt his muscles tense, heard his indrawn breath.

She dropped her hands to his shoulders, then his chest, digging her fingers into his shirt. *She* groaned this time, as she followed her fingers with her mouth, kissing his neck and throat. She worked at the buttons of his shirt. One came open. The next one popped off. And God bless the rest, they retreated without a fight.

Sadie pushed his shirt aside and caught her breath again. He was magnificent. Better than she remembered.

He still wore that strange-looking object around his neck, dangling from a leather cord over his breast bone. It looked to be made of sandstone or wood, swirling lines that appeared to be in constant motion.

An illusion of the disappearing sun.

Or her own emotions, maybe.

"Why couldn't you have been a dork?" Sadie asked with a sigh of resignation.

He pulled back and looked at her though narrowed eyes. "What is a dork?"

Sadie gave him a slow, warm grin. "It's a term of endearment," she whispered, curling her fingers into the mat of hair on his chest. "One that fits you better than that sword you carry around like some medieval warrior."

So quickly that she didn't even have time to scream, Sadie found herself flat on her back on the ground, one very unamused male lying on top of her.

"Don't throw my words back at me, Mercedes."

Pleased to have her brain back in charge of her hormones, Sadie gave him a huge, satisfyingly smug smile.

Morgan did not respond. He had gone suddenly tense, his face raised to the sky, his head cocked to the side as if he were listening for something.

"Do you hear that?" he whispered.

Sadie held her breath and listened, too. And she heard what he had, far off in the distance, the low rumble of an approaching storm.

"That's thunder," she said, turning her head to the western sky. "The front's moving in." She looked back at him and smiled. "We're in for a good soaking, judging by the heaviness of the air. Did you bring a tent?"

He still wasn't listening to her. He released her so suddenly, and scrambled off so quickly, that Sadie couldn't stifle a grunt of surprise. He stood over her, facing west, his hands clenched into fists and his entire countenance as fierce and foreboding as the churning sky.

Sadie scrambled to her own feet and took hold of his sleeve. "It's just a thunderstorm, Morgan. A cold front is moving down from Canada tonight, washing away the humidity."

He shrugged her off and took several steps back. Sadie could only stare at him. This great big bear of a man was afraid of thunderstorms? Lightning flashed on the other side of the valley, and she saw Morgan flinch violently.

She also saw his expression clearly for that one brief moment. Tightly controlled, stone-cold terror was etched into every line of his face.

"Morgan," she said, moving toward him again.

He took another step back, holding up his hands to stop her advance. "Don't come near me, Mercedes," he said, his voice harsh with warning.

Lightning struck high on a mountain across the valley, sending a wave of rumbling thunder toward them. Another flash, farther north, then another, the strikes echoing like cannons along the length of the river. A west wind kicked up, pushed ahead of the arriving storm, sending a flurry of leaves into the air around them. The rain arrived with surprising force, beating more leaves from the trees and adding to the chaos.

Morgan suddenly pivoted on his heel, strode to his canoe, and picked up his sword. Sadie ran after him.

He whirled back toward her. *"Falbh!"*

She stopped on the spot at the sight of that sword pointed at her.

"Begone!" he shouted, waving his weapon toward the woods. "Go back to your camp."

She could only stare at him in shock and confusion. He suddenly slid his sword back into its sheath and settled it over his shoulders onto his back. Lightning flashed again, closer this time, sending the smell of ozone through the air as thunder shook the ground with resonating force.

Sadie blinked against the brightness of the lightning and the driving rain, then blinked again when she realized she was staring at nothing.

Morgan MacKeage was gone.

Chapter Twelve

Daar paced the length of his cabin porch, then stopped suddenly to frown at the darkening sky. Lightning flashed in the distance, creating a halo over the mountains to the west.

Another storm was visiting the valley.

There was something happening here, more than just Morgan and Mercedes' conflict over a park being built. For eighty years the balance of good and evil in the valley had been uneven, since the death of Jedediah Plum. The restless prospector still roamed this valley, waiting for justice finally to be served. And in that time the darkness had been building, gathering strength for the inevitable confrontation.

Daar had spent the entire summer trying to learn the reason for this impending clash of powers. Why here, in Mercedes' valley? And why now of all times, just when he was finally getting Morgan settled into a new and promising life?

Daar rubbed the back of his neck and blew out a tired sigh. As best as he could tell, the violent death of Jedediah Plum had gone unpunished, and the murderer's spirit of greed was still alive today in his descendants. An evil had gone unavenged eighty years ago, tilting in its favor the balance of energy in this valley. The blackness Daar and Morgan had seen earlier this summer had been entrenched here since that long-ago murder.

And just recently, in this generation, Daar had learned through his spells that the darkness had gathered even more strength. Other murders, somehow connected to Jedediah Plum, had again gone unpunished.

The yellow light, which symbolized not only Mercedes but also her family, seemed to be equally involved. It was possible that Caroline Quill had been the second victim of the darkness and Frank Quill the third.

And Mercedes might be in danger of becoming the fourth.

Daar had tried many spells over the last few weeks, attempting to vanquish the blackness. But the churning powers would not be budged. It was happening here, now, and to the folly of all who stumbled into its path. The energies needed to be rebalanced. Grievous wrongs had to be righted. A simple, lonely prospector wanted peace.

That Mercedes and Morgan were sitting smack in the middle of this war was beyond the wizard's power to control. He had done what he could to protect them. It was now up to the warrior to unite with the woman against the darkness and lead them both safely through the coming maelstrom.

Daar's delicate cane began to hum in his hand, and he lifted it skyward and waved it at the valley beyond. He saw the glow of a familiar green light, charged with energy, running through the forest, desperate, driven, aimlessly searching for safety.

Daar shook his head. No words of assurance could convince Morgan that he was not in danger of being sent on another journey through time. For two years the wizard had made promises to all the Highlanders, but only Greylen seemed to believe him.

Probably because Grey thought that Daar's banished staff had left him powerless.

The humming grew louder. Insistent. Daar fought to control his staff as it pulled against the turbulence of the approaching storm. Yellow light, as bright and vibrant as the sun, sparked through the wizard's mind.

Daar smiled. Such passion from one so innocent. Such determination and potent vigor. If anyone could capture and hold the interest of Morgan MacKeage, it was Mercedes Quill.

She was a fine match for the warrior—strong, intelligent, and possessing the courage it would take to fight by his side. And for that Daar was glad, because if he understood the signs he'd been reading these last few weeks, Mercedes Quill's search for the gold was sending her deep into the middle of a violent war.

Morgan ran without direction save one: away from Mercedes. He had to protect her from the storm, from the terror of a journey that could send him, and possibly anyone near him, through time.

As much as he wanted to run to Mercedes, not from her—to bury himself in her soft strength and hold on tightly until the storm had passed—he could not endanger her that way.

But if he were gone, who would keep her safe from the darkness that roamed this valley now?

Morgan stopped his flight abruptly on that thought and squinted through the driving rain to get his bearings. Though it seemed like a hundred, he'd traveled less than half a mile from the river. Lightning flashed again, followed almost immediately by ground-shaking thunder. The storm surrounded him. Wind bowed the tops of the taller trees and drove the autumn-turned leaves from the branches of oak and maple and beech.

A voice, high-pitched and insistent, came through the echoing thunder, faint at first but moving closer.

Morgan dropped his chin to his chest and closed his eyes. Mercedes, the maddening little *gràineag*, was searching for him.

He was torn between continuing on for her safety and returning to her for his own selfish reasons. Dammit. They belonged to each other.

He could protect her, be they in this time or another; he could face any challenge as long as they were together.

But did he have that right yet, to choose Mercedes destiny for her? She'd been about to give herself to him, but did she fully understand what that giving meant?

And was he desperate enough—and selfish enough—to wait until after he possessed Mercedes to explain to her the age-old laws of claiming?

He did not care for this modern society's rules of mating. Once he made love to Mercedes, there was no turning back. She would be his until eternity.

Morgan moved into the shelter of a giant spruce tree. The sound of her calling him was closer now, echoing from several directions and carried on the wind. Her voice rang with desperation and concern— and maybe just a touch of anger.

Morgan couldn't keep from smiling. His little *gràineag* was nothing if not tenacious. She'd drown herself searching for him, or possibly catch pneumonia. But she would not give up, he knew, because she was proving herself to be just as possessive as he was.

And for that reason alone, he stepped into her path.

As quickly and mysteriously as he had disappeared, Morgan was suddenly standing in front of her, a dark, formidable specter visible only in the strobe of lightning that pulsed through the sky.

His shirt was still unbuttoned, the leather strap of his sword lying across his chest. Water ran in steaming rivulets over the harsh planes of his face, down his neck, over his powerful body that could have been carved from granite.

For one brief moment, in one particularly blinding flash of light, Sadie saw clearly the danger she was in. Morgan MacKeage would not negotiate. Would offer no concessions. Accept no excuses.

He would demand her complete surrender.

And then he would demand even more.

The air between them crackled with electricity. The object hanging around his neck seemed to sparkle and hum with energy, taking on an ethereal glow of its own. The nerves covering every inch of Sadie's skin came alive. She didn't know if it was the storm crashing around them or the blood rushing through her head, but she was having a hard time keeping her balance. Her heart wanted to jump out of her chest. Her knees wanted to buckle. And she couldn't stop shaking.

Morgan suddenly stepped forward and swept her into his arms, lifting her against him and burying his face in her neck. "Too late, Mercedes," he growled into her hair. "It's happening now. And we both live with the consequence."

She couldn't have denied him even if she understood what he was talking about. She wrapped her arms around his neck and clung to him fiercely. He carried her deeper into the forest, until he found an outcropping of ledge that would protect them from the storm. He stood her on her feet, pulled off his sword, and set it on the ground, then gathered the grass that grew at the base of the ledge, fashioning a soft bed.

He worked quickly, in silence, keeping one guarded eye on her as if he were afraid she'd bolt. Sadie stood rooted in place, unable to look away.

He straightened and turned and took her back in his arms, kissing her with a passion that bordered on desperation. Sadie kissed him for their entire journey to the ground, smelling the rain heating his skin, tasting the woods he was so much a part of, feeling the tension gathering in every one of his muscles.

He covered her with his body, surrounding her completely.

And Sadie welcomed the onslaught of emotion that overloaded her senses. She sent her hands exploring, touching, kneading his flesh. She opened her mouth to him, suckled his tongue, and tugged on his hair in an attempt to get even closer.

His hands were everywhere, pulling at her clothes, rubbing exposed skin that felt to be on fire. In a frenzy of movement, with time suspended despite her urgency, Sadie helped him tear away all of their clothes. The storm receded from her mind, her focus narrowed on just the two of them, sharpening inward until only warmth and light and feelings were left.

He laced their fingers together and lifted her hands above her head, using his mouth to trace a path across her face, down her neck, to between her now exposed breasts. Searing heat followed his lips; shivering anticipation preceded them. He kissed the nipple of her right breast, taking it into his mouth and sucking. Sadie shivered and cried out and arched her back with pleasure.

His mouth moved on, over her breasts, his teeth rasping her skin and sending shudders throughout her. Sadie wrapped her legs around his waist and arched her back again, feeling his erection pushing against her belly.

He lifted himself off her slightly, just enough that he could stare down at her face. The swirling, now brightened glow of his necklace exposed harsh features and eyes sharp with intent.

"Do you take me, Mercedes?" he asked in a low, guttural voice. "And all that I have to offer—do you take me?"

Her mouth suddenly desert-dry, she could only nod.

He pressed himself forward against her belly, then retreated again. "Say it, Mercedes. Say it out loud, so all can hear. Do you take me?"

"Yes, Morgan. Everything you offer."

Some of the tension eased from his face at her words. His muscles relaxed slightly, and it felt as if he all but melted against her. His mouth returned to hers in a kiss that was different this time. More possessive.

"Take my shoulders, lass, and hold tight," he whispered. "It will be unpleasant for only a moment, I promise."

Unpleasant?

How could anything that had to do with this be unpleasant? Sadie was shaking with the need to feel him inside her. "Get on with it, Morgan," she whispered huskily.

A slow, maddening smile lifted one corner of his mouth. "So you can find the words when you need them, huh, *gràineag*?" he said, moving back and reaching one hand between them, guiding himself between her thighs.

Sadie sucked in her breath and held it as he slowly pushed against her. His mouth returned, his hands trapped hers, and his hips finally moved in the direction she wanted.

Weighted tension. Unbelievable pleasure. An awareness of stretching, filling, spiraling heat. The moment he had spoken of lasted a lifetime measured in seconds.

And suddenly he was completely inside her.

It was Sadie who moved then, lifting her hips to accept him, digging her nails into his shoulders, and reaching up to capture his mouth again. She swallowed his moan that came the moment he began to move, rocking them both in a rhythm that shot repeating currents of fire throughout her.

The pleasure doubled. Tripled. With a cry of pure joy, Sadie turned her mouth onto his shoulder, feeling his straining muscles against her teeth as she tightened around him.

Morgan stopped and reared up and threw his head back with a shout.

Her eyes widened when she saw the stone at his neck suddenly flare to life as if struck by lightning, blinding her to everything but feeling. And what she felt now was Morgan, so very deep inside her, pulsing against the throbbing of her womb.

With a groan like that of a wounded bear, Morgan dropped his full weight to his elbows, brushing back her hair and kissing her tenderly on the nose. His heart pounded against hers. His breathing was labored. And she became aware of every steaming inch of him that touched her naked skin.

The storm returned to her consciousness. The rain continued, but the thunder was moving away now, the flashes dulling to mere hints of light. But it was enough for her to see clearly the gleam of triumph dancing in Morgan's eyes.

Chapter Thirteen

He had one hell of an apology to make.

No better than a rutting animal, he had just taken his woman in the woods, in the middle of a damned storm. What should have been the most pleasant experience of Mercedes' life had most likely been her greatest disaster.

She was frighteningly still but for the faint trembling he could feel coursing through her body beneath him. The apology would have to wait. He needed to get her warm, get her up and dressed and hustled back to their camp in a hurry.

As carefully as he could, Morgan lifted himself off Mercedes and rose to his knees. She immediately scrambled away, crossing her hands over her chest, frantically searching for someplace to hide.

Morgan was stricken by the sight. Much more was needed than a damned apology. He would gladly give up his sword arm for this not to have happened.

He groped on the ground until he found his shirt, shook it out, and attempted to put it on Mercedes.

She flinched, rose to her knees, and almost scrambled away before he could catch her. He wrapped one arm around her waist and hugged her to his chest, feeling her shiver. He closed his eyes and silently prayed for forgiveness, and then he whispered those same petitions to her.

"I'm sorry, lass, for what I've done. But you've got to let me get you dressed. You're going to catch cold."

"I can dress myself."

Her voice was faint. Distant. And without emotion. Morgan grew alarmed. Her shivering had turned violent now, her whole body as cold as snow.

"You can rail at me tomorrow, *gràineag*," he said, returning to his chore of dressing her. "You even have my permission to use my sword, if you still have the strength to lift it," he added, hoping like hell she did have the strength, that she wouldn't catch pneumonia.

She was amazingly strong now and fought him, trying to squirm out of his hold. But it wasn't until he wrapped his hands around her back that Morgan fully understood why Mercedes was so frantic to escape him. She immediately twisted away and kicked out with her feet.

It was those damned scars she was trying to hide from him. Mercedes was horrified that he might see them and be disgusted.

He immediately moved away from her. "Easy, Mercedes. I'll let you dress. Here," he said, gathering up her soaked pants and shirt. "Here's your clothes.

They're wet, but I'll have you back in front of a warm fire in minutes. Just get dressed."

Morgan then stood, shaking out his own pants and stepping into them. He shuddered as the wet cloth grated against his skin. He put on his boots and set his sword over his shoulder before he shook out his shirt and held it up to Mercedes once again.

"Here. It's wet, too, but it's wool. It will add some warmth to your own clothes."

She was only half dressed. She had thrown her shirt on with haste and had buttoned it crooked. Her pants were pulled up, and she was now fighting with the zipper. Her trembling hands were making the chore nearly impossible.

Morgan lost what patience he'd been trying to hold on to. He wrapped his shirt over her shoulders and swept her into his arms.

Her first reaction was to squeak.

Her second was to take a poorly aimed swing at his head.

"You're going to kill us both," she grumbled. "I'm too heavy."

He couldn't stifle a laugh. "Ah, *gràineag*. When the day comes that I can't carry you, I'll be three years in my grave." He hefted her slightly, settling her comfortably. "Now, be quiet and save your strength," he added, giving her a quick kiss on her dirty forehead. "Because tomorrow, Mercedes, we are having a much-needed talk about the rules of this match."

He was planning a lecture, most likely.

Sadie lay in the warmth of Morgan's embrace and

stared up at the ceiling of her tent, most of which Morgan MacKeage was filling.

It was quite nice, she decided, to wake up and find herself snuggled securely against a sleeping bear.

It was also a bit disconcerting.

The guy was completely naked.

It seemed she'd fallen in love with an exhibitionist. She'd probably seen Morgan naked more often than dressed.

She was just the opposite, wanting to keep herself covered up to the chin.

Hence the upcoming lecture.

She expected Morgan was planning to scold her for acting so insanely modest, even to the point of foolishness. She knew he had been worried last night that she'd been wet and cold.

So she'd shut up, let him carry her back to camp— that had been an experience in itself—and then she had washed, dressed in layers of dry clothes, and crawled into bed. She had even remained silent when Morgan had crawled into the tent and settled beside her.

Now she was staring at the dawn-lighted ceiling, wondering how she was going to extricate herself from both his embrace and the mess she'd made of their flaming affair.

But first there was the matter of her body sock. It was lost in the forest someplace, muddy and wet, along with her bra. She had other bras with her, but that was her only camisole, and she wanted it back.

Holding her breath, Sadie carefully lifted Morgan's arm off her waist and gently set it beside her. With painstaking care, she pulled the zipper on her sleeping bag down, cringing at every metallic click it made. She moved first one leg and then the other one free of the bag and silently rolled to her knees and backed her way to the door.

She stopped, though, caught by what she was seeing. The man was lying on his stomach, completely naked. His entire body was tanned, sprinkled with a downy coat of sun-bleached hair. There was a wicked-looking scar just above his right buttock, crossing his waist in a six-inch raised welt of light-colored skin. And another one on his right shoulder, not as long but obviously just as old.

His feet were dirty, thick-skinned with calluses. He apparently didn't wear boots any more often than he wore clothes. And at his side, almost as tall as he was, lay his sword. Sadie stifled a snort. Why wasn't she surprised he slept with the thing?

She continued her study.

His hand rested relaxed on the spot where she'd been lying. It was a large hand, strong-looking, blunt. His huge body took up most of the tent, his feet touching the door and his head all but touching the end. He had to be nearly six and a half feet tall. Beautiful. Magnificent. Completely naked but for the leather cord he always wore around his neck.

Sadie shook off her lusty thoughts, turned, and slid down the tent zipper just enough to crawl through. She continued to crawl all the way to the now smoldering fire Morgan had rekindled last night. She stood, only to realize that she wore only socks and that her boots were someplace in the woods with the rest of her clothes.

Damn. She walked to her dry packs sitting beside her tent and picked up one of the bags and carried it back to the fire. Then she pulled out her spare sneakers and slipped them on. One minute later she was back on her feet and running through the forest, trying to remember where in these woods she might have left her most intimate clothing.

Morgan took his time dressing. He was pretty sure he knew where Mercedes was going, and he suspected it would take her some time to find her way. She hadn't been paying much attention last night to where in the woods they had made love.

She'd been too busy being appalled.

He would set Mercedes down today, once he got her back to camp and filled her belly with food, and have a nice little talk with her about this new and hopefully peaceful life they had begun last night.

He would be understanding but firm.

Patient but insistent.

Calm but determined.

She would get over her modesty.

She would respect his authority.

Morgan snorted to himself. Aye. Mercedes would accept his dictates with all the grace of a *grāineag*.

With that thought lifting the corner of his mouth, Morgan set his sword over his back and headed into the woods at a trot. In less than a minute he picked up her trail and followed its aimless wanderings for nearly a mile.

He heard her sneeze before he actually saw her.

Dammit. She was catching a cold.

He stopped a good twenty paces away and watched as Mercedes scattered leaves with the toe of her shoe. She'd already gathered her boots, their socks, and both of their underwear into a pile. She was now pushing at the leaves and sticks littering the ground but stopped suddenly and reached down to pick up a thin shirt that looked more like a rag than clothes.

She suddenly stiffened and whirled toward him, hiding both her hands behind her back like a guilty child. Morgan pulled away from the tree and walked toward her.

She took a quick step back, realized what she'd done, and stepped forward again, her chin lifted at him. Morgan made sure his smile didn't show what he thought of her actions.

"What's so important that you felt the need to sneak off this morning and come here?" he asked.

Her chin went up another notch, and her beautiful blue eyes narrowed. "Nothing. I didn't sneak off, I walked."

"Then what was that you picked up from the ground just now?"

Her entire face flushed red, and her chin lowered slightly. "That's my business. I came here alone because I wanted some privacy."

He slowly shook his head at her. "Privacy no longer exists between us, Mercedes," he said, stepping closer. "It ended last night." He reached out a hand. "Show me what you're holding."

She took two steps back. "You don't understand!"

Ah, but he was quite sure that he did. "My hands covered every inch of you last night, woman. I know exactly what you look like under your clothes. And exactly how you feel."

Her eyes widened, and her blush paled—and Morgan continued with a determination grounded in truth. "I also know that you have no reason to feel vulnerable with me, Mercedes. Because I don't see scars when I look at you. I don't feel them when I touch you. I only experience your beauty."

He pounced on her then, before she had time to realize his intent. He had to tackle her to the ground to keep his shins from being bruised, and he had to grab her hands before she pummeled him to death. In the end, he was a bit muddy but victorious. He turned them both until he was sitting on the ground, Mercedes was on his lap, and the rag she'd been hiding was in her hands being held by his.

And seeing it close up, he was also quite sure what it was.

Morgan sighed and rubbed his forehead with his free hand. Damn. They were going to have their talk on an empty belly.

"This has to stop, Mercedes. There is no room for modesty or shyness between us." He pointed at the finely knit shirt she usually wore like a second skin, now clutched in her hand. "And it is a sin for a wife to keep secrets from her husband."

Her gasp was expected.

Her sharp little elbow driving into his ribs was not.

Before he could catch her, Mercedes was off his lap and standing over him, her hands balled into fists at her sides, her eyes snapping fire, and her complexion so red it was a wonder she didn't explode.

"That's a sick joke, MacKeage."

He slowly stood up and carefully brushed the mud from his pants, not once taking his gaze off her indignant face. "Joke? What are you talking about, a joke?"

"I'm talking about what you just said. A wife not having secrets from her husband, as if that pertained to us. Well, damn you, when I find a husband, I'll be sure to remember your advice."

It hit him then, like the blow of a mace, that this spitting-mad woman was actually the confused one here. Morgan rubbed his forehead again and closed his eyes while he prayed for strength—and plenty of patience.

"Mercedes," he finally said, in as calm a voice as he could manage when he looked at her again. "I wasn't making a joke to you just now, because you already are my wife."

"I am not."

He nodded. Curtly. "Aye, you are. The ceremony took place right here," he explained, waving his hand at the ground. "I remember asking you, quite clearly, if you took me. And," he continued more forcefully when she opened her mouth to protest, "you quite clearly said that you did."

"I wasn't marrying you! I was trying to get an affair started between us."

"It's done. We're husband and wife."

"But there was no minister. No witnesses, for crying out loud! It won't hold up in a court of law."

"It will damn well hold up to God's law. You're my wife, Mercedes. You are no longer a Quill but a Mac-Keage. And God save anyone who thinks different."

He stepped forward and firmly took hold of her chin, getting close enough so she would feel the finality of his words all the way down to her toes. "And that includes you, wife. Because this will not be one of your modern-day marriages. You will defer to your husband and respect my word. And to that end we will have a peaceful union if I have to take the flat of my sword to your backside."

That said, Morgan pivoted on his heel and strode away from the scene of his dictate, leaving Mercedes to come to terms with what she had just heard. Because, like it or not, he was holding Mercedes to her words of last night and keeping her as his wife.

And he'd even be generous, dammit, and allow her a few days to get used to the idea.

Holy spit. What had taken place here last night? How had they gone from friendship to marriage in less than a week?

And what had happened to her flaming affair?

Sadie folded her knees and sat down on the ground, clutching her camisole to her chest. The man couldn't be serious. Married? As in setting up housekeeping and living together?

Naw. The guy must be touched in the head. He was like his cousin, Callum, a bit old-fashioned was all. Yeah. Morgan was acting like a Neanderthal, being possessive and maybe feeling guilty for last night, and he was trying to make her feel good about the whole fiasco.

Naw. That wasn't it, either. He was just insane. Because there hadn't been one ounce of compassion in him just now, only a menacing threat lacing his whisper-soft voice and snapping in his forest-green eyes.

Take the flat of his sword to her backside?

The man was a throwback.

Either that, or she had fallen down a rabbit hole.

Sadie suddenly realized she was being watched and looked up to find Faol sitting just ten feet away. He was holding a stick in his mouth this time, her favorite glove nowhere to be seen.

The hulking wolf whined like a puppy and stood up and stepped toward her, wagging his tail as he advanced. Sadie scrunched her knees up to her chest and held her breath. She was in no shape right now to deal with another arrogant male.

Faol stopped just in front of her, opened his mouth, and let the stick fall onto the ground at her feet. It sounded like metal striking rock, and Sadie flinched.

And she flinched again when the wolf's tongue suddenly shot out and touched the hand she had wrapped protectively around her knees. The sensation of moist heat sent a tingle straight to her heart.

Faol stared at her, not backing off, not advancing. Tentatively, with great trepidation, Sadie slowly reached out and touched the side of his face. His tongue immediately shot out again and washed her hand.

He bent his head again to pick up the object he'd dropped.

It wasn't a stick but something metal. A large spoon, it looked like. Sadie took it from him, and Faol backed up several steps, lay down, and started washing his paws.

Sadie turned the spoon over in her hands, examining it. It appeared to be an old mixing spoon with half of the bowl rusted off. She pointed it at the wolf.

"This is not a fair trade for the glove, big boy."

He stopped his chore in mid-lick, his tongue looking stuck to his paw as he lifted his canine eyebrows at her. Satisfied that she understood that he didn't care, he went back to washing his feet.

Sadie went back to examining his gift. Using her sleeve, she rubbed some of the rust from the spoon and squinted at what looked like initials scratched into the bowl.

J.L.

Sadie stretched out her legs and straightened her spine. *J.L.?* Jean Lavoie? Was this the old cook's spoon from one of the logging camps? She looked back at the wolf.

"Where did you get this?" she asked, waving it at him again, not wanting to question the fact that she was talking to a wolf. "Can you show me?"

He stood up, wagging his tail as he stared at her. He suddenly turned, trotted down through the woods, and stopped and looked back at her. He let out a sharp bark, took several more steps, and whined.

Her worry over finding herself married suddenly forgotten, Sadie hastily folded her damp camisole and scrambled to her feet. She quickly picked up her boots and forgotten clothes and ran after the wolf.

But she slowed to a walk the moment she realized the treacherous beast had led her back to her own camp. The one where Morgan MacKeage was waiting, sitting by the now roaring fire, cooking breakfast. She stopped at the edge of the clearing and frowned at her gear sitting beside her tent. How was she going to pack her things without having to face the delusional man?

"You should have something to eat before we leave," he said without taking his eyes off his chore.

Sadie stormed into camp and walked past him to her tent. She crawled inside and quickly rolled up her sleeping bag, backed out, then zipped the door closed and carried her gear to her dry bags.

She continued to pack in silence, all the time feeling two sets of piercing green eyes watching her every move. Sadie willed her frazzled nerves to settle down; she needed for her hands not to shake, her throat not to close, and her eyes not to blur with tears.

Sadie MacKeage.

Mercedes Quill MacKeage.

She made a fist and hit the clothes in her bag, driving them deeper. Dammit. She didn't care if it sounded nice. She was not that man's wife. They couldn't be married just because he said so.

Sadie snapped her bag closed with a violent jerk, picked it up and tossed it over her shoulder, and headed to the river.

Morgan MacKeage stood up and blocked her path.

She stared at his feet.

"You'll eat breakfast first, wife."

She brushed the hair out of her face and glared at him. "Stop calling me *wife!*" she shouted, shaking her fist at him. "And stop telling me what to do! I'm not a child, we are *not* married, and so help me," she hissed, taking a step back and pointing her finger when he advanced toward her. "If you tackle me again, I'm going to bloody your face."

Morgan dropped his head so she wouldn't see his smile and was careful not to hurt her when he pounced on her again, twisting so that he took the brunt of the fall when they landed.

And he held her tight as she cursed him again, all the time thinking he must have been drunk on her kisses the night he'd stood on the mist-shrouded cliff and claimed her as his.

He could see now, this was not going to be a peaceful union.

Morgan grabbed at her flailing arms, buried his face in her neck, and smiled again. Who the hell cared if life was peaceful? He was just pleased she was no longer looking as if she wanted to cry.

He pinned both her hands between their bodies, holding her firmly on top of him with his arms wrapped around her back, and let her struggle in vain until she finally tired herself out.

Only then did he gently brush the hair off her face. "You're making threats again, *gràineag*, that you can't back up." He kissed her flushed, angry cheek. "This recklessness must come from not having older brothers who plagued you as a child."

"Let me go," she whispered, trying to get free again.

Morgan rolled them over and sat up, pulling her onto his lap. "As soon as we negotiate a truce," he promised, settling her comfortably but still keeping her trapped.

"You don't negotiate."

"This once, wife, I will try." He touched the end of her nose. "But if you wish my cooperation in the future, don't make me sorry this time. Now, which one of my sins would you like to begin with?"

He felt her take a giant, shuddering breath, and when Mercedes finally lifted her face to look at him, Morgan realized she was trying very hard to appear calmer than she was feeling.

"This married thing," she started, her voice trembling.

Morgan fought the knot in his gut. "What about it?"

"You can't just decide that we're married, just like that," she said, trying to snap her trapped fingers. "It takes two people to make a marriage. Two *aware* people."

"I asked you," he countered. "Do you not remember saying the words to me?"

"I thought you were asking for permission to . . . to . . . well, to do it," she ended on a faint whisper, looking down at his chest. "Not if I wanted to marry you."

"Then I'll ask you now. Will you marry me, Mercedes?"

"No."

He didn't think so. Morgan lifted her chin to look at him. "Then we have a bit of a problem, lass. I consider the deed done."

Her eyes widened, then suddenly narrowed. "And if I don't?"

He gave her a huge grin and once more touched the end of her nose. "I'll give you the answer to that in one week."

Her eyes widened again. "What happens in one week?"

"We will sit down and discuss this marriage then. But for the next seven days," he said quickly, before she could examine his plan too closely, "you will consider yourself my wife."

He gave her a gentle squeeze. "I'm sorry for last night, Mercedes. It shouldn't have happened."

Her head snapped up. "It shouldn't?"

"Not that way," he clarified. "Not under a ledge in the middle of such a violent storm. That was not well done of me."

"I started it," she blurted out. "I mean, I followed you. And I . . . I wanted it, too."

"Ah, yes. This affair you spoke of."

She gave him a frown. "What's wrong with a good oldfashioned flaming affair? Most men would jump at the idea."

"But not most women," he countered. "You demean yourself."

"Yeah, well. How many frogs have you had to kiss?"

"What is it with you and frogs?"

"Never mind. I have another question. Why are you so hell-bent on us being married, anyway? Do you want to sabotage the park so badly that you're willing to get married to do it?"

"Sabotage?"

He felt her exasperated sigh move through both of their bodies. "That's the only reason you're here, isn't it?" she said. "You went on a blind date with me because you knew I was building a park. And you're here now, demanding to be my husband, so you can stop me from finding the gold that will fund it."

Holy hell. The woman had a warped mind—and a

very low opinion of him. No, this was not going to be a peaceful union.

"There will be no park," he replied. "And the gold has nothing to do with it, because I'm not selling my land to your group of people. And without that land, there will be no park," he repeated, just in case she hadn't heard him the first time.

He gave her a less than gentle squeeze. "And the park has nothing to do with our marriage," he continued fiercely. "I want you, and now I have you. It's that simple."

"Well, I don't know why," she said, her voice quivering. "I can't even do it right."

"Do what?"

"M-make love," she whispered. "When you stopped," she said, somewhat louder this time.

Morgan could only stare at this poor, confused woman. She really did know nothing of men. Without thinking how she would react, he threw back his head and let out a deep laugh.

"It's not funny. I'm apologizing here."

"Ah, lass. I'm not really laughing at you," he said with a lingering chuckle. "Well, I am, but mostly I'm laughing at myself. I stopped because I was done, Mercedes."

"Done what?"

Well, hell. He could see that he was going to have to be blunt. "I was done making love to you. The shout you said I made was really a sound of pleasure and fulfillment, when I poured my seed deep inside you."

"You poured your . . ." She suddenly snapped her

mouth shut. Her eyes crossed, and her face sort of turned green—just before it went completely white.

"You . . . you didn't use any protection, did you?" she asked in a whispered squeak.

"No."

Her face turned green again. Morgan leaned back when he saw her hand go to her belly, afraid she was about to be sick.

"I could be pregnant." She looked at him, her glare angry enough to make him lean back even farther. "Dammit to hell. I will not get pregnant."

She jumped off his lap, making him grunt in surprise and cup himself protectively. She whirled and pointed her finger at him.

"I will not make my mother's mistakes!" she all but shouted, her anger flushing her face back to a flaming red. "And I'm sure as hell not making my baby sister an aunt before she's even three months old."

She stomped off after that outburst, in the direction of the river. Morgan leaned back and scrubbed both his hands over his face, attempting to wash away the still lingering echoes of their anything but successful truce. But then her last words finally caught his attention. What baby sister? He counted nine months forward on his fingers, then subtracted three.

And finally it dawned on him what her words meant.

Well, hell. Charlotte Quill was pregnant.

Chapter Fourteen

Charlotte Quill paced the length of Sadie's cabin porch, the concern obvious in every taut line on her face. Callum stood in the door of the ransacked cabin, watching his woman work herself into a fine state of worry.

She stopped in front of him. "Who would do such a thing?" she asked with motherly outrage. "And where's my daughter? Callum, there was blood on the floor," she whispered, digging her nails into his arm.

Callum reached out and pulled her into a mighty embrace. "It's old blood, Charlotte," he assured her. "And Sadie is fine, I promise you," he added. He pulled back and leaned down to look her in the eye. "I know for a fact that Morgan was coming out to see her. And this was the act of only one man, so you've nothing to worry about."

Charlotte pulled free, took a step back, and stared at him. "How do you know that?"

"The muddy footprints he left. This happened this morning, after the storm."

She resumed pacing, rubbing her hands up and down her arms, but stopped again and whirled to face him. "I'm going to find my daughter," she suddenly announced. "I won't have any peace until I see for myself that Sadie's okay."

Her tone was that of a woman expecting resistance, and Callum kept his smile to himself. Charlotte was almost as predictable as the sunrise. In fact, he'd already been mentally planning their camping trip into the valley since the moment he'd seen the destruction to Sadie's cabin.

The first sign of trouble had been the door torn from its hinges. The second thing had been the odor of freshly opened food emanating through the gaping hole. The family of raccoons, whiskers caked with crumbs, had come running out of the cabin the moment Callum's boots had hit the steps.

Charlotte, ignoring his command to go back to the truck, had silently followed him inside and silently looked around at the destruction. Furniture was over-turned, a window was smashed, the bed slashed by a knife. But it wasn't until Charlotte had seen the model of the valley that she had helped Sadie build that she had finally found her voice. She'd become a mother on a mission then, to avenge the violation of her daughter's home. She was mad, worried, and just daring him to contradict her plan.

Callum reached out and pulled Charlotte back into his arms. "I'll drop you off at home so you can pack your gear," he told her, freeing his smile when she gasped in surprise. "I'll get my own things together and then pick you up again." He pulled back and looked at her. "Any idea where Sadie might be headed?"

Still looking shocked that he was being cooperative, Charlotte could only shake her head.

"Doesn't she carry a cell phone?" he asked.

Charlotte nodded but scowled. "She does. But I haven't been able to reach her on it once in these last ten weeks. She's either misplacing it, breaking it, or letting the batteries run down."

She pulled away from him, her motherly outrage returning threefold. "I swear that girl has the sense of a pine cone sometimes. She spends her time walking around with her mind in either the past or the future but never in the present. If she's not wallowing in guilt, she's planning absolution for her imagined sin." She angrily waved at the woods surrounding the cabin. "Like this stupid park she's trying to build. It's not a work of joy for her but an obsession to obtain her father's forgiveness."

"Forgiveness for what?" Callum asked, trying to follow the woman's logic.

"For killing Frank and Caroline."

Callum was stunned. "Sadie didn't kill her da," he said. "Or Caroline. I thought it was a house fire."

"That she started. Sadie went to bed and left a candle burning in the study."

"But Frank died only three years ago."

"From a weak heart," Charlotte explained, worry and lingering grief etched into the lines of her face. "The fire damaged his lungs, and he never fully recovered."

Standing stone-still and staring at his woman, Callum was appalled. "Do you blame your daughter, Charlotte?" he asked.

Outrage returned, and Callum watched as she balled her fists against her sides, as if restraining herself from striking him.

"Of course not," she snapped. "I love my daughter."

Charlotte's anger suddenly deflated, and she threw herself into his arms, burying her face in his shirt with a loud wail of anguish. "Oh, Callum. I don't know how to help her. She's lived so long with this guilt, and nothing I say or do will change her mind. And now this obsession has turned dangerous. Somebody ransacked her cabin," she ended with another wail.

Callum clutched her to him and rocked her back and forth. "Ah, woman," he soothed. "There is nothing you can do. This is Sadie's journey to take." He pushed Charlotte back, wiped her hair from her face, and gave her a warm smile. "But she's not traveling alone anymore, little one. Morgan is with her. He'll keep her safe from whoever did this."

He gave her a quick kiss on the forehead and then smiled at her again. "And if I know my cousin, he'll have your daughter so distracted she won't have time to dwell on either the past or the future. She'll be too busy trying to cope with the present, and with his undivided attention."

She looked as if she wanted to believe him, as if she wanted to put her faith in Morgan MacKeage. Callum kissed her again, this time on the lips, this time much more passionately.

Aye, but he loved this woman who'd come storming into his life just six short months ago when she'd accidentally dumped an entire bowl of baked beans in his lap at the grange supper.

He hadn't been looking for love at the time. Hell, he hadn't even thought it possible. Since the storm had brought them all here six years ago, Callum had tried to keep himself detached from this strange new world, to stay strong in the face of fear and uncertainty and the loneliness that came with both.

Charlotte Quill had scattered every one of his vows to the wind when her dinner had landed in his lap. Charlotte had thrown a fit of worry. She had been like the blow of a mace to his chest that night. Which was why Callum had taken Charlotte up on her offer and had taken his soiled clothes to her home the next day for her to clean.

Now he would use this camping trip to his advantage. Hell, he just might keep Charlotte out here until she agreed to marry him.

He wasn't worried about Sadie, because Callum knew for a fact that Morgan was with her. He knew because his cousin's dangerously spoiled war horse was staying at Gu Bràth while Morgan was away. Callum just hoped that Ian wouldn't finally give in to his urge and shoot the contrary beast.

Reluctantly, Callum pulled away from Charlotte and set her firmly from him. "Don't tempt me, woman," he said through a tight smile. "We have a trip to plan and gear to put together."

It seemed the woman had lost her tongue. Charlotte was just staring at him, starry-eyed and disheveled.

Aye. This was going to be a most rewarding adventure.

Sadie wasn't sure how it had happened, but it seemed she had agreed to be Morgan's wife for the next seven days. Of all the foolish notions a man could have, where had he come up with the idea that they were married?

Sadie dipped her kayak paddle into the water with lazy strokes, letting the current of the river do most of the work. Her attention was divided between the wolf jogging along the river bank and the man paddling his canoe in front of her.

The more she got to know Morgan MacKeage, the more she couldn't figure him out. He was simply strange. She didn't care what lame excuse he'd come up with, carrying a sword everywhere he went was a damned odd thing to do.

And this married thing. What kind of medieval notion was that, that two consenting adults making love constituted a lifelong commitment?

But more important—and the thing that scared her the most—was that she had so easily agreed to go along with his outrageous plan.

Was she in love?

No. But she was in lust. And for that reason alone, she had decided to spend the week pretending they were married, if that was the only way she'd get to have an affair with Morgan.

Which brought her right back to where she'd been last night before the storm had arrived, back to trying to figure out how to make love and still keep her shirt on.

★ ★ ★

And Morgan was trying to figure out how to get Mercedes to talk. Her silence worried him. He'd bungled things last night, claiming her the way he had. And this morning he'd managed to dig the hole he was standing in deep enough that he might never be able to crawl free. Mercedes Quill was not a woman who liked being told what to do or how to do it—even when it was for her own good.

She was determined to build her park.

And he was determined to stop her to protect his gorge.

That damned wolf was not helping his cause. Faol had brought Sadie a tool of some sort and was now leading them to the place where he had found it.

And that place was near the mystical stream that ran through his gorge.

Morgan looked to the east, to Fraser Mountain, trying to decide if the tall trees were visible from this vantage point. He decided they were, but only because he knew to look for them. The gorge itself was deep, and because of that the tall trees appeared nearly level with the neighboring forest.

The mist, however, rose like the smoke of a smoldering fire before it slowly dispersed on the northwest breeze. But it was autumn, it was cold this morning, and mist was also rising from the river they were on.

Morgan absently trailed his oar in the water to guide the boat around a bend in the river. And that was when he found himself bow-to-nose with an equally startled bull moose.

Now, in his experience, moose of either sex did

not care for surprises. And this hulking bull was no exception. The great beast reared upward, churning the water with his front hooves, and charged toward him.

Cursing the lumbering weight of his loaded canoe, Morgan dug his oar deeply into the river and tried to power his way against the current, out of the path of the charging bull. The hit, when it came, struck with enough force to send the boat backward, splintering wood and knocking the oar out of his hand. Morgan grabbed the gunnels for balance and rode the storm of choppy water.

The bull reared again and charged a second time. Morgan dove for his sword, rolling in the bottom of the boat as he scrambled to unsheathe it. Mercedes' cry of alarm came to him over the sound of more splintering wood and the snorting of the enraged moose.

He was getting a little enraged himself.

A large antler appeared over him, just as two large hooves smashed down on the gunnel. The damned moose was trying to climb into the boat and kill him.

Morgan lifted his sword, grabbed the antler, and pushed it away. He drove his weapon deep into its neck. The bull jerked violently and bellowed in anger. His wife's shout ended abruptly and turned to a blood-curdling scream.

The bull kicked out, slashing a razor-sharp hoof into his thigh. Morgan twisted his sword, driving it deeper, feeling it slip past the shoulder blade until it found the animal's heart.

Now in its death throes, the shuddering, heavy

moose slowly slipped into the water, its only triumph that of finishing the destruction of his canoe. The boat snapped in half and rolled over, pulling Morgan and all his gear into the river.

Still holding the hilt of his sword, Morgan kicked his feet and pushed at the now dead moose, guiding them both toward the river bank. His feet touched bottom, and he turned, dragging the moose by the antlers. Once the animal scraped gravel, he let it go, pulled his sword from its body, and threw himself onto dry ground.

He lay on his back with his eyes closed, exhausted, breathing heavily, his muscles still quivering with battle-tense energy, reciting a list of curses that might have God striking him dead. He suddenly felt the coolness of a shadow fall over his face. Still he kept his eyes closed, loath to look up, not wishing to see the accusing glare of his obviously tender-hearted wife.

A warm tongue suddenly licked the side of his face, lapping the river water dripping from his hair. Morgan snapped his eyes open and sat up, shoving Faol away with another curse, this one out loud. The wolf backed off and went instead to inspect the kill.

Morgan looked around for Mercedes. She had beached her boat and was standing beside it, staring at him with eyes wide and her face completely drained of color.

Morgan closed his own eyes and cursed again out loud. His woman had just witnessed a violence that she didn't understand and might never be able to forgive.

"I cannot show mercy to anything bent on destroying me," he said across the twenty paces separating them.

She continued to stare in silence.

Morgan wanted to howl.

But it was Faol who lifted his nose into the air and let out a primeval cry that echoed up the sides of the valley.

Morgan looked back at Mercedes, only to find her suddenly standing just two feet away. Her dark blue eyes still huge and unblinking, her face drawn and pale, she continued to stare in silence. He followed the direction of her gaze to the bloody sword he still held in his right hand.

He opened his fingers and let it drop to the ground as he looked up at her. She took a step back. He rolled and stood up, and Mercedes quickly took another step back.

He wiped the blood from his hands on his wet pants as he moved toward her, matching her every retreating step with one of his own. He reached out and took her shoulders, ignoring her flinch, and held her firmly.

"Say what you're thinking, Mercedes," he instructed. "Give voice to your thoughts, so I can respond."

He watched her swallow and saw her eyes move to the carcass of the moose. He shook her, making her look back at him.

"When God gave man intelligence and free will," he told her, "he was giving us the means to survive in this world. Killing an animal for food or in self-defense is an act of nature, Mercedes, not malice."

Unable to look at her stricken expression any longer, Morgan pulled her into his embrace and hugged her fiercely. "That bull acted according to his own law, lass, set down by the blood of his ancestors," he continued more gently. "That the two of us clashed today was nothing more than the journey of life playing itself out."

He squeezed her tightly when he felt her begin to tremble. "Say something, Mercedes," he entreated once again. "Give me either your anger or your hurt."

"Will you be just as ruthless when you protect this valley from me?" she asked into his shoulder, her voice void of emotion.

Morgan closed his eyes on the realization that this woman knew him more than he cared for her to, that she now understood he would never compromise when it came to protecting his home.

He tugged on her hair, forcing her to look at him. "When the time comes, wife, I will do what I must to keep this valley safe. And also to keep you safe," he quickly added when she tried to pull away. "Because you and this land are all that is important to me now. Without either, I am nothing."

"Who are you, Morgan MacKeage?"

"Your husband."

She tried to pull away again, but he held her firm. "I'm also your greatest ally, Mercedes. Give me your trust now, and we will find a way through this."

Well, it seemed she needed to think about that for at least a minute. And in that time Morgan saw emotions flash in her eyes that ranged from hope to suspicion—before anger finally won the battle.

"Dam—"

He kissed her before she got the curse out, canting her head and covering her lips with his, swallowing her words as he swept his tongue inside. She made a mewling noise, and he couldn't decide if she was welcoming him or protesting. Nor did he care, as he found himself spiraling downward, deeper into the magic of her spell.

She tasted sweet, fresh, and so wonderfully alive. She felt vibrant in his arms, strong enough to possess his heart, solid enough to anchor his wandering soul.

He had traveled eight hundred years to find her, and he would let nothing come between them.

His spirit soared when she suddenly melted against him, raised her arms, and tugged on his hair to deepen their kiss.

Morgan flinched as pain suddenly shot through his body.

They pulled away at the same time, Mercedes with a gasp of surprise, Morgan with a groan. He shot a hand to his leg, covering the gaping hole in his jeans.

"You're hurt," she said, pulling his hand out of the way. She gasped again. "You're bleeding."

In a frenzy of movement, Morgan suddenly found himself sitting on the ground, Mercedes unfastening his pants at the waist. Unable to keep from smiling, he leaned back on his elbows and let his now distraught wife tend to his wound. He lifted himself up enough that she could pull his wet pants down to his boots, where she suddenly stopped and frowned. She grabbed his hand, making him fall completely flat, and slapped it over his bleeding thigh.

"Keep pressure on it," she hissed, now beginning to work on the laces of his boots.

It took her a few minutes to strip his legs bare, and then she carefully lifted his fingers and examined his wound. She looked up at him then, her eyes dark with concern against her pale complexion.

"It . . . it needs stitches," she whispered, as if the news might undo him.

He wanted to laugh but didn't dare. Mercedes was the one beginning to panic. Her hand covering his was shaking, her quivering jaw was making her teeth chatter, and her eyes were glistening again with unshed tears.

"Do you have a needle and thread, then?" he asked, stilling her jaw by clasping it with his hand, into which she slowly nodded.

He nodded back and gave her a reassuring smile. "I promise not to howl like the wolf, lass, when you sew me up. Now, do you think you can find my pack before you go looking for your thread? There's a nice bottle of Scotch in it that just might make the job a bit easier."

"I have painkillers in my first aid kit," she said. "But you can't mix them with alcohol."

Morgan lifted a brow. "The Scotch is for you, wife. I prefer your hands steady when you take a needle to my flesh."

He gave a grunt of surprise when she suddenly pushed herself to her feet, and another grunt—this time of approval—when she balled her fists on her hips and glared down at him.

"It's not funny, Morgan. Stitching a wound like that

is nothing to joke about. You belong in a hospital."

He scanned the river bank they were on and let his gaze stop on their one remaining boat before he looked back at her. "Any suggestions on how we get to this hospital?" he asked.

"My cell phone," she said, suddenly brightening. "I can call my mother to come get us."

She ran to her kayak and rummaged around in the front hatch. She straightened with her cell phone in her hand, but her smile suddenly disappeared.

"It doesn't matter, Mercedes," he quickly assured her. "I'm not needing a hospital. Sew me up and bandage my thigh, and I'll be good as new in a few days."

She still refused to look at him. She bent over and rummaged around in the hatch again. She straightened, a small red bag in her hand, and finally returned to him.

And, like the idiot he was, Morgan just couldn't seem to keep himself from asking, "What's wrong with the phone?"

"The battery is dead."

Morgan started undoing the buttons of his soggy shirt. He stripped himself bare, except for his wet and now muddy boxers, keeping them on only because he didn't want his wife distracted when she sewed him up.

She handed him two small pills. She looked up and down his now nearly naked body, then suddenly reached into her bag, took out one more pill, and placed it in his hand with the others.

"These are for pain?" he asked, examining them.

"They will dull it."

"And my head? Will they dull my thinking, too?"

"If I'm lucky."

He handed them back to her. "Keep them, then. I can't afford to be slow-witted right now."

She tried to give them back. "You need these. I can't sew you up without them." She lifted one perfectly arched brow. "Afraid I'll take advantage of you?"

He tapped the end of her insolent nose. "Nay, lass. That worry never crossed my mind." He looked upriver and then back at her, suddenly serious. "We're not alone in this valley, Mercedes. The Dolan brothers are here, looking for the gold. And I have no wish to be drugged should they suddenly appear."

"They're harmless," she said, waving his concern away. "They've been searching for Plum's gold as long as I have. It's a hobby for them. Almost a game."

"They're also armed with powerful rifles," he countered. "And last I knew, gold was not a dangerous prey to hunt."

"How do you know they've got guns?"

"I've seen them."

"You've met Harry and Dwayne?"

"In a way," he said, nodding. "I met them, but they didn't meet me."

"You spied on them?"

"I thought they might be poachers," he said. "That day I asked you to stay out of the woods, I was trying to learn their purpose here."

"Did it ever occur to you just to ask?"

Morgan gave her a broad grin. "What fun is there in that?" He reached up and ran his finger down the side of her cheek. "Why don't you go find my gear before it floats any farther downriver?" he told her. "I really could use a drink of that Scotch."

She hesitated, looking torn between getting him a drink and wanting to stab the needle she was holding into his thigh.

"I'll be fine, Mercedes. I'll keep pressure on it until you return."

She finally stood up, started for her kayak, but stopped and looked back. "I'm sorry you got hurt, Morgan. I thought the moose would just bump your boat and run off."

"I know, lass. I expected that, too. And don't worry about my hurt, Mercedes. I've had worse. I'll be fine in a few days."

Her expression suddenly brightened, and her eyes sparkled. "You stay put," she said, pointing a threatening finger at him. "Or I'll come up with some consequences of my own."

He solemnly nodded, then waved her on her way, watching her climb into her odd little boat and expertly guide it into the current.

He leaned back on his elbows again, letting the weak autumn sun warm up his skin as he watched Mercedes slowly disappear past the bend in the river. He couldn't quit grinning. He liked that she wasn't afraid to throw his words back at him. He liked her sassiness and her determination to match both wit and will against him.

But mostly he liked her ass. Mercedes had the nicest, firmest, most delectable bum—and the longest legs he'd ever seen on a woman. Aye, she pleased him in all ways, with her body as well as her spirit.

They'd make great babies together. She'd give him strong sons who would grow to love and cherish this land as much as their parents did. He was glad now that the old priest had talked him into building a home here. He was also glad that Grey had had the foresight to banish Daar's cane into the pond.

Because, like his brother, Morgan was now decided that he never wanted to leave this suddenly interesting new world.

When Mercedes finally disappeared around the river bend, Morgan set the needle and thread to his flesh and quickly repaired his wound—before his wife could return and make a mess of the job.

Chapter Fifteen

"You need to stay off your leg."

"No. I need to keep it from stiffening up."

"Faol is eating your moose again."

Morgan muttered a few Gaelic words as he threw a rock at Faol to drive him away from the moose carcass still lying on the river bank. Faol gave a snarl of protest, then trotted off into the brush.

"We need to find a game warden and report the kill," Mercedes said from the campfire, drawing his attention. "And you need to put some clothes on. The sun's setting."

Morgan stopped tugging on the antler of the now gutted moose and scratched his bare chest as he looked at his clothes drying by the fire. He had pants on, but they were covered with moose blood. He had already carried the entrails far enough away that they wouldn't be bothered by scavenging animals, and he was ready to wash up. The problem was, all his clean clothes were still wet from their dunk in the river.

He looked at Mercedes' dry packs sitting by the tiny tent she had already erected so that it would be dry by nightfall. He needed to get himself some of those bags, since he'd likely be spending time camping with his wife and children in the future.

Mercedes seemed so at home here in the wilderness, so comfortable sitting on logs, cooking over an open fire, and sleeping on the ground. She guided her boat as if she had been born with a paddle in her hand and hiked these woods with the confidence and excitement of a wanderer determined to embrace life.

Morgan realized how lucky he was to have found such an old soul in this modern time.

"Why do we need to find a game warden?" he asked, walking over and picking up one of his still damp shirts.

"Because it's illegal to kill a moose out of season. And even then you need a permit."

He slipped into his shirt and sat down across from her. "But I'll have it quartered and carried to Gu Bràth by tomorrow afternoon. No one need even know about it."

Her eyes narrowed. "That makes you a poacher."

He didn't care for that title any more than he cared to hear it coming from his wife's mouth. "I am not. The animal is dead through no fault of my own. I didn't go hunting for it. But that doesn't mean I intend to let the meat go to waste."

"The warden will probably let you keep the moose,

once we explain what happened. He won't want to see it go to waste, either. What's Gu Bràth?"

"It's my brother's home," he told her.

"I thought it was called TarStone Mountain Resort?"

"That's the business name. Our home is called Gu Bràth."

"Is it Scottish? What does it mean?"

"Forever," he told her. "It means that we're here now, forever."

"But you don't live with your brother anymore?"

"No. I built my home on Fraser Mountain just this summer."

She scooted closer, suddenly interested. "Does your new home have a name?"

Morgan leaned back against a rock, crossed his arms over his chest, and grinned at her. "I thought I'd leave that chore up to my wife."

She frowned and scooted away, giving her attention back to the food she was preparing. She stirred the powdered soup she had dumped out of a foil pack and added more water.

Morgan stood and picked up his sword and a few clean clothes, then took the water bottle from her. "I'm going to find a place to wash up and refill our drinking water," he said. "Before it gets too dark."

"You need to stay off that leg."

He took hold of her chin and lifted her face up. "What I need is for you to spread our sleeping bag at the base of that ledge over there and stuff a thick bed of dry grass under it."

He watched her eyes suddenly widen. "What . . . what's wrong with the tent?" she whispered.

"I don't like tents," he said succinctly. "They keep me from seeing into the woods."

"They keep you dry when it rains."

He bent down and gave her a quick kiss on her arguing mouth. "Nature provides our shelter. That ledge will keep us dry tonight. Now, are you gripping my leg because you don't want me to go or because you're looking to leave another mark on me?"

She swatted his knee and pulled her chin free, glaring up at him. "I want you to tell me why you're always so guarded. You act as if the entire world is out to get you."

Morgan settled his sword over his back as he looked down at her. "I didn't come all this way to die at the hands of fools." He bent at the knees so he was level with her and took hold of her chin again. "And you must be on guard as well, Mercedes. There is a storm brewing in this valley, and it has nothing to do with the weather. There is danger here."

She tried to pull away again, but Morgan wouldn't let go. "I'm not jesting, Mercedes. The Dolan brothers are not to be trusted. You need to be just as guarded as I am."

"You expect me to trust you without question, don't you?"

He grinned and spread his fingers to encompass her entire face. "I expect obedience, *gràineag*, when it comes to your safety."

She suddenly leaned forward, grabbing his shoulders and pushing him off balance. They both ended up on the ground, Mercedes stretched full-length on top of him. She kissed him, her tongue slipping inside his mouth as she sensually wiggled her sexy body against his.

Morgan immediately placed both of his hands on her luscious bum, pulling into his erection with a groan of frustration. He wanted her again.

But not like this, with nothing but dirt for a bed.

Going against every urge he possessed, Morgan took hold of her shoulders and lifted her away. His teeth clenched in restraint and his gaze locked on her swollen lips, he set her on the ground beside him.

"Tonight, wife, we will finish what we began last night."

She blinked at him, then scrambled away. With another curse, Morgan stood up and walked into the forest without looking back.

And Sadie couldn't decide if she had just been rejected or threatened. Or if she should be insulted or scared.

And she couldn't decide if Morgan kept calling her wife to rile her or if he thought she needed to be constantly reminded of that disconcerting fact.

She would like to be his wife. Maybe. She could imagine what it would be like waking up beside Morgan every morning for the rest of her life, her in her nightgown buttoned up to her neck, him buck naked and beautiful.

Sadie snorted, went back to the fire, and stirred the soup. She was weaving a dream fantasy for herself. But she hadn't felt this alive, this excited about what the future might hold, since before the house fire.

And that was the one thing keeping her from realizing her dream. That stupid fire. She had killed two people she loved. Her carelessness, her inattention to detail, had resulted in a tragedy so horrific she could never be forgiven. Her scars were nothing compared with their deaths. She deserved every horrible one of them.

What she didn't deserve was a husband as beautiful as Morgan MacKeage. But that didn't mean she couldn't at least love him, couldn't be married to him if he continued to insist on it.

It didn't mean he couldn't eventually love her back.

Sadie caught a glimpse of movement out of the corner of her eye and turned to see a canoe come into sight, two men paddling it toward the shore where her kayak was beached. She stood up, scanned the woods for signs of Morgan, then slowly walked over to greet Harry and Dwayne.

Morgan began to limp the moment he was out of Sadie's sight. He rubbed his throbbing thigh and cursed his bad luck for getting hurt.

But then, better him than Mercedes. His chest tightened at that thought. She could have been in the lead boat, battling the moose, and him not able to reach her in time.

Or she could have been out here all alone, as she had been this past summer. Anything could have happened to her. She could have fallen during one of her ribbon-planting hikes, have drowned running some of the more violent rapids on the river, or simply have taken a fever with no one to tend her.

He knew from experience that Mercedes was reckless. She didn't always think before she acted. Hell, what if it had been some other guy she'd taken pictures of, instead of him? What dangers might she have faced?

The woman needed a keeper.

Morgan stopped at a stream that ran into the river and looked down into the crystal-clear water that slowly disappeared into the slightly brackish Prospect River. He turned and started upstream, lifting his gaze to the mountains ahead.

He knew where he was, and he didn't like it. This was the same stream that flowed from the cliff, through his gorge, then eventually into this valley. And he and Mercedes were camped not half a mile away.

He didn't want her to see this stream. Didn't want her to realize that it was special. Once he had her allegiance, then he could show her the waterfall.

Faol silently stepped into his path, planting his feet and curling his lips into an almost human smile.

"You scavenging dog. You leave that moose alone, or I'll have your hide tacked on the wall beside it."

Faol dropped his head, stepped into the stream, and began to lap the water, not the least bit bothered by the threat. Morgan remembered he was supposed to be looking for drinking water himself. He moved above Faol and knelt on the bank, submerging the bottle and letting it fill. He capped it, set it on the grass, then leaned down to take his own drink.

A sharp, crackling sensation shot through his body the moment his lips touched the water. Morgan grabbed the burl dangling from his neck into the stream that was now vibrating with the force of a thousand bees taking flight. He straightened abruptly as heat seared through his body and sparks of green light danced in his eyes.

The wolf gave a yelp of alarm and shot past Morgan, knocking him backward onto the river bank. The tingling lessened, and the burl settled into a soft hum.

Morgan lifted it from his chest to see it better. The cherrywood was swirling, pulling against his hand in the direction of the stream.

Well, hell. The magic was seeking its own. It felt the lure of Daar's old staff coursing through the water. Morgan lifted the burl over his head, gripped it in his fist, and touched his hand to the water again.

Needles of energy shot up his arm, through his chest, spreading to every inch of his body. The wound on his thigh throbbed as heat gathered around it like the touch of a hot poker.

He pulled his hand back, and it stopped.

He opened his fist and stared at the swirling, vibrating burl that glowed with intense light. What had the *drùidh* said? That this burl carried the magic and that Morgan must find a way to add to its strength?

Well, it seemed he just had.

Not that he understood it. He'd gotten the burl wet many times since receiving it, but this was the first time it had touched this particular water. And that was the secret. This magical stream that the towering trees drank from, that grew big fish, and that now sent energy coursing through his body.

Morgan slipped the burl back over his head and stood up. He unbuttoned his shirt and threw it on the ground, then stripped off his boots and pants and tossed them beside the shirt. He ripped the bandage off his thigh and examined his wound.

The skin around it was pulsing, pulling against the stitches he'd set. The jagged edges of flesh were tingling, swelling, throbbing together as if trying to become one again. The knots of thread suddenly snapped, sending pain shooting all the way to his teeth.

Morgan waded into the stream up to his waist, then sat down until all but his shoulders were submerged. The burl dangled in the water. Sparks shot from it in every direction, scattering bubbles of light around him. He closed his eyes and let the energy course through him, leaning back until only his face remained exposed to the air.

Color swirled through his mind. Warmth wrapped his skin in a blanket of heat so intense that breathing was difficult. The humming grew louder. The water boiled, bubbles exploding around him like sparks from a bonfire.

Morgan sank below the surface, twisting and kicking his feet in an attempt to outswim the chaos. He felt as if he had the strength of a legion of men, as if he possessed the power to bend the laws of nature.

And the ability to heal himself.

He twisted again and sat up, brushing the hair from his face and letting the water cascade down his back. He grabbed the burl into his fist and pictured his wound in his mind's eye, sending the heat there, willing his flesh to seal itself up. He flexed his left knee, pulling against the skin on his thigh.

And he suddenly felt no pain.

Nothing but the warmth of pliant flesh.

Morgan opened his eyes and looked around. The sparks had disappeared. The water was calm again, gently making its way down to the river. His body was cool, his breathing even, his muscles relaxed.

And he felt wonderfully alive.

He opened his fist and looked down at the burl. It, too, was calm, softly humming in his hand. But it felt different to his touch now. Smoother. Smaller.

Dammit. It was smaller. He'd used up some of the magic.

Morgan stood up, let the burl fall back against his chest, and waded over to the bank. He threw himself onto the ground and lay face-up, staring at clouds colored red by the lowering sun. He stayed there motionless for several minutes, trying to come to terms with what had just happened.

He sat up suddenly and looked down at his thigh. There was no wound, no stitches, not even a scar. He rubbed the balls of his fingers over the smooth, hair-covered flesh.

Well, hell. How would he explain this to Mercedes?

Faol came slinking out of the brush much more silently than he had left and nudged Morgan in the back. The wolf let out an agitated whine and trotted several paces down the stream bank.

The animal stopped, turned back to him, and growled, his head lowered and his hackles raised in an aggressive posture. He lifted his nose in the air, sniffed, and took several more steps toward the river before he stopped and let out a bark.

Morgan grabbed his clean clothes and quickly dressed. He snatched up the water bottle and his sword and trotted after the wolf. Keeping in the shadows of the tall brush that lined the stream, he stayed alert to whatever was making Faol travel with the stealth of a hunter.

They both worked their way back upriver to where he'd left Mercedes, and Morgan heard the voices as he neared camp. He hunkered behind the protection of an outcropping of ledge, behind a dense bush, and watched as his disobedient wife strolled to the river and warmly greeted the very men he had told her to avoid.

"Why, if it ain't Sadie Quill," Harry said, waving his paddle at her. "Haven't seen you in a year of Sundays. I thought you'd gone off to the big city to be a weather girl."

Sadie grabbed the bow of their canoe to keep it from hitting a rock, then stepped back when Harry stepped out. Together they pulled the heavily packed boat halfway up onto the beach, pulling a grinning Dwayne with it.

"Hi, Sadie," Dwayne said, nodding and smiling and shaking a finger at her. "You trying to beat us to Plum's gold?"

"And I'm winning, too," she shot back. "I'm a full day ahead of you two lazy prospectors."

Dwayne giggled and scrunched his shoulders. "Not this time, missy," he said with another giggle, his eyes nearly disappearing into his grin. "We got something better than a map this time."

"Dwayne," Harry snapped. "Get out of the boat before you roll it."

Dwayne scrambled up the length of the boat until he found himself unable to get past their gear. He solved his problem by simply stepping into the water and wading ashore. Sadie moved back, worried he might shake himself dry like a dog, and smiled when she saw his gaze drift down the shore and his eyes suddenly widen in surprise.

"You got a dead moose!" Dwayne said, pointing at the moose. He started running toward it. "You killed a moose, Sadie!" he yelped as he ran, stopping at it so suddenly he almost fell. He looked back at her and pointed his finger again, this time waggling it like a mother lecturing a naughty child. "You ain't supposed to kill these, missy. It's illegal."

Sadie ambled after Harry, who had followed his brother to view the moose. "I didn't kill it," she told Dwayne. "My husband did." Now what on earth had made her say that? "The moose attacked his boat, and he was defending himself."

"You got a husband?" Harry asked, first looking at her in surprise, then scanning the campsite for signs of the man. He looked at her again, his eyes narrowed. "You bring back one of them city fellows from Boston?"

Sadie slowly shook her head, still reeling from the thought that she had just told these men that she had a husband. "No. He's a local. Morgan MacKeage."

"We heard of them MacKeages," Harry said, his eyes still narrowed. "They own the ski resort."

"They're an odd bunch," Dwayne piped in, though

he appeared more interested in the moose than in the conversation. He suddenly stopped handling an antler and looked at her, his grin still in place. "What made you go and get hooked up with one of them, Sadie?" he asked. "I heard they're a big, mean-looking group of fellows that keep to themselves."

"They are big," Sadie agreed, unable to keep herself from grinning back. Dwayne's unflappable cheeriness was always contagious. "That's probably why I married Morgan. He's taller than me."

Dwayne's gaze scanned her from head to toe. He suddenly straightened to his nearly six-foot height, puffed out his chest, and shot her another crooked-tooth grin. "Well, hell's bells, Sadie. If I'd known you was looking for a husband, I would have offered to marry you. I don't even care about your scarred hand or nothing. I think you're right pretty just as you are."

God save her, Sadie could feel her heart melting at his sincere offer. "Thank you, Dwayne," she replied, nodding with gratitude. "But Morgan beat you to it. You're going to have to let a girl know sooner that you find her pretty."

Dwayne bobbed his head, his face flushed red as he nervously darted a look around the perimeter of her camp. "I hope your husband didn't hear that," he whispered. "I don't want him thinking I was poaching on his property."

Sadie waved Dwayne's worry away, then tucked her arm through his and led him toward the campfire. "He won't take offense," she assured him as they walked. She guided him to a rock and sat him down, then motioned for Harry to take a seat on the log. "Now, how about a trade, gentlemen?" she said.

"What you needing, Sadie?" Dwayne asked. "You running low on supplies?"

"No," she told him, shaking her head while she quickly scanned the woods herself, looking for Morgan. She hoped he had walked a fair distance to find a spring and that he wouldn't suddenly come barging in waving his sword like a heathen. All she needed was another twenty minutes, and then she could send Dwayne and Harry safely on their way.

"I was thinking of trading you two some supper for a peek at what you've got that's even better than a map," she said, hunching down and stirring the soup, sending the delicious smell toward them.

Both sets of eyes staring at her narrowed, and the smile finally disappeared from Dwayne's face. He waggled his finger at her again. "We ain't telling you spit, missy."

"Why you still looking for the gold, anyway?" Harry asked. "You don't need it none. Them MacKeage fellows are rich."

"They are?" she asked, lifting one brow.

Both men nodded. "They own most of the land in these parts, all the way up to Canada," Harry continued, waving toward the west side of the valley. "And they got that fancy resort."

"I'm still after the gold," Sadie told them, "because it never was for me. You know that. Dad was hunting for it only to prove the legend. He intended to donate the gold to a good cause." Sadie lifted her other brow. "What are your plans for it?"

Dwayne was suddenly smiling again, rubbing his hands together. "We're going to buy ourselves some wives," he said, nodding to show he was serious.

"Some what?" Sadie asked with a gasp. Of all the things she'd been expecting—like a new truck or maybe fixing up their house—wives were the last things she thought these two old bachelor brothers would want.

"Wives," Harry echoed, frowning at her shocked expression. He resettled himself on his log and gave her a defensive glare. "We found this catalog where you can buy women. They even sell trips to Russia, so you can meet them."

"We get our pick," Dwayne added, leaning forward, excitement lowering his voice to a whisper. "They throw this fancy party, and all the women come, and we get to meet them and then choose."

"But you gotta marry them," Harry explained, also lowering his voice in reverence. "They ain't whores or nothing. They're respectable women."

"They're down on their luck, is all," Dwayne added. "And so they're wanting to marry rich men and move to America."

"And once we find that gold," Harry said, straightening his back, puffing his chest, and running his thumbs under his suspenders, "we'll be rich Americans. We'll have enough money to go to Russia, buy our wives, and bring them here to look after us in our golden years."

"And we'll get to diddle without having to pay for it," Dwayne interjected, only to slap a hand over his mouth suddenly and turn beet red, realizing what he'd just said to her.

Sadie snapped her own mouth shut, realizing she was gaping like the village idiot. She felt heat rush into her cheeks. These two old goats were buying wives? From Russia?

"All this time . . . you've been hunting for . . . ? You think to actually *buy* wives?" she finished with a squeak.

She snapped her mouth shut again, took a deep breath, and fought to hold her composure.

"We'll make good husbands," Harry said defensively. "We'll take right good care of them women."

Sadie held her hands up in supplication. "I don't doubt you will," she quickly agreed. She looked from Harry to Dwayne. "All these years you've been searching for Plum's gold," she started again. "This has been your reason the whole time?"

Both men nodded, but it was Dwayne who spoke. "We never could stomach our own cooking," he admitted. "And we get lonely sometimes, especially in winter."

"And that's why we ain't sharing our secret," Harry said, drawing her attention again. He shook his head. "We ain't getting any younger, and we need to find that gold this fall."

"Why now, after all these years?" she asked.

" 'Cause we want children," Harry explained impatiently, sounding as if she should have figured that out by herself. He puffed up his chest again. "A man wants to leave a bit of himself when his time comes to depart this earth."

Sadie had to cough to cover up the fact that she was choking. Children? Heck. Both brothers were nearing sixty years old.

"Ah, Sadie?" Dwayne said. "I don't suppose that if you find that gold first and are wanting to donate it to a good cause like your papa intended, you would think Harry and me are good causes?"

"You wouldn't have to donate all the gold to us," Harry said, warming to his brother's idea. He leaned forward and rubbed his hands together. And she'd swear that she could almost see the beginnings of an idea forming behind his puckered brow. "We could pool our information and hunt for the gold together. Then split it."

Dwayne was shaking his head, frowning at his brother. "We already tried that with her papa, remember?" he told Harry. He looked at Sadie. And damn if he didn't waggle his finger at her again. "No offense, missy, but since we're wanting to buy two wives, it's going to take all the gold. We gotta have some left for when we come home, so we can take good care of them."

Harry frowned back at his brother, not liking that his plan was so quickly shot down. He darted a look at Sadie, then suddenly stood up. "We gotta go now," he said, prodding his brother to get him moving. "We need to make camp before it gets dark."

"Why can't we just stay here?" Dwayne asked, once he was standing. "She's already got a fire going."

Harry shook his head and nudged Dwayne toward their canoe. "She's got a husband," he reminded his brother. "She might want some privacy."

Dwayne, suddenly grinning again, turned a dull shade of red. "Oh," he whispered to Harry, not intending for her to hear. "You mean they might want to diddle."

This time Harry's nudge was not so gentle. He gave his brother a mighty shove into the river. Dwayne caught his balance by grabbing the canoe, then continued to wade out and climb into the stern. Harry grabbed the bow and shoved the boat toward deep water, then quickly climbed in and picked up his oar.

Dwayne waved his paddle into the air. " 'Bye, Sadie," he said. "We'll let you know where Plum's claim is after we take out all the gold," he said as they turned into the current, letting it carry them away. He twisted in his seat, still waving his paddle, still grinning. "We might even give you a nugget, just so you won't be skunked."

They began to slip toward the bend in the river, but still Dwayne kept waving and talking. "Say hi to your husband for us!" he hollered. "And remember, missy. If he don't treat you right, you come see me and Harry. We ain't afraid of them MacKeages."

Harry, apparently not liking his brother volunteering him for such dangerous service, slapped the water with his oar, soaking Dwayne. Dwayne sputtered something under his breath while wiping the river off himself.

The last Sadie saw of them, both men were paddling furiously, Harry determined to outrun his brother and Dwayne determined to catch him, apparently forgetting they were both sitting at opposite ends of the same boat.

Chapter Sixteen

$\mathcal{S}$taring at the spot where Dwayne and Harry had disappeared, Sadie fought the bubble of laughter that was threatening to burst from her belly.

Buying wives. For all these years those two old goats had been hunting for gold because they were sure they had found a way to make the long winters less lonely.

Shaking her head in disbelief, Sadie walked back to her camp, continued past the fire, and stopped just in front of a giant boulder. She crossed her arms under her chest and smiled at the tall clump of brush beside it.

"Now do you understand why they're harmless?" she asked the dense honeysuckle.

Morgan emerged from behind the honeysuckle to stand in front of her. And he didn't appear anywhere near as amused as she was.

"Do you suppose a man can *sell* a wife in this catalog they spoke of?" he asked, his eyes gleaming in the last light of the setting sun. He suddenly sighed and rubbed the back of his neck. "Not that I could get very much for you," he added tiredly. "A disobedient wife can't be worth a hundred dollars."

"They're good men, Morgan," Sadie continued, deciding to ignore his not so subtle threat. "Between the two of them there isn't a mean bone in their bodies. Either of them would give the shirt off his back to someone in need."

"I will admit they do appear more a danger to themselves than to anyone else." He took hold of her shoulders. "But when it comes to gold, even the most timid of men turn lethal, Mercedes. They become blinded by the promise of riches. They act without thinking."

"Not Dwayne and Harry." Sadie shrugged free and walked to the campfire, pulled the now boiling soup off the grate, and set it on the ground to cool. She picked up her spoon and pointed it at Morgan.

"They're my friends," she told him, accentuating her words by poking the air with the utensil. "And you will trust my judgment," she added. "Marriage is supposed to be a partnership, Morgan. Tell me, do you think I'm stupid?"

"What?"

"Do you think I'm stupid?" she repeated. "That I'm a simple-minded woman who needs a man to look after her?"

His eyes narrowed at her question, and his jaw flexed while he thought about his answer. Sadie almost laughed out loud. The poor guy looked like one of those men who'd just been asked by his wife if her pants made her ass look fat. He understood that any answer he gave would be the wrong one.

Sadie stopped pointing her spoon and used it instead to stir the soup, hurrying the cooling process along. Their overcooked dinner was starting to look like mush.

"I don't think you're stupid," he finally said, his voice guarded. "I just think you're too trusting."

Sadie slumped her shoulders. Wrong answer. "Too trusting," she repeated. "As in the way I'm trusting you?"

She watched Morgan take a deep breath and let it out with a harsh sigh. He rubbed his hands over his face before he looked at her again. He slowly shook his head.

"What is it you're wanting from me, Mercedes?"

"I want you to respect my judgment when it comes to Dwayne and Harry. Until either of them does something that proves different, I want you to treat them kindly. And," she said, pointing her spoon again when he started to speak, "I want you to trust me."

He snapped his mouth shut and started thinking again. Sadie took a careful sip of the soup and nearly gagged. She turned the pot upside-down and dumped their ruined dinner onto the ground, then rummaged around in her dry pack, pulled out two granola bars, and tossed one to Morgan.

He caught it, examined the bar with a critical glare, then turned that glare on her. Sadie lifted her shoulders.

"Hey. You probably wouldn't get fifty dollars for me. You beginning to rethink this marriage thing?"

"I'm beginning to think it's time to go to bed," he

said, standing up and tossing the granola bar on top of her dry pack. He walked toward the sleeping bag she'd laid out by the ledge, pulling his sword off his back as he went. Sadie quickly scrambled to her feet.

"There's one more thing I want, Morgan."

"And what would that be?" he asked, turning his head to look at her, lifting one arrogant brow.

Well, damn. She didn't know how it had happened, but she was pretending to be this man's wife for the next seven days, and she assumed that included sleeping with him. Not that she minded. Truth told, she kind of liked the idea. But they needed to get a few things straight first.

"A-about our sleeping together," she started, nervously wiping her hands on her thighs. "I want to . . . but . . ."

He turned fully to face her, and Sadie nearly lost her nerve. But she squared her shoulders and lifted her chin. By God, this gorgeous, hulking, perfect example of man was not going to intimidate her.

"I want to set some ground rules," she finally told him. "I keep my shirt on, and my back is off limits."

Instead of an argument, Morgan simply shrugged his shoulders and nodded in agreement before turning back to their bed. He set his sword down beside it and began taking off his clothes. Sadie tossed her own granola bar onto her dry pack and walked into the darkness toward the river.

She took her time washing up before she rolled her bra, body sock, panties, and glove into her jeans. Then, wearing only her flannel shirt, she headed back to camp—and her waiting husband.

★ ★ ★

Morgan gritted his teeth as his wife crawled under the covers beside him and stifled a groan as her long naked legs slid against his. Sweat broke out on his forehead. Blood rushed to his groin. And with only the barest bit of control, he kept his hands to himself.

"What is your necklace made of?" she asked, her hand going to the burl at his neck. "Is it covered with some sort of glow-in-the-dark paint? It seems to always be shining."

He wanted to jump her beautiful bones, and the woman wanted to talk. Morgan took a calming breath. Maybe talking was not such a bad thing. She obviously needed some time to get used to sharing a bed with him, and he could use the distraction to get his urges under control.

"It's made of cherrywood," he told her, lifting it from her hand and holding it up between them. "And I don't know why it swirls like that. It must be a play of the light," he said, ignoring the fact that the light had left with the sun.

"Why do you wear it?"

"It's a gift from an old friend."

"It looks just like the cane Daar was carrying," Sadie mused, frowning at the burl. "It was cherrywood and had knots in it just like this one."

"It is from Daar," Morgan admitted. "That crazy old man said it was a good luck charm. I think he's touched in the head."

"Yet you wear his gift."

"He's old. I have no wish to hurt his feelings."

She patted his chest, apparently pleased by his

answer, then left her hand there, her fingers lightly caressing his left breast. Morgan closed his eyes and prayed for patience.

Then snapped them open the moment her lips touched his.

The cagey little vixen had managed to capture his hands and was holding on to them with the desperation of a woman determined to have her way. She pushed his arms over his head, kissing him senseless as she wiggled to maneuver her body on top of his.

As she had promised, she was wearing only her shirt and was completely naked from the waist down. Every inch of her exposed skin touching his made the muscles in his body tighten in response. She weighed nothing, but still he was having a hard time catching his breath.

His manhood jutted into her belly, and Morgan was unable to keep from lifting against her. She squeezed her knees into his thighs and rubbed against him in slow, sensuous motions.

He groaned into her mouth and pulled his hands free in order to grasp her hips, hoping to slow her down.

She tore her mouth away from his, then placed her lips along his throat, and lower, where she lightly kissed back and forth over his chest.

He groaned again as Sadie straddled his lap. She was being so passionate, so honest about her desire for him, and he didn't want her pulling away with worry that **he** wouldn't keep to their bargain.

Dammit. He just wanted to make love to her.

"Slow down, Mercedes," he said between clenched teeth.

"But I want you. Now," she said, squirming against him. "I want to feel you inside me again," she added in a husky whisper, feathering her fingers over his shoulders.

He held back a groan when her hands moved down the insides of his arms, along his ribs, and stopped to stroke his hips.

Had he really expected his disobedient wife to listen? And why was he second-guessing his luck? He liked her aggression, her honest and unskilled passion. He especially liked that she seemed to have forgotten her shyness with him.

She moved restlessly above him and kissed him with open-mouthed abandon. Morgan simply gave up then, taking her with him as he rolled them over until he was on top. He nudged her thighs open and settled between them and captured her hair so that he could still her wandering lips just long enough to kiss them.

He rocked his hips in sensual circles, using his arousal to build her desire. She groaned into his mouth, dug her nails into his back, and wrapped both of her legs tightly around his waist.

He leaned up and stared down at her, barely able to see her expression in the pale moonlight. "Do you trust me, Mercedes?" he asked. "To the point that I can touch you anywhere but your back?"

"Yes," she whispered, nodding as she strained against him.

He rolled so that he lay beside her, cradling her against him. He started with her belly button, gently stroking and teasing with his fingertips, waiting for either her resistance or her acceptance. She lifted herself into his touch, making a sound of pleasure that sent a shiver coursing through his body. He splayed his hand wide, spanning over her belly from hip to hip, and moved lower, laying pressure with his palm on her most sensitive place.

She dug her fingers into his chest, raised her head to meet his lips, and kissed him.

Morgan moved his hand lower, cupping her, curling a finger inside her. He swallowed her gasp, captured her restless knee between his, and used his thumb to send waves of pleasure spiraling through her. He felt her tighten against his hand, felt her lift her hips in search of more.

He pulled away and reached under the edge of their sleeping bag, remembering her worry about getting pregnant. He was in no hurry to start a family, not until they both agreed to it.

He found the foil packet he had stashed there while she was washing up and quickly placed the protection between them. Then he rose up over her, spread her thighs with his knees, and slowly slid into her welcoming warmth.

He'd just found his guaranteed spot in heaven. She was so warm, so perfectly built, so well matched to him. He covered her face with kisses as he slowly moved back, then thrust forward, then back, creating a rhythm that had her tightening again.

Morgan lost what was left of his control. He thrust deeply into her, more forcefully, and withdrew only enough to do it again. He brought her with him this time to that blinding place of white energy he had found last night. Mercedes convulsed around him, shouted her pleasure, and sent him spiraling into the maelstrom with a rewardingly arrogant shout of his own.

He dropped his head to her shoulder, only to find himself touching the flannel of her shirt instead of soft skin. He lay unmoving, breathing heavily, savoring the feel of her lingering tremors.

Reluctant to move but knowing she needed to breathe, Morgan finally rolled onto his back, welcoming the cold night air rushing over his damp skin. She immediately followed, tucking herself up against him, wrapping one arm around his waist and settling the other one near his head so that she could run her fingers through his hair.

And he lay there. And he waited.

It was a good five minutes before she spoke.

"That was wonderful," she whispered, squeezing him.

He grunted in answer, rubbing his hand up and down her flannel-encased arm. Aye, it was wonderful but somehow not quite as fulfilling with cloth standing between them. And that was the reason for his sudden black mood. He wanted nothing between them. Not cloth, and especially not her scars.

She needed time. And patience. That is what it would take to cure her shyness.

"And because we're married, we can do this whenever we want?" she asked.

"Yes," he told her, wondering where her thoughts were headed.

"And as often as we want?"

He tilted his head just enough to see her expression

and almost burst into laughter, his dark mood suddenly gone. Mercedes looked quite pleased with the idea of making love to him as often as she wanted. He tapped the end of her nose, then tucked her firmly against him so that her head rested on his shoulder. He pulled the sleeping bag over her back and used it to swaddle her tightly.

"Not quite that often, wife. A woman is weak after making love. She needs at least until morning to gather her strength."

She fell silent again, and he couldn't decide if he should be glad or worried. She suddenly yawned, apparently accepting his ridiculous statement as truth, and snuggled against him like a contented, well-fed cat.

"Morgan?" she sleepily whispered into the silence.

"Aye?"

"When I find the gold, I'm giving some of it to Harry and Dwayne."

Chapter Seventeen

There were advantages to this marriage thing, one of which was having such a large, very warm body to snuggle against.

"Good morning, wife."

Yes, it was morning—the morning after, to be specific. What does a woman say to a man she was intimate with just a few hours ago?

Sadie decided to follow his example.

"Good morning, husband."

His grin broadened. "Have you regained your strength?" he asked, his voice husky, his eyes dark with obvious intent.

"It—it's daylight."

He nodded. "Aye. It is daylight."

"We can't . . . we shouldn't . . . no, Morgan, I'm still quite tired."

He stared at her for another overlong minute, then suddenly brushed back the covers and stood up, picking up his pants as he straightened. "Too bad," he said as he slipped into them. "I was planning to take you to the site of an old logging camp I know of that's not too far from here."

He shrugged again and began to put on his shirt. "I thought it might be the one you're looking for and that Faol was leading us to. But if you need more rest, then go back to sleep."

Sadie shot upright and was standing before she remembered that she was naked from the waist down. Her cheeks—on her face and her backside—threatened to blister with embarrassment. Sadie jerked down her shirttails to cover herself. This time their state of dress was reversed. Now she was the exhibitionist, and he was the one looking on with interest.

"Turn around."

"No."

Why wasn't she surprised by his answer? "Don't you have a moose to cut up or something?"

"The job would be easier with a good morning kiss."

"No."

Unlike her, he seemed sincerely surprised by her answer. "Why not?" he asked, crossing his arms over his chest and glaring at her.

"Because if you kiss me, one thing will lead to another, and I'll be flat on my back in less time than it takes to sneeze."

One corner of his mouth kicked up in a smile. He uncrossed his arms and tucked both hands behind his back. "I promise not to lay a finger on you, lass. Just my lips."

"I'm not kissing you. Not until we are both fully dressed and I've had some breakfast to build up my strength again." She shot him a seductive smile to let him know that she hadn't been fooled by last night's claim that women were weak. "Although I'd bet my boat that you're needing the nourishment more than I am."

Apparently not caring to have his words thrown back at him, Morgan spun on his heel and headed downriver, disappearing into the brush.

Sadie breathed a sigh of relief. She brushed the hair off her face and smoothed down the front of her shirt. She suddenly smiled. Well, spit. She had just survived a second night of sleeping with Morgan MacKeage.

And she thought things had gone quite well. Heck, she was actually feeling proud of herself. She had managed to make love to the man without embarrassing them both, she hadn't bitten him again, and she had just won an important battle of wills. She was feeling quite wifely this morning and beginning to think this marriage just might work out after all. She could survive living with Morgan.

She could even get used to the idea that he was strange. So what if the man carried a sword everywhere? He obviously knew how to use the weapon. He had skillfully killed that moose yesterday afternoon. It shouldn't matter to her why that was his weapon of choice, only that he didn't choose to use it on her.

A breeze suddenly kicked up, lifting her shirttail and sending a shiver past her bare bum and up the length of her spine. Sadie realized she was still standing on her sleeping bag, still naked but for her flannel shirt.

There was actually frost on the ground this morning. She hurried to find her clothes, then hurried even more to get them on. Only after she was finally dressed did she straighten from tying her boots to look around the tiny meadow she was in.

Leaves rained from the trees and wafted through the air like drunken butterflies, having given up the battle to hold on to their branches. The frost and then the abrupt heat of the rising sun had snapped their stems and left them to fall to their inevitable end, to become fodder for next year's growth of new flora. The cycle of life was playing itself out.

"I see breakfast isn't looking any more promising than last night's supper."

Sadie spun on her seat and shot Morgan a smile. She grabbed one of the granola bars, now frozen solid, and tossed it to him.

"When I'm traveling I only make one hot meal a day," she explained, her smile widening as she watched him frown at his breakfast. "Mostly I just graze on trail mix, granola bars, or jerky until supper."

Voices traveled in on the breeze just then, and both Morgan and Sadie looked upriver to discover the source of the sound. Sadie shot to her feet the moment she recognized her mother's voice. Charlotte Quill was sitting in the bow of the approaching canoe, paddling and smiling and talking to Callum sitting in the stern.

Sadie's mood took a sudden dive into the dirt. She slapped her hands over her face to cover her gasp and could only stare in mute shock through her fingers.

Dammit. Her mother was here.

She spun on her heel and ran to Morgan, grabbing him by the shirt and standing on tiptoe to get her eyes dead level with his.

"Not one word about our being married," she whispered urgently, clutching the front of his shirt. "Understand? No kissing in front of my mother. No calling me wife. And hide that damn sword!" she finished on a whispered shout, pushing away and running to their bed.

She quickly rolled up her sleeping bag, ran to her unused tent, and threw it inside. She went back to the ledge, kicked around the matted dry grass she'd put there for padding, and frantically scanned the campsite for any other telltale signs.

Dammit. What in hell was her mother doing here?

Morgan still hadn't moved one muscle, much less done as she'd instructed and hidden his sword. She did that for him, running back to the ledge and kicking some of the dry grass over the weapon. Then she smoothed down the front of her shirt, took a calming breath, plastered a smile on her face, and sedately walked to the river to welcome her mom.

Morgan just didn't have the heart to tell his wife that no amount of deception would ever disguise the guilt she was feeling at the sudden arrival of her mother. Mercedes' face was blushed red; she was embarrassed to the soles of her feet despite her efforts to appear otherwise. She didn't seem to realize that any person in her right mind, especially her mother, would consider finding her daughter sharing a campsite with a man anything but innocent.

Morgan mimicked Mercedes' amble and slowly made his way over to Callum and Charlotte. He grabbed the canoe and pulled the boat sideways to the bank, then reached in and lifted Charlotte out so she wouldn't get her feet wet.

Charlotte squeaked much the way her daughter was prone to do and blinked up at him with eyes the mirror image of Mercedes'.

Morgan stepped onto the bank and carefully set Charlotte down, then shot Mercedes a grin. Quickly recovering from her fluster, Charlotte ran to her daughter and gave her a motherly hug.

"I've been so worried," Charlotte whispered loudly enough for everyone to hear. She pulled back and took her by the shoulders. "Your cabin was ransacked."

Mercedes reversed their positions, taking her mother by the arms. "Someone broke into my cabin? When?"

"Yesterday morning," Callum said, straightening from pulling the canoe onto the beach. He looked at Morgan, then at Mercedes. "We were coming out to visit you, lass, when we discovered the destruction. And your mother," he said, waving a hand at Charlotte, "would have no rest until she knew you were safe."

Mercedes turned her shocked gaze back on her mother. "Who would do something like that? I had nothing worth stealing."

"It looked to be more vandalized than robbed,"

Callum said before Charlotte could respond. "It appeared as if the man was looking for something."

"The Dolan brothers were a half day behind us," Morgan interjected. He looked at his cousin. "You said one man."

Callum shrugged. "There might have been more. I could find only one set of footprints. They belonged to a small but heavy man, maybe two hundred pounds."

"It was not Harry and Dwayne," Sadie said, glaring at Morgan. "It was a stranger."

"What makes you so sure?" he asked. "Do you have any idea who would have done this? Other than the Dolans, is there anyone else looking for this gold?"

Sadie shook her head. "Not that I know of. For years the only people who even believed Jedediah's mine exists were my dad, the Dolans, and Eric Hellman."

Morgan walked over to her. "Now you will take my warnings seriously, Mercedes?"

Before she could answer him, her mother was poking her in the arm, trying to get her attention again. "There's a dead moose over there," Charlotte whispered, pointing down the beach.

Sadie quickly looked back at Morgan, nodded, then turned and led her mother over to see the moose. As Morgan and Callum followed, Morgan let his gaze scan the area. Morgan suspected that the danger he had seen in the *drùidh's* vision was coming closer.

Callum nudged Morgan's shoulder and motioned with his head that he wanted to speak to Morgan alone. Morgan looked to see that the two women were deeply engrossed in a discussion over the dead moose.

Satisfied that they would have some privacy, Morgan walked a short distance away, and his cousin followed.

"Tell me how I can help," Callum said quietly, keeping a small part of his attention on the women. "I've brought guns if you need them."

"What makes you think I need a gun?" Morgan asked.

Callum grinned. "It's been more than eight hundred years, cousin, but not so long that I've forgotten that look."

"What look?"

"You're guarded, Morgan. Feeling hunted. And you're wearing the look of a man who is about to turn the tables and do some hunting of your own." Callum rubbed his hands together, suddenly looking downright cheerful. "And I wish to help. Nay, I demand to help. I could use a rousing fight just now."

"I am not hunted," Morgan snapped, darting a look at the women to make sure they hadn't heard him. They had moved back to the canoe Callum and Charlotte had arrived in and were rummaging through the gear. He looked back at Callum.

"It's Mercedes who's being hunted. That her cabin was ransacked is proof enough. And I think the gold is the reason she's in danger. Either that, or someone doesn't want the wilderness park to be built."

"Besides you?" Callum drawled.

"That's different. I can stop the park from happening without endangering Mercedes."

"Why are you so against this park to begin with? It's only a small part of our land."

"My land," Morgan shot back. He let out a tired sigh

and attempted to rub away the tension slowly building in his neck. He needed to make Callum understand.

"That gorge is special," Morgan told him, deciding it was time to reveal his secret to Callum. Only then would his cousin be able to comprehend the scope of the problem.

"The waterfall comes from that mountain pond where Daar's staff was thrown," Morgan continued. "And everything around it has changed somehow. The trees have grown taller, the trout are the size of salmon, and even the granite of the gorge itself has been altered."

Callum took a step back. "By the *drùidh's* magic?" he whispered, his face drawn pale.

Morgan nodded. "Aye. From his old staff. But Daar has no wish for Grey to know this. He fears what my brother might do."

"Grey will likely dynamite that pond," Callum said, nodding agreement about their laird's determination that Daar's staff never reappear. "So this is why you asked Grey for that land? To protect the old priest?"

"Something like that," Morgan muttered, looking back at the women. They were unpacking the canoe, and by the looks of the gear, Charlotte was planning to stay for a month. He turned back to Callum. "People would wander out of the park and discover the gorge. And that would bring even more people."

Callum could only shake his head. "If Charlotte ever discovered that something like this was connected with us, she would never agree to marry me."

"You don't intend to tell her about our past?" Morgan asked.

Callum looked downright appalled. "Hell, no," he ground out, shaking his head again. "You saw what happened when MacBain told Mary Sutter. The woman ran away and got herself killed."

"Grace knows," Morgan reminded him. "And she still married Grey anyway."

"Grace is a scientist," Callum said, getting defensive. "And scientists are used to discovering wonders. They understand that there is something driving the forces of nature that can never be explained. Tell me, are you intending to tell Sadie about your past?" Callum asked quietly, turning the question back on Morgan.

"I do not like deception," Morgan said. He sighed and kneaded the muscles in his neck again. "I don't know," he said more calmly. He grinned. "I thought about getting her pregnant first," he admitted.

Callum looked appalled again. "And you don't think that's deceptive?"

"It might be a good plan. I've already claimed her. A babe would only bind us together more tightly." Morgan broadened his grin. "Are you saying you haven't thought that maybe a bairn would hurry your courtship along?"

Callum actually looked sick. "I could never do that to Charlotte," he whispered. "She had to get married at sixteen when she became pregnant with Sadie. I could not force her into another marriage that way."

Morgan didn't have the heart to tell Callum that it was too late, that Charlotte already carried his child. Besides, that was Charlotte's duty.

"I could use your help," Morgan said, changing

the subject. Telling their women they were eight hundred years old was a personal decision that each of them eventually would have to make. But not today. "I need to get that moose taken care of," Morgan continued. "And it seems I have to notify the authorities that I killed it. If you could help me do that, I would be grateful. I have no wish to leave Mercedes unguarded right now. Not with the news you've brought us."

"You killed the moose with your sword?" Callum asked, knowing full well that Morgan rarely carried a gun. "Tell me, what does Sadie think of your weapon?"

Morgan shrugged. "She seems to be getting used to it."

"I swear I'd give all my teeth to have my sword back," Callum said. "I've felt naked for six years." He suddenly grinned. "Although there is something to be said for a good rifle. You needn't get close to an enemy to dispatch him."

Morgan let his gaze scan the landscape again. "That works both ways," he said, looking back at Callum. "Neither does your enemy need to be close." He rubbed his neck again, the tension having suddenly doubled. "Hell. Someone could be watching us right now, with his gun trained on Mercedes."

"Do you honestly believe there is that kind of danger?"

"The *drùidh* warned me there was a presence roaming this valley. Something dark," Morgan carefully explained without coming right out and telling Callum about the vision he had seen. "Mercedes might be in danger. This is why I'm with her now. I want that damn gold found, and then I want to settle this park thing between us."

"In a way that won't expose your gorge?" Callum surmised.

Morgan nodded. "She's going to have to be content with just owning the land and not opening it up to people."

Callum gave Morgan a staggering pat on the shoulder. "For an ancient man, you can be foolishly young sometimes, cousin. Living with a woman who's had her dream taken away does not bode well for a peaceful union. Hell, it can be downright dangerous."

"Yeah, well," Morgan said, pivoting on his heel and heading back to Charlotte and Sadie. He hoped Charlotte was a better cook than her daughter. There had to be breakfast fixings someplace in all that gear she'd brought. "You'd better start putting some of your own long-lived wisdom to work," Morgan said quietly over his shoulder as he walked off. "You've got your own female problems to deal with, and I'm thinking they might turn out to be just as troubling as mine."

Chapter Eighteen

There was another advantage to having a husband, Sadie decided later that morning. He carried the bulk of their gear.

Sadie slid her unusually light backpack off her shoulders, absently letting it drop to the ground as she studied the old logging camp that lay before her like a slumbering beast forgotten by time. This was it. Camp number three.

The last place Jedediah Plum had been seen alive.

Sadie could easily make out the remains of what must be the cookhouse. The roof was gone except for the rafters, the door and several of the windows were broken, and good-sized poplar trees were growing inside, spilling the last of their leaves like yellow flakes of unmelted snow. Rotting into the forest floor just to the right of the cookhouse, not twenty feet away, were two bunkhouses running perpendicular to the cookhouse. Both were long and narrow and set low to the ground with the rusted remains of a stove pipe jutting crookedly against the middle rafter of one of them. Several of the giant logs that made up the walls had come free of their moorings, the ravages of time and nature working them into peat dust to litter the ground around the cabins. Young spruce grew in the acrid peat, reaching for the sunlight filtering through the few towering trees that had escaped the woodcutter's blades.

The building that housed the saw was far off to the left, set away from the living and eating area. Probably so that one group of men would be able to sleep in relative peace while another group worked.

Sadie knew from her years of studying journals and history books that the sawmill usually ran around the clock in ten-hour shifts. Maintenance was done during two-hour breaks; the saws were changed and sharpened, the machinery oiled, and the bark and debris from the previous shift cleared away to make room for the next round of sawing.

Sometimes the trees were sawn on sight and the lumber hauled to town over the frozen ground, and sometimes the whole logs were simply driven downriver in the spring. This site, apparently, had been a portable mill. Which meant it would have been a small, self-sufficient town unto itself.

Sadie slowly turned in a circle, studying the site, unable to believe what she was seeing, shaking her head in wonder.

"I bet my daddy's mill processed some of this timber," Sadie said, finally looking at Morgan. "Only it would have been Grampy Quill who ran it then."

Morgan was shaking her head. "It was more likely your great-grandfather," he corrected with a smile. "This site is at least eighty years old."

Sadie looked around again. "I can't believe this has been sitting here like a ghost town all these years, its location never documented."

Morgan shrugged. "Why would anyone bother? They moved in, harvested the trees, then got out. There was nothing here to lure people to settle, other than the timber. And once that disappeared, so did the camps."

He turned her to face him. "You can properly thank me now, wife, for finding this camp for you," he said, an arrogant smile lighting his eyes.

Not one to deny a person his due, Sadie leaned up on her toes and kissed Morgan the way she had wanted to since morning. His tongue swept inside her mouth, his body hardened against her, and that shivering tingle returned to her chest as Sadie melted against him.

Yeah, husbands definitely had their advantages.

She was trembling like a poplar leaf when she finally pulled back, still making sure that she stayed within his embrace. Her heart was threatening to fly out of her chest, and she was quite pleased to see that Morgan was equally affected.

"Thank you for bringing me here," she said, toying with a button on his shirt. She looked up. "And thank you for getting rid of mom so diplomatically. She's pregnant and doesn't need to be in the middle of this. Having her and Callum take the moose back for you was a brilliant idea."

"Ah. So you do believe you're in danger."

"I believe that someone besides us and the Dolans might be out here and that they might be looking for the gold."

"So, if I were to ask you to stay here with Faol today and explore only this camp, you just might obey me?"

Sadie thought it was past time Morgan's vocabulary got an adjustment. "*Obey* is one of those words women don't really care for, Morgan. But I might be inclined to go along with your *suggestion*," she offered instead.

He pulled her back against him, tucking her head under his chin and rocking her gently. His laughter made her chest tingle, and Sadie closed her eyes and leaned into his strength. Yeah. She really liked being married.

"Ah, Mercedes. I'm starting to have hope for us," Morgan whispered, kissing the top of her head and squeezing her tightly. "You can spend the rest of your life making me into a modern husband, if that is your wish." He lifted her chin. "While I work just as hard to make you into a suitable wife."

His eyes darkened, sending her heart racing again, this time with anticipation. Now that she knew what making love could be like, she wanted to experience it again. Tonight. Just as soon as the sun set, she was going to attack this man like a woman possessed.

"You enjoyed yourself last night, wife?"

Sadie had to look away from his intense gaze, so she turned her attention to fingering the cherrywood knot hanging around his neck. "That depends," she whispered to his chest. "Did you?"

All she got for an answer was silence.

Sadie felt heat climb to her face. Dammit. He'd better give her the right words. She tugged on the cord that held the cherrywood knot. "Did you?" she repeated.

"Almost," he said quietly.

Sadie snapped her head up. "Almost? What does that mean?"

He tapped the end of her nose, dropped his arms to his sides, and stepped away. "I'll tell you what it means in six days," was all he said before he pivoted on his heel and strode off through the woods.

Sadie stared at his back until he disappeared around the cookhouse. Almost? How can someone almost enjoy something? Either he did or he didn't.

She was almost ready to scream.

It amazed Sadie how quickly she had grown accustomed to sleeping with Morgan. And as she set up their new camp, she thought again about her decision to pretend to be Morgan's wife for the week. Had she managed to sabotage her heart, making it impossible to walk away in six days?

For the first time since the fire eight years ago, Sadie had the hope of a future that included a husband, children, and a cozy home of her own. If nothing else—if she did have to walk away at the end of the week—Morgan had returned that possibility to her. He had made her realize that the fire may have taken half her family, but it had not taken her future.

She could still hope.

She could still dream.

She could still love.

But could she *be* loved?

Sadie finished spreading out their sleeping bag and stretched out on it and stared up at the tops of the trees. Morgan hadn't once mentioned the word *love,* for all his peculiar vocabulary. Sadie dismissed the fact that she hadn't exactly brought the word up, either. He was the one talking about marriage; he should be the first one to say it.

He acted possessive, like a caring husband.

He worried about her safety.

And he *almost* enjoyed having sex with her.

Sadie touched the fingers of her right hand together, feeling leather touch leather. Would he *completely* enjoy their lovemaking if she had no scars? What would it be like, to go to Morgan fully naked, flawless, and beautiful?

Would he say the words to her then?

I love you.

Sadie closed her eyes and let her escaping breath turn into a smile, letting those three little words echo though her mind like a promise. And she decided then that she was not walking away from Morgan MacKeage in five days.

Sadie woke with a start, unable to orient herself for several seconds. As the treetops towering over her head came into focus, she realized that she'd fallen asleep. Feeling a bit embarrassed for having a nap in the middle of the day, she sat up and scanned the area for Morgan.

He was nowhere to be seen. Sadie decided this was

her chance to have a bath while she still had some privacy. She gathered her toiletries and some clean clothes and looked around the logging camp. There had to be a water source nearby, a spring or a small brook. She hadn't seen any signs of a dug well during her exploration of the camp earlier.

She headed into the forest, hiking north along the west side of Fraser Mountain, figuring that if she walked far enough, she would eventually run into a stream.

She ran into Morgan instead.

He stepped from behind an outcropping of ledge and used his impressive body to block her path. Sadie's heart started to race at the sight of him. He was so incredibly handsome. So large and solid. And so damned sexy, standing there like a god of the woods.

She smiled at him.

He didn't smile back.

"I stink," she said, her smile rising a notch at the incredible look he gave her. "And I'm not kissing you until I wash my hair and change into clothes that can't stand up by themselves."

"You'll catch a cold."

"I don't care. I'll catch fleas if I don't have a bath."

He actually took a step away from her at that possibility. Sadie walked up to him, tapped him on the nose, and continued past him with an insolent sway of her hips. Morgan fell into step beside her. And as they walked in companionable silence, Sadie thought about the history of this area.

Jean Lavoie's diary mentioned that Jedediah Plum

had visited camp number three for several days and had taken to wandering off at night. But he was always back in his bunk each morning, which meant the prospector hadn't traveled far.

Jean had followed him once but had lost his trail when Jedediah's footprints had become mixed with the tracks the horses had made that day hauling logs. Jean also mentioned that he hadn't been the only one stalking Jedediah that night.

But on the fourth morning the prospector had not returned. His body had been discovered sticking out of a snowdrift about a mile north of the logging camp.

"That's it," Sadie said, pulling Morgan to a stop so abruptly he stumbled backward.

"That's what?" he asked.

Sadie brushed the hair from her face and shifted her bundle of clothes to her right arm. "I was thinking about Jedediah's gold mine," she said. "And when he died." She looked around the forest they stood in. "It was near here, according to the cook's diary I have. Someplace just north of the logging camp."

Morgan also looked around, frowning. "North? How far?"

Sadie shook her head. "The diary said about a mile or so but wasn't specific. But I remember from my dad's research that Jedediah's body was found near the base of a cliff that was at least a hundred feet high. Only we were never able to find that cliff because we never knew where the logging camp was."

She shot Morgan a bright smile. "Until now. Thanks to you and Faol, I can discover exactly where

Jedediah's body was found. And I'd bet my kayak that the old prospector died close to his gold mine."

"A tall cliff?" Morgan whispered, looking north. "About a mile from camp?"

Sadie dropped her bundle of clothes and threw her arms around Morgan's shoulders. "Forget our swim," she said with a laugh of excitement, hugging him tightly. "Let's go north and look for that cliff."

Morgan slowly untangled her arms from around his neck, setting her away from him. He bent down, picked up her clothes, and gently placed them back in her arms. He smiled at her, but his face was drawn, his expression tight.

"We have the rest of the week to look for that cliff," he said, his voice even-toned. "After our swim."

Sadie could only stare at Morgan, confused by his reaction. Why wasn't he excited about this?

Morgan took hold of her hand again and started them walking down the mountain, west, away from where she really wanted to go. Sadie followed along meekly and thought about her pretend husband's sudden change of mood.

With Mercedes' hand firmly tucked into his, Morgan headed to where his magical stream ran into the Prospect River. Sweat broke out between his shoulders and ran in a trickle down his back. His right hand involuntarily curled into a fist, and his feet felt like stones as every step he took led him closer to the magical stream he wanted to keep secret from Mercedes.

Of all the hundreds of square miles in this valley, why did Plum's accursed mine have to be located in his gorge? And why now, after all these years of searching with her father, did Mercedes have to be the one to find it?

The *drùidh's* vision rose in his mind, and Morgan started to shake with the force of his thoughts. He released Mercedes so she would not feel his trembling. He walked ahead in silence, holding back branches for Mercedes when the trail became thick.

They broke from the woods and stepped onto a sandbar jutting into the magical stream. Upstream the water rippled with gentle current over gravel worn smooth by time. But the stream's path bent around the sandbar and eddied into a deep pool of calm water—perfect for swimming, Morgan decided, and for making love to his wife.

Mercedes wasted no time. She dropped her bundle of clothes onto the sand and quickly followed it down, immediately unlacing her boots.

"Go away," she told him succinctly, pulling off her boots and then her socks. Her hands went to the snap on her pants. "Find your own swimming hole farther downstream."

Morgan pulled his sword from his back and set it on the ground, then unbuttoned his shirt and took it off, letting it fall beside his sword. Mercedes turned her head to discover he had not obeyed her order. She frowned at him.

He smiled at her. "I stink, too, wife," he said, wrinkling his nose. "And I like this swimming hole," he added, unbuckling his belt and pushing his pants down to his ankles.

His wide-eyed wife suddenly squeaked and turned

to face the stream. "It's broad daylight, Morgan. You can't . . . we can't just . . ."

Morgan ignored her flustered sputtering and stripped naked, setting the rest of his clothes neatly beside his shirt. He hesitated, then took the cherry-wood burl from around his neck and set it on top of his pile.

He didn't need its help today to froth up the water. He and Mercedes could do that all by themselves.

Stretching his muscles against the cool autumn air, Morgan strode past his speechless wife and waded into the stream. He slipped under the water and kicked his way to the center of the pool before he turned and resurfaced. He let his feet sink to the bottom and stood facing Mercedes, the water only as deep as his chest. He brushed back the hair from his face and smiled at his still gaping wife.

"Hide in the trees to change," he told her. "And wear only your shirt if you feel you must hold on to your modesty."

He sent a splash of water toward her. "It's not cold, Mercedes. Hurry up and join me." He bobbed his eyebrows and spider-walked his fingers through the air. "I'll wash that beautiful hair of yours if you want."

She darted a nervous look up and down the length of the stream, then suddenly jumped up and ran for the forest. Morgan lay back in the water and floated, smiling up at the deep blue sky. For all of her shyness, Mercedes seemed to be a willing wife, playful and energetic and eager.

And so comfortable here in these woods.

Now, if he could only get her comfortable with him.

Morgan watched from the corner of his eye as Mercedes silently tried to sneak into the water. The little *gràineag* had emerged from the forest a good fifty paces from where she'd entered. Now she was tiptoeing up the stream toward him, trying not to make any noise or ripple the water.

Morgan closed his eyes, smiled, and waited.

Strong feminine hands—both of which were naked, he was pleased to feel—landed on his shoulders with surprising force and drove him under the water. Morgan twisted and reached for the tails of Mercedes' shirt, pulling her down with him.

His mouth captured her squeal under the water as she wrapped her arms around his neck and pulled their bodies together, snaking her legs around his waist and trapping him tightly. Morgan shouted, still underwater, the moment his groin came into contact with the naked, delicate, down-covered folds at the juncture of her thighs.

He ravaged her mouth while she stole the breath out of his body. Her hands tugged at his hair and dug into his shoulders. She wiggled her hips, further arousing him, setting him on fire as he hardened to stone.

They needed air.

Not that he cared at the moment. But Morgan had a thought that Mercedes' eagerness might drown them both.

He planted his feet and stood, keeping his very passionate wife firmly locked against him. They both tossed their heads back the minute they surfaced, taking in large gulps of air. But before he could catch his breath, the little *gràineag's* mouth was covering his. Morgan fell forward, sinking them both to the bottom, placing Mercedes between the gravel and his now rock-solid manhood.

And that was when Morgan suddenly remembered the foil packet that was still in his pants. On the beach. Much too far away right now. But Morgan simply didn't care at that moment. This woman was his. He was hers.

He kicked his feet just enough to bring them to the edge of the pool, lifting Mercedes' head above water and resting it on the shore. Still covering her, still locked in the embrace of her legs, he slid down just enough that he could touch the tip of his manhood to her feminine center.

Her eyes opened, blinking the cascading water away, and Mercedes smiled in anticipation of the passion he offered. Her hands dug marks into his shoulders as she used the heels of her feet to lift her hips against him, opening herself to receive him inside.

But he hesitated and pulled back.

"We don't have protection, wife," he said, closing his eyes against the urge to drive forward. "I need to go to my pants."

"I don't care," she whispered, lifting her hips again and trying to pull his mouth back down to hers.

Morgan held fast. "Well, I do, *gràineag*. I will not have you crying foul in two months. You'll say the words in front of a priest before I put a babe in your belly."

She gave him a fierce shove. And before he could right himself, Mercedes was up and running toward his clothes. Morgan didn't know if she was going for his pants or his sword.

"Why didn't you bring it into the water?" she growled as she knelt down and rummaged around in his pockets, making a mess of his neatly stacked clothes.

Morgan stood up and backed deeper into the pool while he appreciated the view of her beautiful backside. Soon she had the foil packet in her hand and was running back to the stream, her wet flannel shirt clinging to every delectable curve of her body, her long legs making short work of the distance between them.

Morgan heard the rifle shot the instant Mercedes lunged into his arms. When she landed against his chest, she was dead weight. He dove them both into the water, holding on to her with desperation. He covered her back with his hand and sank to the bottom of the pool, feeling the warmth of her blood against his palm as she lay limp and unmoving against him.

Morgan rose to the surface and frantically waded to the sandbar, turning to shield Mercedes from the direction of the sniper. He crossed the sandbar in less than three strides and ducked into the forest just as another shot cracked through the air, hitting the dirt at his feet.

Morgan kept running deeper into the woods, heading downstream toward the sniper, hoping the villain wouldn't expect him to move in that direction. Morgan ran a few hundred yards, then finally stopped and set Mercedes gently on the ground.

She was a bloody mess, nearly all of her flannel

shirt soaked red, both front and back. The bullet had gone straight through her body.

With shaking hands, Morgan popped all the buttons on the shirt and spread it open, revealing a small wound just below Mercedes' right breast. Her breathing was labored. She was unconscious, her face as pale as a winter's moon, her eyes already sunken beneath eyelids that were blue with the promise of death.

Morgan forced his hands to remain steady as he worked the shirt off her shoulders and held her in a sitting position. He wrapped the blood-soaked flannel around her back and over her breasts and the wound, using the sleeves to tie it as tightly as he dared.

Swiping his forehead with a trembling and bloody hand, Morgan looked up and cocked his head, listening for sounds of the sniper moving in for the kill.

He took a deep breath, trying to calm his racing heart. They were miles from nowhere, and Mercedes would bleed to death before he could get her to civilization. He had to get to Daar's magic burl and the stream to heal her before it was too late.

He heard a sound then, on the other side of the valley, the distinct shout of a man being surprised. A wolf's growl was followed by another shot, but this time the muzzle was pointed in another direction.

Confident that the sniper was now occupied elsewhere, Morgan gently picked up Mercedes and ran through the forest again, back upstream. He kept to the woods and passed the sandbar, running until a bend in the stream concealed him from the other side of the valley. He set his wife down gently on the gravel and then ran back to the sandbar.

With only a negligent look across the valley, Morgan stepped onto the sand and gathered up his clothes and his sword, quickly draping the cherry-wood burl around his neck as he ran back to Mercedes.

He tossed everything onto the ground beside her and picked her up, wading into the stream until it was deep enough for him to sit down. The moment the burl got wet, it started to hum against his chest. The water began churning, frothing around them and sparking to life with thousands of bubbles that rose to the surface as exploding green light.

He untied the shirt and pulled it from around her waist. Mercedes moaned, arching her back in pain. Morgan clasped her to his chest and lay back, sinking deeply into the stream. His body felt on fire as blinding green light blazed around him. He tightened his arms around his wife's limp body and held her head just above the surface for a good ten minutes, gritting his teeth against the heat assaulting him.

He sat up finally and looked at her wound. It was still bleeding, frothy red bubbles oozing from it. She'd grown paler, more limp.

Morgan roared. The magic wasn't working. "Dammit! I command you to work!" he shouted, grabbing the burl and tearing it from his neck.

Supporting her with his knees, Morgan tied the leather cord around Mercedes' neck and straightened his legs to lower her into the water.

The green bubbles suddenly turned yellow, snapping with angry pops that filled the air with steam. Morgan lifted Mercedes just enough to see her wound.

It wasn't throbbing as the cut on his thigh had, but the bleeding seemed to have slowed.

It still wasn't enough.

She was still dying.

Faol stepped out of the woods but stopped at the edge of the water. Morgan looked up to see the panting wolf frantically dancing from foot to foot, as if agitated. Faol whined, then barked, then trotted several paces upstream.

Morgan turned his attention back to his dying wife. Faol barked again, louder. He stepped into the water, then retreated, trotting upstream again, his bark turning into a keening howl.

Upstream.

The waterfall.

Nearer the *drùidh's* magic.

Morgan stood up and gently settled Mercedes against his chest. He waded out of the water and followed the wolf, who was now trotting quickly up the edge of the stream.

The desperate journey seemed to take forever before he finally reached the waterfall. Morgan simply kept walking until he was standing shoulder-high in violently frothing water.

This time the light snapping around them was neither green nor yellow but a pure, blazing white that forced Morgan to close his eyes or be blinded. Heat radiated from Mercedes in waves so intense his arms and chest felt scorched.

The mist rising around them warmed the air with summerlike heat, making sweat break out on his forehead and scalp. Morgan stood solid against the assault, reciting prayers he'd all but forgotten since he had been a lad on his mother's lap.

And he prayed, willing the *drùidh's* magic to save Mercedes' life, to heal her wounds and bring her back to him whole and hearty and spitting mad. He stood until his muscles trembled with fatigue, willing Mercedes to live.

"I had a wonderful dream."

Morgan snapped open his eyes and stared down at the woman in his arms. She was smiling sleepily up at him, her face flushed pink around heavy-lidded blue eyes.

"And what was it you dreamed about?" he whispered, his voice shaking as violently as his legs.

"I visited Daddy and Caroline. We had a picnic high up on a mountain overlooking a beautiful valley."

Sweat broke out on his forehead again when Morgan realized that Mercedes had actually died for a while. She'd been with her father and sister and very well could have ended up staying.

"Caroline doesn't blame me," Mercedes whispered, drawing his attention again. "She told me the fire wasn't my fault."

"I'm glad you saw your family," Morgan whispered. He shook her slightly. "Don't go to sleep again, Mercedes," he softly commanded when she closed her eyes.

"I'm so tired, Morgan. My muscles feel like jelly," she mumbled, turning her face into his chest. She smiled again, snuggling comfortably against him.

Morgan waded to shore and fell to his knees on the sand, still clasping Mercedes tightly, finding himself unable to set her down. He knelt there for several minutes, silent tears rolling down his face. Over and over he repeated his thanks to God that his wife was alive.

Faol suddenly appeared and quietly padded up to them and nuzzled Mercedes' hair, his tongue washing the entire side of her face. Morgan didn't send the wolf away but let the animal see for himself that Mercedes was okay.

And still Morgan couldn't put her down.

Faol started to whine and dance from foot to foot again, turning in circles, trotting to where the pool emptied out of the cliff-surrounded grotto they were in. He barked sharply and sat down, whining as his tail thumped the edge of the stream.

"I don't care," Morgan said softly to the wolf. "I will find our sniper and deal with him later. Mercedes needs my attention now."

Faol yipped again, standing and looking nervously downstream.

"Go, then," Morgan told the wolf. "Stand guard."

Without further urging, Faol whirled and shot out of the grotto, his tail disappearing from sight in a blur.

Morgan looked down at Mercedes.

She was still sleeping, her eyes no longer sunken into her head, her cheeks a warm, healthy pink. He looked around for a soft place to set her down, inching forward on his knees just a bit before he gently laid her on a carpet of thick green moss.

He straightened, brushing back the hair from her face, feeling the heat of life on her skin. He traced the shape of her cheekbone, letting his finger trail over her chin, then down the length of her throat.

He halted and stared at the empty piece of leather tied loosely around her neck.

The cherrywood burl was gone.

Morgan turned to look at the pool. The waterfall dropped from the cliff at the far end, sending a cloud of mist into the air that settled over the entire grotto. The water gently rippled with floating stardust that glittered and winked in the unearthly light that scattered its rainbow through the mist.

The magic was spent, the burl destroyed.

And Mercedes' life had been saved in the process.

Morgan turned back to his wife, continuing his inspection with a still trembling hand, needing to assure himself that she really was okay. His gaze went immediately to where the gaping wound had once been, but he saw only smooth, milky-white flesh that carried just the hint of a blush from her own inner heat. His hands settled around her waist, and Morgan closed his eyes with relief.

She was perfect. Flawless. Completely healed.

With a sharp intake of breath, Morgan pulled back, staring at Mercedes' body. He reached out, lifted her right hand, and turned her palm toward him.

No scars. Nothing but pink, healthy skin. He looked back at her left arm, then turned her just enough to see her back. There was no puckered skin. Nothing but flawless flesh.

Mercedes was completely healed.

Completely.

Morgan sat down on the ground and scrubbed at

his face, shaking his head and grinding his palms into his eyes.

Now how in hell was he supposed to explain this?

His wife was going to wake up to find herself lying in this magical gorge, completely naked and flawless. It was bad enough he wouldn't be able to explain why she hadn't died from her bullet wound. But her old scars?

Morgan twisted to see the scar he had on his shoulder from a battle that had been waged more than eight hundred years ago. And he turned more, to feel for the long ridge of flesh on his waist, where a sword had nearly cut him in half.

They, too, were gone. Disappeared.

He looked out over the still shimmering water and shook his head again. Was he dreaming? Why hadn't the *drùidh's* magic taken his old scars away the other day in the stream, when it had healed his thigh?

The light had been green then, not the pure, blinding white of today. The magic was more powerful here. Special. The strength of Daar's thick old staff flowed into this grotto and was soaked up with the mist to nourish the towering trees.

It also had nourished both himself and Mercedes and given them perfect bodies.

And now he was left with the task of explaining to this modern-born woman just what had happened to her. And to do that, he would have to explain his own magical existence here.

Chapter Nineteen

She was dead.

She remembered the force of the bullet slamming into her back. Remembered falling against Morgan. Remem-bered the disbelief, the pain, and the regret that she would not get to spend a long and happy life with this man.

She'd died instead.

But Sadie didn't know if she'd landed in heaven or hell.

Or maybe this was the purgatory she'd heard about.

It was hot. She was hot. But she was in the most beautiful place she'd ever seen. Towering cliffs of gray-speckled granite formed a half-circle around her. Mist hung overhead in a suspended cloud, blanketing her in muggy summer heat. The roar of water falling from a great height echoed off the tall granite walls, and she was bathed in a fog-amplified white light.

She still had all five of her senses. She could hear,

see, feel the tickle of moss beneath her, smell the warmth of the mist-soaked spruce mingled with pine. And she could even taste Morgan lingering in the back of her mouth.

Sadie slowly rolled over to face the sound of the falling water and widened her eyes as her gaze traveled up and up and up, following the stream of crystalline water that appeared to be shooting out of the side of the cliff like a giant faucet turned all the way on.

She scrambled to her knees and stood up, turning in a circle with her head thrown back, looking at the cathedral-like room surrounding her. Spruce and pine and oak and cedar rose so high over her head that their tops disappeared into the mist. Ferns grew so lush in long-feathered spikes that they looked prehistoric. The moss she'd been lying on was as thick as sheep's wool and so green it was almost fluorescent.

It should have been dark from the abundant canopy of growth, but there was light shimmering everywhere, the source coming from the water instead of the sky.

Sadie raised her right hand to brush the hair off her forehead, only to halt with her hand suspended in front of her face. She stared at her palm, at the perfect flesh that should have been covered with ugly scars.

She looked down at her body and gasped again at the realization that she was naked. She instinctively covered herself, folding her hands over her breasts.

And that was when Sadie noticed her arm.

The scars on the inside of her left arm were gone.

She twisted enough to see her back. The wide, jagged patchwork of skin grafts was gone. She tucked her chin and peered at her right shoulder. There was no scar peering back at her. Pink, flawless skin covered her back from her shoulder to her waist.

Sadie folded her legs and sat down, covering her face with her hands.

She *was* dead.

She would never see Morgan again. He was back in their valley—all alone, mourning her, cursing his inability to protect her.

Sadie pulled her hands from her face just enough to look down at her hand. What was the point of having such a perfect body if Morgan was not here to enjoy it with her?

Sadie threw herself facedown on the sand and burst into tears. She didn't care anymore that she'd been scarred. Better to have flaws and have Morgan than to be perfect without him.

Sadie cried loud, wrenching tears, mourning all that she'd lost. She'd come to this beautiful place, becoming beautiful herself, to spend eternity alone.

And that was when Sadie decided she'd landed in hell.

She lifted her head at the thud of something hitting the ground. She looked up to see Morgan, fully clothed, standing beside where the pool spilled out between the towering trees. At his feet was her bundle of clothes and her boots, his pack, and his sword.

Sadie jumped up and ran toward him but came to a stop several paces away when she noticed the look on his face.

He was as pale as snow, the skin drawn back on his cheeks in tight lines of tension. His eyes were the color of winter spruce, and his fists were clenched at his sides.

Sadie threw herself at him. She kissed his face, his hair, his mouth, whimpering her approval when his arms tightened around her.

"I think we're dead," she whispered into his ear. "I'm sorry, Morgan, that we've died, but I'm so happy you're here with me. I love you so much," she continued, kissing him again.

It took Sadie a full minute to realize he wasn't kissing her back. And that he'd gone even stiffer the moment she'd started to speak.

He didn't know yet, that they'd both died. He didn't understand what had happened to them.

She unwrapped her legs from his waist and stood, dancing away from him and twirling in circles with her hands out.

"Look, Morgan. I'm whole. I'm as naked as the day I was born and just as perfect." She spun to present her back to him, showing off her flawless skin. "The scars are gone, Morgan. I'm me again," she said with a laugh over her shoulder.

He didn't move. Didn't speak. He didn't so much as blink.

Sadie rushed back to him and unbuckled his belt. "Let me show you," she said, unsnapping his pants and pulling them down to his knees. "You're going to be perfect, too."

Sadie took his fisted left hand and set it over the spot on his thigh where he'd stitched up the wound from the moose. "There. See? It's gone," she said, looking up at his face.

He wasn't looking at his thigh. He was staring at her. Sadie gave him a huge smile, straightened, wrapped her arms around his neck again, and kissed him soundly on the mouth.

"I truly am sorry we died, Morgan," she whispered. "But we're together, my love." She rained kisses over his face as she spoke. "I was so afraid I'd lost you forever."

Sadie felt him reach down and pull his pants back up before his arms came around her again. Morgan swept her off her feet and carried her back to her spot by the pool. He set her down and then sat beside her, unbuttoning his shirt, shrugging out of it and handing it to her.

"Put this on, lass," he said softly, his gaze quickly roaming over her naked body before he turned his head and looked out over the pool.

"I wish you'd take your clothes off instead," she said, disgruntled but doing as he asked. She slipped into the shirt and buttoned it up to her neck but stopped at the feel of something dangling over her collarbone.

Sadie lifted the leather cord and gasped, sending her gaze to Morgan's chest. "This is the cord you wear." She tucked her chin and pulled the leather out to see better, feeling for the wood that should have been there. "Oh, no. I lost the cherrywood knot that was on it."

She turned, frantically searching the ground for the wood. Morgan grabbed her by the shoulders, then leaned them both over until he was lying on top of her. He brushed the hair back from her face.

"We're not dead, Mercedes," he said, his mouth mere inches from hers, his eyes dark and unreadable as he stared at her. "We are both very much alive."

Sadie blinked at him, pressing her head into the ground to focus better on his face. "We . . . we can't be, Morgan. I don't have any scars. And neither do you."

"You're alive, Mercedes."

"But I remember the bullet. The pain. I remember falling against you. I was shot, Morgan. I . . . I died."

He slowly nodded his head, his eyes never leaving hers. "Aye, lass, you did die," he whispered, bringing one hand up to finger the leather cord on her neck. "But the old priest's magic brought you back to me."

"M-magic?"

He nodded again. "Aye." He let go of the leather and waved at the air around them. "This place, the mist, the very water that flows from the cliff. It's special, Mercedes. It comes from a pond where the *drùidh's* staff was thrown two years ago."

"D-drùidh?"

Sadie pushed at his chest, struggling to get up. He rolled off and sat up as she scrambled to her feet and turned to stare down at him.

"What are you saying?" she whispered, fighting the fear that was rising inside her. She took a step back. "Are you . . . are you saying you're a . . . a witch or something? A warlock?"

He shook his head and then quickly stood.

She took another step back.

"I'm only a man, Mercedes," he said, keeping his distance. "I know nothing of magic."

"Then how . . . ." She fingered the leather cord at her

throat, swallowing the lump that had lodged there. "Then how did you heal me?" she finished on a disbelieving squeak.

He nodded in the direction of her neck. "The priest's gift," he said. "The cherrywood burl and this water healed you," he told her, waving at the pool behind her.

Sadie darted a cautious look at the water, turning just enough so that she could see it without losing sight of Morgan.

"Wh-where is the burl now?"

He waved his hand again. "Gone. Dissolved. The magic was spent saving your life."

Sadie dropped her chin and toyed with the button on Morgan's shirt that she wore. What he was saying was fantastical. But, more important, why was he saying it?

Could he not accept that they'd died?

"Morgan," she said, looking at him, taking a small step closer, and holding out her right hand, palm up. "Do you see this?" she asked. "The scars are gone. And that's not possible. There's no such thing as the kind of magic you're talking about. A person can't get shot and then just . . . just heal. And eight-year-old scars can't disappear as if they never existed."

"Then explain to me what has happened," he softly demanded, his eyes now piercing points of solid green flint.

"We died. Both of us, or you wouldn't be here with me now. That cut on your leg wouldn't be gone. It's the only logical explanation, Morgan. We're dead." She suddenly smiled. "And we've landed in heaven."

He took a step toward her. "Mercedes."

Sadie beat him to it. She ran and jumped into his arms, laughing up at him. "And we're going to make love now, husband, before God realizes his mistake and kicks us out of here," she finished, planting her mouth on his. She pulled him down to the ground until she was sitting and straddling his waist.

Morgan let out a sigh that all but filled her lungs and settled his hands under his head. "That still might happen," he said, smiling up at her, only to sober suddenly as he softly feathered a trembling finger across her cheek. "I was so afraid I'd lost you, wife," he whispered.

Sadie covered his hand on her face. "Me, too. I love you so much, Morgan. I couldn't live without you." She shot him a smile. "I couldn't die without you, either."

She leaned down and kissed the frown on his forehead. She stretched out full-length on top of him and wiggled until her nose was even with his beautifully naked chest, grinning again when she heard him moan.

Sadie traced circles with her fingertip through the furry mat of hair covering his chest. She had a fair amount of area to cover and let it tickle her palm as she ran a lazy path over his muscles. She stopped and explored a nipple, heard him moan again, and ran her tongue over the silky-smooth circle. Hair tickled her lips as she gently suckled, and Morgan sat bolt upright and held her away.

Sadie smiled at his ferocious scowl, patting the spot she'd just licked

"I promise to let you do the same to me in a minute," she told him. "But I want my wicked way with you first."

"I'll disgrace myself," he said through gritted teeth.

She pushed him back and leaned over him again, her nose inches from his. "We've got an eternity to practice, husband," she said, sitting up and unbuttoning her shirt.

She watched his eyes go from her face to her breasts, and his scowl relaxed. He set his hands behind his head again as she slid the shirt off her shoulders and let it fall to her back.

Sadie cupped her breasts, pushing them together as she leaned forward and let them dangle over his chest. She slowly brushed them back and forth, only to find that now she was the one building with a tension that started in the pit of her stomach and spiraled outward and down to the very center of her femininity.

Sweat broke out on Sadie's forehead. She felt flushed and wet between her thighs, and she couldn't seem to stop shaking with the need to feel Morgan inside her.

His hands came to her breasts, replacing hers that were now digging into his shoulders. He gently fondled her, setting her completely on fire. She may have cried out, Sadie wasn't sure, but she did know that she couldn't make her hips stop moving against him.

His hands left her breasts but were quickly replaced by his mouth. Sadie shouted then, louder than the roar of the waterfall. Morgan lifted her and pushed off his pants, and suddenly there was nothing between her and her husband's rock-hard erection.

Searing heat pushed against the folds of her womanhood, and Morgan's strong hands grabbed her hips and lifted, settling her more intimately onto him.

Sadie felt herself stretching, accepting, taking Morgan inside. She moaned this time, loud and deep and keening, when she felt his mouth cover her breast. He used his hands on her hips to set them into a rhythm, suckled her nipple until she thought she was going to explode.

And she did, gloriously, shouting her pleasure to the granite walls of their wondrous heaven, gasping as each rocketing spasm took her spiraling upward. Morgan shouted his own pleasure, tightening his grip on her hips to help her ride out the light storm they'd created together.

Sadie sprawled on top of him, tucking her head into the crook of his neck, feeling the lingering pulse of her pleasure still throbbing around him.

And they lay together that way, both breathing hard, until their racing hearts stopped trying to out-thump each other.

"It kind of sneaks up on you, doesn't it?" Sadie mumbled into his chest.

"What does?"

Sadie tilted her head back and opened one eye to the sleepy laughter she heard in his voice. "The passion. I thought I was going to spend an hour driving you insane. But I was the one who didn't last five minutes."

He patted her bottom affectionately. "I'm guessing we'll calm down in about thirty years," he said with a chuckle. He rolled them both over until she was beneath him, then kissed her on the forehead. "We'll practice until we get it right."

He brushed the hair from her face with repeated, gentle strokes, staring down at her with shining eyes.

"I love you, Mercedes," he whispered. "As God is my witness, I love you more than life itself, lass. Will you marry me, Mercedes? Just as soon as I find that crazy old priest, will you do me the honor of making our vows legal?"

Sadie stretched her arms over her head like a lazy cat and thought about making Morgan wait for her answer. But she was too sated, too happy, and too much in love with him to let him suffer one more second.

"There must be a priest somewhere around here," she told him. "And as soon as you find him, I'll marry you, Morgan. Do you think we can make babies in heaven?"

He rolled off her and stood up, then leaned down and picked her up. He waded into the shimmering pool until the water reached his waist and dropped her without warning. Sadie sank to the bottom, retaliating by touching him intimately and kissing his erection.

She could hear his shout even under the water.

They practiced getting it right three more times, moving from the warm, shimmering water to the sandy shore to the far side of the pool under the thick spray of the waterfall.

Sadie lay exhausted on top of Morgan on the rocks, not even possessing enough strength to let out a respectable sigh. Morgan, though, could still manage enough energy to stroke her bottom gently with a lazy hand.

He lifted her chin to look at him. "You're a scary woman, wife, when you lose your shyness."

She wrinkled her nose and tiredly patted his chest. "You ain't seen nothing yet, husband."

Sadie didn't know where the man found the strength, but he lifted her away from him and gently set her on the rocks beside him. She looked out over the waterfall. They'd ended up underneath it somehow, and the unusually warm water ran in a curtain that sparkled like sun-washed glass before it crashed into the pool at their feet.

Sadie's stomach rumbled, and she laughed. "I guess you can get hungry in heaven," she said, rubbing her belly. "But I'm simply too tired to eat."

"And I'm too tired to hike back to the logging camp right now and get our stuff," he said, standing and holding out his hand. "How about a small nap first, then I'll go get our stuff?"

She took his offered hand and stood up, looking around the water-walled chamber they were in.

"Oh my God!" She gasped, shaking off his hand and walking in small circles, staring at the ground.

She was walking on small pebbles of gold.

"This is it, Morgan!" she squeaked, whirling to face him. "Jedediah's mine. We found it!"

He scuffed at the ground with his bare toe, bending down and picking up one of the nuggets so that he could hold it up to the light of the waterfall.

"It seems we have," he said softly, his voice barely audible over the noise of the falls.

Sadie walked back to him and examined the nugget in his hand, letting out a weary sigh. "Fat lot of good it does me now," she grumbled. "The park will never be built."

Morgan looked at her, his smile sad and his eyes dark. "What would happen if we were not dead, Mercedes? What if you were alive and had all this gold at your disposal? What would you do?"

"I'd build the park."

"And then what would happen to this magical place?" he asked, dropping the gold and turning her to face him. "If we're alive, and this place really exists, then what will happen to it when all the tourists come to visit your park?"

She frowned at him. "It's a moot point. We're dead."

He shook her slightly. "But if we weren't," he persisted. "What would happen to this gorge?"

She had to think about that, and she didn't like what she was thinking. "It would be ruined," she told him. "Once it was discovered—and it would be—then the people would trample over every square inch of this ground, trying to get to the gold."

He nodded and released her shoulders. "That's right, they would. Your park, your father's legacy—it would all be forgotten, overtaken by the mystery of this special place."

"But we're dead, Morgan," Sadie insisted. "Simply based on the fact that nothing like this can exist in the real world. It isn't possible."

Morgan said nothing more. He took her hand and led her around the edge of the waterfall and along the shore of the pool until they were back on the sandy beach. He picked up the shirt she'd discarded and settled it over her shoulders, wrapping her up and grasping it closed over her breasts. He kissed her nose.

"Let it go for now," he softly entreated. "There will be plenty of time to worry about this later. We both need some sleep first. Then I'll find us something to eat, and we'll deal with our problems on full bellies."

He used his grip on her shirt to pull her down as he spoke, and Sadie happily let him. She cuddled into his embrace the moment they landed, closed her eyes, wrapped her arms tightly around him, and quickly fell asleep.

Chapter Twenty

Sadie awoke to the strong odor of a wet dog. She opened her eyes and reached up to push Faol's tongue away from her face, but her hand stopped in mid-reach and changed direction to poke Morgan in the shoulder.

"We've got company," she whispered, quickly wiggling to sink farther behind him. "Father Daar's here," she squeaked a bit louder, poking him harder.

Good Lord. She and Morgan were as naked as the day they'd been born, her shirt thrown off and lying behind her. And if they weren't dead already, the scowl on the old priest's face likely would kill them.

"Ya have two minutes to get up and get dressed," Father Daar snapped, pointing an age-bent finger at them. "Or you'll be saying your wedding vows naked."

Morgan sat up and used his body to shield Sadie from the scandalized gaze of the priest. She took advantage of his broad back and quickly found his shirt and slipped it on, buttoning it all the way up to her neck.

"Turn around, old man," Morgan growled. He waited until the priest complied, then looked to see that Mercedes was modestly covered. He grinned at her furiously blushing face.

"Are you ready to say the words, lass?" he asked, feathering a finger over her red-hot cheek.

Mortified beyond any ability to speak, Sadie nodded.

Morgan stood up, sauntered past the still waiting priest, and gathered the clothes he'd dropped by the end of the pool. Sadie scrambled to her feet and made sure she was decently covered to her knees, thankful that Morgan's shirt had long tails.

Her soon-to-be-for-real husband wasn't the least bit shy about his own state of undress, nor did he seem worried that they'd been caught sleeping together—naked—by the priest. He carried her bundle of clothes back to her, frowning at Father Daar as he passed him.

Sadie quickly dressed, pushing Faol out of the way several times in order to tie her boots.

She suddenly gasped. "Faol was killed, too!" she yelped, just now realizing what the wolf's presence meant. She gasped again. "And Father Daar. You're dead!"

The priest turned and looked down at himself. "I am?" he echoed in dismay.

Morgan sat beside her, putting his own boots on, but he stopped and looked at her.

"You're not dead, old man," Morgan said impatiently. He waved one large hand in the air. "Mercedes thinks she's died and gone to heaven," he explained. "Thanks to your magic."

Looking more confused than relieved, Father Daar turned his attention to Sadie. "What makes ya think we're all dead, girl?" he asked.

Sadie held up her right hand, palm toward him. "I'm healed, Father. All my scars are gone. And I was shot. I felt the bullet rip through my body, but I don't hurt, I'm not bleeding, and I don't have any scars anymore. So I'm dead."

The priest darted a quick look at the still shimmering pool, then turned his penetrating gaze to Morgan as he lifted one bushy white eyebrow. "Ya used the burl again, didn't ya?" Father Daar said in a low voice, waving at the water. "Ya exposed our secret to save your woman's life."

Sadie looked at Morgan and saw him nod.

"And being a modern, she don't believe this is possible?" the priest continued, drawing Sadie's attention back.

She looked at Morgan, and he nodded again.

Sadie stood up, deciding she could speak for herself. She walked up to the priest and pulled her shirttail from her pants, lifting it high enough to expose her stomach.

"The bullet went into the middle of my back," she told him. "And came out my side," she added, turning and pointing at her back. "And I should be covered with old scars here, from the fire that killed my sister."

She dropped the shirttail and crossed her arms under her breasts. "I'm completely healed, Father."

She heard Morgan sigh again right beside her and looked to see him rubbing a hand over his face.

"We can't say our vows until she understands," Morgan said to the priest. "She has to realize what she's getting for a husband."

"Then explain it to her," Father Daar said. "And be quick about it." He pointed at Sadie's middle. "At the rate you two are going, your firstborn will be sprouting teeth before ya're properly wed."

Sadie stepped back, covering her belly with her hand. "What firstborn? What are you talking about?"

"Are ya telling me it was an innocent nap you two were just having?" Father Daar asked.

Sadie felt her face heat to near flaming.

"We'll say our vows as soon as she understands," Morgan repeated.

"You'll say them now before me and God, or I'm going home and washing my hands of ya. There's a terrible storm brewing in this valley that's needing your attention. But not until you're properly wed."

Still unable to raise her mortified eyes above Morgan's belt, Sadie waited for him to decide if he really wanted to marry her or not. If they were all dead, what did it matter?

And if they were really alive?

"If—if you don't want to get married, we won't," she said to his chest, still unable to raise her eyes any higher, fearing what she might see in his. "We'll forget the rest of the week and just go our separate ways now."

She was suddenly hauled up against Morgan's side, turned to face the priest, her ribs crushed so fiercely it was a wonder they didn't crack.

"Begin!" Morgan snapped to Father Daar.

As a declaration of love, that one word sounded magical to Sadie. Yes, they would begin their life together right now. And they'd have the most blessed union heaven had ever seen.

Their vows would be real this time, in this wonderful place that was more beautiful than any church Sadie had ever seen. They would have a storybook marriage that would last for eternity.

Father Daar had taken a small book out of his pocket and had already begun reading their vows. Sadie smoothed down the front of her flannel shirt and decided she probably should pay attention. But the moment she started listening, she realized she didn't understand a word the priest was saying.

She squinted and leaned forward to see the book he was reading from, and she didn't recognize any of the words. She covered the page with her hand, making him frown up at her.

"What language is that?" she asked.

"Gaelic," Daar said, moving the book from under her hand and holding it up again.

"But I don't know what you're saying," she interrupted, making his frown deepen. "Can't you translate it into English? And why are you using Gaelic to begin with?"

He cleared his throat, turned his frown into a glare, and shot it at Morgan, then back at her. "Because it's our language, girl," Father Daar said impatiently. "And since we outnumber you two to one, we get to choose the vows."

Sadie waved at the book. "Then say them. But we're going to add our own vows—in English, so I know what I'm promising."

With a lift of his eyebrows at her impertinence, Father Daar raised the book up and began reading again. The words sounded more like curses than pledges to Sadie, with sharp consonants and guttural vowels that were more spat than spoken.

Faol had come to view the proceedings and was sitting beside Sadie, leaning on her leg, his tongue lolling out and his eyes a sappy iridescent green as he stared up at her. Morgan, disturbingly silent beside her, had her right hand clasped so tightly Sadie thought he was afraid she'd change her mind before the service was over.

Father Daar suddenly quit speaking and turned expectant blue eyes on her. Sadie guessed she was supposed to say "I do."

She took both of Morgan's hands into hers, straightened her shoulders, and started her vows.

"I love you, Morgan MacKeage. And I promise to be your wife for all eternity, to cherish you, to honor your spirit, and to guard with my soul this love that we've found."

She squeezed his hands. "And we'll have lots of babies together and raise them in a house overflowing with love. We'll teach them the wonders of nature and bring them up . . . bring them up . . ."

She couldn't go on. Her heart was near to bursting,

she was getting all mushy inside, and a lump the size of a basketball was caught in her throat. She shook her head and swallowed and forced herself to continue.

"And I promise to love you forever," she finished on a choked whisper.

That finally said, Sadie sucked in her breath and waited for Morgan to say his vows.

"You're mine," he growled, pulling her so forcibly into his chest that the air rushed out of her lungs with a gasp.

You're mine?

That was it?

Morgan's mouth covered hers with that same downright possession she'd seen in his eyes. He kissed the outrage right out of her before it could gather a foothold. And he kissed her some more, until the impatient coughing of a scandalized priest broke them up.

"It's done, then," Father Daar said with finality, rather loudly. "Now, let's eat. We'll have us a wedding feast of nice tasty trout. Stop mauling your wife, Morgan, and catch us some supper."

But her husband wasn't paying the priest any mind. Sadie pinched Morgan in the side to get him to come up for air.

"Go catch us some trout from one of the cooler pools below, Morgan," Father Daar said, taking Sadie by the arm now that she was free of Morgan. "We'll build a fire, cook your catch, and then you and I will set our minds to convincing your wife that we all have many years left before we finally see heaven," he added, walking her toward the sandy beach by the pool.

He looked back over his shoulder at Morgan and crackled with laughter. "Not that you have any chance of getting there yourself, warrior. They rarely allow pagans through the gates."

Sadie didn't know what surprised her the most, that the priest had called her husband a pagan or that he'd called him a warrior.

Morgan picked up his sword and settled it over his back, his glare fierce enough to fry Father Daar where he stood.

"You may begin the explaining without me, old man," Morgan said. "Faol. *Tàr as. Falbh,*" he added, waving the wolf toward the exit of the pool, then walking through the towering trees himself.

Staring at the spot where he'd disappeared, Sadie posed her question to the priest. "What did he just say?"

"*Tàr as?*" Father Daar repeated. "It means 'move off' or 'go.' And *falbh* means 'guard.' " He started walking around the cathedral-like grotto and picked up small pieces of wood. "He's set the wolf to guarding the entrance," he said as he continued his work, putting the branches into a pile. He straightened and looked at her. "I told you befriending Faol would come in handy one day."

Sadie put her hands on her hips and faced the priest. "So you're saying this Maine wolf knows Gaelic?" she asked. "A language that's been dead for hundreds of years?"

He sat down on the moss near the pile of branches he'd made and looked up at her. "It's not dead, girl. Gaelic's still spoken in some parts of Scotland." He suddenly grinned. "Now, watch," he said, touching the branches with his skinny cane while he muttered some words under his breath.

The wood erupted into flames, and Sadie stepped back. She quickly stepped closer, glaring at the now crackling fire.

"That's not magic," she said. "Not in heaven. Anything's possible here," she said, waving at the tall granite walls.

Father Daar sighed loudly enough to be heard over the noise of the waterfall and rubbed his hands over his face. He looked up at her and patted a place beside him. "Come. Sit with me, Mercedes, so that I can explain what has happened to you."

With a sigh of her own, Sadie sat down beside the crazy old priest and stared at the softly crackling fire.

"Do you remember my visit last week?" Daar asked, using his cane to push more wood onto the fire. "And your feet? Were the cuts not healed the next morning when you woke?"

"They were gone," she admitted, frowning to herself.

"And were you not alive when that little miracle happened?"

She looked at him. "It wasn't a miracle," she disputed. "Miracles are big things that happen to deserving people."

"And you're not deserving?"

"That's not the point. God wouldn't trouble himself with small cuts on my feet. He has much more important things to worry about."

Daar harrumphed and scrubbed his face with his

hands again, shaking his head. He finally looked at her, his expression confounded. "The whole world is still sitting out there, Mercedes, just beyond those trees," he said, pointing at where Faol and Morgan had disappeared. "Your valley, your mother and Callum, your two simple-minded friends, and the man who shot you. All are still there, all still waiting for you."

Sadie looked toward the trees. She hadn't even thought about trying to leave. "Then, if I'm not really dead, will my scars return if I leave here?" she whispered. "Will I be ugly again?"

"Ya can't be what you never were," Daar snapped. He blew out a tired breath. "But no, the scars are gone for good." He frowned. "Which will be hard to explain to your mother, I'm guessing. She's a modern, too, and won't be able to understand any better than you can."

"What do you mean, 'a modern'? You say that as if you and Morgan are ancient or something. And Morgan's not in the military. So why did you call him a warrior?"

Daar kneaded the back of his neck and finished by scratching his beard. "Because that's what he is. Or, rather, what he was," he said. "I had a little mishap with the magic six years ago and brought Morgan eight hundred years forward in time."

"You *what?*"

He frowned at her incredulousness. "I made a mistake," he said, lifting his hairy-white chin. "I was only wanting to bring Morgan's brother, Greylen, forward, but nine other men came with him, including Callum and Ian and Morgan. And MacBain," he added with a scowl.

"Callum?" Sadie squeaked. "Are you saying the man my mother is going to marry is like . . . like Morgan? That he's old . . . and also a warrior?" Sadie scrambled to her feet and balled her hands into fists. "What are you saying?" she shouted.

Father Daar lifted his cane into the air and began muttering words softly to himself again. Sadie's eyes widened as she saw the cane grow to nearly double its size and start to hum with gentle vibrations.

"Take hold of this, Mercedes," Daar said, holding it out to her. "If ya want to understand, hold this, and I'll show you."

She stepped back. "No."

"Aw, come on, girl," he cajoled. "Where's your spirit of adventure? Do ya not want to know who your husband truly is?"

She didn't understand any of this. What he was saying was impossible. But her scars were gone, she was in a veritable rain forest that shouldn't exist anywhere near Maine, and the old priest's cane was now glowing like a finger of lightning.

Hesitantly, but with more curiosity than fear, Sadie reached out and took hold of the surprisingly cool cane.

Light entered her head, flashes of brilliance that should have blinded her. But she was able to see something slowly appear in her mind's eye. A scene out of a picture book. Men on horseback, carrying swords and dressed strangely. Actually, some of the men were naked. They were fighting a mighty battle.

She could smell the dust being kicked up by the trampling feet of the horses. She could hear the clash of the swords striking each other. Sadie immediately recognized Morgan. And Callum. She could see Callum trying to unseat a man whose face was covered in paint. Lightning flashed over their heads. Thunder boomed. The very air around them became charged with the energy of a quickly descending storm.

A torrential rain suddenly blanketed the chaos, darkening her vision. There was an intense explosion of light, the detonation making Sadie flinch in surprise. She tightened her grip on the priest's cane. Suddenly, there was only silent white light as pure as the center of the sun, muted spectrums of color shading the edges.

The men reappeared, no longer fighting but scattered in dazed disarray on an earth that was the same but different. It was more lush. Greener. There were buildings. Cars and trucks were zooming by.

Sadie looked for Morgan. He was first holding his head, covering his eyes with his hands, then suddenly patting his body as if he didn't believe he existed. She cried out at the fear she saw on his face, the confusion, the very terror of what had happened to him.

Horses lay scattered around the men, dazed with terror and screaming, trying to stand. Sadie watched Morgan run to one of them and recognized the horse he'd been riding the first day she'd met him.

"What's its name?" she softly asked the priest standing and watching beside her in her mind's eye.

"Gràdhag," Daar answered. "It means 'pet.' "

Sadie let go of the cane and stepped back. The

vision left as mysteriously as it had come. She turned and stared out over the still shimmering pool made by the waterfall.

"That's why Morgan is afraid of thunderstorms," she said. "He was caught in one and ripped from his home and brought . . . brought here."

"Aye. He did not care for the journey," Father Daar said from right beside her, also looking out at the waterfall. "Nor has he cared much for the new life he's found himself living."

He took hold of her shoulder and gently turned her to face him. "Until now, child. He's found you, Mercedes. And he's not going to let anything come between the two of you. Not my magic, not the blackness visiting this valley, not even your own inability to believe. He's said his vows before God and man and claimed you as his. You belong to each other now. So accept what I have shown you for the gift that it is."

"Morgan called you *drùidh*. What does that mean? Who are you?"

"I'm what your modern language would call a wizard, and I'm nearly fifteen hundred years old."

"A wizard?" she repeated, taking a step back.

He frowned at her. "And a priest," he said defensively. "And a hungry one at that," he tacked on, looking toward where the pool spilled into the valley. He walked back to the fire and sat down again, working it back into flames.

Sadie stared at the cane he used as a poker. What he was saying, what she had just seen, it was . . . it was the stuff of fantasies and ancient legends that continued to survive despite modern science explaining it away.

But science couldn't explain her missing scars or the very fact that she was alive right now. And neither could she. Her dead theory made more sense, but she hoped with all her heart that she was alive. She had a new baby sister coming soon, and she wanted to be here when she was born. She wanted to see her mother get married. She wanted to have babies of her own.

So, yes. She wanted to believe in the magic.

Morgan stepped through the towering trees just then and stopped and stared at her. There were several trout hanging from his belt, his sword was still on his back, and if she looked hard enough, she could see that same warrior from the vision the priest had given her.

And Sadie knew then, no matter what means had brought them together, that she loved Morgan.

She launched herself into his arms, breaking into overjoyed laughter, confident that he would catch her and hold her safe—forever.

"We're alive, Morgan." She laughed into his startled face, which she couldn't stop kissing over and over. "Wonderfully alive, thanks to a wizard's magic."

He held her so tightly that her last words were squeaked rather than spoken. He buried his face in her neck, his whole body trembling with what she suspected was relief.

"I swear you two spend more time cuddling than looking to practical matters," Father Daar called from the fire. "Ya have a lifetime for that foolishness, Morgan. I want my supper."

Still crushing her tightly to him, Morgan carried

her over to the fire and set her down by the priest. He tore the trout from his belt and tossed them at Father Daar's feet.

"Eat, then, old man," Morgan said, darting a look at Sadie and then back at the priest. "I haven't the time right now. I've got to go find our sniper before he finds us again."

Sadie was standing before she finished gasping. "You will not! The man has a gun, and all you've got is that . . . that sword," she said emphatically, waving a hand at the inadequate weapon sticking up past his head. "You're staying right here."

Morgan took hold of her shoulders and pinned her with his eyes. "As beautiful and warm as this place is, we cannot hide here forever, gràineag. We have to leave eventually, and we cannot do that until I'm sure we'll be safe."

He pulled her against him gently and cupped the back of her head into his shoulder. "I'll be careful, wife. He won't even see me coming."

"It—it's not Dwayne and Harry," she muttered into his shoulder, trying to wiggle back to look at him. But he wouldn't loosen his hand. "Don't hurt them. It's someone else."

"I know, Mercedes. I will not hurt them." He finally leaned back to look at her, now holding her hair in his fist, his grip emphasizing his words. "In return, you must promise to stay here with Daar. You'll be safe with the drùidh."

He was holding her so tightly she couldn't even nod. His entire body was filled with tension.

"I'll protect Father Daar," she told him instead.

Father Daar snorted at her response.

The right corner of Morgan's mouth curved in amusement. He kissed her soundly on the lips, then stepped back.

"Wait." Sadie turned to the priest as she untied the leather cord she was still wearing. "Father Daar. Give Morgan another cherrywood knot to take with him," she said, handing the leather to the priest.

Father Daar clasped his cane to his chest protectively, fingering the empty leather cord now in his hand. "I can't," he said, darting a look from her to Morgan. He lifted his shoulders in a shrug. "I've only one decent-sized burl left that would have enough power to do any good," he explained. "And if I take it off, my staff will be useless."

"Then give him your whole cane," Sadie insisted, reaching for it.

"Nay!" Daar yelped, quickly tucking the cane behind his back. "He's liable to set this entire valley on fire. The magic's too powerful for mere mortals."

"Well, he needs something."

"I have you, wife," Morgan said, turning her to face him. "Nothing can stop me from coming back to you, Mercedes."

"You'll have your clan's help," Daar interjected. "Callum and Charlotte stopped by my cabin yesterday on their way to Gu Bràth. Callum said he'd return with Greylen and Ian." He waved in the direction of the valley. "They're probably already out there, hunting for whoever broke into Mercedes' cabin."

Morgan gave Sadie a reassuring smile. "See? You have nothing to worry about."

"Does your brother or Callum or this Ian fellow have guns?"

"Aye. We all do."

"Then where's yours?"

"Home in my gun cabinet. I'll be okay, *gràineag*. Now, make our priest some supper," he said, kissing her quickly on her still protesting mouth. "And try not to kill the man with your cooking," he said as a parting shot, turning and loping into the darkness at the end of the pool. He disappeared before Sadie could tell him at least to take Faol.

She turned back to Father Daar.

"Did you know that burned trout is an acquired taste?" she asked the man of the cloth who was still eyeing her suspiciously, still guarding his cane behind his back.

"I do know what that word is now, that you asked me about the other day," the old priest said instead, his clear blue eyes suddenly sparkling with mischief.

"Gray-agch?" Sadie whispered, stepping closer. "What? What does it mean?"

The old man rubbed his beard with the end of his cane and sent her a satisfied smirk. "Well, girl. *Gràineag* is Gaelic for 'hedgehog.' "

Chapter Twenty-one

*M*organ stepped through the towering trees that protected the pool and out into the cold night, letting his eyes adjust from the bright glow of the grotto to the darkness of the forest. Faol whined beside him and stood up, his tail wagging and his eyes glowing green with their own inner light. The wolf was licking his lips, finishing off the trout Morgan had given him earlier.

"You be ready, my friend," he told the wolf in Gaelic. "I give Mercedes only an hour before she comes sneaking out here. Guard her, and keep her from wandering off the side of this mountain and getting herself killed."

He hunched down and ruffled the wolf's fur. "It seems we've gotten ourselves a *gràineag*, wolf, who has more heart than common sense sometimes. Nothing else can explain her acceptance of us."

Morgan smiled into the night as he thought about the afternoon he'd just spent with Mercedes. She'd been so playful and passionate when they'd made love. And so open with her now perfect body. Not an ounce of shyness did she possess, now that she felt beautiful. He would give his sword arm to have possessed her that way before she'd been healed. He'd never have that chance now, thanks to the magic. He would never be able to prove to Mercedes that love did not come with conditions.

Morgan stood up and let his gaze scan the quiet forest. "I'm going to find Greylen and the others," he told Faol. He reached into his pocket and pulled out a fistful of gold nuggets he'd taken from the pool. "I won't go after Mercedes' sniper. Grey and Callum and Ian can do that. I'll set out bait and wait for them to push our prey into my trap."

He gave Faol one final pat and a warning. "Be alert," he told the wolf. "And keep our woman away from the river."

And then Morgan walked into the night, towards the dark force that roamed his valley.

Though Sadie didn't know it, her husband's prediction was off by a good two hours. Sadie paced to the edge of the pool and stared down at the shimmering water which continued to glow with magical intensity. It appeared to be daylight within the confines of the granite cliffs, but when she looked skyward, the mist rose into blackness. It was the deep of night outside her own little heaven, and Sadie couldn't stop thinking about her shooter and the danger Morgan was walking into.

Sadie wished she had bought a handgun. But even

if she had, it most likely would be back at the old logging camp, with the rest of her stuff.

And that was another thing that was bothering her. The logging camp and her backpack. Jean Lavoie's diary was there as well, with the section pertaining to this cliff, and its approximate location, circled in red ink. If whoever shot her stumbled onto it, he would know where to look for the gold.

And he would find this mystical gorge.

Sadie skirted the edge of the pool, walking beneath the waterfall and scooping up a handful of gold. She turned and looked out over her small piece of heaven.

If this place were discovered, it surely would be destroyed.

In order to keep this magic a secret, she would have to build the wilderness park farther down in the valley and find another way to access it instead of through MacKeage land.

But she would have to worry about solving that problem later. Instead, Sadie set her mind to the bigger problem at hand now. She had to go to the logging camp and retrieve that diary before it was found.

Sadie tucked the handful of gold into her pocket and walked over to the slumbering old priest. She eyed the cane in his hand. She needed some sort of weapon that could protect her if she ran into trouble. It was only two miles to the logging camp and back. With luck, she'd be gone less than an hour. She'd have Father Daar's cane safely tucked back beside him before he woke up, and she'd be sitting here like a dutiful wife long before Morgan returned.

Being as careful as she could, Sadie slowly slipped

the cane from the sleeping priest's hand. She quickly straightened, clasped the warm wood to her chest, and turned and set off at a jog through the magically giant trees.

She nearly ran over Faol when she stepped into the darkness of the forest. The wolf jumped to his feet, whined, and started wagging his tail.

"Shh. You're going to wake Father Daar," she said, giving him a pat on the head. "Feel like a hike, big boy?" she asked, blinking her eyes at the darkness.

It took her a few minutes to locate the North Star and get her bearings and another few minutes for her eyes to adjust completely to the night forest. And then Sadie started south along the edge of Fraser Mountain, toward logging camp number three. Faol trotted ahead of her, his bushy tail wagging like a flag leading the way.

In less than half an hour they reached the camp, and Sadie ran toward the tent her mother and Callum had left standing in wait for her and Morgan's return.

She heard Faol's warning growl at the exact moment a gunshot cracked through the air, the muzzle blast flashing from a tree beside the tent.

Faol's yelp of pain was drowned out by her own scream of surprise. There were several shots in rapid succession, and all Sadie could see was the scurry of moving shadows where Faol had been standing. Another yelp, then the growl of an enraged beast, followed by another crack of gunfire.

Sadie screamed and threw herself toward the tent. She unzipped it and dove inside to find her pack and the knife she usually carried. She pushed around her sleeping bag and dry packs but couldn't find her back-pack.

"Looking for this?"

Sadie whirled at the sound of the familiar voice. The beam of a flashlight sliced over her face. She held up her hand to see beyond the glare and gasped.

"Eric!"

He dropped her pack and grabbed her by the hair, pulling her out of the tent. With a yelp of her own, Sadie scrambled on her knees until she could stand up. She watched as Eric quickly scanned the forest with his flashlight, looking for Faol.

"Where's the MacKeage guy that dog belongs to?" Eric asked, turning the flashlight back on her.

"H-he's dead."

"He's not. I saw him carrying you from the water. You were the one I shot." He sent the beam of light over her body.

Sadie gasped, trying to step back, but was pulled up short by his grip on her hair. "You were the one shooting? But why?" she cried, struggling to get free.

He held her tightly. "I was aiming for MacKeage. I wanted him out of the way."

"Out of the way for what?" she whispered, holding herself perfectly still.

"He was distracting you from your hunt for the gold. I'm sure I shot you by mistake," he said, giving her hair a vicious tug.

"You just grazed me. Th-that's why I have this cane," she said, pointing at the cane on the ground by the tent. "But the bullet went into Morgan, and he used up the last of his strength getting me to safety."

"You wouldn't be here if MacKeage were dead. You'd be in town." He tugged her hair again. "Where is he?"

"O-okay, he's not dead. But he's wounded. I have him tucked down by the stream. I'm here to get my phone so I can call for help."

"The phone's not in your pack, Quill. I checked."

"It's got to be." She pulled from his grasp and bent down to her pack, pretending to look for the phone. "I know it's in here."

"No, it's not. And neither is your knife," he said, jerking her upright again. "I have it now. And I also have the diary, including the page you circled."

He released her and pulled his gun out of his belt. "You found the gold, didn't you? That's where MacKeage is now."

"No. No, we didn't find anything. He really is hurt."

Eric shoved her in the direction she'd come from. "The diary says the gold is north of here. So let's just go see."

Sadie bent, picked up Daar's cane, and pretended to use it as a crutch. With a final look over her shoulder at where Faol had disappeared and a prayer that the wolf wasn't too badly hurt, Sadie started limping back toward the stream.

"Why are you doing this?" she asked as she set a course slightly northwest of where Father Daar was. "I want this park as much as you do. I would have told you the moment I found Jedediah's gold."

Eric laughed. "The park's not important to me, Quill. Granted, I'll make a good chunk of money off my land once the park's in operation, but I'd much rather find the gold. Why in hell do you think I talked the consortium into hiring you?"

Sadie stopped and whirled on him. "You shot Morgan over some gold that might not even exist? Are you nuts?"

He aimed the beam of his flashlight down the trail behind them, then poked her with it to get her moving again. "My great-granddaddy wasn't nuts," he said, walking behind her, keeping his beam scanning the woods. "Old Levi Hellman financed the store I now run with what gold Plum was carrying on him when he died."

"Your great-grandfather? Did he . . . was he the one who murdered Jedediah?"

Eric shrugged. "Who the hell knows? Or even cares now? I just know that the Hellmans came into a good chunk of money eighty years ago, and there were stories passed down in our family that speculated about where it came from. And I'm guessing your daddy had heard the rumors, too. That's why he never would discuss his search for the gold with me. And I know he was close to succeeding when the fire destroyed all his research."

"How do you know that?"

"I knew he had Jean Lavoie's diary. I saw his copy."

"When?"

"The night of the fire," he said, his voice low and angry. "And if your sister hadn't caught me, I would have gotten it then."

Sadie whirled on him again, stumbling back when he bumped into her. "What are you saying?"

She could just make out Eric's sneer in the glow of

his flashlight. "I'm saying that your sister didn't burn in the fire, Quill. She was already dead."

She lunged at him with a shriek of anger, one hand coiled into a claw, the cane raised to strike in the other. They went tumbling to the ground, and Sadie tried to reach for his gun as they fought. He hit her on the side of her head with the flashlight, momentarily stunning her with the blow.

Eric rolled to his feet, his gun back in his hand, and kicked her. "After the fire, I spent the next five years trying to talk Frank into resuming his research," he continued as if nothing had happened. "But he'd lost his passion for the hunt. He wouldn't even tell me where he'd found the diary when I alluded to it. I couldn't come right out and mention the diary, because I wasn't supposed to know he had it."

"Then how did you?" Sadie asked, rising onto her hands and knees, clutching the cane in her fist.

"I only knew Frank had found something important. He couldn't wait for you to get home from school. He was like a kid with the key to the candy store."

Sadie glared at him past the flashlight beam. "So you broke into our house and tried to steal what he'd found."

Eric nodded. "But then Caroline came into the study. You really had left a candle burning, Quill," he continued derisively. "Your sister was covering your ass. But we struggled, and that's how the fire started. We knocked over the candle, and Lavoie's diary burned before I could get to it."

Sadie stood up, and Eric took a guarded step back, raising his gun.

"You're a murderer," she said in a low voice. "You killed my sister eight years ago, and you tried to kill me yesterday."

She could just make out that he was shaking his head. "No. It was Morgan MacKeage I was aiming at. Why in hell would I want to kill you?" he asked incredulously. "You're the only one who knows this valley."

"And now I know you're a murderer."

He nodded. "That doesn't matter now. Where's the gold?"

Sadie realized then that he intended to kill her. And that she needed a way to stall for time until Morgan could get here. Surely he'd heard the gunshots. "So where did you really find the diary you gave me?"

He laughed again, somewhat insanely. "I searched every museum in this state for eight years. But those bumbling Dolans managed to find it first. They came into the store last winter bragging their fool heads off that they had the next best thing to a map. And that's when I started making plans to get you back here."

"Why didn't you just work out a deal with Dwayne and Harry?"

He scoffed, waving the gun in the air. "With those two? Between them they don't even have a full brain."

"They found the diary."

"And I found a way to get it from them. Now, where's the gold, Quill?"

"It doesn't exist," she said. "I've already searched this entire side of the mountain. I found the cliff mentioned in the diary, but there was nothing there."

"You're lying." He took a threatening step toward

her, his face twisted in anger in the beam of his flashlight.

"But I did find placer gold in a stream near here," she quickly amended, taking a step back.

He stopped and was silent for several seconds, apparently trying to decide if he believed her or not. Sadie held the cane up in supplication and reached into her pocket with her other hand. She slowly drew out one gold nugget and held it up for Eric to see.

"This is what I found," she said in a voice that belied the anger she felt, handing him the nugget. "It's large, Eric. It must have been close to the source. You could probably be rich just panning that stream. I don't think there's an actual mine, Eric. I think Jedediah found only this heavy placer gold."

He put the nugget into his shirt pocket, then took his flashlight and waved it at the trail. "Then let's go, Quill. Show me."

Sadie turned and started them back in the direction of the stream, frantically thinking of what she should do next. Where the hell was her husband?

And where should she lead Eric? To Prospect River? Or to the stream? She could buy a couple of hours waiting for Morgan to show up by taking Eric to the stream well below the pool and then pretend to search for the exact spot where she'd found the nugget.

Sadie clasped Daar's cane protectively to her chest, then remembered it was supposed to be her crutch. She started using it like a cane and tried to think of a way to make the magic work for her without blowing them all to kingdom come.

What had the old priest mumbled to the cane when

he started the fire? She needed to be able to speak to the cane. And the only word she knew in Gaelic was *hedgehog*.

Morgan snapped his head up at the sound of gunfire echoing down the mountain. It was coming not from where Mercedes should have been waiting safely for him but from the old logging camp, where she'd probably gone.

He knew she wouldn't stay put.

Morgan turned his gaze down the mountain to where Grey and Callum were trying to drive anyone lurking in the woods toward him. But they probably still were a couple of miles away. Ian had been posted at the river, protecting everyone's back.

Sweat now covering his forehead, Morgan abandoned his post and started running upstream at an angle that sent him toward the logging camp, hoping to intercept whoever had fired those shots.

As they finally neared the stream, Sadie began speaking to Eric again, her voice loud enough that she hoped it would warn Morgan of her presence and that she was not alone.

She hoped Morgan had heard Eric's gunshots. An hour was enough time for Morgan to run to her rescue, wasn't it?

And Sadie worried about Faol. Was the wolf fatally wounded? Dead? Or was he quietly following them?

"How did you find the logging camp?" Sadie asked, still walking with a pretend limp, still trying to stall for time.

"That pack you picked up last Sunday," Eric said. "I sewed a transmitter into the bottom of it."

Sadie stopped and looked back. "A transmitter?"

"I sell them for hunting dogs," he told her, nudging her shoulder to keep her moving. "They're good for more than two miles."

"But why, Eric? Why leave me alone for ten weeks and then suddenly start interfering?"

"Because the Dolans arrived. And I heard about your date with MacKeage, and I didn't like the distraction he was making for you. So I decided it was time I intervened."

"Why ransack my cabin? It was you, wasn't it?"

"Because you always keep a journal, and I hoped you had made notes from Lavoie's diary. That day I brought you the photos, I was going to look for it."

They finally reached the stream, and the anger of knowing she'd been forced to walk and talk calmly with the man who had murdered her sister threatened to boil over. Sadie stopped beside the water and turned, forcing herself to be calm.

"This is it," she said in an even tone, using Daar's cane to point at the stream. "This is where I found the nugget."

"Where?" he asked, scanning the rippling water with the beam of his flashlight.

"Just up there." Sadie pointed at where she could hear the water churning over a sharp drop of ledge. "There's a tiny bowl that forms an eddy just below that ledge. And the bottom of the pool is littered with nuggets."

She led him to the small eddy. Sadie turned so

that Eric wouldn't see her reach into her pocket and palmed a handful of the nuggets, hiding them in her fist as she made her way to the edge of the small pool over the falls.

"There!" she yelled over the noise of the rippling cascade, throwing the nuggets into the churning water. "Shine your light there, at the eddy."

As she had hoped, Eric took one last cautious look around and tucked his gun into his belt. He scrambled over the strewn boulders to the edge of the eddy and shone his flashlight into the pool of water.

Faint bits of gold sparkled back at him.

Sadie took a small step away from him, into the blackness of the forest, but stopped when Eric turned his flashlight on her.

"Get down here," he said. "Hold the light for me."

Taking a look around, Sadie sighed and climbed down to Eric. Where in hell was Morgan? She may have foolishly gotten herself into this mess, but he was supposed to get her out of it.

She crouched beside Eric. The moment he tried to hand her the flashlight, Sadie took Daar's cane and smacked him over the back, putting all the force of her anger behind the blow. She heard Eric splashing in the pool as he tried to get back to his feet in the water. He shouted for her to stop, but she continued to run until gunfire erupted and tree bark exploded beside her. Sadie stopped and slowly turned around. Eric was standing in the pool, water dripping from his hair and clothes, the beam of his flashlight glinting off the barrel of his gun. He cocked the hammer to fire again, and aimed the weapon at her chest.

"Wait," she said, "I lied. This is nothing," she added, waving at the nuggets in the water. "There's more gold upstream than you could carry in a lifetime. But it's hidden. I can show you were it is."

Eric was silent for several seconds, then suddenly he waved the gun. "Then let's go. But if you run again, Quill," he added in a snarl as he stepped out of the pool, "I won't miss next time."

Chapter Twenty-two

Sadie led the way toward the magical pool, where she hoped Father Daar and his Gaelic words would make the cane do something magical to save them.

Where was Morgan? And Callum and the others? Why wasn't this mountain teeming with warriors, dammit?

Sadie saw the glow of the grotto ahead and breathed a sigh of relief.

"What's that light?" Eric asked from behind her.

"It must be coming daybreak."

"We're on the west side of the mountain," he countered, moving up beside her and peering through the tall trees. "The sun won't reach here for hours."

"It's a very high waterfall. Hear it, Eric? It sends up a mist that the sun's rays must be touching. It's filtering the light down."

Sadie led him through the trees until they reached the edge of the large, shimmering pool. She inconspicuously searched for Father Daar, but the priest was nowhere in sight.

Suddenly, she spotted him on the far side of the pool, just to the left of the waterfall. He was frantically tugging on the branch of a cherrywood tree. Sadie immediately led Eric to the right side of the pool and spoke loudly, trying to warn Father Daar of their presence.

"Wait until you see it, Eric. The entire floor of the cave is covered in gold nuggets."

She saw Father Daar shoot upright and whirl to face them. And then the old priest ducked behind the tree he'd been tugging on. He quietly pulled on a back branch instead.

"Where is it, Quill?" Eric asked, stopping and staring up at the towering cliffs surrounding them. "Where's the gold?"

"It's there, hidden by the falls," she said, using the cane to point to the far end of the pool. "Just walk behind it."

He nudged her forward with his gun. "You go first."

"I can't," she said, leaning heavily on the cane. "Just let me rest here for a minute."

She started to sit down, but Eric grabbed her arm and pulled her along after him. There was a loud snap from Daar's direction, and Sadie watched in horror as the branch he'd been tugging on broke free and fell on top of him.

"Who the hell is that?" Eric hissed, turning his gun toward the priest.

Sadie rapped Eric's hand with her cane, but he didn't drop the gun, instead whirling to pull her off balance. At the same time, an angry roar came from the lower end of the pool. Sadie saw Morgan standing with his sword in his hand at the entrance to the grotto.

And Faol was standing just in front of Morgan, his hackles raised and his teeth bared. Blood slowly oozed from where Eric's bullet had grazed his chest, but the wound didn't keep Faol from growling at Eric.

With his arm now firmly around her neck, Eric started backing away, pulling her deeper into the pool. "I'll kill her, MacKeage!" he shouted, touching the barrel of his gun to her head. "Slowly walk over to your right, to the cliff wall."

"*Tàs as,*" Morgan hissed at Faol, using his knee to push him to the right. In unison, Morgan and the wolf moved toward the cliff.

"Remember the magic, girl!" Father Daar shouted.

Having forgotten about the priest, Eric whirled in his direction, spinning Sadie with him.

Father Daar pointed a finger at her. "Use it!"

Sadie was violently turned around again at the sound of a growl, and a gunshot rang out beside her head. Sadie screamed when she saw Morgan, running toward her with his sword raised, fold in half and fall to the ground. Faol lunged from the edge of the pool, and Eric stepped back and fired again.

Sadie slammed her cane into Eric's ribs. "No!" she screamed, striking him again, struggling to get free and reach Morgan.

Faol knocked them both off balance enough that Sadie was able to push Eric away and scramble to the edge of the pool. She reached Morgan just as another gunshot sounded, the bullet ricocheting off the ground beside them. Morgan rolled in a blur of movement, pulling Sadie with him as he grabbed the cane out of her hand.

He rose to his knees with his back to her, one hand grasping the cane, the other hand covered in blood pressed against his side. He held the cane over his head, pointed it at Eric, and shouted something in Gaelic.

Lightning suddenly cracked with blinding brilliance through the air, charging the mist with a rainbow of colors. The ground beneath them began to tremble. The cliffs began to groan and rumble. Large chunks of granite broke from the towering walls and fell into the water with thunderous splashes.

Eric's gun fired several more times. Light swirled through the grotto, and Sadie could no longer see Eric as he became surrounded by black whorls clawing at him through the mist.

Sadie screamed, not understanding what was happening.

Morgan continued to shout, the cane in his hand sparking with blinding energy. The mountain groaned louder, violently shaking as if trying to shrug off the chaos. Huge blocks of granite fell around them. Uprooted trees came crashing down, vibrating the earth with deadly shivers.

Black fingers chilled with the stench of death swirled past her, the howl of their rage making Sadie's ears hurt. She saw Eric clearly for one blinding moment, running to where she had told him the gold was, as the fingers reached him, clawing menacingly. She could hear his screams.

And her own. She could hear the mountain growling as it crashed around them. Morgan turned and pushed her, telling her to run.

But Sadie couldn't move.

Morgan slammed into her, throwing them both back against a large piece of the fallen granite wall. He used his body to cover hers as chunks of debris rained down around them with such relentless violence that she could no longer hear her own screams. The air detonated with the percussion of a sonic boom, and the cane in Morgan's hand whispered a mournful sigh before it simply dissolved into ash.

And the chaos suddenly stopped.

Silence replaced it. The air was still. The earth no longer rumbled, and the sound of the waterfall had ceased.

Sadie blinked in the dim light of dawn breaking over the summit of Fraser Mountain and looked past Morgan's shoulder. Destruction lay everywhere like a volcanic eruption. A gaping hole had opened several hundred yards deep into the mountain, and the sharp cliffs that had formed the grotto now lay crumbled into talus. The waterfall had been sealed off, the gold and most of the pool now deeply buried beneath boulders. The giant trees, most of them uprooted, some of them still standing but with their tops snapped off, littered the ground like discarded toothpicks.

The destruction was complete.

"Morgan!" she screamed, grabbing his shoulders and wiggling out from under his limp body. "Morgan!" she repeated, shaking him. "Answer me!"

There was a cut on his head, but his side was bubbling red with blood from one tiny hole from Eric's bullet. More blood spread at the ground beneath him, soaking his shirt all the way down to his pants. His eyes were closed. His breathing was shallow. His face was pale as death.

Sadie dug at the boulders pinning his legs, whimpering with frustration when she couldn't budge them.

Father Daar stumbled over and knelt beside them.

"Do something!" Sadie shouted at him. "Use your magic!"

"I have none!" Daar snapped back, adding his own weight to hers. "It was used up in the destruction."

Sadie spotted Morgan's sword lying beside him. She grabbed it and started prying at the boulders.

The sword suddenly broke, sending both Sadie and Father Daar stumbling backward. Sadie lifted the hilt that she was still holding, staring in horror at what she had done.

"Oh my God. I broke his sword."

She scrambled back and knelt down to cup Morgan's face. "Hold on, my love," she whispered, touching her lips to his ear. "You hold on," she ordered when he didn't respond.

Sadie was suddenly grabbed by the shoulders and pushed away so violently that she swallowed her gasp. A tall, dark-haired giant with eyes the exact same color as Morgan's replaced her at Morgan's head, running a large hand over her husband's face.

"We'll have you out in a minute," the stranger said, putting his shoulder into the larger of the two boulders.

Callum suddenly appeared and set his own shoulder to the rock, both men grunting and straining and cursing. Sadie sat on the ground and placed her feet just below their hands to add her own strength. Even Father Daar used smaller rocks to hold up the boulder each time it moved.

The stranger stopped, catching his breath, and looked at the situation. He walked to the back of the rock and started working, throwing debris out of the way. Callum found a stout branch and set it to pry against the boulder, only to stop suddenly and lift out the broken tip of Morgan's sword.

"I hope ya can run fast," Callum said. "Because just as soon as Morgan is well enough to stand, he'll come after you."

"Oh, please hurry," Sadie whispered. "He's bleeding to death." She turned to the priest. "Isn't there something you can do?"

Both Callum and the stranger—Sadie realized he was Morgan's brother, Greylen MacKeage—looked at the priest with Sadie. Father Daar slowly shook his head. "My staff was destroyed, and so was the waterfall. There's nothing left."

Faol suddenly appeared, limping over and washing Morgan's face, whining and pawing at the boulder.

"Get that beast away from him," Greylen said harshly, moving to kick the wolf.

"Nay," Father Daar said. "He's only worried about his son."

"His son?" Greylen whispered, his face paling as he snapped his eyes back to the priest.

Daar turned red in the face. "I'm guessing, MacKeage. But I have a notion Duncan's been visiting us this summer," he said, waving at the wolf.

All four of them turned to stare at Faol, who was now looking at them with unblinking green eyes. He whined again and pushed at the boulder with his nose.

Greylen and Callum went back to work. They were suddenly joined by another pair of large, strong-looking hands, and Sadie looked up to see an older man, with red hair and graying beard, putting his weight into the boulder.

"Ian," Greylen said. "Be ready to pull him out the moment there's room. Woman," he snapped, looking at her. "Help him."

Sadie quickly moved more debris out of Ian's way, making room for Morgan to be pulled free. With a lot of grunting and another fair amount of cursing, Callum and Greylen put their backs into the task. The boulder moved mere inches, and Ian roughly pulled Morgan free of his prison, continuing to drag him until his feet were clear of the boulder.

Sadie immediately crawled to Morgan and ripped open his shirt. Blood gushed into her hands.

Greylen grabbed her by the shoulders again and roughly set her to the side. "You've done enough to him. Get her out of here, Daar."

There was such anger emanating from Morgan's older brother that Sadie backed away on her own. She wiped her husband's blood on her pants and turned to Father Daar.

"There has to be something we can do. What about the magical water? Th-that puddle's still shimmering."

The priest slowly made his way to the puddle, bent down, and stuck his finger in the water. He looked up to where he'd been standing when she and Eric had arrived. Sadie followed his gaze. The cherry tree he'd been trying to break was splintered into a thousand pieces. He looked back at her.

"You can get there better than me, girl," he whispered. "Go look for a cherry burl in that mess. The tree's been growing in blessed water for more than two years now. Maybe some of the magic is hiding there."

Sadie crawled over the rocks to the far edge of what had once been the pool.

"Find a big burl!" the priest shouted. "From the root if ya can."

It took all of her strength, but Sadie was able to dig a knot free from the roots of the cherry tree. She hurried back to Father Daar and handed him the small piece of wood.

"This is all I could find," she whispered, anxiously glancing toward Morgan.

Greylen had taken off his shirt and wrapped it around Morgan's wound. He was now checking Morgan's legs for broken bones. Sadie looked back at the priest.

He was frowning. "I don't think it's enough," he said, sadly shaking his head. "It's wanting the strength of the water and my old staff. Already I can feel it losing its vitality."

Sadie reached out and touched his arm. "Please. We have to do something. We'll never get Morgan to town in time."

The moment she touched him, Daar's eyes widened in surprise. He covered her hand with his own, his mouth suddenly lifting into a smile.

"It's in you, girl," he said in a voice filled with awe. He turned to face her and touched her with both hands, holding the knot of cherrywood against her skin. "There's magic left. It's here," he said, turning her right hand palm up. "In you."

"What do you mean?"

"When ya were healed," he told her, rubbing her unscarred palm with his finger. "The burl dissolved because its energy went into you."

"And—and I can give it back?"

"Aye," he said, looking into her eyes. "Ya can."

"And I can heal Morgan?"

"Aye. I'm thinking it should be possible."

That was all she needed to know. Sadie jumped up and ran to her husband, pushing her way past his lethal-looking brother. Greylen stood up, took hold of her shoulders, and shook her.

"Ya've done enough," he snapped.

"I can do more!" she shouted, giving him a direct glare. "I have the wizard's magic in me."

He released her as if burned, stepping away and looking at the priest who had walked up beside them. Father Daar nodded.

"She has, MacKeage," Daar confirmed. "Your brother healed her with my own magic. She's carrying the energy of my staff in her body."

Greylen looked torn between wanting to believe it was possible and not wanting to let her anywhere near his brother.

"Please. Bring him over to the water," she entreated, taking the small cherry knot from Father Daar and walking to the water herself. "At least let me try," she added, holding out her hand. "He—he's my husband."

Again, Father Daar nodded confirmation to Greylen. "Aye, MacKeage. I married them myself just yesterday."

Greylen scanned the destruction around them, then looked down at his dying brother. He bent and picked Morgan up and carried him to the small puddle of water. Callum and Ian quietly followed. Faol trotted past her and around the puddle and lay down with a whine, his nose touching the water.

Sadie stepped into the puddle and sat down, holding open her arms to receive Morgan. Greylen gently settled him on her lap.

Father Daar came over and crouched beside her. "There's just one wee little problem, Mercedes," he whispered.

Greylen and Callum and Ian leaned closer to hear what the priest was saying.

"What's that, Father?" Sadie asked, not caring if they did hear.

"The magic . . . well . . . I don't know what will happen to ya, when ya give it up to your husband."

Sadie snapped her gaze to his. "Will I go back to when I was shot?"

Father Daar nodded hesitantly. "Aye, that is possible. But I don't really know." He shrugged. "I can't predict what the energy will do when passed through a mortal."

Sadie realized all three men standing over her were collectively holding their breath, waiting for her decision. They couldn't know that there simply was no decision to make. She didn't care if she bled to death right here in this puddle. She was not letting Morgan die.

She took the cherry knot and held it against Morgan's chest, brushing the hair back from his face with her other hand.

"No, girl. Hold the burl with your right hand," Father Daar instructed. "That will have the most powerful energy."

Sadie switched hands but hesitated, holding the knot just off Morgan.

"Wh-what will happen?" she whispered. "How do I know I won't kill him? Look what happened to this beautiful place when Morgan had your cane. What if all I create is just more destruction?"

Father Daar was shaking his head before she finished her question. "The wood is only a conductor of energy, Mercedes. Morgan was desperate and angry when he held the cane, and it was his wrath the magic brought down on us. But you're yearning for something good. Ya won't kill him."

Sadie set the knot of cherrywood over Morgan's wound, closed her eyes, and wished with all her heart for him to be healed.

The palm of her right hand suddenly started to warm. Light arced around her, filling her head with colors. She started to tremble as her whole body tightened with prickly heat. She could hear the blood rushing through her veins, feel it pulsing down her arm and into her hand, smell the halo of ozone that suddenly wafted around her.

Her belly churned. Her back felt on fire, the intense heat shooting through her middle. A sharp pain stabbed down the length of her left arm. Her lungs and ribs felt crushed.

She could feel her flesh burning, almost smell it.

A hand touched her shoulder, and a voice whispered beside her ear. "Send it into him, Mercedes," Father Daar instructed from a great distance. "Push, girl. Send the energy to Morgan."

Sadie concentrated on moving the heat. She held her palm fiercely against Morgan's side, pushing the knot of wood into his wound. Fire shot through her body. Her muscles trembled. Sadie fought not to lose consciousness, to keep the energy flowing to Morgan.

And slowly, ever so slowly, his heartbeat grew stronger.

And that made *her* stronger.

Sadie focused her thoughts. She pictured Morgan being healthy in her mind's eye, saw him laughing, glowing with the fire of passion as he made love to her. She saw him swimming naked in the lake, felt his patience even when he was angry with her. And she heard him calling her *gràineag* in a tone that was anything but endearing.

And Sadie sent him her love.

The green light that had faded in the destructive storm suddenly flashed and throbbed around her, sparking to a brilliant white before settling back into the gentle and steady glow of winter spruce.

"I had a dream," came Morgan's whispered voice.

Sadie pulled the sleeve of her shirt over her right hand and brushed the hair from his face as she smiled down at him.

"Did you see your mother and father?" she asked softly.

"My mum," he answered. "Da wasn't there."

Because he's here, Sadie thought to herself, peeking at the wolf who now had his nose tucked firmly against Morgan's arm.

"I'm so sleepy, wife," Morgan muttered, closing his eyes.

"Then sleep, husband," she whispered, stroking his chest in comforting circles. "And know that I love you."

Chapter Twenty-three

$\mathcal{D}$aar sat on a rock in the middle of the destroyed and deserted grotto and glared at the rubble created by Morgan's desperate attempt to save his wife's life.

It seemed all the magic was not gone. He could still feel something quietly humming, energizing the air. The wizard kicked the splinters of cherrywood at his feet. A small branch from one of the trees that had grown here must have escaped the destruction. He just couldn't find the damned source of the hum.

With a weary sigh, Daar sat down on one of the smaller rocks and stared at the dig marks Morgan had made. When the warrior had awakened from his sleep and had been told that Mercedes had run away, Morgan hadn't flown into a rage as they'd all been expecting. No, he'd simply gotten up, stared at the destruction he'd wrought, and asked what had happened to Eric Hellman.

Greylen had silently pointed to the pile of rubble

that had once been the cliff at the far end of what had once been the pool. Morgan had walked over, pushed a few rocks out of the way, and started digging until he had amassed a small pile of gold nuggets. He'd tied the nuggets up in his shirt and then climbed the rubble, using his considerable strength to finish the destruction. Morgan had rained a final avalanche of boulders down over Hellman's grave, then dusted off his hands and walked away.

Daar continued to search for that small hint of magic that seemed to have survived. He needed a new staff, and it would be nice if he could find a branch from this place. The cherrywood growing here had soaked up the magical energy from the waters that had flowed from the high mountain lake. This was blessed wood, and a cane from here would be much easier to train.

Daar wanted one now more than ever. He didn't care to be powerless when it came to dealing with the MacKeages. For mere mortals, they were proving themselves powerful enough in their own right.

Faol suddenly stepped into sight, trotting over to one of the small remaining puddles. He took a drink, lazily lapping at the water for several minutes, before he lifted his head and stared at Daar.

"Duncan, ya old warmonger," Daar said, not unkindly. "Your sons have found themselves good lives here. There's no need for ya still to be hanging around."

Faol rumbled a growl from his chest and turned and started climbing over the rubble. The wolf briefly disappeared from sight. He reappeared just off to

Daar's right, holding a two-foot-long stick in his mouth.

With a shout of surprise, Daar jumped to his feet. "That's my old staff!" he yelped, quickly scrambling over the rubble to reach the wolf. "The half Grey threw away two years ago. Give that to me!"

Faol trotted toward the valley.

"Hey! Get back here, you damn dog!" Daar shouted, awkwardly following him. "That's my staff!"

His tail wagging like a banner of victory, Faol picked up his pace and continued down the winding and now dry streambed, Daar's staff held in his mouth like a prize of war.

The aging wizard ran until he was out of breath and couldn't go on, bending over with his hands on his knees, tiredly panting, overjoyed to know his old staff had shot free of the waterfall before it had closed, and frustrated that it was still out of his reach.

A howl came to Daar then, climbing up the side of the valley toward him in maddening echoes of triumph.

Daar sat down on a nearby log, pulling his white collar from his frock and undoing three buttons. God's teeth, but he was reaching the end of his patience. He kept losing his magic.

He shook his weary head in dismay. He'd had that old staff with him for more than fourteen hundred years, a gift from his mentor when Daar had been a young man of seventy-nine. And in only two years the MacKeages had managed to destroy not only it but the new staff he'd been training for Greylen and Grace's unborn daughter, Winter.

All that remained of his magic was now being

carried away by a mean-spirited wolf. And just what was Daar going to tell Grey's seventh daughter, Winter, when she came to him a grown woman ready to become a wizard?

Daar stood up finally, having caught most of his breath back. He needed that two-foot piece of his old staff. Faol couldn't actually take it with him when he went back to wherever he came from. Spirits crossed over; material things did not.

With a disheartened sigh filled with self-pity, Daar stopped chasing the wolf and started walking instead in the direction of Michael MacBain's home. Perhaps it was time he got better acquainted with MacBain and his young son while he searched for his old staff, which he was determined to find. Until then, he was staying the hell away from the MacKeages.

It took Sadie two hours to make it to the logging camp, and for every step of the way, she wished she had the old priest's cane. Not for its magic but for the help it would give her to walk.

She had sneaked away from the MacKeages and Father Daar like a thief, not wanting to face Greylen's wrath any longer—and definitely too cowardly to face Morgan when he woke up.

The beautiful gorge he'd tried so hard to protect was completely destroyed, thanks to her. He'd revealed its location and its magic in order to save her life and then had destroyed it saving her life a second time.

And she had nothing to give him in return. She didn't even have her beauty anymore, which he had so greatly enjoyed yesterday when they'd spent the afternoon making love.

Even the gold was out of reach now.

But for that she was glad.

Morgan was right. Gold made people do terrible things. It turned them into murderers.

Sadie unzipped the fly on the tent to pulled out her sleeping bag, which she tied to the pack Eric had left discarded on the ground. The pack, the sleeping bag, and the food would allow Sadie to survive for the next few days, until she could decide what to do.

For the entire next day, Morgan quietly followed his wife, patiently waiting for Mercedes to get over her bout of self-pity. He was anxious to bring her home and finally start their peaceful union, but he was keeping his distance for now, for her sake. It appeared she needed this time to think about everything that had happened over the last couple of days.

And so he sat in the shadows of the night, watching her sleep. He'd seen her bathe this morning, and his worry had lessened that the magic she had given him to save his life would take hers. He had seen the scars from the house fire covering her body again and the place where Eric Hellman's bullet had pierced her skin. And Morgan had silently thanked God that not all the magic had been pulled from Mercedes' body. Enough had been left to make healing only a matter of time. Already she had gained back most of her strength.

But the scars that had killed half of her family would always remain. Morgan didn't care as long as she was well.

She cared, though, he feared. She'd been so open with him that day in the pool after the magic had healed her body. Morgan sighed, wondering if Mercedes would ever be that free with him again.

He would demand that she be.

No. He would beg.

He loved her more than he loved life and was growing tired of this directionless pilgrimage his strong-minded wife insisted on traveling. How the hell long did it take to realize her heart belonged to him?

Morgan settled himself more comfortably against the tree, pulled his plaid more warmly around him, and closed his eyes with another sigh. If she didn't soon come around, he'd have to give Mercedes a bit of a push and see what sort of results he got. His *gràineag* would either run deeper into the valley or come up spitting and swinging and cursing.

He hoped with all his heart it would be the latter.

Sadie rolled out of her sleeping bag and quickly danced to the fire and stirred it up, adding first kindling and then large branches to coax it back into flames. She set her battered pot full of water on the grate, willing it to hurry up and boil as she rubbed her hands together and held them over the stingy fire.

It was time that she quit sulking. She would go to Morgan today and explain to him that no matter what had happened, they belonged together.

But first she had to find the Dolan brothers. She still had a bit of gold left in her pocket, and she'd give them the nuggets and let them know there was nothing left.

Sadie drank her coffee, broke camp, and headed south along the bank of the Prospect. Her resolve to set Morgan straight on how things would be between them added momentum to her pace.

But within ten minutes, Sadie realized she was being followed. And within another three minutes, she recognized her stalker.

"Come out here, big boy," Sadie cajoled with an eager laugh, clapping her hands to call him.

Faol stepped into her path not five paces in front of her, his big green eyes looking sappy, his tongue hanging out of his mouth, his ears perked forward, and his tail wagging a mile a minute.

"I'm so glad you're okay," Sadie said, walking forward and patting his broad head.

Sadie continued along the bank of the Prospect with her silent traveling companion, until she finally came to a large green canoe pulled up onshore. She stopped to signal Faol to stay back, only to realize the wolf had disappeared. Sadie turned from the river and traveled inland about a hundred yards.

"Hello the camp!" she called out. "Don't shoot. It's me."

"Missy Sadie Quill—oh, I mean Mrs. Sadie MacKeage," Dwayne said excitedly, bolting to his feet and running to greet her, waving like crazy. "What brings you out here today? I thought you'd be home cooking dinner for your new husband." He waggled his finger at her. "Feeding Morgan is going to be a full-time job."

Sadie narrowed her eyes at Dwayne. "It's Morgan now? What happened to 'that MacKeage guy'?"

Dwayne reddened in the face slightly. "He said we could call him Morgan, Sadie." He suddenly grinned. "I like your new husband. He ate my stew and belched loud enough to wake the bears."

It was Sadie who got red in the face all of a sudden, and it wasn't embarrassment. "Morgan was here? When?"

"Yesterday," Dwayne told her, frowning. "Didn't he tell you he was coming to see us? And what he was doing?"

"Ah, yeah. He did mention it," she quickly prevaricated.

Dwayne suddenly snapped his mouth shut, his frown turning into a glare as he waggled a finger at her again, this time scolding. "You just never mind, missy. I don't know nothing."

"Where's Harry?" Sadie asked, looking over Dwayne's shoulder at the camp behind him.

Dwayne stepped to the left to block her view. "Harry's in town buying us some supplies."

Sadie sighed and rubbed her forehead. "It's okay, Dwayne. The reason I'm not home cooking for my husband is that I'm checking to see if Morgan really did come visit you and that he did what he said he was going to do."

Her convoluted words nicely confusing him, Dwayne frowned again. He thought for a minute, shook his head, and suddenly smiled at her.

"I guess I can show you. Since the gift's really from you and all," he whispered, as if afraid even the trees might hear what he was saying.

He shot a suspicious look around the rim of his

campsite, then excitedly waved Sadie over to some boxes stacked by a honeysuckle bush. He put his finger to his lips for her to be quiet and looked around again just before he crouched down on his knees.

Sadie took a look around herself and then bent to see what he was doing. Dwayne pushed several of the boxes out of the way and started digging in the dirt.

"We hid it good, didn't we?" he whispered, pawing the sand away like a groundhog.

"You surely did," Sadie quietly agreed, shrugging her pack off her back and kneeling beside him.

Sadie gasped when Dwayne pulled a quart-sized Mason jar out of the ground and brushed the sand off it. "You hid it real good," she whispered in awe, blinking at the jar full of gold nuggets.

Dwayne continued to pet the jar, reverently cleaning every speck of sand off it with a slightly trembling hand.

"Morgan told me and Harry this was all the gold," he said, his voice still quiet and reverent. He looked at her, clutching the jar to his chest and grinning like a child at the circus. "That you and him found Jedediah's gold, Sadie, and that you want us to have it. That you don't need it none, being you have a rich husband now."

Unable to speak, Sadie nodded, feeling her face heat again. Dwayne suddenly grabbed her around the neck and noisily and very wetly kissed her shocked mouth.

And then he scrambled back, the gold still clutched to his chest, his own face as red as a sunset. He shot a look around his campsite with wide, horrified eyes.

"I—I didn't mean to do that!" he yelped, his entire

neck and face now blistering red. "I mean, I . . . but . . ." He looked around the campsite again. "I don't want your husband to think I was . . . that I was . . ."

Sadie patted his arm and stood up, finally gathering her wits enough to smile at him. "It's okay, Dwayne. Morgan understands that you and Harry are my friends. He wouldn't take offense even if he were here. Which he isn't," she assured the still worried man.

Sadie reached a hand into her pocket and curled her fingers over the two gold nuggets she still possessed. She had planned to give them to Harry and Dwayne, but now the gesture seemed lame, considering she had apparently already given them a fortune.

Why had Morgan brought this gold to them?

And just where had he gotten it? Everything had been destroyed. The gold had been buried under thousands of tons of granite.

"Did Morgan tell you why he—I mean, why we gave you the gold?" Sadie asked, waving her hand at the jar Dwayne was still clutching.

"Because you don't need it none," he repeated, crawling on his knees to the honeysuckle bush. He put the jar back in the ground, carefully covered it up with sand, and set the boxes back over it.

"Did he tell you where we found the gold?" Sadie asked.

Dwayne looked at her and frowned. "No. We asked, but he wouldn't tell us nothing. He just said this was all of it, that there weren't no more."

He stood up and brushed off his hands, suddenly narrowing his eyes in suspicion. "Was he telling the truth, Sadie? Is this all of it?"

She nodded. "Best as we can tell, Dwayne. There wasn't really a mine. Jedediah had only found a large deposit of placer gold, not the source."

"Where?" he asked, cocking his head and squinting one eye. "Was it close to a logging camp? Say, about a mile or so north of the camp?"

Sadie shook her head. "Nope," she lied, smiling while she did, having already decided it would be best to guide the Dolans to look elsewhere. "It isn't even in this valley, Dwayne." She pointed toward the mountains. "It's in the next valley over, almost in Canada."

"The next valley!" Dwayne shouted, only to look quickly around himself again. He stepped closer, lowering his voice. "You mean, we've been searching the wrong valley all these years? Even Frank?" He narrowed his eyes again. "Your daddy thought it was near the Prospect. And Harry and me even found flakes of placer gold here."

Sadie shrugged. "We all thought it was here, Dwayne. But if you were to look in the valley to the west, you'd probably find several old logging camps."

"Where?" he whispered, taking another step closer. He set his face into a puppy-dog look of pleading. "Can you at least give me a hint, Sadie?"

"Why? It's all gone, Dwayne."

"But there might be more."

"Why do you need more?" she asked, waving toward the honeysuckle bush. "There's enough there to go to Russia and bring back a dozen wives if you want."

Dwayne was startled by the idea. "We don't want a

dozen," he said, looking horrified again. "We only need two." He suddenly grinned. "Morgan helped us pick them out."

"He what?"

Dwayne strode over to his tent, picked up a magazine, and came running back to her, leafing through the pages as he ran.

"Here," he said, slapping the page with his dirty, callused finger. "Morgan said I should pick this one."

Sadie leaned away to focus on the page that was now being held in front of her face. A fortyish woman was smiling back at her, looking shy and a whole lot scared.

Dwayne suddenly pulled the magazine back and turned to another page. He held it up to her again. "He said Harry should pick this lady," Dwayne said, pointing to another woman.

This one was a bit older, a bit more worn-looking, also smiling with what appeared to be . . . hope.

Sadie smiled at her old friend. "They're pretty, Dwayne," she said. "They look like they'll make you and Harry fine wives."

Dwayne moved beside her, held out the magazine, and leafed through it again. "I liked this one," he said, showing her the picture of a twenty-something woman. "I think she's beautiful."

"She is."

Dwayne looked over at Sadie, his mouth lifted at one corner, his dusty gray-hazel eyes shining with wisdom. He was shaking his head at her.

"Morgan said she wasn't beautiful," Dwayne told her with authority, nodding his head in agreement with her husband. "Morgan said beauty isn't here," Dwayne elaborated, tapping the young woman's face. "That's it's here," he explained, quickly turning the page to the woman Morgan had chosen for him. Dwayne touched his finger to the older woman's eyes, then let it trail down to stop just below the photo, where her heart would be.

"Morgan said me and Harry have to look really deep below the surface to find beauty in a woman. That if we're wanting good wives, we won't be tricked by a pretty face." Dwayne squinted one eye at her, letting the magazine drop to his side. "Like you, Sadie," he said.

"Like me? Morgan said like me?"

"Naw," Dwayne said, shaking his head again. "I'm saying it. Look at your hand," he told her, waving toward her gloved right hand. "And I know you got other scars. But that didn't stop Morgan none from picking you." He smiled and touched her hair. "Because you got yourself a wise husband, Sadie. He looked real deep and saw your beauty."

A lump the size of a boulder got stuck in Sadie's throat.

Dwayne let his finger slide down her hair until he could tug on the end of it, his grin warm and his voice tender. "You're a beautiful lady, Sadie," he said in a whisper. "I only hope my new wife is half as pretty as you are."

Sadie threw herself into Dwayne's arms and struggled to hold back tears born of the fear and uncertainty of the last three days. Her old friend wrapped his arms around her, squeezing her tightly, and frantically apologized.

"Hell's bells, Sadie," he growled. "I didn't mean to make you cry!"

"You didn't," she said. "Morgan did."

Dwayne quickly set her away from him and scanned the bushes surrounding the campsite.

"I—I wasn't saying you're pretty because I want to steal you!" he shouted, backing away from Sadie as he spoke. "I was only trying to explain myself."

Sadie couldn't keep from smiling. "Oh, Dwayne. I didn't mean Morgan was here," she said. "What you said made me think of him, and that made me cry."

Dwayne relaxed slightly and lifted his brows at her. "Just thinking about your husband makes you cry?" he asked incredulously. He took a step closer. "What happens when you actually see him in person?"

"I smile."

Her answer confounded him. He scratched his dirty hair and squinted one eye at her.

"Does Morgan tell you you're beautiful?" Dwayne suddenly asked.

"Every day," she told him truthfully. "Without words."

"How's he do that?" Dwayne wanted to know, stepping closer.

"By his actions," Sadie explained. "By caring and worrying about me. By scolding and lecturing and bossing me around. By making me so mad sometimes I want to spit. He also teases me every chance he gets. He carries all the heavy supplies in his pack, lightening my load when we hike. He also makes sure I'm warm at night. And safe. And by doing all that, Dwayne, Morgan is telling me every minute of every day that I'm beautiful."

"Hell's bells, Sadie. Am I going to have to do that kind of stuff for my wife?"

Sadie wiped another threatening tear away and nodded. "You are. And you're going to love doing it, Dwayne. Because your wife will understand by your actions how much she means to you. Each small deed will tell her you think she's beautiful and that you cherish her and are glad she's agreed to share your life."

Dwayne suddenly frowned at the ground. "I probably will have to show her instead of tell her, like your Morgan does." He looked up, his expression confounded again. "Because I don't know Russian, Sadie. Me and Harry got us some tapes to listen to, but we just can't get the hang of the language. And, according to the book that came with the tapes, their alphabet is missing some letters and has some other ones that look mighty weird."

"The language of love is universal, Dwayne," Sadie assured him, walking to her pack and slinging it onto her shoulders. She walked back to Dwayne and touched his arm. "It's also timeless, I've discovered. Don't worry. You and Harry are going to do all right. Because," Sadie whispered, leaning over to kiss his blush-heated cheek, "*you* are beautiful, my good friend, deep down inside where it counts."

Sadie walked out of Dwayne's camp then and decided it was time she found her husband.

Chapter Twenty-four

$\mathscr{S}$adie knew the first rule of searching for someone was that the searchee had to stay put in order for the searcher to find him. If both parties wandered around in the same hundreds of square miles of forest, they likely would pass within yards of each other and not even know it.

But that theory only worked if the searchee really wished to be found, and it depended on how determined and tenacious the searcher was.

Sadie was very determined.

After wasting most of the afternoon hunting for Morgan, wearing out her boots and getting a sore throat from hollering his name over and over, Sadie finally conceded defeat. She knelt in front of Faol, who had suddenly appeared when she walked out of Dwayne's camp, and held his big head between her hands and pleaded with the animal to help her.

"You've got to find Morgan, big boy," she entreated,

getting her nose within inches of his. "Before he finds me first. It's important that I go to him with my heart in my hand and remind him again that he loves me."

Faol whined, darting out his tongue and lapping her chin, his wagging tail shaking his whole body. Gripping the tufts of hair on the sides of his face, Sadie held him away.

"Can you do that? Can you find Morgan for me?"

He tried to wash her face again, then barked when she wouldn't let him. Sadie let go and stood up, waving her hand at the forest.

"Go on, then. Go find Morgan," she told the wolf, giving him a nudge with her knee.

Faol barked again, spun on his feet, and took off at a run down the trail. Sadie tightened the waist belt of her pack and started jogging after him, the thrill of the chase lifting her spirits until she was laughing out loud.

Sadie lost sight of Faol but heard him bark someplace to her left. She turned off the trail and ducked under limbs, slowing to avoid getting poked in the face by low-hanging branches. She couldn't see Faol anymore, but the wolf was making enough noise to wake the dead.

Sadie broke onto a narrow game trail, this one obviously used by moose more than deer. She was able to stand upright and pick up her pace again, and within twenty minutes Sadie realized exactly where Faol was leading her.

And she laughed again, at the irony of what was happening. Because it wasn't all that long ago that she had been running down this very same trail—only away from a madman instead of toward him.

Faol had stopped at the edge of the lake. He was sitting down, his tail wagging the ground clean, and looking over his shoulder at her. He darted a look at the lake and then back at her, whining and standing up and padding over to touch her fingers. He carefully grasped the fingertips of her glove in his teeth and gently tugged.

Sadie took the hint. She pulled off her glove, knelt down, and took hold of his face again. "I know, big boy," she whispered. "I might be hardheaded sometimes, but I eventually figure things out. I—I'll take good care of your son, Mister MacKeage," she whispered. "I'll see that he's happy and very glad he came to live in this time. We'll give you some grand-babies and tell them all about your visit with us."

Faol whined and lapped her chin, then pulled his head free and turned and looked out at the lake again. He lifted his nose into the air and sent a howl over the valley that carried into the mountains on tremulous waves.

Faol then trotted off into the forest without looking back.

Sadie stepped to where the wolf had been standing and stared at Morgan sitting on the boulder in the middle of the cove, facing her, his large hands braced on the edge of the rock and his feet lazily stirring the water.

He was naked, of course, despite the fact that there was ice lacing the shore of the lake and the air was below freezing. Steam wafted from his wet shoulders, his breath puffed in gentle billows around his head, and the water dripping from his long blond hair made icicles on the rock beside him.

"I'm beautiful, Morgan."

"Aye, Mercedes, you are."

"And I'm your wife."

"I remember our vows."

"I—I'm a modern."

"Nobody promised us a perfect world, lass."

"I'll continue to be strong-minded . . . sometimes."

"Aye. But only sometimes, *gràineag.*"

"I know what that means now. And it's not an endearment."

"But it fits you so well, wife . . . sometimes."

Sadie scowled, thinking this wasn't going well. Not that she'd had a plan when she'd come searching for Morgan, but she had thought the man would be more . . . well, at least more eager to see her. Sadie took a deep breath and continued.

"I broke your sword."

"I noticed that."

"And your waterfall was destroyed."

"I noticed that, too."

"All the magic is gone, Morgan."

"Nay, lass. It's more powerful than ever."

"Dammit, Morgan. I want you to forgive me."

"I did that two days ago, Mercedes."

"Then why didn't you come for me?"

"Because you needed to forgive yourself first."

With trembling hands, Sadie swiped at the tears that had escaped and flowed down her cheeks. This was proving even harder than she'd thought. He was just sitting there like a turtle on a rock waiting for the sun to warm him, his infuriatingly patient and calmly given responses making her insides quake.

Maybe he was a turtle, and she was the sunshine he was waiting for.

"I'm beautiful."

"Aye, Mercedes, you are."

"And you love me."

"I must."

"Dammit, Morgan. This is hard."

"Only because it's important, Mercedes."

"I love you."

"I'm glad. But it's not me you must love, lass."

"I'm beautiful."

"Aye, wife. You are very beautiful."

With hands more shaky than useful, Sadie un-cinched the belt at her waist and let her pack slide off her shoulders, catching it and gently setting it on the ground without taking her eyes off her husband.

Morgan lazily watched her as she sat down and unlaced her boots and pulled them off. She tucked her socks inside them and then stood, her trembling hands going to the buttons on her shirt. It took her a long time to get the shirt open, and even longer to work up the nerve to slide it off her shoulders. She let the shirt fall to the ground, reached behind her back, and unhooked her bra, pulling both it and her body sock off, letting them fall to the ground.

And still she watched her husband.

And still he sat there, not saying a word, not moving, not taking his eyes off her.

Sadie unbuckled her belt and unsnapped her pants, pushing them down to her knees and stepping free.

She couldn't quit shaking, and she knew it wasn't the cold making her tremble. Every nerve ending, every taut muscle, every inch of her skin felt as if it were on fire.

She straightened her shoulders and forced her hands to her sides, now facing her husband as naked as he was.

"Do ya see that sunset behind me, lass?"

Sadie could only nod.

"I was sitting here waiting for you to come to me, and I was thinking how the sky is the color of your eyes. It's a very beautiful shade of blue, don't you think?"

She nodded again.

Morgan stood up and held out his hand. "Then come to me now, Mercedes. Bring your beauty into my life."

She took a step forward, and then another. Each step was a bit easier than the previous one, and soon Sadie was running to Morgan.

Until she was up to her knees in the ice-cold water. Sadie screamed at the feel of the icy water on her legs.

"Goddammit, MacKeage! This lake is freezing!" she shouted, scrambling back to the shore.

Morgan dove into the lake and swam until he could stand up. He rose, water cascading down his tall, masculine body, and waded toward her.

Sadie took a step back. Morgan had never looked more like a warrior to her, even though she'd seen him like this before. He was different somehow.

Or maybe she was.

Or maybe it had something to do with the unholy gleam in his eyes, the look of a warrior about to possess the prize of his hard-won battle.

Sadie took another step back.

Morgan had certainly waged a fine war, if not a subtle one. But then, Sadie suddenly thought, stepping toward him instead of away, the prize he was receiving was well worth the effort.

She ran and threw herself into his arms, grabbing his wet hair and kissing his wet face, laughing with the joy of knowing she was about to begin a dream life with this man. He wrapped his powerful arms around her and gently lowered them both to the ground, growling into her ear as he rained kisses through her hair.

With lusty words and whispered promises, Morgan told Sadie as much as he showed her just what he thought of her body. His hands roamed over her skin with feather-light touches, his lips following the trail of his fingers.

Sadie mimicked his actions and his words and made a few lusty promises of her own. She arched her back when his lips grazed her nipples, pushing her breasts into his mouth, yearning to be touched everywhere.

Nothing was off limits any longer. Nothing stood between them, nothing obstructed the pleasure of loving each other. Passion took precedence over shyness, and Sadie was able to give herself freely to the wonder of love.

They played and loved as they had that afternoon in the beautiful, mystical pool filled with the *drùidh's* magic. And Morgan hadn't been lying a moment ago when he'd said the magic was more powerful than ever.

The magic was stronger, their love a brilliant rainbow wrapped around the pure white light of their passion.

Pocket Star Books
Proudly Presents

Only With a Highlander

Janet Chapman

Now available in Paperback

Turn the page for a preview of
Only With a Highlander. . . .

Winter MacKeage lost the thread of the conversation the moment the large male figure stepped into view. Rose continued talking, however, oblivious to the fact that the most gorgeous man ever to set foot in Pine Creek had just stopped to look at the painting hanging in the front window of Winter's art gallery.

"Tell her I'm right," Rose demanded, nudging Winter's arm. "Tell Megan that no one is whispering behind her back. Hey," Rose said more loudly, grabbing Winter's sleeve to draw her back into the conversation. "Your sister thinks everyone in town pities her."

Winter looked away from the divine apparition in the window and blinked at Rose, trying to remember what they had been talking about.

Rose sighed. "Darn it, Winter, help me out here. Tell Megan she's not the center of town gossip."

The tiny bell on the gallery door tinkled, drawing everyone's attention. Just as Winter began to turn, she noticed that Rose was staring at the door in utter disbelief. Megan's eyes had gone equally as wide and her jaw had gone slack.

Winter spun fully around and actually took a step back. Who wouldn't feel a punch in the gut when finding herself in the presence of such incredibly virile . . . maleness? The man was just too stunning for words.

Which seemed to be an immediate problem for Winter, as she couldn't even respond when the tall, handsome stranger nodded at her—though she did hear Rose sigh, and she did feel Megan poke her in the back.

"Ah, may I help ya," Winter finally said.

Enigmatic, tiger-gold eyes met hers, and it took all of Winter's willpower not to take another step back. The man was standing just inside her spacious gallery, yet he seemed to fill up the entire space.

"Is the painting in the window by a local artist?" he asked.

The deep, rich timbre of his voice sent a shudder coursing through Winter, and another sharp poke in her back started her breathing again. "Ah, yes," she said. "She lives right here in Pine Creek." Winter waved a hand at the east wall of her gallery. "Most of the paintings are hers. Everything we sell is by local artists," she finished in a near whisper, unable to stop staring at his beautifully rugged, tanned face.

He simply stared back, his eyes crinkled in amusement.

"Feel free to look around," she added with another half-hearted wave, thankful that her voice sounded normal this time. "I can answer any questions ya have."

"Thank you," he said with a slight nod before turning to the wall of paintings.

As soon as he looked away, Winter spun around to face Megan and Rose. Neither woman noticed her warning glare, however, as they were too busy gawking at the man. Worried that he'd turn around and catch them, Winter grabbed them both by an arm and hustled them ahead of her into the back room.

"Cut it out," she quietly hissed. "You're being rude."

"Did you see how broad his shoulders are?" Rose whispered, craning around to look back at the gallery.

Winter moved the three of them farther away from the door. "Rose Dolan Brewer, you're a happily married woman with two kids. Ya shouldn't be noticing other men's shoulders."

Rose smiled. "I can still look, as long as I don't touch."

"Did you see his hair?" Megan whispered, her eyes still wide, not a trace of a tear anywhere in sight. "He's wearing a suit that probably cost more than my entire wardrobe, but he's got a ponytail. What sort of businessman has long hair?"

"And those eyes," Rose interjected before Winter could respond. "They're as rich as gold bullion. My knees went weak when he looked at you, Winter."

"That does it. Out," Winter said, crowding them toward the door that connected the back office of her gallery with Dolan's Outfitter Store. "You're going to scare off my most promising customer today."

Rose snorted and stepped into her store, combing her fingers through her short brown hair. "I doubt anything could scare that man," she muttered, smoothing down her blouse as she turned to Winter. "Send him over to my store after," she said with a cheeky grin. "I'll, ah . . . fit him into more suitable clothes for around here."

"Do you suppose he came in on that plane that flew over?" Megan asked. "We saw it bank for a landing at the airport. It looked like a private jet." Megan sighed. "My God, he's handsome. Maybe I should stay and help you set out the figures Talking Tom brought in this afternoon."

Winter didn't have the heart to remind Megan that she had sworn off men—handsome or otherwise—when she'd come home from her field work in Canada last month, abandoned and two months pregnant. It was rather nice to see her sister's face flushed from something other than tears.

"Thanks," Winter said with a tender smile, "but I think I'll wait and put out Tom's carvings tomorrow."

Megan took one last look toward the gallery door, sighed, then followed Rose down the aisle of camping equipment. Winter softly closed the connecting door, ran her fingers through her own mass of long red curls, straightened to her full five-foot-six height with a calming breath, and headed back into the gallery.

Mr. Tiger Eyes was still facing the wall. He had worked his way down the wall to a painting hanging toward the front of the store, his arms folded over his broad chest and his chin resting on one of his large, tanned fists. The pose pulled the material of his expensive suit tightly across a set of impressively wide shoulders. He glanced only casually at Winter when she stepped up to the counter, then went back to studying the painting.

He was looking at a large watercolor she had painted last spring, that she had titled *Moon Watchers*. It was a nighttime scene set deep in a mountain forest awash with moonlight. Three young bear cubs were gathered around a thick old rotting stump, their harried mother catching a quick nap as they played in the shadows. One of the cubs was perched precariously on top of the stump, its tiny snout raised skyward as it brayed at the large silver disk in the starstudded sky, its siblings watching with enchanted expressions on their moon-bathed faces. And if one studied the painting long enough, he or she would eventually notice all of the other nocturnal creatures hidden in the shadows, curiously watching the young bears watching the moon.

It was a painting that usually drew the attention of women more than men, what with its endearingly familial subject and somewhat playful and mystical mood.

Winter slid her gaze to the man standing in front of it.

He was at least as tall as her cousin Robbie MacBain, and Robbie was six-foot-seven in his stocking feet. This man's shoulders were equally as broad, his legs as long and muscled beneath that perfectly tailored suit, his hands just as large and blunt and powerful looking. He had the body of an athlete, which said that whoever he was, he didn't spend all of his time sitting in board rooms or merely shuffling papers around.

Like Megan, Winter found herself questioning his choice of hairstyle, if he truly was the successful businessman he appeared to be. His hair was thick and smooth and soft, neatly brushed off his face and tied at the nape of his neck with a thin piece of leather. It wasn't overlong; Winter guessed that when loose, it would fall just past his shoulders.

"The artist," he said, nodding toward the wall of paintings. "Does she take commissions?"

"Ah, yes. Yes, I'll take commissions."

One of his dark, masculine brows arched. "These are your paintings," he clarified softly, more to himself than her as he looked back at the wall. He studied the large watercolor for another moment in silence, then turned fully to face her, his deep golden gaze locking on hers. "I'll take *Moon Watchers*," he said. "But I would like to leave it here until I have a wall to hang it on."

Winter drew her own brows together in confusion. "A wall to hang it on?" she repeated.

He took several steps toward her, then stopped, his

mouth lifting in a crooked smile that slammed into Winter like another punch in her gut. It was the smile of a cajoling little boy, and it didn't belong on a face that . . . that . . . *masculine*.

"I'm building here in Pine Creek," he explained, "and I would like to leave the painting with you until my home is finished." He nodded toward the wall without taking his gaze off hers. "You can keep it on display if you wish. That way I can come in and look at it whenever I want. Just put a sold sign in place of the price. Would that be okay?"

She had to stop staring into his eyes! She couldn't think, much less keep up with the conversation. Well, curses. She was acting sillier than Megan and Rose. Winter tore her gaze from his and searched the counter until she found her sales book under Tom's list. Then she found a pen.

Then she found her wits, and then her voice again. "I don't have a problem with ya leaving it here. Tell me, what is it that drew ya to *Moon Watchers*, Mr. . . . Mr. . . ." she trailed off, her pen poised to write his name at the top of the slip.

She looked up when he didn't immediately answer, and found him standing just two feet away, his golden eyes once again locking on hers. "It's Gregor," he said softly, his deep voice sending another shiver down her spine. "Matt Gregor. And I've always had a fondness for bears."

Okay, this was bordering on the ridiculous. He was only a guy. Granted, he was a stunningly gorgeous guy, but she was acting like she'd never even spoken with a man, much less been attracted to one. Winter again forced her gaze from his and wrote his name on the slip. She wrote the title of the painting, and then started to write the price beside it.

One large, unbelievably warm hand covered hers, and Winter stopped breathing. She looked up to find Matt Gregor smiling that little-boy smile again, and she could only helplessly smile back.

"Twenty percent discount if I take a second painting," he said, his beautiful, golden eyes sparkling with challenge. "I also want to buy that small watercolor of the panther."

Winter very slowly—trying very hard not to let him see how disconcerted his touch made her—slipped her hand from under his. "I'm sorry, but the panther's not for sale," she told him. "It's part of my personal collection. It's only on display because I had an empty space on the wall I wanted to fill."

Matt Gregor's expression instantly turned from that of a little boy to a fully engaged hunter. His eyes stopped smiling, their penetrating stare sending Winter's heart racing in alarm. "I'll pay as much for the panther as for *Moon Watchers*," he said with quiet force. "No discount on either."

Double curses! When he looked at her like that, she wanted to *give* him every painting in the gallery—*especially* the panther. Winter just barely caught herself from snorting out loud. It was obvious Matt Gregor was used to getting what he wanted.

But then, so was she. "*Gesader* is not for sale," she told him, shaking her head to strengthen her words. "Choose something else that ya like, and I'll give ya a discount on it."

He leaned his weight back on his hips, crossed his arms over his chest, and studied her much the same way he had studied her paintings. Winter felt a warmth creep into her cheeks, but she stubbornly held his stare, determined not to let him see her discomfort. And she decided then that this would be a lesson to her—stunningly gorgeous didn't automatically mean nice. In fact, it could sometimes be downright rude.

Then again, it could also be exhilarating. Winter couldn't remember the last time she had felt this provoked by a man. Or this warm and fuzzy inside. Or this challenged.

She set down the pen and stepped from behind the counter, walking past Matt Gregor to the east wall of her gallery. She stopped in front of a tiny pastel drawing and crossed her arms under her breasts. "If ya like cats, I have this drawing of a Maine lynx."

She sensed him moving to stand beside her, but she continued to look at the drawing of a confounded lynx that was searching for the hare it had been chasing. In the background, its head just slightly showing above a snow-drift, was a perfectly camouflaged snowshoe hare watching the lynx. "If you're building a house here, Mr. Gregor, ya might consider works depicting local wildlife. We don't have panthers in Maine, but we do have lynx and bobcat and bear."

"Where did you come up with the name *Gesader?*" he asked, not addressing her suggestion.

Winter looked down the wall until her gaze fell on the small watercolor of the black leopard napping on a large tree limb, and she smiled affectionately. "It's Gaelic for 'Enchanter.'"

"Gaelic," Matt Gregor repeated, stepping around to face her. "I thought I detected a slight accent. Are you Irish?"

"Nay, Scots," she said in an exaggerated brogue. She nodded toward the information card pinned next to the drawing, and held out her hand. "Winter MacKeage."

His own hand swallowed hers up, his grip warm and firm but not overpowering. "My pleasure, Miss MacKeage." He lifted one brow again. "Or is it Mrs.?"

"Miss. But it's 'Winter' to my patrons."

His grip tightened only perceptibly. "I'm not a patron yet, Miss MacKeage. We haven't concluded our negotiations."

Winter forced herself to leave her hand in his. "Full price for *Moon Watchers*, and you can have *By a Hare's Breadth* for half price," she offered, nodding toward the lynx drawing.

Matt Gregor, still holding her hand, let out a soft sigh. "Nothing I offer you will get me that panther, will it?"

She finally slipped her hand free, tucked it behind her back, and rubbed her fingers together as she slowly shook her head. "I'm sorry, but he's not for sale. Do we have a deal?"

"Deal," he said, turning to look at the lynx drawing more closely. He pulled the tag from the wall, then moved over to *Moon Watchers* and pulled its tag. He walked back to the counter and set them down next to the sales slip she had started to fill out. Winter walked around to the back of the counter and picked up her pen.

"About that commission," he said when she started to write.

She stopped and looked up. "What is it ya want? I must warn ya, I don't do paintings of mechanical things."

He folded his arms back over his chest. "It's not a painting I want from you, Winter MacKeage. . . ."

FINALLY
A WEBSITE
YOU CAN GET
PASSIONATE
ABOUT...

Visit
www.SimonSaysLove.com
for the latest information
about Romance from Pocket Books!

READING SUGGESTIONS

LATEST RELEASES

AUTHOR APPEARANCES

ONLINE CHATS WITH YOUR
FAVORITE WRITERS

SPECIAL OFFERS

AND MUCH, MUCH MORE!

Love a good romance?

So do we...

Killer Curves
Roxanne St. Claire

He's fast. She's furious.
Together they're in for the ride
of their lives...

I Hunger for You
Susan Sizemore

In the war between vampires
and humanity, desire is the only
victor.

One Way Out
Michele Albert

Suspense crackles as two
unlikely lovers try to outrun
danger—and passion.

Close to You
Christina Dodd

He watches you. He follows
you. He longs to be...close to
you.

The Dangerous Protector
Janet Chapman

The desires he ignites in
women makes him the most
dangerous man in the world...

Shadow Haven
Emily LaForge

She followed her heart home—
and discovered a passion she
never dreamed of.